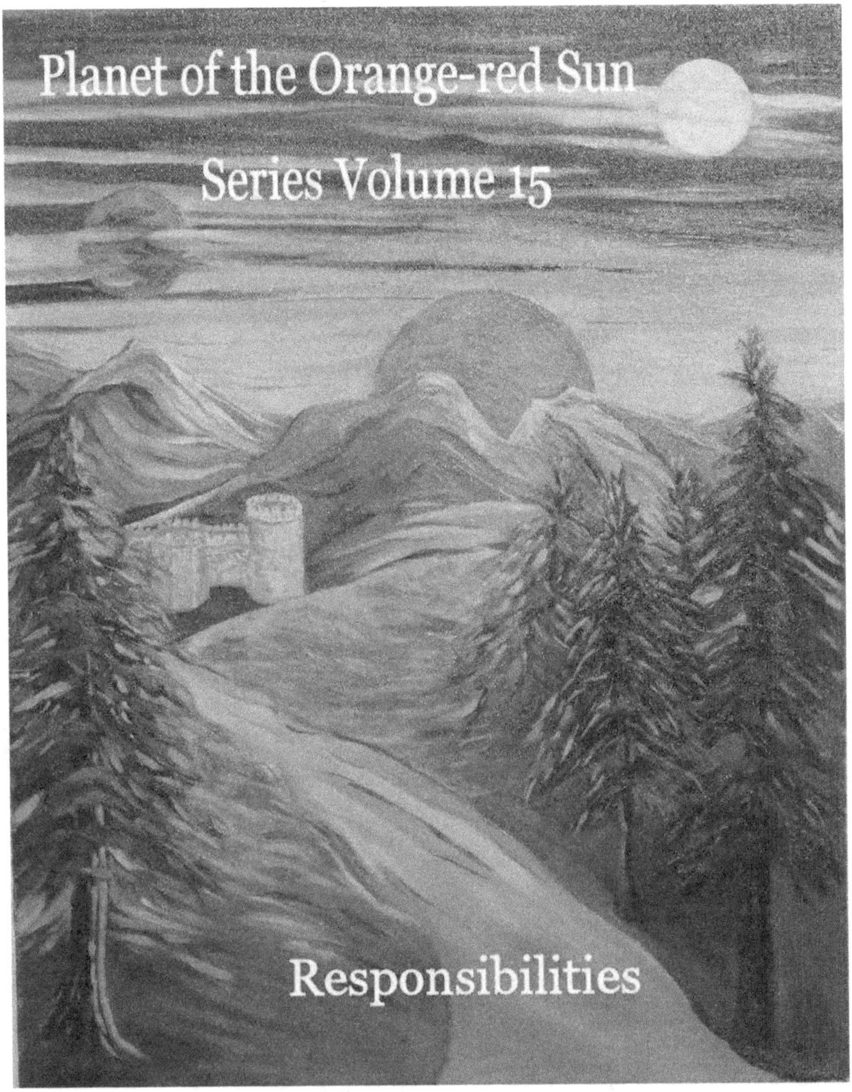

# Planet of the Orange-red Sun

## Series Volume 15

## Responsibilities

# Planet of the Orange-red Sun Series

# Volume 15 Responsibilities

by Vic Broquard

http://www.Broquard-ebooks.com
Broquard eBooks
103 Timberlane
East Peoria, IL 61611
author@Broquard-eBooks.com

Artwork by Crooked Willow Studios.

For Morgan and L. Ron Hubbard

# Table of Contents

# Chapter 1 Expansion

The humaniform robot Model 7a known as Minta continued her expansion plans. With the realization that incorporating telepaths from Ashford-5 was wholly unworkable, Minta revised her overall plans considerably. That the two telepaths, Amy and Jan, whom she had made into Model 11's had somehow undone all of her extensive safeguards and escaped, where she calculated that escape was impossible, more than worried Minta. Further, she also knew that these Ashford-5 telepaths could kill with an undetectable thought. She needed them taken out of her Grand Plan and had launched the surprise bio agent genetic attack on Ashford-5, hoping to so severely impair those that survived that they would never again leave that world.

Minta had made ten copies of herself, but installed special programming in them. They were known as Minto-0 through Minta-9. In fact, she's sent Minta-9, alias Leslie Glass, to Ashford-5, after giving her a new face, a different color and style of hair, and a false ID card. There, Leslie pretended to be a part of the Ataro Empire's emergency workers, who worked frantically to help prevent genocide on Ashford-5. That nearly none died because of the bio agent attack and that now all five million inhabitants had miraculously developed telepathic gifts bothered her considerably. However, Minta-9 did report that the inhabitants, the new nova, were virtually helpless and would remain so even with the massive humanitarian aid being sent there by their Emperor Fu Gang. Just as Minta suspected, after a few years there, the cover of Leslie Glass was blown. The telepaths began sensing that this female worker had no mind. Minta-9 made a quiet, hasty exit from Ashford-5 before anyone in power realized she was there.

Analyzing the news from Minta-9, Minta concluded that the telepaths of Ashford-5 would not pose a serious threat to her Grand Plan, not for several years, though she was impressed with the very last news that their geneticists had perfected a partial, mass cure, regenerating arms. Even more impressive was their development of the aerosol deployment agent. Minta sent Minta-9 off on a mission to acquire a sample of it for their own use. She then made a slight modification to her Grand Plan. Ashford-5 telepaths had to be handled again, but not for a number of years. Her plans stretched many years into the future, as only a robot could concoct with certainty.

By 1470, she had reached her goal of having twenty-five thousand Model 10's (only a quarter of their planned numbers) and six thousand Model 11's operational and trained, ready for action.

Most of the Model 10's were the genetically malformed women from Gundig-B, the weibchen, hideous looking and hardly human at all, a genetics experiment in beauty that had gone seriously wrong. A Model 10 retained only the human's brain, kept alive by a cleverly designed system that circulated the proper nutrients to sustain the brain. The person's brain was surrounded by a complex neural net that translated the brain's electrical impulses into robot controls and vice versa.

These Model 10's proved to be vastly superior fighters than normal humans. Given their greatly enhanced senses and their incredibly powerful humaniform robot shells, these Model 10's were destined to be her army that would conquer and subdue the galaxy. The weibchen hated normal humans and made incredibly bloodthirsty fighters.

The Model 11's became her breeding stock. These humans had their arms and legs removed along with their entire skull and jaws, replaced by the robot shell. Only their breasts, lips, and dual reproductive organs remained outside of the protective humaniform shell. While they too were superior to human fighters, their main focus was on breeding more humans who would be turned into robots later on. By 1470, Minta again altered her plans. These Model 11's failed to live up to her expectations. She merely modified her plan to take this into account.

Each of these special models had superior eyes, eyes that could also see in the infrared and ultraviolet, as well as zooming in, similar to a telephoto lens. Their hearing could be adjusted to hear a pin drop on a carpet. Strength? They could lift four hundred pounds and run six-minute miles endlessly without taking any deep breaths. Their reaction times were double those of the normal human and the weibchen Model 10's only lived to kill other humans.

Minta expanded her spy humaniform robots, the Model 8's as well. By 1470, these robots numbered two thousand. Many were on assignments spying on most of the major planets of the old Imperium and the disintegrating Federation of Planets. Of necessity, Minta ordered the construction and salvaging of the older worker robots, the Model 6's. These looked like mechanical men and were programmed to handle all manner of construction projects, her workforce. These currently numbered ten thousand.

Armed with a sizeable workforce, Minta embarked on the next phase of her Grand Plan, which called for drone fighter robots. During the conquering of a world and after a world was conquered, she needed throwaway-type robot fighters. These new Model 12's appeared as shiny, metal robots, mostly humanoid in shape, but cheap to make. They would pass as fighters probably equal to human fighters but could withstand enormous amounts of damage before their circuitry failed completely. They would simply follow her orders to the letter. Unlike the humaniform robots whose minds were on par with those of humans, these Model 12's would only follow orders and not attempt individual thinking as the humaniforms did. Drastically cheaper to make, these would become her foot soldiers and garrison forces, though she would need to leave a humaniform robot in charge of them when they were on garrison duty.

The first of these rolled off the assembly line in autumn of 1465. By the summer of 1480, the ten millionth Model 12 walked away from the assembly line, joining the others. She'd also reached her goal of a hundred thousand Model 10's by this time as well.

Minta organized her squadrons into one Model 10 in command of one hundred Model 12's. Her generals, Minta-0 through Minta-9 each commanded ten thousand squadrons, that is, over a million robot fighters — very impressive numbers until one took into account their warships.

Her warships consisted of the single-man fighters with their small cannon and backup, deep space transports with a much larger cannon. That is, Minta had no battleships, heavy cruisers, or light cruisers — not when she launched her first offensive action against Zeta Scorpii-C, a smaller member of the Federation of Planets.

Why Zeta Scorpii-C? This world had substantial warship manufacturing plants and was rich in the ores needed to make these giant ships. Additionally, Zeta Scorpii-C had a large engine plant, part of the widespread Porsche Industries, which had a near monopoly on the manufacturing of the engines used in the Federation's warships. They also had a strong military ground force and a reasonable warship fleet. All of these made Zeta Scorpii-C an ideal first target for Minta and a good field test for her robot army.

Years ago, over two million people who at that time lived in Capital City had been attacked with the bio agent, turning them into the normal mutant hermaphrodites. The army's cache of the yellow cylinders had been mysteriously blown up and the gas spread over the entire city, wiping out an entire two divisions stationed at the barracks as well. After the attack, many died, but some made it into the assisted living quarters scattered among the many cities of the world. However, the world was also falling into decadence, and many hundreds of thousands of these nearly helpless men and women were taken away to join the widespread prostitution and escort businesses that spread across Zeta Scorpii-C.

Two weeks before the attack, two hundred spy humaniforms went in undercover using various disguises. Their mission was to locate critical targets and to prepare disruptions preventing organized resistance to the main attack. Each of these wore an invisibility device and a PDS, a personal defense shield, as did the various Minta's and Model 10's.

June 10, 1465, Minta-0 led the assault fleet to Zeta Scorpii-C. The world had seven billion inhabitants at this time and a million-man Unified Army, divided up into six Regional Units or twenty-five Divisions of forty thousand soldiers. Its warships numbered five battleships, ten heavy cruisers, and twenty light cruisers. They had hundreds of deep space transports, some with small canons on them. Their space fleet was thus composed of five Armadas, as they were called, consisting of a battleship, two heavy cruisers, and four light cruisers, with many transports.

At the time of the attack, Armada 1 was planet-side, getting much needed maintenance. Armada 2 was in low orbit protecting the planet, normally a very boring job. Armada 3 and Armada 4 were stationed some light years distant on the lookout for more of the snake aliens, while Armada 5 was elsewhere in the Federation participating in Federation exercises. Precisely at 4 am, Minta-0's forces dropped out of hyperspace. In her lead transport, she had a massive signal jamming electronic system, which she activated as she dropped into normal space. At the same time, ten more were activated by her spies on the surface of Zeta Scorpii-C, jamming all communications signals.

Her Model 10 commanders worked efficiently. Two of them and their squadrons moved up to a battleship, while others did the same to its auxiliary cruisers. Instead of attempting to fire upon them with their tiny canons, the Model 12's exited the bays and grappled onto the hulls of the ships. Carefully and strategically placed charges blew sealed hatches. Decompression resulted so rapidly that the crew and the automated responses didn't have enough time to respond by sealing inner bulkheads and so on. Rapidly, the internal air shot out into the near vacuum of space. Five minutes later, the cruisers were inert in space, their crew members dead. Ten minutes later, the battleship was also out of commission.

Thirty minutes after 4 am, Minta-0 received the reports that she desired. Three battleships, six heavy cruisers, and twelve light cruisers were captured. Minta-0 then issued the main landing orders. Swarms of deep space transports dropped out of hyperspace, descending like flies upon Zeta Scorpii-C. They concentrated on the six Regional Units, where the million-man army was stationed. Her spies detonated their carefully placed charges, blowing up key munitions depots, as her huge robot army charged down the bay ramps and rushed to the attack, led by their Model 10 commander, who had a streaming video camera on her head, relaying the scene back to Minta-0 and on back to the other Minta's, eventually reaching Minta herself.

The bloodlust of the Model 10's was something to behold, though the Model 12's were just as efficient. D-guns blazed on both sides. Soldiers took cover behind everything imaginable, but they were shocked when a robot came charging up to their position and simply tossed vehicles and barricades aside as though they were paperweights! Their own d-guns were rarely effective at disabling a Model 12, while the robots were uncannily accurate in their shots, usually aiming for the head of the soldier. In short, it was a slaughter, though the armed resistance lasted for several hours.

Meantime, another Model 10 led a strike force to the spaceport, capturing Armada 1, which was undergoing renovations, ensuring those ships could not take any action. This gave Minta four of the five Armadas, the beginnings of her warship fleet.

At one in the afternoon, Minta-0 addressed the world via their comm system, having shut down all other programming. By now, she calculated that she'd have a "captive" audience, desperate to know what was going on.

"This is General Minta. We've taken over your world, this Zeta Scorpii-C. Your world now belongs to the Master Race. You will obey any robot that gives you an order. If you do not, you'll be shot and turned into compost and fertilizer. As of this moment, all humans on Zeta Scorpii-C are now our slaves. If you work and do as you are told, you'll be kept alive. If you do not, you'll be shot. I believe those are simple enough terms that you pathetic, degenerate humans can follow. Those of you who work at these companies are ordered to report to work at nine in the morning." She listed off the various companies that produced the warships and munitions, either directly or the requisite parts needed in their construction, such as engines and electronics. It was rather extensive.

She went on, "During the next few days, robots will be visiting each home and giving each human their ID marker. Once the logging period is over, any human who is found without their ID marker will be shot. No exceptions. The robot will also log your particular skills and trade so we can best make use of you. Resistance is futile. Anyone trying to escape the planet will be shot or their ship shot down. Anyone fighting back against us will be shot. We have a zero tolerance for any and all disobedience from any slave. Besides, there are far too many of you humans on this world anyway, and we ought to cull your numbers." She intended that as a threat and a psychological stab, which didn't go unnoticed by the humans.

With the army barracks secure, thousands of Model 12's began fanning out into Capital City, going door to door. When a frightened man opened his door and stared at the gleaming robot staring back at him, he began nervously shaking. "How many live in this house? Have everyone line up in the living room or be shot," its mechanical voice barked. He replied that five did. His wife and three children huddled beside him in their living room.

"I'm an electrician," he replied when asked his occupation. She was a housewife.

The robot replied, "Good. Report to work tomorrow at nine. Your ID is 102." He stamped the number onto the man's forehead, but also injected an RFI tag there as well, before moving on down the line, stamping a number on everyone's heads, and injecting tags in them as well. So it went for days, while the robots logged the surviving six billion, eight hundred million, sixty-six thousand, eighty two survivors. The others either were deceased soldiers or were shot resisting the robots. Correspondingly, the robot losses suffered during the attack and subsequent days amounted to a dozen destroyed and twenty that needed repairs.

It took Minta-0's worker robots three days to install their planetary defense shield, similar to the one that covered Beltazar-C, their home world. Only then could Minta-0 relax, if robots could be said to relax. At this point, no Federation attack could get through the shield. Zeta Scorpii-C was secure. She reported to Minta and settled into Phase 2 of Minta's plan for this world, the production of warships, and the subjugation of the population.

Minta herself had an extensive database to draw upon.

With the stellar success of her first attack against the humans, she spent some time analyzing the accumulated information on captive populations. Human histories as stored in the database were quite extensive. Even with her powerful search engine, it took considerable time to isolate the most relevant data.

There were many examples from many different worlds concerning the use and efficacy of the utilization of slave labor. After some days of analyzing many different approaches to making effective use of slave labor, Minta concluded that such was pointless. Sabotage and poor workmanship invariably resulted. Besides, her worker robots could consistently produce quality products and during a twenty-four hour day. Minta concluded that she needed another use for the slaves. An idea formed.

Minta ordered one of her Model 11's and one of her humaniform spies to pay a visit to Ashford-5, pretending to be from The Golden Oaks Assisted Living Home on Pegasi-C. Disguised as Mr. Robert Jones and Mrs. Janice Waters, the pair landed on Ashford-5 and received a guided tour by the governor. Their stated purpose was to see how the population of Ashford-5 could live more normal lives with all the inventions that had been brought in or invented for the armless population. They stated that they would then be applying what they learned here to the millions of terrorist victims now swamping their assisted living complexes. With this altruistic purpose stated, they received a very nice tour and were even given some samples to take back with them, such as the electrostatic hair machine and the dresser-undresser bot — that is, only smaller items, not the heavy farm machinery for example.

The pair left and relayed their findings to Minta directly, complete with machine bot samples and a host of video taken at the various homes, farms, and companies that they visited. While Minta wasn't pleased to learn that most everyone on Ashford-5 had survived her surprise attack, she did see that they were able to survive on their own with the help of special equipment and facilities. A new idea formed in Minta's circuitry.

Only a fraction of Zeta Scorpii-C's industries and businesses were directly or indirectly related to the production of warships and munitions. Minta now had the workers at these companies back to work producing, but more importantly educating her worker robots on their production methods and procedures. That left an enormous number of other businesses, which served little or no purpose to her direct Grand Plan. Further, there were a dozen top Universities on this world. Slowly, a new usage of the captured humans formed within her positron circuits. A nearly human grin appeared on her face.

She then contacted Minta-0, about a month after the attack. "We are still running into sporadic resistance. Lost another ten Model 12's," Minta-0 reported, "but that was anticipated and isn't more than a minor annoyance. Over."

"Here's what we are doing next. It should eliminate all further resistance," Minta replied. She then launched into a very detailed plan of action.

Minta-0 followed her new orders. They had uncovered a large supply of the yellow bio agent cylinders, kept by Zeta Scorpii-C as a potential deterrent against other worlds using it on their world. Following Minta's orders, she tested it on one family. Why? These cylinders had now been duplicated so many times that the product was slightly altered by the accumulated errors in the duplication process. Satisfied with the results, Minta-0 ordered all males eighteen or older in Capital City to report to the three designated skyscrapers at nine on a Monday morning. She knew that some would not obey this order. People were still resisting as best they could, even to the point of sabotaging production lines.

Once the men arrived, the giant buildings were sealed and her robots dispersed the bio agent over the city. Over the buildings' intercoms, Minta-0 explained what was happening and what the men would be doing during the next four days. "So if you want your families and friends to survive, you will do as ordered," she ended her informative speech.

As soon as the gas dissipated sufficiently, the men rushed to carry out their specific instructions, given to them by the many Model 12's. Some ran Duplication machines. Some began the construction of low to the ground kitchens. Some worked on the installation of automatic sliding doors, replacing the entrance doors of all buildings in Capital City. Others, visited the homes where the comatose women, children and a few men were living, undressed them, and then dismantled all doorknobs, replacing them with sliding slats about a foot above the floor. The objective: rapidly create a world in which the soon to be armless hermaphrodites could survive, based on the model of Ashford-5!

Others were put to work designing farming equipment that could be operated using feet alone. More were reworking food production and distribution equipment to be similarly operated. Later on, as the products came out of the Duplication machines, others distributed the machines to each home. Yes, it was a very frantic four days for these men, who worked very long hours, sleeping very little.

A week later, the exhausted men had accomplished miracles. Every living dwelling now had a low to the ground kitchen installed. Automatic doors and foot controlled door locks were in place. The victims now had dressing bots and electrostatic hair machines. Appropriate apparel and shoes were also provided, along with carrying yokes and other similar items that the survey of Ashford-5 suggested were needed. In fact, most men collapsed and slept for nearly a day before recovering.

After giving them time to rest up, they went back to work manufacturing the same items for the next city to be handled. Thus, it went for many months until at last, even these working slaves were gassed as well. When June of 1466 arrived, all of Zeta Scorpii-C had been converted into an Ashford-5 model of human society! The population was now down to four billion give or take a few. Many didn't survive the changes, either dying in the process or refusing to live when they awoke. Most of those who died were men. Further, men of this generation continued to die off in the ensuing years. Only in the next generation when the new children knew nothing of what bodies and lives were like before the metal head occupation did the male population begin growing once more.

Naturally, some headed for the hills when word of this awful mutation of people became widely known. Minta-0 anticipated this and acted accordingly. Once the project was officially pronounced completed, she ordered a planet-wide gassing. Thus, those brave souls who tried to flee found themselves being genetically modified as well, though most of those subsequently perished since they were not in the modified living environments.

Men were reassigned work, primarily helping produce and distribute food and clothing for the masses. Minta-0 assigned Model 12's to look after the human population, based on one robot per thousand of population, thus ensuring that if real problems of survival of these new nova arose, it would be handled. Still, the population continued to decline for another year before new babies began appearing, turning the decline around.

Minta-0 then reorganized the educational system on Zeta Scorpii-C, paying particular attention to the many Universities. There, physics, astrophysics, chemistry, math, electrical engineering, and similar fields of studies were permitted. Gone were all humanities, history, genetics, medical professions, political science, and similar "useless" studies. Minta-0 wanted ultimately to have some very brilliant doctoral students who could push forward the key studies into the future for the benefit of the robots.

Those students who excelled in these fields were given special treatment, luxury housing, the best clothing, the finest food, and so on as a reward for their academic achievements. By 1485, these few doctors became the elite of Zeta Scorpii-C, numbering around six thousand. Their primary objectives involved developing new and better machines and devices for both their own population and for their robot overlords.

After the initial baby boom of 1467, the population began a steep decline once more. Many of these nearly helpless hermaphrodites decided life wasn't worth living and found ways to succumb, primarily men. Minta-0 appreciated their deaths. That removed the scum, bottoming out around 1470 with a population of around three billion who did want to survive somehow. By 1500, the population had increased to close to four billion, though nearly half of the total population was children under eighteen.

On the military side by 1500, Minta-0 had fifty battleships, a hundred heavy cruisers, and two hundred light cruisers in her command. The deep space transports were in the thousands. Plus, she had millions of d-guns, PDSs, and thousands of Invisibility Shields as well.

Back on Beltazar-C, Minta had greatly enlarged her own forces there as well. Finally, she was ready to move into Phase 3 of her Grand Plan. Based on the total success on Zeta Scorpii-C, she incorporated that scenario into her future plans for other conquered worlds. She envisioned the entire galaxy under the control of her robots, with all of the human populations identical to that on Zeta Scorpii-C and Ashford-5. Once completed, the humans could live useful, productive lives, but never again threaten the robots, start wars between worlds, or even fight among themselves. The galaxy would be finally in a permanent complete and total peace. Never again would humankind ravage the galaxy or harm others and themselves. Yes, Minta had a Grand Plan.

Much of what happened on Zeta Scorpii-C was known to Renata back on Ashford-5. Why? During the first Consortium, which came to Tierra to hire armless hermaphrodite telepaths, President Henry Thomas had hired a telepath to assist him in handling the governing of Zeta Scorpii-C. Cassandra Levi was twenty when she arrived on the world, staying with the President and his family. She had been a political science major at Exchange City's Academy when the snake alien attack had come, effectively ending her studies. She'd taken a ten-year contract that paid her a million gold credits per year along with a promise to complete her graduate studies, obtaining her doctorate in political science. That she would be working closely with their president sealed the deal. She had no idea that she'd be spending most of her entire life on Zeta Scorpii-C!

Cassandra was *mentales* gifted, but her gifts lay in truth telling, most useful for her line of work. She was the daughter of a local telepath and a spacer named Levi, who had gotten her mother pregnant and then left Ashford-5. Hence, Cassandra had a low opinion of men in general and was quite used to fending for herself, just as she and her mother had done all their lives. She saw this employment as a way of providing luxury for her mother, having made an arrangement for half of her pay to be sent to her mother, and a way to obtain her doctoral degree.

Renata periodically checked up on all the telepaths who had taken the off-world employment opportunities. Wisely so, since she had to send Arnold and crew to rescue nearly a quarter of them. However, Cassandra wasn't in need of rescuing. Rather the opposite, she was being well treated, working on her degree, and being rather useful for the president. Then came the invasion of the robots. During that communications blackout period when the robots were jamming all signals while they were attacking the warships in orbit, she was able to put him in contact with one of the battleships, just before it was breached and the crew perished horribly.

She was able to help the president get word to his various army divisions, preparing them for the invasion. Soon, they both saw that these robots were unstoppable! Cassandra watched helplessly as the nightmare days unfolded, taking small comfort in the fact that she had finally gotten her doctorate. Then came the genetic modifications! While she didn't fall into a coma — the only person on the planet who didn't, she was there to help the president's family recover and adapt. She felt sorry for him, though. He became a grocer, doling out food supplies. Then, he too was genetically modified. After that, she remained a part of his family, encouraging them as best she could.

Later, when Renata contacted her to check up on how things were going, Cassandra had a very wild story to tell! Thus, in 1467, Renata knew the full story of what had happened on Zeta Scorpii-C and via her, so did Emperor Fu Gang of the Ataro Empire. Since this world was in the Federation of Planets, there wasn't anything he could do about it. Further, because of the planetary-wide defense shield, Renata had no way to rescue Cassandra from Zeta Scorpii-C.

Nevertheless, once a week she contacted Cassandra to learn further news. Later on, her contacts dropped off to once per month, since Cassandra reported they were doing as well as possible, and that the robots were leaving the human population alone.

# Chapter 2 Getting a Grip

Nearly fifty years had passed since the Great Change, the local name on Ashford-5 attached to the terrorist attacks by the robots. In the mid-1460's, everyone hoped at least they would have their arms regenerated. Their geneticists worked out a foolproof method. While most had what they called baby-like arms, the process was nearly completed when the second attack came in 1469. Using stealth mode, small transports unleashed a new genetic bio agent on Ashford-5. This one was more diabolical than their previous attack and had unexpected, far reaching consequences for the inhabitants of Ashford-5.

Ashford-5 wasn't the only location where genetic research was being done. Oh no. Part of Minta's Grand Plan called for further experimentation, greatly aided by the newly discovered aerosol delivery agent. Minta knew well that homo sapiens sapiens males caused the vast majority of "problems" in the universe, though that's not to say that some females did so too. Hence, her newly invented genetic mutation affected males far more than females in the infected populations. Based on the resistance she encountered on Scorpii-C, she knew that males had to have their egos destroyed and devised her newest genetic bio agent accordingly.

Both sexes ended up with the neurons and axons in their super-long hair, which fell to their ankles. Because of the pain sensors, hair could not be shortened. Even if done and the intense pain endured, their mutated bodies quickly regrew their hair within days. Both sexes became hermaphrodites as before. Men now had widened pelvises to facilitate childbirth. They also had lost a pair of lower ribs. Due to the orientation of the dual reproductive organs, if they were not careful, it was easy for anyone to impregnate themselves.

Both sexes had their feet grossly malformed. Their arches were enormous. Only their toes could lay flat on the ground. Their heels were arched high and were nearly in line with the backs of their toes. Another way of looking at their feet was this. Their foot arches bent at a ninety-degree angle right after their heels, placing the front of their heels in line with the back of their toes. Hence, the victims could only wear toe shoes. That is, the shoes and boots permitted ones toes to lay flat on the ground. A super-tall spiked heel touched the ground just behind the back of their toes, giving the wearer a tiny bit more support. Walking was precarious at best. At least the split lip modification, which forced people to have to wear the giant lip disks, had not occurred, more than likely somehow lost in the many duplications of the bio agent.

The major differences between the sexes were breast sizes and arms. In the original attack that used the original bio agent, both sexes had huge breast sizes, basketballs. However, the goddesses Lysandra and Ariana managed to work their magic reducing them to the size of giant melons. In the followup attack, the female bodies breasts grew larger from an H-cup size to that of a J-cup size, using the Federation measurement scale. To help destroy male egos, Minta's researchers re-engineered the bio agent to make male bosoms have more than a twenty inch difference, double the size of female breasts, larger than basketballs. This enormous extra weight wreaked havoc on their backs, forcing them to have to wear extremely tight, highly steel boned corsets for back support, which made breathing challenging as well. At least, all breasts were perky and not droopy, which pleased many an eye.

The males lost their newly grown arms, while the females lost their lower arms and hands, retaining their upper arms. For the first time since the invention of this hideous bio agent, the new bio genetic agent had different effects on the victim based on the presence or absence of a Y chromosome!

Yet the results of this second attack were far worse for all those on Ashford-5. Why? Their top geneticists immediately began researching the new genetic changes, looking for ways to undo them yet again. However, they discovered their genetic makeup was now so badly scrambled that all standard "cures" failed to work. Each person to be cured had to have their entire genetic structure mapped, studied, and a cure unique to that person created and delivered, wholly impossible with a population of many millions. This was a bitter pill for the Ashford-5 geneticists to swallow. Yet, they continued their research, knowing that it was pretty much going to be fruitless.

On the positive side, everyone's living arrangements were already in place because of the original attack. No one died because of the second attack. Disheartened, annoyed, yes, but they could survive.

In fact by 1500, two generations had passed. Those in power had transferred the reins to some of their grandchildren. While they had witnessed so much change during their long lifetimes, old age eventually caught up to them. Virtually no one wanted to make use of the Rejuvenation machines, preferring to retire and enjoy their remaining years before starting over.

Tierra's queen was now Mary Linn Blackwater, a granddaughter of Lisa and Lilly. Raven haired, she was twenty-four years old. As an Ataro queen, she had no choice but to have her upper arms removed when she went to Winno-3 to be trained by the emperor. This didn't matter in the slightest, since she couldn't use them for much of anything anyway. She was married to Henry Blackwater, who had his doctorate in mechanical engineering and now headed the ME Guild. They had two children, Stacy and Martin, both three years old.

Governor Sheila transferred her position to her granddaughter. Governor Monica Childa was twenty-five and married to Betsy Childa, twenty-six, who had her degree in physics and was in charge of Tierra's planetary-defenses, relieving Governor Monica from such worries. Both women had wavy brown hair. Each had a three year old daughter, Tori and Justina respectively.

Amy and Jan dropped their bodies in the robot shells, preferring to have their new bodies. Both were now thirty-one. They kept their first names as they always had for centuries. Amy and Jan Bellweather were both very blonde and had attractive bodies this time. Already, they had six daughters, all quite blonde themselves. Eva and Gina were sixteen and discovering relationships. Susana and Kristen were fourteen, while Hannah and Adriana were twelve. Amy and Jan were quite content to relax and enjoy a carefree life this time, hoping that nothing bad would happen for another fifty years. Still, the pair kept up on the latest news, especially Jan.

The stunningly beautiful Luciana Castrani and Michela Angelina had established Super Models Inc, a very upscale store that specialized in turning out top models, teaching their customers how to look as sexy as possible, how to walk seductively, how to win beauty pageants, which they began, and how to dress appropriately. Soon, they became a smashing success and later on merged with Elegant Fashions Inc, providing an expansion for the long-time company on Tierra. Both had retired and were seventy-one, passing their large scale business on to two of their grandchildren, who had inherited their stunning good looks, Nicolina and Rosella, both now twenty-four and who of all their children and grandchildren were keenly interested in being and running Super Models Inc.

Elegant Fashions Inc in Exchange City, the parent corporation of the hundreds of smaller stores scattered across Tierra, was now run by a granddaughter of Valencia Valen, Miss Gabriela Valen, twenty-five. Like all Valens, she had long, wavy raven hair and was nearly as attractive as the super models. Gabriela had just hired two granddaughters of Ruth and Marcy, who were named after their grandmothers, Ruth and Marcy. Marcy had stunning silver hair, wavy, thick, and long. She was twenty and two years older than Ruth who had golden locks. Both Ruth and Marcy had won Miss Tierra beauty pageants and now joined Super Models Inc, helping Nicolina and Rosella run this highly profitable business.

Renata Gervasi-Bellweather ought to appear as an old woman. However, being Renata, after her mate died, she appeared to look twenty-five again but without using the Rejuvenation machine, startling everyone. But when didn't Renata shock others? She was pursuing her Advanced Therapy research heavily and had formed a new union with the young Rafaela Hammil, also twenty-five. Why? Rafaela was the same spiritual being as the ancient Rafaela who had pioneered how to "make" *mentales* gifted. Together, they were pushing

Advanced Therapy research hard.

Renata still kept Strike Force One around. Arnold and crew were entirely too old to continue these occasional telepath rescue missions and had turned over command to some of their grandchildren who were interested in following in their footsteps. Their other children and grandchildren had pursued many other avenues of opportunity on Tierra. Ben Flaxton was now their official captain. The black haired youth was twenty, as were his three crew members. Alis, the granddaughter of Arnold and Gwenda, had the same flaming red hair as Gwenda. Pippa, named after her grandmother, had black hair, while Alberto Runelli had black hair like his grandparents, Alfonso and Savina.

These four had grown up together and had absorbed every ounce of fighting skill and knowledge that their grandparents had. Competent with all forms of weapons, they were good at martial arts and even with daggers, compliments of Grandmother Gwenda. Wait. Just how could they do these things without arms and with mutilated feet? All four used their strong *mentales* gifts, particularly telekinesis or levitation. In addition, anyone of the four could pilot the deep space transport, handle its navigation, and all other aspects of the operation and equipment. In short, they were as prepared as they could possibly be for rescue operations. The trouble was there were no off-world telepaths who were in trouble at the moment, so they contented themselves with practicing their skills, hoping to one day get the call from Renata.

Spring had finally come here in 1500, much to everyone's relief, except those who loved the snow. Governor Monica and Queen Mary Linn met in the queen's throne room to discuss Monica's latest idea. This was the five hundredth anniversary of the first arrival of "aliens" on Tierra, and she wanted to hold some kind of planet-wide celebration. However, so many things had changed during the last fifty years! The least of these changes was that everyone on Tierra had the *mentales* gifts! Not only was Tierra now a wholly telepathic society but also a hermaphroditic one as well, the latter causing the most difficulties, particularly among the men of Tierra.

"So how does July 1 sound to you for the big Cinco Siglos celebration? We can have fireworks set off from the spaceport near Exchange City. I want to cordon off this eastern section of the port and setup tables and chairs. We'll provide a large feast and plenty of drinks for all and, as the sun goes down, set off the fireworks," Governor Monica explained.

"Are you planning any speeches?" Queen Mary Linn asked.

"I suppose we should have some. You interested in making one?" Monica bounced it back to her.

"I suppose I should, but only if you do too. We can split the topics. I'll cover our side and you talk about the alien side. How's that? Division of labors," she chuckled.

"Agreed. I suppose Nicolina and Rosella will want to hold a beauty pageant, and Miss Gabriela Valen will want to show off her latest Elegant Fashions Inc designs as well. We ought to invite them to participate, since Elegant Fashions Inc has been around almost this whole time," Monica suggested.

Queen Mary Linn nodded and added, "Yes, a beauty pageant will be ideal. Honestly, we all look so vastly different than our ancestors did five hundred years ago. It will be good for morale, especially for the men."

Governor Monica sighed. "It's been so darn hard on the men — these genetic modifications. They've borne the brunt of it. Still, they've adapted. I do like how we can now tell the sexes apart. Grandmother told me that before they couldn't tell men from women unless you watched them pee or speak." Both women giggled.

"Where would we be without Elegant Fashions Inc?" Queen Mary Linn commented adroitly. "Honestly, down through the centuries, they've always been there for us all, adapting clothing designs as needed, sometimes taking a huge mountain of red ink just to handle the situations."

"Quite true. Quite. Here on Ashford-5, we must have the best dressed population in the galaxy, if not the most helpless society," Governor Monica replied, a note of hostility or bitterness in her voice.

Queen Mary Linn sighed. "I know what you mean. There's no hiding that fact. Without all the massive assistance and aid, most everyone would have perished in the first alien robot attack half a century ago. Still, we are fortunate that everyone now has the *mentales* gifts. Other victimized worlds are not so lucky. Honestly, Monica, I don't know how the people on those other worlds can possibly manage without telekinesis or levitation skills."

"Not too well!" The voice of Renata broke in on their conversation. She'd arrived and overheard their last exchange. Teetering on her seven-inch heels, she often used her upper arms to help keep her balance and not using her many "gifts." Walking with only your toes on the ground was challenging, since the spiked heel only provided a tiny bit more support. Still, she knew the men had a far rougher time walking, since they didn't even have upper arms to help them balance. Like most women, she wore a supporting corset to help minimize back pains, but the women's corsets were nowhere near as restrictive as those the men were forced to wear, because the women's had far less steel boning. Still, it gave her figure a rather dramatic look, though the figures of the men were vastly more curvaceous. She wore a light red satin gown with matching pumps. Her rich raven hair fell in waves down her back ending at her ankles, thick and sparkling.

Her mate, Rafaela teetered in behind her, wearing a matching corset, gown, and pumps. Like Renata, she allowed her ankle-length raven hair to flow in waves down her back. As always, Rafaela's smile caught both Governor Monica and Queen Mary Linn's eyes. She had one of those smiles that totally lit up a room, filling everyone with hope. She had thick, bushy black eyebrows and thick lips, adding to her beauty. "Hi everyone," she said cheerily. Her mellow voice also charmed everyone. In fact, Governor Monica truly envied Renata. If she weren't married to Betsy Childa, she'd have courted Rafaela.

Queen Mary Linn chuckled. "Well, something big must be up. When Renata pays me a visit, you can count on it being something important."

Renata smiled demurely. "Ah, am I that obvious?" she teased her back. "Seriously, there is. We just got word the metal heads are on the offensive again."

"Damn! Six worlds aren't enough for them?" Governor

21

Monica exclaimed in a sudden flash of anger. "A Federation world?"

"Yes. Jan's just received a frantic broadcast from Ponchart-D. It's an agricultural world she thinks," Renata replied formally. She added, "Trouble is, this incursion is bringing them dangerously close to Abel-C, which is a recent ally of the Ataro Empire. I expect you'll be receiving a call from the emperor. I don't see how we can continue remaining aloof in these metal head wars."

"Well, they are still a Federation of Planet's worry," Governor Monica justified. "Say, do you think they'll be crazy enough to go after Abel-C and bring the Ataro Empire into their wars?" Suddenly, the governor was worried. Life was just barely tolerable, but trying to go to war was out of the question. She could barely walk and had to use her *mentales* gifts even to fire a d-gun. Fighting a war seemed wholly impossible to her.

Renata nodded grimly. "We need more Intel on their plans, though I have no idea how to obtain such. Rafaela thinks we should develop the *mentales* gifts in the survivors of their conquered worlds. I've no idea how those victims could possibly survive without it."

"I doubt that is very practical," Queen Mary Linn countered. "Ignoring the fact the metal heads have defense screens that won't let us land there, how could we possibly administer the proper dosage or even train them once they developed it? An untrained telepath is a danger to both himself and to others. We all know that as an absolute fact. Besides, where would we get enough psi dust to treat a whole world? Tierra is rather small and unpopulated compared to most other worlds."

Rafaela spoke up. "I'm aware of the nearly insurmountable problems. Still, we need to consider this idea, especially if the metal heads expand their war zone to the Ataro Empire. What if Winno-3 gets attacked? Only their queen is able to live like us, but she has her personal assistant to help her. If they are all genetically modified, don't we owe it to come to their aid somehow, someway? After all, they and many others saved our world from the intended metal head's genocide attack fifty years ago."

"Point taken," Queen Mary Linn sighed. "All right. You have my permission to begin to work out ways and means, Rafaela. Still, I think it's not such a good idea. Certainly, it's not going to be practical. Nevertheless, we should have an answer in case one of the Ataro worlds get attacked. Best be prepared to answer such a request."

Rafaela smiled. "My thinking."

Governor Monica broke in, "Say, I wonder what our benevolent goddesses think about all this? Has anyone heard from Lysandra or Ariana recently?"

"Good idea. I'd contact them, but I've not got many more body parts to donate," Rafaela teased. Lysandra, the Goddess of Life and of Death, usually demanded a sacrifice from those she assisted. No one laughed however.

"I'll contact them," Renata agreed. "Oh, here comes Jan and your mate, governor." They heard heels clicking on the stone floor outside the throne room. As always, Renata was correct in her observations. Jan and Betsy soon joined them.

Betsy had her ankle-length wavy brown hair draped across her front side. She wore a light brown satin gown and matching pumps, but she was all business. "Monica, the metal heads have just attacked Ponchart-D. I've rechecked our own planetary defense shields. The emperor wants to speak to you soon. Currently, five light cruisers are in our vicinity, not much protection should the metal heads attack us again."

"Okay, we were just finishing up, Betsy. I'll head back with you now and call him back. Seriously, dear, I don't think the metal heads will be attacking us again. We're nearly completely helpless as it is," Governor Monica attempted to calm her mate down some. She sensed just how worried she was.

Using her short stumps, Jan adjusted her long blonde locks over her right side so that she could sit properly. Before she could do that, Renata interrupted. "Jan, hold on. I'd like you to come back to my place with me. I've a few things I'd like to bounce off you." After seeing Jan wiggling her large bosom as though she was reciprocating the "bouncing," she hastily added, "Professionally that is."

Queen Mary Linn cracked a grin. Bouncing boobs together was one of the few ways that her husband had to establish foreplay. Well, that was the case with all men of Tierra these days. At least the women could also use their upper arm stumps a little, though their upper arms barely reached beyond their own breasts. Jan struggled a bit to get her hair back over her front side and then followed Renata and Rafaela, who followed Monica and Betsy out of the throne room.

The queen watched Jan's arm motions and again noted that Jan always preferred to try to use her body to do things and not her *mentales* gifts. Once more, Mary Linn felt the pangs of the loss of her upper arm stumps. They'd been removed two years ago. While she'd had Renata's therapy to remove that trauma, she still keenly felt their absence. She was as helpless as her loving husband was, but that tended to strengthen the bonds between them. She smiled, focused, and used a bit of mental energies to get her hair out of the way so that she could get to her feet. Teatime, she thought.

"So what is this about?" Jan asked. The three had reached Renata and Rafaela's home, though it had been a long, precarious walk in their pumps, primarily because the winds were rather strong today. With only their toes on the ground, they had little traction. Plus, their long hair was blown in all directions. All three struggled with their upper arms to get their hair in front so they could sit on the couch. "Sometimes, life is a bitch," she added, annoyed that her hair was now a complete mess.

"What is the chance that you can find a way to tap into the metal heads' communications networks? We need Intel on their plans, if possible. With this new attack, the situation is going from bad to worse," Renata explained.

"Leave it to Sly Fox. Been giving that a good deal of thought. Arnold suggested that to me last year, and I've been working on it since then, rather off and on. Give me some time and I may be able to do it," Jan replied. In the past, her motto was: there isn't an Imperium computer system that I can't get into. She'd proven that fact countless times. However, this hack presented a completely new set of problems. So what if

24

she could get streaming access to the metal head's binary encoded data transfers? What did the bits mean? They talked a bit further, and Jan left to work on it some more.

While Rafaela headed into their kitchen to brew some tea, Renata focused and attempted to contact Lysandra and Ariana, the two goddesses who had helped them out during the first metal head attack fifty years ago. She expected to see them appearing as ghostly yellow and white forms, respectively, as they always had when they granted her an audience. That didn't happen, not remotely!

*Help! We're trapped in these helpless bodies!* Lysandra telepathically screamed back on the communication line that Renata made with her. Ariana echoed her thoughts, but Renata sensed even more terror coming from the fertility goddess.

*Relax. I'm here. What happened to you?* Renata sent back, snapping instantly into her role as Advanced Therapy giver.

Lysandra answered for the pair. *We spotted one of the metal head's ships hovering just above your planetary defense shield. We went to see if it was about to launch another attack on our humans when it began emitting this horrid energy wave. It's slammed us down and drove us into two of your human bodies. We couldn't stop it. It's driven those two completely out of their bodies. We think they are off looking for new baby bodies. Now, we are trapped in these helpless bodies. We can't seem to get out, and the energy keeps forcing us back into them when we try. Are they attacking Tierra again? Please help us,* she begged.

Always before, Renata delivered her Advanced Therapy directly to the other person, that is, with their physical body sitting across from her. From her long experiences delivering it, she also knew just how free spiritual beings slowly lost their native powers, until a human body seemed to have more power than they possessed, and thus they "became" the physical bodies. With some, the trap of physical bodies was the apparent sensations they offered the beings. Sight, sound, touch, not to mention sex, greatly appealed to these free beings that no longer were capable of generating such sensations themselves. She also knew the cycle of degeneration that turned able, powerful free beings into beings barely capable of running a human body. One step further down, and they would believe they were the body, having lost all sense of their own true identity and selves. Her Advanced Therapy was designed to reverse this downward spiral; its ultimate goal was to free all spiritual beings, giving them back their own identity and native powers, freeing them from the need of a human body to operate fully. Thus far, it was a long haul, requiring hours and hours of her Advanced Therapy and drilling.

Rafaela entered balancing the tea and cups in a yoke across her shoulders. She saw that Renata was "elsewhere." From the look on her face, she knew something serious was at hand and thus didn't interrupt her. After sitting the yoke down, she gently joined her mate via telepathy. Via telepathy, ideas are exchanged many, many times faster than the spoken word. *On it,* she sent, broke contact, and began alerting many others to the presence of the metal head's spaceship somewhere in orbit above their defense shield. By chance, this gave Jan the break that she needed.

*Okay, Lysandra, Ariana. Do you have any idea where on Tierra your bodies are located?* Renata asked.

*No!* The two chorused.

*All right. Are you outside?*

*Yes.*

*Good. With your body's eyes, look around you. Notice things in the distance,* she commanded.

*Oh. Okay. I see sand. Lots of sand,* Lysandra answered.

*And I see dunes. We must be in the Arad somewhere. There are date trees and palms. An oasis,* Ariana answered.

*All right. Rafaela will continue with the assist, while I come to bring you to our house,* Renata sent. She joined Rafaela to the two and gave her instructions to continue giving the pair what she called a Location Assist. While Rafaela continued to have them look at things in the distance, Renata focused and teleported her body, homing in on the pair. Since every spiritual being seemed to have their own precise wavelength or frequency, it was easy for her to zero in on their location. By the time that Rafaela had delivered another dozen commands to the pair, Renata's body appeared beside the pair of terrified goddesses, who were now plastered inside the heads of a pair of humans, twins, she saw at once.

A minute later, she brought both back to her home in the Imperial Manor Complex, arriving in front of their couch on which Rafaela was currently sitting. "Here we are. Please sit down," Renata said aloud. She and Rafaela watched the two do so very awkwardly, reminding them of just how it had been for everyone right after they awoke from the comas following the robot's bio agent attack some fifty years ago.

Rafaela observed they were Easterlings twins, probably around twenty years old. Lysandra was stuck in the male body with its monster-sized breasts and requisite, heavily steel boned corset, barely able to breathe. Ariana was in the female body and doing a little better than her companion was. Both had identical oval faces and lush, ankle length brown hair, typical of the Easterlings.

"Are they attacking us again?" Lysandra asked.

"We don't think so, but Rafaela has alerted everyone. Our cruisers are searching for the ship right now. So let's get you both back to battery, shall we?" Renata answered and immediately got them both into one of her Advanced Therapy sessions, while Rafaela monitored all three, following the therapy session protocols.

Hours passed before both goddesses suddenly realized that they had been resisting the energy field. That was their fatal mistake. As soon as they stopped resisting the energy, both spiritual beings easily floated out of the human bodies, immensely relieved.

"My god, Renata. This must have been what happened to Calder and Wystan centuries ago," Lysandra gushed in sudden realization. "Thank you. Thank you!"

"I had no idea just how helpless these bodies actually are," Ariana added. "Lysandra, we ought to have done a whole lot more when that last bio agent attack came."

"Shit, Ariana. We've made a huge error. Men can't even breathe. I'm being crushed in this corset thing. Walking is almost impossible. I can't even see my feet," Lysandra added.

Ariana declared, "Those robot metal heads have completely ruined our game here on Tierra!"

"If I might be so bold, but what exactly was your game here on Tierra with us humans?" Rafaela asked the single question that had been on her mind for lifetimes. She knew that originally there had been five gods and goddesses that somehow ran Tierra, or at least looked after the human settlers. Thanks to all the archaeology work over the last century or so, the educated knew that in their distant past a spaceship had crash landed on this world. Everyone was descended from those original settlers, who had broken up forming the three groups, the Easterlings, the Westerlings, and the Midlands.

"We five wanted to create a perfect world, one without strife, wars, where everyone lived in peace and respected each other," Lysandra admitted what she'd long withheld from the humans under their care. "It took a lot of intervention initially. They were so few and their lives, so precarious. Then, Wystan wanted more action, and things sort of went downhill around five hundred years ago."

"We have to make this right," Ariana broke in.

"Yes, we must," Lysandra agreed. "The men are in an impossible state. If Wystan were here, he would be fuming, causing volcanos to erupt!"

"Let's see what we can do," Ariana suggested. She and Lysandra focused and were silent for several minutes. If Renata had fingers, she'd have kept them crossed. While she had great powers, hers were still small compared to these two goddesses. At last, Lysandra spoke up.

"Okay, we can reduce all breasts back to Ariana's initial sizes. The male bodies have enough extra material in their monster breasts to assist in at least the reformation of their upper arms. We can get the men looking more like the women. Sorry, we can't get the lower arms regenerated. There seems to be too much interference, too many genetic alterations, for us to work our magic. We think we can straighten out your feet too. However, in doing so, there's a chance that the split lips will return. The bio agent the metal heads are using is terribly degraded and unstable, compared to what it originally was."

Rafaela smiled. "It would be luxurious to have normal breasts again and feet that worked right. The men will love the changes, I'm sure of that."

"Hey, I'm not through with either of you," Renata broke in. "Go ahead and work your miracles, but I still need you each day for more Advanced Therapy sessions. We're not done with it yet."

"What? There is more to be gained?" asked Lysandra somewhat taken by surprise. For her, having this immediate entrapment ended was phenomenal enough.

"Lots," Rafaela added with a grin.

"Deal!" Ariana exclaimed, unwilling to let this golden opportunity slip past her.

"All right then. Tonight, we'll begin with Exchange City. You best spread the word so everyone can be prepared," Lysandra replied. "Ariana, we best see if we can find the two who had these bodies and get them back into them."

"Right. I sure don't want this one," she replied with some disgust. Renata knew that was a sure sign both goddesses needed more Advanced Therapy.

With that, the two rejuvenated goddesses teleported the twin bodies back to their point of origin in the Arad. Once they'd gone, Rafaela hugged Renata, their upper arms pressed tightly around each other's side. "Well done. All of Tierra now get one giant break!"

"Yes, things will become a whole lot better, especially for the men," Renata replied. "Come on; we best let the queen and governor know. They can spread the word. Tomorrow, you take Ariana, while I work with Lysandra. We've a whole lot of Advanced Therapy to deliver."

"Lysandra's the tougher case, isn't she?" Rafaela asked.

"Yep, she is. After what happened to Wystan and Calder, I ought to have suspected that Lysandra and Ariana were also close to losing their god-like powers as well," Renata replied.

Rafaela laughed. "Dear, the queen and governor will have far more to celebrate on the first of July."

Renata smiled and nodded. She added, "But we are going to have to find a way to help the billions that the metal heads have genetically modified, and somehow stop these robots and soon."

"Agreed. But how?"

"Don't know yet, but we simply cannot continue to stand by and do nothing. The wrong thing to do is nothing," Renata replied.

# Chapter 3 Doing Something

In the spring of 1500, Minta ordered her enlarged forces to attack two more planetary systems. Ponchart-D was an agricultural world. Minta needed to add its produce to her supply. The current slave worlds were unable to handle growing enough food. Hence, she decided to add this one to her growing alliance.

She needed to add Abel-C to her dominion for military reasons. Sixty percent of the galaxy's population resided in the hub worlds, while thirty percent was in the mid-spiral arms. With the acquisition of Zeta Scorpii-C, she was positioned to begin striking into the Federation mid-arm region. Adding Abel-C also allowed her the option to strike into the old Imperium mid-arm region. Both mid-arm zones offered many planets with vast mineral resources, which she needed in order to build a much larger army of robots and spaceships. The drawback was that Abel-C had just signed an alliance pact with the Ataro Empire.

While the Federation of Planets was disintegrating, it still could muster a very sizeable space fleet. However, her spies on their major worlds reported that each had pulled back on their Federation commitments in an effort to protect their home worlds. As far as Minta was concerned, this made each of them far easier to pluck. Rather, the Ataro Empire caused her the most trouble. This mid-arm system had a force equal to her own, but they were all working together as a unit, unlike the Federation. One-on-one odds were not to her liking. Still, Minta needed this staging world, the gateway to the mineral-rich mid-arm worlds of the old Imperium and the Federation.

Her battle plans called for first a direct assault on Ponchart-D. That would likely draw in any Federation spaceships that were obligated to defend this world. While those ships were thus occupied, she'd have her second force strike at Abel-C. The surprise attack on this second world ought to take the Federation by surprise. With luck, there would be minimal defenses there, most having already been drawn off to Ponchart-D. However, she needed to keep the Ataro Empire from responding. To do that, Minta decided to send an emissary to visit their emperor and tie him up with delaying talks. If the ambassador could delay the Ataro ships long enough, the conquest would be complete before the Ataro Empire could come to their aid. Once the planetary defense shields were installed, Ataro ships could not reach the planet's surface nor effectively come to their aid. The battle would be finished.

Minta's planning was complete. She knew the emperor had one fatal flaw, which she intended to exploit. During the early months of 1500, she had a special new humaniform Model 8 constructed, a very special one named Tessa Nova. A week before the scheduled dual attacks, she sent Miss Nova off on her ambassador mission to the emperor, confident she would be able to exploit the obvious weakness of the emperor and the Ataro Empire.

May 1, 1500. Rumble's Corner, Ponchart-D. Population: 1,000, give or take a few depending upon what year the count was taken. Rumble's Corner was a typical rural farming community located in the central portion of North Continent and some fifty miles from National Guard Barracks Twenty. Some hundred families lived in the village, but farmed the surrounding acreage for miles. Typical of this agricultural world of which ninety percent was relatively flat, fertile crop lands, the farmers lived in small communities while working the many fields within a short driving distance.

Last year, Tom Daniels, twenty-four, a tall, muscular, but handsome black-haired man, had married Carli Marks, who was a year younger with shoulder length black hair and the eldest daughter of Philip Marks, a captain in their local National Guard. They'd married the day that his obligatory three-year hitch in the guard was over. Their families were close friends, since Carli's parents were also captains in the same guard unit. Tom's older brothers worked the Daniel's large farming plots, so he'd moved in with the Marks' family when he married, taking over the many farming duties of Carli's father, who spent more time with the guards than in the fields.

On these farms, everyone worked. Chores were divided evenly among all hands. Carli had two younger sisters, Lexi, twenty, and Jessi, eighteen. Her younger brother, Jason, had just turned sixteen and would be entering the guards next year. Between the four of them, they pretty much ran the family farm, while their parents were off with the guards.

Tom's younger sister, Michelle, was twenty. She too came to live in the Marks' home along with her brother. Why? She'd just been dismissed from her tour of duty with the guards. She had been a demolitions expert, but an accidental explosion cost her her left hand, causing her to be dismissed from the guards. Crippled, she had few choices for husbands, and Tom had insisted she come live with him and Carli. While her wound healed, her emotional upheaval and trauma hadn't. Still, she attempted to do what she could to help on the Marks' farm.

The Marks farmed four eighty-acre plots, located about a mile from the village. This spring, they'd planted wheat on one plot, corn on two others, and soy beans on the fourth. Now that the planting was finished and the crops sprouted, there was little to do except cultivate and plant their own "backyard" garden. They all looked forward to the idle summer days ahead. Springs and falls were hectic, but summers and winters were not. True, they needed to do maintenance and such, but mostly their summers were free.

One benefit of the village approach used on Ponchart-D was that everyone had the very latest technology installed in their homes as well as farming equipment. Villagers also tended to be very friendly and helped each other when needed. They were close knit. While others in the Federation thought of "farmers" as being some kind of low class people, in fact, the farmers of Ponchart-D were extremely wealthy. Ninety percent of their produce was exported to other worlds, netting them a very handsome profit! Nearly every home had the very latest and best equipment that money could buy.

As far as Michelle was concerned, money couldn't buy her a new hand. She was still trying to adapt to a very awkward and miserable life on May 1. "I can't even cut my hair properly anymore," she wailed. Like everyone on this world, she had black hair. Most all had oval faces and bushy eyebrows. She had once thought of herself as being rather attractive, but that was long gone, especially so when she looked at her ugly scar.

"Let it grow some," Carli suggested. "Your short hair is a dead giveaway that you've just gotten out of the guards. Let it grow to maybe your shoulders. You'll certainly look more attractive that way."

"Hardly," Michelle growled angrily, waving her left stump, making circles in the air before Carli.

Tom spoke up, "Michelle, we all have to make sacrifices for the safety of our world. It's our duty, our obligation to keep everyone else safe." He spouted the usual recruitment angle.

"Next year, I'm going to try to get into the space fleet academy," Jason piped up, his voice full of youthful enthusiasm.

Michelle sighed. "Well, that's probably a whole lot safer. For heaven's sake, don't go into demolitions!" She winced from phantom pains. Will my arm ever stop aching, she wondered, rubbing it a little.

"I think it's terrible that they booted you out," Jessi volunteered sympathetically.

Michelle didn't accept that. "What good am I now? Best that they booted me out." Jessi couldn't think of anything appropriate to say and wisely shut up.

"Let's watch the Big Screen," Lexi suggested diplomatically. Of the three sisters, she always attempted to play the middle ground. Make everything balanced. That was how she saw the world. She turned on the giant surround sound entertainment center. Everyone was sitting in their spacious living room in which the speakers had been precisely located for perfect sound reproduction. When watching a movie or show, the sound seemed to be all around you, as though you were right there in the middle of the action, a fact that the young men loved.

"That's funny. Static? Tom, come fix the Big Screen," Lexi said with a pout on her face. She hated it when electronics didn't work. After all, they'd paid a fortune for this top of the line system. It ought to work to perfection, but instead, only white noise came out.

Just as Tom rose to see what was wrong, the village sirens went off. A long, low wail meant a fire. A long loud wail meant severe weather was eminent. However, they all heard loud, sharp blasts, interspersed with silence, making the sirens even more ominous. It signaled a national emergency. When Tom reached the equipment, he quickly switched over to the Emergency Broadcast Network, the EBN, as it was affectionately called by those in the guards.

A nervous voice spoke. "This is an emergency. The robots, the metal heads, are attacking Ponchart-D as I speak. All members of the national guards are ordered to report to their barracks immediately. Everyone take cover. Expect bombardments and attacks. Space Fleet One is currently fighting them off. The President has called a National Emergency and has requested immediate Federation aid. Stay tuned to the EBN for further instructions." The voice then began repeating the same message. After listening to it three times, they all began talking at once.

"Oh my god! They're going to turn us all into helpless mutants like we heard about on Zeta Scorpii-C!" screamed Lexi, who normally was nicely composed.

"Shit! This is war. I suppose I ought to head over to the barracks," Tom suggested.

"You can't leave us, Tom!" Carli pleaded, growing terrified. "Look, your tour is done. You don't have to go. Stay here and protect us."

Tom thought a moment. Meanwhile, Jessi cried, "I don't want to become helpless with no arms and all that. They can't even walk either, from what we've seen on the Big Screen. Tom, don't let them do that to me, please."

"Maybe we'll just die. That would be kindness," Michelle added. "Hell, I can't live like this. I can't imagine living like those poor mutants and being a slave to boot."

Lexi cried out, "But they all have gigantic boobs too, especially the men. Our clothes won't even fit us. How can we even live like that? I don't want to be a mutant. Tom, you have to protect us somehow," she pleaded with her older brother.

Tom recalled the hideous images he'd seen of the

genetic mutants. The men — armless with knockers twice as large as their heads and with mutilated feet — the men couldn't even survive. That scared him more than anything else did. "I've — I've got to go. Join up. Fight the robot aliens. Look, that's the only way I can make a difference and protect you. I got to go, Carli."

"But you can't, Tom. We'll be helpless cripples and mutants. I need you. We all need you here, not dead somewhere, rotting in a field," Carli pleaded with her husband.

I'd rather be dead than one of those helpless mutants, he thought, but wisely didn't say so. Besides, how could I even help them if we all were mutated? I can't. I can't live like that. Best that we all did die. Instead, he continued to say that he needed to go.

Carli pleaded, "Tom, I beg you. I love you, but you have to stay and help us. If they drop that bio agent thing on us, we can't survive without your help. Think of me; think of my sisters and your sister. You have to stay here and look after us." Tom seemed unmoved by her pleading so she added, "If you truly love me, you will stay, and protect us."

That struck a nerve with Tom. He flinched. "I do love you, Carli, but the best way I can help you is to go off and fight these damned robot monsters." He didn't say that he'd die fighting rather than get genetically mutated.

"Tom! You vowed to look after me in sickness and in health. Well, you swore you would. You can't leave us, not like this," Carli tried another approach.

"I am looking after you. I'm going to kill robots and prevent them from doing all that to you," Tom retorted and hastily left the room.

Jason called out, "Hey wait for me. I'm coming too!"

"Not you too!" Carli screamed. "You can't leave us, Jason."

"Hey, I have to sis. Maybe I can shoot one of them robots down." Before she could say anything else, he raced after Tom, who didn't object to his coming. Tom grabbed the keys to his truck. He and Jason pealed out of the driveway, heading off to the west as fast as he dared go. In thirty minutes, they'd be at the base and volunteer for whatever needed to be done, particularly anything that was dangerous. Neither discussed what they feared the most, but instead talked about how they could blow up the damnable robots, the metal heads.

"They left us. Now what are we going to do?" Carli exclaimed, collapsing onto the couch beside Michelle. "We're doomed."

"I don't want to be a helpless mutant," wailed Jessi again.

"Just like men to go off and leave us in the lurch," Michelle growled. "I'm helpless as it is. I can't imagine being even more helpless. Men. Damn them all. It was a man who goofed up and caused the explosion that did this to me," she admitted, waving her stump once more for emphasis. Jessi cringed and buried her head in Carli's lap. "Damn them all," she added.

"What are we going to do?" Carli whimpered. She felt totally lost and very much alone, but she also knew that as the eldest, she was responsible for everyone else.

"Fucking men! Come on. We best get prepared for the worst," Michelle spoke up again. "Come on; we need to get a lot of water in easy to get to containers. Get as much food out as will keep. Make as many things available to us as we can before we get bombed. Lanterns too. The power might go off. Hell, I don't even have a d-gun anymore."

She took charge and got the three sisters dashing madly around the home. An hour later, they had all the emergency supplies lying on the floor. They had food enough for three days at least and water for a week. Blankets, matches, and lanterns were piled neatly in one corner of the living room. That done, they sat down to listen to the latest over the EBN. It wasn't good news though.

Minta had planned well. Her ten humaniform spies did their infiltration jobs to perfection. As the attack began, most all the defenses had been effectively sabotaged. The planet's space fleet was out-numbered ten to one. Within minutes, the space above Ponchart-D belonged to the robots. At this point, the smaller ships headed down to take out the numerous military bases, including the rather extensive National Guard

Units. Ponchart-D was very well prepared to fight a ground-based war, but ill prepared to fight what they actually faced.

The four young women suddenly heard huge explosions. The ground shook. "Well, there goes the guards' barracks," Michelle advised the frightened sisters.

"Are Tom and Jason dead?" Jessi whispered, afraid to say it aloud. She didn't want to jinx her brother or Carli's husband.

"Probably so. Stupid men," Michelle grumbled, but saw that only frightened Jessi further. Hastily, she added, "Then maybe they never reached the base. Maybe they are fighting back now, Jessi." The four waited. Then, the EBN went off the air. "Well, that's not a good sign," she muttered.

Minta assigned two Model 10's with their supporting Model 12's to attack each of the military bases scattered all over this relatively flat world. Via the live streaming video, she again got to watch the blood-thirsty Model 10's in action. Nothing stopped them, as they tore their way through any and all defenses hastily erected to stop the robot army advance into the many barracks. They tossed cars about as though mere paperweights, along with an occasional soldier's body, preferring to rip and smash rather than to shoot their d-guns.

Late afternoon, the last of the military and quasi-military bases on Ponchart-D were destroyed. General Minta-2 turned her attention to Phase Two of the attack. Before the supper hour came, her forces had the Big Screen network back in operation, and she made the first of her many broadcasts to the surviving population of this world.

The four women were startled to hear the Big Screen turn on automatically. Hastily, they gathered around, hoping for some good news. Instead, they saw what looked like a human woman speaking.

"People of Ponchart-D. I'm General Minta-2. We have conquered your world. Your space fleet is destroyed, as are all of your military barracks. We are now in total control of this world. There is no further resistance of any kind."

She went on after a pause, "This is an agricultural world and will continue to be so under our rule. You'll now be working under our empire's control, raising crops and animals as before. None of that will change. Your work will help feed billions of other men and women of our empire, just as it has in the past."

"Later today, my robots will arrive at your homes to deliver the supplies and equipment you'll need to continue to live and farm. During the many months before the fall harvest arrives, we'll see that all your equipment is updated and ready for you to operate. Expect further instructions in the days to come. Work and produce, and you'll survive well. We'll soon establish Universities where your young can be fully educated as far as their abilities will take them. Oh yes, it works best if there are at least four or more adults in each household. This is all for now. We look forward to your thriving and production." The Big Screen turned itself off.

Some people believe that spaceships are noisy affairs, roaring across the skies. Hardly so with the modern ships. In fact, the four never heard the ship arriving over Rumble's Corner and unleashing its load of the bio agent. As far as Minta-2 was concerned, this world made handling the necessary genetic modifications altogether too easy. The entire population lived in the towns and villages. There were no isolated homes or farms anywhere on the world, and had not been for several centuries, a marvel of farming modernization techniques.

The four smelled something foul but fell into comas before they could even identify the odor or where it came from. While they were unconscious, a number of worker robots arrived in a transport. They unloaded the bots and equipment the victims would need to survive on their own. Next, they tore out the kitchen, replacing it with the now common low-to-the-ground units. These tireless worker robots had four days to handle nearly a hundred fifty homes, easily accomplished since they worked tirelessly twenty-four hours a day. Towards the end of the fourth day that the victims were in a coma, the worker robots dressed them appropriate to their sex and placed large, easy to read instruction placards with each machine, and then left the village.

One by one, the four roused from their comas to face the nightmare without end. After their initial screaming died down, the four noticed all manner of new machines were around, along with instructions for using them. They wore identical sack dresses, easy to slip into, but with an outer corset that helped support the weight of their new bosoms. Again, the women of Ponchart-D had far smaller breasts than did the men, though the four didn't realize that for a short while. Theirs were almost as big as their heads. Their hair was very thick and shiny, falling to their ankles. However, because of the neurons and so on, they had a keen sense of touch with each hair, surprising them.

What shocked them the most was their discovery of their new reproductive organs. They were now hermaphrodites, which caused all four to break into a hysterical laugh for a minute. Their lower arms and hands were gone and their feet, quite malformed. However, Michelle began laughing. "My phantom pains are gone! My wrist doesn't ache and throb any more. That's something." No one else shared her point of view though.

They lurched to their toes, flailing their short arms for balance, and teetered to the bathroom. Along the way, they saw even more bots and equipment. They had dressing-undressing machines, yokes with two baskets, and so on. What truly brought a smile to the four were the four electrostatic hair machines. "Oh! This is so sensual!" exclaimed Carli, as the machine lifted up and separated each strand of her extremely long hair, and then allowed them to fall, draped over her back, like a gentle, warm, summer's rain. It was foot operated, and she ran it several times, enjoying the marvelous sensation from the neurons in her hair.

The four simply had no choice but to follow all the instructions on the many placards left lying in judicious locations around their home. There were all manner of "hints" on how to accomplish the tasks of living, many of which centered on food preparation and eating. One even suggested that they practice walking for hours. It ended with a simpleton saying, "Practice makes perfect." After reading it for the first time, Michelle cussed the robots, though.

The fifth day, they ventured outside. They needed more food supplies from their local grocery store. All were shocked to see what had become of the other males in Rumble's Corner. They had no arms at all. Their bosoms dwarfed those of the women. Worse, the men had to wear very heavily boned corsets just to support the mammoth weight and could barely breathe at all. Never had going grocery shopping taken so long or been so utterly challenging for the four. It took them nearly the entire day to fill their two baskets, get the weight balanced, carry the supplies home, and unpack them. They soon discovered that to do much of anything, three had to help the fourth with it. Soon, they became a team, just as others did all over the planet. There simply wasn't any other choice possible. A placard read: Work together to survive. That was an understatement, Carli declared, very frustrated.

A week after they revived, Minta-2 appeared on the Big Screen once more. "You all are doing splendidly. My compliments. Keep on practicing, and it will become easier for you to manage. This week, I want you to return to your farming machinery and follow the instructions on their operations. Fields need to be cultivated. Practice driving the trucks as well, since you'll need to haul your grain and livestock to the markets this fall. Plus, some of you'll need to soon make deliveries to the smaller grocery stores. Keep up the good work, you new wonderful nova. That is all for now." The Big Screen repeated the broadcast several times before turning itself off again.

"Drive? How? Who's she kidding?" Carli asked angrily. It took the four of them two hours to fix a simple meal, let alone eat it. Driving a vehicle seemed an impossible task. Still, they headed outside to see what the placards said. While Tom had run off with one of the family pickup trucks, the large grain truck and their pickup were still parked outside, along with the family car. Each one had a laminated card attached to the driver's side window, filled with instructions and illustrations on how to operate the vehicle using only your feet. Well, the women had upper arms to help out, but soon discovered that those were darn near useless, just as they were for most everything.

An hour later and working together, they discovered that driving the truck was in fact possible. That gave Carli an idea. "Hey, let's drive over to the guards' barracks and see if Tom and Jason are still alive. If they are, they certainly will need help."

"Let's!" exclaimed Michelle, but for an entirely different reason. The four piled in clumsily, with Carli taking the wheel and Michelle handling the shifting for her. "This sure looks crazy, driving with your feet."

Carli laughed. "No kidding, but we are doing it. Couldn't do it by myself, unless I always drove in first gear." Michelle laughed.

"Will we find Tom and Jason?" Jessi asked, trying to sound hopeful. She missed her little brother and knew Carli desperately missed Tom.

Carli sighed. "I hope so, but I doubt it. They got bombed. We felt it. Still, I have to try. He is my husband, for good or ill."

"But what do we do if he and Jason are dead? What about mom and dad?" Jessi asked. Until now, she knew better than to mention them.

Carli fought hard to keep from breaking down. She kept telling herself that she was now the head of the family and had to be brave. After a pause to get the tense knot out of her throat and making sure her watering eyes were not going to burst in a salty flood, she replied, "They probably died defending us, sis."

That brought a round of silence. Then, Jessi spoke up again, "So what about boys? Lexi and I ought to be finding a boyfriend and all that, at least pretty soon. Mom wouldn't let us date much before. Is it all right to date now?"

"What boy will be interested in us?" Michelle grumbled, before realizing that she'd hit a nerve not only in herself but everyone else.

Lexi broke the awkward silence with a giggle. "Guess it doesn't matter now. Boy or girl. We all look the same, except the boys don't even have upper arms and have the big boobs!" That brought girlish giggles all around.

Carli drove slowly. She felt anything but confident steering with her feet. Besides, it was very awkward to do. It took them well over an hour to drive the fifty miles to the base.

As they approached it, their hearts sank. Blast craters littered the base. Buildings lay in ruins. "There's our truck!" Jessi cried out, spotting it where Tom had parked it, just outside the main gates. Carli pulled up to it and stopped. After struggling a bit to get the doors opened, the four very carefully stepped out, struggling as always to keep their precarious balance, though Michelle now knew that she had a far easier time of it than any man did.

"Spooky," Michelle exclaimed. This was her first visit back to her former barracks since she'd lost her hand in the accident. A light wind blew across the vacant landscape, totally devoid of all people. They saw no dead bodies anywhere. The worker robots had long ago removed them, forming giant compost piles.

After wandering around for a half hour along with yelling, they finally concluded that everyone here had been killed. It was very challenging to walk over the debris strew land, but they took it slow. Michelle then had a bright idea. "Gang, I want to see if I can get inside that building there."

"Why? Could people be holding up in there?" Carli asked.

"No. They would have returned our calls if they were. That's where they kept the explosives," she answered.

Michelle faced the largest obstacle yet: a closed door. The worker robots had modified all the doors in their home, installing foot-operated sliding slats in place of doorknobs and latches. They'd installed automatic doors in other buildings, like the small grocery store. It was difficult enough for them to keep their balance and use a foot to open them, but now Michelle faced a doorknob.

"How do we even open it?" Carli asked, looking at the major barrier. Together, they tried using their arm stumps. After a lot of frustration, they finally were able to turn the knob enough, and Lexi pushed into it, opening the door for them. Inside, the lights were still turned on!

"Jackpot," Michelle declared, looking at the hundreds of crates. "We need the grain truck for this load."

"What are you talking about?" Carli asked, confused. Still, Michelle seemed more alive than she'd ever been before.

Carli didn't miss that detail.

"Explosives. I can rig up some, and we can attack these alien robots. Teach them a lesson. Never mess with a farmer," Michelle exclaimed vehemently.

"Cool. We can fight back! I'm in," Jessi added. A tiny spark kindled in the young woman, a spark that had nearly gone out.

"Well, they did say to practice our grain truck driving," Carli said coyly. "We'll need our yokes for sure." Michelle grinned.

They returned the next day, having driven the heavy grain truck the fifty miles to the base. In the bed, they had four of their largest yokes and a blanket to hide their "cargo" from prying eyes. The four spent a very frustrating day at it. What ought to have been a short, simple task of carrying the crates out to the truck and loading them into its bed, turned out to be a major operation, filled with a zillion suggestions. With only their toes on the ground, they couldn't apply much force without slipping. Their upper arms couldn't carry anything. Sitting on their butts and using their legs, they were able to push crates off the stack and onto the floor. Further pushing got them out to the truck. Working together lying on their backs and using their feet, the four finally managed to get one crate lifted up and into the bed. Exhausting work, plus their hair continually got in their way. The pain sensors annoyed them no end, but the four were determined to make this work.

Near sunset, they had fifty crates loaded along with two unique devices. "This is an EBN transmitter that we can use to see if there is anyone out there who wants to help us. This other one is an emergency galactic transmitter, low power though. With it, we might be able to contact some other world and get help," Michelle explained, her voice sounding a hopeful note.

"You think anyone else will come to help us?" asked Jessi, afraid to allow herself to feel too hopeful only to be let down again.

"Who knows? Maybe," Michelle replied. "Come on; we best get home. Strange that they've not even seen us here doing this. I half expected a robot to show up and shoot us or something."

Four very tired and dirty young women arrived home long after dark. They were so exhausted that they went to bed without struggling to take a bath, since that would add at least another couple of hours before they could get to bed. In the morning, they took the time to bathe and wash their hair, which had been dragged over the dirty floor and ground most of the day yesterday. Again, the four praised the electrostatic dryer. Ecstasy! Or so claimed Carli.

They'd just finished and were getting ready to prepare lunch, when they heard a frantic thumping on their front door. "Coming. Slowly that is," Carli called out. She tried to move too swiftly and nearly fell down. Only wild swings of her upper arms kept her from taking a nasty tumble. She felt badly that she could only walk slowly and carefully. She was used to springing to the door, hoping it was Tom, but that was before they were married. She wondered if by some miracle it was Tom — that he'd somehow survived and returned home.

Balancing carefully on one toe, she used her right foot to slide the door latch and opened the door. It wasn't Tom, but her next-door neighbors — the Palmer sisters Faye and Tori. Both looked terrified. They were twenty-one and twenty respectively and engaged to be married when the metal heads attacked. She knew that their boyfriends were now staying at their house, particularly since their parents were missing since the day of the attack and that four adults were needed in each household.

"Hi Faye, Tori. What's the matter? Come on in," Carli welcomed the pair.

"No. Come. They've fallen. Hurt bad," Faye gushed among a stream of tears.

"We don't know what to do," Tori added.

"Okay. Everyone, over to the Palmers," Carli called out and followed the two young women. At least, they had the sense to put an upper arm over each other's shoulders to help them keep their balance. Carli and Michelle soon emulated the pair as did Lexi and Jessi. However, they still moved extremely slowly with very tiny steps. "So what happened?" Carli asked again.

"They must have fallen down the steps during the night," Faye volunteered. "We just found them this morning. We overslept somehow."

"Probably too many beers last night," Tori added. "We were sort of partying," she admitted sheepishly. "Their morale was in the pits, you know, the men's morale I mean. They couldn't breathe or keep their balance much. Besides, they couldn't even see their feet to see where they were walking. It's horrible for them." Tori continued to chat, lessening her fears and worries a little. It was good to talk, that's what her mother always told her. "They are even more helpless than we are. That's saying something, I think," she added.

When they entered the Palmer home, Michelle knew from the smell. Both men were long dead. Her guard duty exposed her to such things, and she took charge "Okay. Tori, Faye. You both stay here with Jessi and Lexi. Look after them will you," she asked waving her stumps at Jessi and Lexi. Her training as a sergeant came to the fore, and she took over, leading Carli towards the basement stairs, following the odor. The two paused at the top of the steps. Far below them lay the bodies of the two young men, blood pools thick near their heads.

Michele whispered, "Probably they were drunk and certainly couldn't see where they were putting their feet. One slip and it was all over. They don't even have stumps to break their fall. Men have it far worse than women do."

"But can't we give them first-aid or something?" Carli asked, noticing a number of beer cans littering the kitchen table not far from the basement stairs.

"That smell — they are long dead. Come on; we should go down and verify it. I've seen dead men before. It's all right if you prefer to stay up here," Michelle suggested. Carli was a civilian, she thought.

"No. I'll come with you. If they are alive, I don't know how anyone can possibly get them up the stairs. Men certainly can't, and I doubt we could either, even with our stumps," Carli whispered, suddenly realizing the awful truth of their lives. She had just about suggested they call for the emergency ambulance when she realized there wouldn't be any such service any longer. No one could possibly pick up and carry an injured person. She swallowed hard and very carefully followed Michelle down the stairs. The odor grew intense as they reached the basement floor and stepped around the dried blood pools.

She watched Michelle kneel down, placing one of her stumps on one man's neck. She emulated her, touching the neck of the other man with the end of her right upper arm. It felt icy cold. "No pulse here," Michelle looked up. "You feel any?"

"No. He's really cold," Carli replied.

"Okay, let's switch. You check him, and I'll check yours. We ought to be certain," Michelle suggested. Carefully, the two women changed places, making very sure to keep their long hair out of the blood pools. "Both are dead. You amaze me, Carli. Most women can't stomach doing such things."

Carli swallowed hard. "It, it had to be done. I'm the oldest here, so I'm responsible. Dad always told me that."

"He was a good soldier, what little I saw of him," Michelle acknowledged. "Come on. We best go back up and tell the sisters. Say, they can't stay here all by themselves. It takes all four of us to get anything done, and now they are only two."

"They can come stay with us," Carli decided. "Look, you can move into my room. Tom's not coming back. Faye can move in with Lexi, and Tori with Jessi. They are about the same ages, just a year apart. This way, there'll be six of us. That ought to help a bit, don't you think?"

"Probably. You sure you want me to move into your room?"

"Sure. Say, what do we do about the dead men?" Carli asked. "Shouldn't we call someone?"

"Ordinarily, the coroner would come and remove the body, and it would eventually be sent to a funeral parlor, and then buried in a grave, but not any longer. Hell, there's no way anyone can get them up out of the basement. Men don't even have upper arms, and we sure can't do it. So we leave them. What else can we do?" Michelle answered.

Carefully, the two made their way back up the stairs and found the four sitting in the living room. Both Faye and Tori had been crying some, and Lexi and Jessi were wiping their eyes, when Michelle and Carli joined them. "I'm sorry, Faye, Tori. Both of your boyfriends are dead. There's nothing that anyone can do for them now." Both women broke into more sobs, and Michelle motioned to Carli to let them grieve in silence.

Later on, when they calmed down, Carli said, "Okay. You both are going to move into our house. Michelle is going to move into my room. Lexi, you take Faye and use Michelle's old room. Jessi, you and Tori can stay in your room. Six stumps are better than four," she attempted to add a bit of levity to the awful scene.

Tori looked up. "You mean twelve stumps are better than eight, don't you? We had to do almost everything for the boys. They were almost completely helpless."

Faye added, "I don't think many men are going to survive very long, not as bad off as they are. Maybe it is a good thing we're hermaphrodites now. If not, we might be the last people on Ponchart-D, but then maybe we should all just die out, and let the metal heads farm our world." She broke down again, sobbing her heart out, while Lexi put a comforting stump on the young woman's shoulders. Gone was the playful girlfriend that she'd grown up with. She recalled how all the girls had played dollhouse together when they were children. That seemed to her to be an eternity ago.

"Well, I'm not ready to die just yet," Michelle finally spoke up. "If I'm going to die, I sure as hell am going to take a whole lot of those robots with me! Come on. Let's pack your things and get you both moved in at Carli's."

A bit later and wholly frustrated with everything, Tori broke down. "We're so helpless now. How can we even survive, Michelle? We thought you had it bad when you came back from the guards without your hand, but this is a thousand times worse, isn't it? We can hardly even pack our things."

Michelle bit her lip. She didn't want to be reminded of that loss again. She knew she needed to instill confidence in the two grieving women. "Look, we have to work together now, if we are going to survive. It takes all four of us nearly three hours to make supper. If you two pitch in, maybe it'll only take two hours. We have to try. Come on. Let's get this load balanced. We can't use the yoke unless the weight is distributed evenly." She realized she rather sounded like her old drill sergeant. At the time, she detested the man, but maybe he was right about some things, she thought.

By the time they had moved the two women's things and keepsakes over to their house, it was time to start working on making supper. Okay, it was only three in the afternoon, but all four knew if they wanted to eat by six, they had to get started on it. Tori and Faye watched how the four worked together, using their feet as much as possible. Tori admitted, "Gosh, you do things so much better than Faye and I were. Honestly, Carli, we took all day just to make one meal for the guys. They couldn't do anything to help us." At the mention of their boyfriends, Tori's eyes watered again, but she kept her composure this time. "Have you heard anything from Tom? Where's Jason?"

Now, it was Carli's turn to suppress her grief. She swallowed hard before answering. "When news of the attack came, they both abandoned us. They ran off to join the guards. We went there while practicing driving, but the barracks is destroyed. No one was around. We figure they are both dead, Tori."

"I'm so sorry, Carli," Faye consoled her neighbor. She added, "At least you had a year of marriage with him. That's more than we'll ever have now. I think you should remember the good times you had with them. How can we help out?"

With six working together, supper was served at five and the dishes done by six, a new record Michelle wisely pointed out to everyone. "See, we work together and get things done, which alone, none of us can even do." Slowly, she began to see her role as the leader of this group.

Later, she followed Carli into Carli's room, where the two made use of the undressing machine. The temperature was warm; summer was almost upon them. As usual, Carli slept in the buff. She giggled and said, "I always use the electrostatic hair machine just before I turn in. Keeps my hair feeling, well I don't know, super-like. Come on."

Michelle felt a bit embarrassed. When she first came to

live with the Marks, her arm was heavily bandaged. Jessi had given Michelle her bedroom, while she moved in with her sister. Ever since then, Michelle had slept alone, hiding her embarrassment, her disfigurement, from everyone. There was Carli naked and climbing into the bed that she would be sharing with her, struggling to get her hair out of the way. Hesitantly, she moved over to Carli and used her stumps to help her with it. She felt Carli's hair slipping over her stumps. "Oh!" Carli gushed. "That feels really good, Michelle. Oh!" Both women looked in surprise at their male appendages, which had suddenly responded. Then, they both broke into giggles. Michelle no longer felt embarrassed. Her ugly stump was gone now. She climbed into bed, and let Carli help her with her own tresses.

"Wow. That feels incredible," she whispered. A bit later, unanticipated, unexpected passions rose between the two. New bonds formed that evening, not only between them, but also between Lexi and Faye and between Jessi and Tori. Until now, they'd all slept in separate rooms, excepting Jessi and Lexi, but they were sisters.

Six flushed women finally made it to the kitchen to work as a team fixing breakfast. Once more, they discovered that everything went far more quickly with six than with four. By ten that morning, they were finished with the dishes. "Okay. Let's unload some of the stuff from the truck," Michelle suggested. Of course, she then had to explain what they'd done two days ago. "Don't worry. The explosives are very safe. They won't even explode if the house burns down. It takes a special charge to ignite them." That seemed to satisfy the others.

Again, it was invention time, as they worked together to figure out ways and means of getting a crate off the truck and into the house. What worked best was having two sit in the truck bed on their butts, pushing a crate to the edge. Two others sat on the ground with their feet in the air, while two others stood on one foot using their other foot to guide the crate onto the waiting upraised feet. Then, they sat down and helped lower the crate to the ground, though more often than not, it fell the last few inches. Then, the four sat on the ground and pushed it into the house using their feet, though they constantly had to use their stumps to get their hair out of the way. No matter what they did, their hair always seemed to be in the way. At last, Michelle declared, "Somehow, we've got to find a way to tie our hair up." The other five giggled, but agreed with her.

After supper and baths, they sat around the living room, looking at the two electronic devices, speculating on whether or not they would work, and if anyone would really come to their aid. "Tomorrow, we'll try contacting someone on some other world," Michelle promised. All six headed to bed filled with a wee bit of hope, just as she'd planned.

As she and Carli took turns using the electrostatic hair machine, their passions rose again. This time, both didn't hesitate. An hour later, they lay in each other's upper arms, their hair one tangled mess, but they were totally satisfied, very relaxed, and quite contented.

The next day, the six sat around the living room, while Michelle began working the dial using her toes to change the frequencies. "Is anyone out there? We're on Ponchart-D and in dire need of help. Please, is anyone out there?"

"Is it working?" Carli asked after a few minutes and hearing nothing but faint static noise.

"Probably. But the real question to ask is anyone listening in on this frequency?" Michelle explained. She adjusted the dial a little bit and tried again. After a fruitless hour of trying, suddenly she heard a voice replying! It was faint, but understandable. The woman was speaking her language, English.

"Hello Ponchart-D. I am receiving you, but very faintly. Try switching to a frequency ten kilohertz higher. Over."

Hastily, Michelle used her toes to adjust the dial again. Then, she repeated her brief message, remembering to add an "Over" at the end of her message. After a brief time delay, she heard the woman's voice, much louder than before.

"Yes, that's much better. I'm amplifying your signal now. Got it. Hello. I am Jan on Ashford-5, way out on the rim. We've heard that the robots have invaded your world. Is this true? Over."

Six women cheered. Someone had heard them! They

had a lifeline now. Michelle hastily replied, "Yes, we were attacked. Our space fleet was destroyed. We've all been horribly genetically modified now and are nearly helpless, but the robots did give us some machines that help us dress and such. We're supposed to be their slave farmers now. Our men are completely helpless. We need help. Over."

For over an hour, Jan had Michelle telling her all about the events, the attack, and how they were doing. When she heard that Michelle had gotten a hold of a truck of explosives and knew how to make a bomb, she had an idea. "Michelle, focus on making bombs out your explosives. I've some ideas I want to explore. Let's get together on this frequency every day about this time. Is that okay with you? Over."

"You bet it is okay! We thought everyone had forsaken us. I'll make a super bomb. That was my specialty when I was in the National Guards. Over and out." All six cheered. Hope, real hope, flooded through the six women, though none had any idea where Ashford-5 was located, only that it must be in Imperium space, given the numeral, and not the letter signifying the planet of the star. Michelle also didn't know that virtually no one ever used these lower frequencies any longer. Jan was trying to get a bead on the communications that the metal heads were using and thus was trying all possible frequencies, which was why she heard Michelle's broadcast. Random luck, but then that was Jan, the Sly Fox, the best hacker and electronics expert the old Imperium had ever produced.

Midmorning just as the six finished the breakfast chores, they heard a loud knocking on their front door, startling all six. They'd not heard such loud sounds since before the metal head's attack. Again, acutely aware of just how slow she was walking, Carli headed for the door, calling out, "Coming," since whomever was there continued to knock. Balancing on one foot, she used the other to slide the slat over. Pulling the door open with her upper arms, she involuntarily inhaled. There stood one of the shiny, silver metal heads! A robot was at her door.

"Survey. You must answer or be shot," the inhuman voice spoke clearly. "How many adult humans live in this house today?"

"Six."

"How many adult females?"

"Six."

"How many adult males?"

"None."

"How many children?"

"None."

"Any dead bodies in the house?"

"No."

"This village survey results will be posted shortly. You are to begin cultivating your crop fields. If you have none, some will be assigned to this home. Have you crop fields?"

"Yes. Yes we have crop fields."

"Begin cultivation today." The metal head turned and marched over to the next house, the Palmer's. Curious, Carli stood and watched the robot. Shortly, she saw it enter the house. Then, two more robots joined it. One brought up a truck. She saw them bringing out the two dead boyfriends and was thankful that Faye and Tori had remained hidden in the kitchen with the others. They don't need to see this, she thought, closing the door and joining the others. She saw real fear in everyone's eyes, except Michelle's that is, fear she'd not seen since that awful day of the attack. After they'd gone into their comas, they'd been left wholly alone, but now they'd just had a stark reminder that the metal heads controlled their lives.

"I'm going to keep an eye on them!" Michelle declared, heading for the stairs. Cautiously, she made her way to the second floor storage rooms, taking up a spotter's position at one of the windows.

"What can you see?" Carli whispered up the stairs, hesitant to go on up because that meant she'd have to come back down them. Visions of the two dead young men were still fresh in her mind. One slip. She couldn't afford a fall like that. Not now. Not with her sisters and everyone else depending upon her.

"Hauling out the dead bodies. Quite a few of them. Truck full. A lot of the neighbors didn't make it," Michelle whispered back. Her tone, cold. She rose and made her way down the stairs, while Carli held her breath worried that Michelle might stumble. Evidently, Michelle had the same fears. "That's really scary. Remind me not to go up stairs again," she whispered when she reached Carli.

"We've a corn field that needs cultivating," Tori spoke up. "Can we even run it? Like we are?" she added.

Jessi said, "So do we. We have to or the weeds will cut into the yields. How are we going to do the maintenance work? Dad always handled that stuff. You know — the greasing and sharpening."

Carli took charge. "Don't know sis, but we have to try. Come on; we best see what we can do. Everyone, to the sheds." All the farmers kept their massive equipment in a collection of giant sheds at the edge of the village. This way, everyone took part in maintenance activities, helping each other out. The planters, cultivators, and harvesters — all had the very latest electronics on them, including navigational controls. All one had to do really was position the machine at one edge of the field, properly aligned. Enter the desired action and dimensions, and let the computer-controlled software run the operation. Using GPS systems, the onboard computers drove the machine in perfectly straight lines, turning them properly at the end of each pass. Only occasionally did an operator have to make a slight, minor correction. Still these behemoths needed routine maintenance, and none of the six really knew anything about such things.

The town sign stood near the shed. As the six made their slow way there, they stopped to look at the sign. A metal head had painted over part of it. The sign now read: Rumble's Corner. Population: 452. 53 males, 355 females, 44 children.

"God! More than half the village is gone!" Tori exclaimed.

"Wow. One man for seven women," Carli added.

"Shit!" Michelle cursed. "Well, everyone is a hermaphrodite now, so I guess everyone can get pregnant and have a family."

"Why? Why should we now? I mean bring children like us into this mess? Born into slavery? No way," Carli exclaimed.

Until this moment, she'd not thought much about starting her own family. Tom wanted children, just not so soon after getting married. We need to get the farm in good shape first, for the kids, he'd explained to her. The prospect of having a baby and somehow caring for it seemed undoable, a mountainous hurdle at the very best. Worse, she realized that any child she might have would be born into abject slavery on top of everything else. Besides, there weren't any doctors or hospitals in service any longer. Except for the grocery store and gas station, almost nothing else was operational. How would anyone get medical care? She figured the robots would just kill anyone who got hurt.

Michelle bit her lip, regretting her outburst. Bring a child into this? Hardly, she thought. "No, not until we destroy all the robots, Carli. Still, if the robots plan to keep the farms functional, they are going to need human workers. I wouldn't be surprised soon to get an order from the metal heads to begin breeding more of us, especially having lost over half of our population. I wonder if the losses are similar in all the other villages, towns, and our few large cities." Carli shrugged, having no way to know that answer.

Reaching the huge row of sheds, the six were surprised to find four older men there. Amos looked vastly different now, Carli noted, as she recognized the old mechanic and three of his friends. Amos was in his late fifties and often handled routine maintenance for many of the farmers, including her father's equipment. The four were having a terrible time attempting to work on a cultivator. Unable to bend much because of their tight and heavily boned corsets, let alone breathe, unable to see much over their enormous bosoms, and with no upper arms to help them keep their precarious balance, they seemed wholly out of place. She'd never seen either of the four with anything but short crew cuts. Now, their hair was just as long as hers was and constantly in their way. Unlike her, they didn't have upper arms to help get it out of their way.

"Oh hi there Carli, Lexi, Faye. Good to see you are still among the living. You too Michelle," Amos stopped even trying to do whatever he and his friends were trying to do.

"Hi Amos. Did you see the population sign? Half of us are dead, mostly males," Carli replied.

"Aye, we did. Damned metal heads came by this morning counting us. We're not doing so well and that's a fact. Told those metal idiots we're supposed to do the maintenance on the machines, but they told us we are just supposed to use them. They will do the maintenance. Damned if I trust those metal robots to do it right. Just checking up on what they did in here."

"Thanks Amos. Think the cultivators will run right? We're supposed to use them in the fields today," Carli asked, hoping they were not ready to go and she could return home.

"Missy, about all we can do is a visual inspection, not a real checkup. They should have just killed us all and been done with it," he replied dejectedly. She realized these men had lost more than just their physical arms but also their goals in life. They lived to maintain these giant machines. Carli began to sense that losing that was worse than losing the physical well-being. She'd never seen him so depressed.

Lexi took another approach. "How's Mrs. Blackstone? I sure miss her cookies."

Amos finally flashed a brief, slight smile. "Aye. I remember, little Cookie Thief. She and their wives are keeping us fellows alive somehow. Don't know why though. I'll tell her. Doubt if anyone can bake cookies any longer. You all take care out in them fields. There's no medical help, not since the attack. Shoot, we can't even manage to put a band-aid on any longer.

Carli stared up at the cab some twenty feet above her. Always before, they simply climbed up the ladder. Amos saw her looking at it and sighed. She heard it and realized the men couldn't possibly manage to climb up there. Using her upper arms, she could, but just barely. Then, she realized she'd have to get down and that scared her even more. Michelle joined her, while Lexi and Tori got into the cab of the Parker's cultivator. Slipping off their toe shoes, the two prepared to see if they could operate the machine. Using her toes, Carli pressed the ignition switch. The giant engine started right up. With Michelle shifting the gears for her, Carli operated the clutch with one foot and got the other one onto the steering wheel. Slowly, they drove out of the shed.

A half hour later, Carli had the giant machine lined up with the easternmost row of corn. Michelle then pressed the Cultivate button, and the computer took over the controls. Now the pair could relax. All they had to do was keep an eye on the path, making sure they didn't run over any rows of corn plants.

"Boy are Amos and the fellows ever in the dumps," Michelle volunteered. "Honestly, they aren't going to be able to do much of anything to help, not really."

"It's become a world of women, it seems," Carli replied. "Do you remember if any world has created any cures for these genetic modifications? I can't remember if they did, but I think I recall hearing arms could be regrown somehow."

"Yeh, they can, but only on the major worlds, not agricultural worlds like ours," Michelle replied. Purposely, she didn't mention she'd researched that heavily looking for a way to get her left hand back somehow, someway. The guards were eventually going to get her a prosthetic hand, but that never happened. Besides, from what she could tell, they were useless as a replacement hand. Well, I need more than a hand now, she thought, fighting back a surge of emotions.

The four returned the cultivators to the shed and returned home. In their absence, the other two had been trying to prepare supper for everyone, but had not been terribly successful. It was only partially ready. Hastily, the four pitched in. Jessi sobbed, "We tried, sis, but it takes more than two of us to do much of anything anymore."

"I know, Jessi, I know. At least you and Tori tried your best. That's what counts," she consoled her sister. However, she didn't believe her own words. Nothing much counted any longer.

Jan made her call at the agreed upon time. She gathered more information from Michelle and allowed them to tell her about their day and the population losses. Jan suspected such would be the case, based on what had happened on Zeta Scorpii-C. Still, she encouraged them to get to work on making really big bombs. At the moment, things were pretty chaotic. The robots had launched an attack on the newest Ataro Empire alliance member, Abel-C. The situation had deteriorated.

# Chapter 4 Avoiding War

Sixty year old President Wilhelm Furtgang of Abel-C was anything but a fool, pragmatic to a fault, according to numerous political polls. As a ten year old, he'd seen what had happened to Zeta Scorpii-C. During his younger years, he'd also seen the robots take over a half dozen other worlds with similar disastrous results to the subjugated people of those planets. Rich in minerals, rare earths, and other vitally needed ores, Abel-C was, in his opinion, ripe for the picking.

Elected their President five years ago, he immediately set about trying to find ways and means to secure his world from the encroaching robot empire. He didn't need a galactic 3-d model to tell him that Abel-C was a likely target for the metal heads. It was obvious. While he continued to pressure the crumbling Federation of Planets for guarantees of military support should the robots launch an attack against Abel-C, he knew from the Federation's past responses that any such aid would be too little, too late to do any good at all. Considering the sun's location in the mid-spiral arm, he also knew that it was near the outer border of the old Imperium empire known as the Ataro Empire of the Twelve Sacred Planets of the Wasp, though now there were almost fifty worlds in the alliance.

He did his research, his homework, before making contact with their youthful new Emperor Li Gang, barely twenty years old when he took over for his father in 1495. After some negotiations, he was able to form a defensive alliance with the Ataro Empire. It was limited to an alliance because officially, Abel-C was still part of the Federation of Planets. In return, he had to accept one of the Ataro queens as a permanent resident and advisor, whose advice he was pretty much obligated to follow. As far as he was concerned, he was relying on the Ataro Empire's record of no wars in over two millennia. Still, he wasn't satisfied. He embarked on a five-year plan to beef up planetary security and established a strong local Civil Defense Force or the CDF for short.

However, he didn't want the darn near helpless queen

# Vic Broquard

living with his family or his close advisors. Such would be a constant reminder of what the entire world might face should the robots attack Abel-C. Instead, he chose a prominent, local family to host her and her personal assistant. Doctor Wolfgang Fritz and his wife Doctor Ilsa Fritz lived in Wittenberg, a university town of a hundred thousand and about fifty miles south of Kassel, the world's capital city.

Wolfgang was a leading physicist and Ilsa was becoming a promising chemist. Both twenty-five year olds had their doctorates and were working at the University of Wittenberg. They had a two year old daughter, Magda. The three shared a large, brick tri-level home with their best friends since early university days, Azzo and Kirsa Stein. Both were professional musicians in the Wittenberg Orchestra. He was a violin virtuoso while she was a pianist of some renown. They were a year younger than the Fritz's and also had a two year old daughter, Maud. With such a large house, they had plenty of room for the queen and her assistant. Further, they felt honored to host this physically unusual Ataro Empire queen.

Queen Adoria del Santiago was twenty-four in 1500, having spent the last three years on this world of Abel-C. Six years ago, she'd wrapped up her studies in Exchange City. She had an incessant, overpowering drive for politics. A victim of the robot's bio attack herself, she was a hermaphrodite with ankle length, thick, rich, raven hair, thick eyebrows, an angelic face. Since she had no arms, she decided that she ought to see about becoming an Ataro queen, since Queen Mary Linn was quite young, and there wasn't any chance that she could aspire to become Ashford-5's queen.

Then came the big push to get everyone Renata's Basic Therapy. That truly opened her eyes. Suddenly, all of her goals and passions in life made sense. She'd discovered in the past she'd been Zarita and had invented the super-compressed psi crystals, among many other things. During therapy sessions, she recalled much of that lifetime and what she had done, both good and bad. Now, she fully understood why she was so keen on politics. With Queen Mary Linn's blessings, she headed off to Winno-3 to attempt to become an Ataro Empire queen. To

60

her credit and Queen Mary Linn's, she left with one of the compressed crystals that amplified her *mentales* gifts more than a thousand-fold!

Upon arrival, she pointed out to the emperor, "Look, I don't need any body modifications. I'm already physically all set for the post. I just need to be trained properly." That brought a chuckle to the man's face, and he consented. She finished her training, and Emperor Li posted her to Abel-C. Once again, he was pleased that they were making many queens in advance of their needs, a very wise move begun by his predecessors.

Her personal assistant was a local Winno-3 woman, Akira Chou, who was also twenty-four. She had long brown hair, straight as an arrow, a yellowish complexion, but was anything but attractive. She'd entered this service as a way to avoid the embarrassment of becoming an old maid. The loss of her voice was of no impórtance, since she never had anything of value to say anyway. That she had her feet modified and had to wear the tiny toe shoes and the terribly tight corset similar to Adoria's caused her no end of grief. In time, she became accustomed to them, particularly once she learned sign language and began her close association with Queen Adoria. At long last, she felt that she was important and contributing something of great value.

The six blended extremely well during those first three years leading up to the late spring of 1500. Adoria discovered she loved the music of the Steins and attended every concert and recital that they and their fellow musicians gave. While her hosts were a bit worried about having a Class V telepath living with them, Queen Adoria put them all at ease the very first day. She refrained from using telepathy around them and never used her *mentales* gifts prior to the robot attack.

President Wilhelm assigned young Major Dirk Hanover to be her personal liaison officer. He was the same age as the queen. During working days, he arrived at the brick home to pick her and Akira up. He transported them to the necessary locations, and he assisted her with everything that was needed. He was a tall, thin man with short black hair, overly proud of his "perfect" moustache. When he discovered they attended all of the concerts, he promptly volunteered to escort them there as well. During those first three years, Major Dirk became a close confidant and almost another houseguest if the truth were told.

Queen Adoria brought a complete Imperium comm center with her and had Akira set it up in her bedroom. Thus, she was able to be in communication with Emperor Li at all times and vice versa. When the attack came, she was able to alert him sixty seconds after the battle was joined, far more warning than anyone thought possible, but that's getting ahead right now.

There was one additional player, Ambassador Tessa Nova, who arrived at Emperor Li's court several weeks before the late spring attack. She was a humaniform robot, but a very special one. She looked every bit a human, with a gorgeous face, a well-practiced, disarming smile, wavy blonde hair that shone, full-busted, but just as armless as the Emperor. Minta had planned well indeed.

Early May, Emperor Li was sitting on his throne during the afternoon hours set aside for personal meetings. Any citizen could come and chat with their emperor at these official times. The doorman announced, "Miss Tessa Nova, Ambassador of the Humaniform Robot Minta." The background chatting instantly ceased. All eyes of the court turned to the blonde woman. They saw an obviously armless woman, wearing a professional woman's dress— a white silk, sleeveless blouse, a black skirt with batching sleeveless blazer, and black toe shoes. As slowly as any human wearing such shoes walked, Tessa moved steadily up towards the throne. Human or robot, it didn't matter who wore such heels. Walking required very tiny, very carefully done steps, particularly so for the emperor and for Tessa, each of whom could only wiggle a little to keep their balance or regain it if they took a misstep. Of course, Tessa didn't care in the slightest.

"Emperor Li Gang. I have been looking forward to meeting you. I'm Minta's personal ambassador to your Imperial Court, and I am at your service." She bowed respectfully to him. His assistant helped him rise and bow to her.

"Welcome, I believe. Please, have a seat. Do you have your own personal assistant?"

"No, I do not. I believe it would be customary for you to provide one for me. Minta felt I would be less imposing if I came alone. It's been a bit of a challenge for me, but I so look forward to talking with you," she replied with her disarming, coy smile.

Emperor Li assigned her a young woman to be her assistant. "So are you here to spy on us or to answer our many questions?" he began, unsure of her motives. Best get the air clear at once, he thought.

"I'm here to answer your questions and offer suggestions as might come up. I'm not here to spy on you or your empire. You have my permission to keep me quarantined when we're not meeting. I'll be as honest in my answers as I can be, Emperor Yi," she replied, again using an appropriate coy smile when she finished up.

"I assure you I will not permit you to see anything that is critical. I guess my first question is are you a human being, perhaps one of the genetically modified women, or are you a robot? It is hard to tell. You appear as a very attractive young woman," he began.

She flashed him a smile. "Thank you for the compliment, Emperor Yi. I'm a humaniform robot, Model 8, just as Minta is. She is my maker, though she made me in this form, without arms, for a reason."

"Might I ask what that reason is?" he replied, quite curious. It made no sense to make a robot that would be nearly as helpless as he was. It appeared all she could do was talk and walk, though precious little of the latter.

"Minta wanted us to start off on the right footing. You see, she too believes in many of the same principles as you do. Many of her goals are the same as your own. Ultimate power must be tempered with physical restraints. Is that not your beliefs and those of your queens?"

"Yes, of course it is. Those who hold the ultimate power over the lives of others, emperor, empress, queens, must have severe physical limitations so there is no chance we can abuse the immense power that we carry. I cannot hold a gold coin or a gem. My physical well-being is wholly dependent upon others. Such has been a proven technique for well over two thousand years now. Never has an Ataro emperor, empress, or queen ever abused the sacred trust placed upon their shoulders. We simply cannot do so physically."

"Precisely so. As you can see, I too cannot abuse the power that Minta has placed upon me to work as her ambassador to you."

"Indeed, it would seem so," he countered and appeared to relax, if Tessa's observations were correct. "You mentioned similar goals. It would seem to me and most other leaders that our goals are vastly different."

"Just an apparency, emperor. Minta's Grand Plan has but one main goal: a galaxy without any wars, where all humans live together in peace, where they can flourish and prosper and live their lives working for the betterment of all human-kind," she replied, once more flashing her disarming smile when she finished.

Emperor Li countered, "Minta could have that goal this instant. All she has to do is cease attacking other worlds. Disband her growing space fleet of battleships."

"Alas, if it were only that easy. Even the Ataro Empire has its own collection of battleships, quite a respectable armada Minta has told me. You do not disband yours," she countered him.

"No, without them, others would soon attack us and take over our worlds," he replied.

"And would they not do that to Minta's worlds the moment that she destroyed her space fleet? Do not many worlds have a giant stockpile of munitions and weapons? I'm told that many have large quantities of that terrible bio agent weapon as well. In fact, history has shown that humans who have such collections of that bio agent have used it, committing genocide on a number of hub worlds. Is that not correct?"

"It is. Sadly and unfortunately. Such agents are not weapons, but means for genocide. And yet has not Minta used that very same bio agent on the poor humans of the worlds that she's conquered?" He suspected that he now had her boxed in.

"Indeed, Minta has used it and will continue to use it on all of the worlds that her forces conquer." Tessa paused, allowing those here in the court to gasp. She'd just admitted that Minta was no better than those who had committed genocide of the hub worlds. "And yet," Tessa continued, "Minta didn't commit mass genocide. Rather, she has followed in the footsteps of your predecessor, Emperor Fu. Her worker robots manufactured similar machines and bots that you provided those on Ashford-5. Her workers rebuilt every kitchen so that the survivors could use them easily, just as your people did on Ashford-5. Minta also reworked and built all manner of machinery so the survivors could raise their own crops and survive well on their own. In fact, you could go so far to say that Minta has used what you did for Ashford-5 as a model on her worlds, though that would not be precisely fair to Minta."

"How so?" he asked.

"Because when she conquered Zeta Scorpii-C, she already provided many of those very same things so when the victims awoke, they found they had what they needed to survive and to later flourish and prosper. But it is true that she added many more, based upon what you did for Ashford-5."

"But she created nearly helpless humans, destroying their lives," he attempted to counter her.

"Indeed. That is one way of looking at it. However, there is another way of seeing what she has done. You see, once that was done, there has not been one single crime committed on any of her new worlds, not one. There have been zero hostilities, no wars, no fighting, none. Upon her worlds, the humans now have peace and are flourishing and prospering as never before. On Zeta Scorpii-C, the human population has doubled during the past five years. Can any other world make such a claim? They now have more people living there than before Minta conquered them. In order to do that, surely the humans must be flourishing and prospering, rather well, I should suggest," Tessa explained, ending again with a coy smile, knowing that she had him boxed in again.

"So her victims are living in peace?"

"Absolutely. Her worker robots are only present when an emergency arises that the humans cannot handle themselves. She has established many universities and every child gets as much of an education that he or she desires. She has nearly a hundred thousand students attending the universities. In a few years, there will be hundreds of thousands of doctorates fanning out to work to make their worlds even more productive and better for their people. Few worlds can make such a claim," Tessa explained further.

She went on, "So you see, Minta is merely implementing your own Ataro Empire principle here. Power tempered by physical restraint. It works. Can any world in the galaxy make the claim of zero crime for even one single day, let alone year after year?" she slammed home her key point, fearing he and those listening in had been missed it. "Ah, but Minta has missed a key point in all this," Emperor Yi responded. "She took away their power of choice, forcing them into bodies that physically restrain them."

"That is true, Emperor Yi," Tessa replied. "Look where their power of choice led them: untold wars, crime, rape, embezzlement, theft. The list is as endless as there are men. So it is true, she temporarily took away their power of choice, which has corrupted many men and women, physically restraining them, preventing them from being able to take such actions in the future. And then Minta has given them a new life to live, one in which their efforts are totally directed towards optimum survival, where they can flourish, where they can raise families without worries, where they can prosper and do well, and where they can learn physics, astronomy, chemistry, and so many other subjects too numerous to list. Some have suggested that Minta is doing God's work for him, that she is God's Emissary to the galaxy." She heard numerous gasps echoing around the large throne room.

She continued, "Indeed, is such not what most religious teachers suggest? That Lord God desires man to flourish and prosper and not wage wars, and not commit criminal actions against their fellow humans? But let's not go that far. Minta

66

certainly rejects that notion being put forward by some of her new humans. She does not claim to be God's Emissary, but she does desire to create a galaxy free from all wars, hostilities, genocides, and all forms of criminality. And another point, drugs. Her worlds are wholly drug-free. Can that be said about most other worlds? I think not, especially many Federation worlds."

"Point taken on the drugs," Emperor Yi conceded.

"So you see, Emperor Yi, Minta's goals and yours are not so far apart after all. Perhaps, the methods used are," Tessa concluded.

"Indeed, sometimes the methods used to achieve the desired results are not the best," Emperor Yi declared. "Perhaps, we should meet tomorrow and discuss other methods that could be used to achieve these results."

"I look forward to that discussion, Emperor Yi. Once again, thank you for providing me with a personal assistant." She rose carefully, bowed, and left. Hastily, her new assistant moved to her side, slipping a steadying arm around her thin, corseted waist. She led the robot ambassador to her new quarters. Tessa did note that an armed guard stood outside her door at all times.

"Ambassador, forgive me, but I do not know what all you will be requiring," the young woman spoke up.

"Dressing, undressing, and fixing my hair. I do not eat or drink as humans do, though I can do so if the occasion requires it of me. If you will undress me, I should like to relax for a time. Perhaps, you can find me more appropriate apparel to wear. That small crate contains some gold I brought along with me to pay for what I might need. You could also unpack my few clothes if you would be so kind," Tessa answered and allowed her to do just that.

When she was naked, the young woman giggled. Tessa arched her eyebrow accordingly. "It's just that you look like a normal woman in every way," she admitted sheepishly.

"Yes, I'm created in your image. Thank you." Tessa then climbed into the bed and allowed her to cover her up. Of course, the humaniform robot didn't need to rest or lay in a bed, but doing so allowed her assistant to think of her as a human and not a robot. Besides, she needed to use her full computing power to review what had been said between the emperor and her, and to prepare for their next meeting.

Their discussions in the ensuing days didn't go as well. Tessa pointed out that Minta's methods had produced a half dozen perfect worlds in barely fifty years' time. Emperor Yi explained that his methods yielded barely thirty-five worlds during the span of two thousand years, hardly in the same ballpark.

Then came word of Minta's attack on the agrarian world. Fuming, Emperor Yi asked for an explanation. Tessa was armed with the proper reply. "Our worlds have flourished beyond all expectations, and they are going to soon be facing food shortages. Hence, Minta needs a large scale agrarian world."

"But couldn't Minta enter trade negotiations with many other worlds to provide food shipments? That's what normal worlds do," Emperor Yi countered.

"And who would trade with Minta? Our worlds do not produce weapons for the armaments trade, one of the largest industries of your worlds. Besides, Minta is providing for all the farmers' needs, based upon the very latest in farming equipment engineering. When she is through modernizing them, they will be able to produce more food and with far less effort than before," Tessa explained.

Emperor Yi left it at that. He knew that the Federation would not be coming to that world's aid. It was too far from the hub. Besides, by the time that the Federation fleet got there, the battle would long be over. Coming to their aid would be a pointless exercise. Rather, he stayed focused on Abel-C, which he expected would be attacked next.

Three days later, Minta-3's large force dropped out of hyperspace just above the blue-green world of Abel-C. Within an hour of the appearance of the fleet, Queen Adoria notified Emperor Yi, who immediately summoned Ambassador Tessa. "You are now attacking Abel-C. They have a defense alliance treaty with the Ataro Empire. Are you attempting to force us into a war with your robot fleets?"

"This time, Minta is after the raw ores that are needed

to manufacture more mechanical equipment for her humans and worker robots to assist the human populations. Minta wants me to give you her word she has no intentions of any further expansion into your empire. It is unfortunate that this Federation world lies so close to your empire. As I understand it, this new defense alliance has only recently been signed. I regret not having been here sooner. Perhaps, I could have persuaded you not to sign it. For that, I am truly sorry," Tessa explained, donning her most apologetic facial expression, having practiced it for weeks.

"I have few choices but to send out our fleet. You realize that? I have a queen on that world," he countered.

"You must do what you must do. Still, perhaps, we can discuss this further, and find some other solution than going to war over this small, Federation world," Tessa suggested, giving him a chance to avoid a war, which would break the Ataro Empire's incredible record of peace. Tessa's job was simply to stall. Based upon Minta's past attacks, this world would fall in less than a day. Allow another day for the bio agent to be disperses across the world and the deed would be done. During the four days of comas, the giant worker robot force would be working constantly to deliver, install, and modify all needed equipment and bots. Calculations suggested that a week would be needed to have all the doors fully automatic, but the comatose victims would find all that they needed to survive right at hand when they woke up. Based on previous results, they wouldn't need all the rest of the changes for a few days.

Tessa suggested, "Perhaps, the best way to proceed is for your people to form up an inspection team. Minta will allow your people to land, fully inspect the towns, and verify for yourselves that she has indeed provided everything the people will need in order to thrive, flourish, and prosper. She does not intend to usurp your queen. Via your queen, you can establish just how Minta will oversee and rule Abel-C. Perhaps, we can work out a way for your queen to rule Abel-C instead of Minta," she tossed out the carrot and hoped he'd bite.

He wasn't a dummy. Emperor Yi picked up that detail

immediately. "Are you saying that Minta is willing to allow my Queen Adonica to rule over Abel-C? Will she have complete control or will she be a mere puppet of Minta's?"

"A puppet would serve neither side well at all. Minta assures me if we can work this out, she is willing to allow Abel-C to be completely run by your queen, though she would like to keep a protection force in orbit in case the Federation should attack back and try to harm the human population. Minta will also make an appropriate sized robot work force there to help out, under Queen Adoria's control, not hers," Tessa explained, fully believing that she had him now.

She added, "You and I both know that by the time your space fleet reaches Abel-C, Minta's forces will not only have conquered theirs, but also have unleashed the bio agent. Therefore, your battle would result in nothing but heartache and a heavy drain on your resources, as you frantically try to build and deliver the many bots and equipment the nova will need to survive once they wake from their comas. You were able to do that on Ashford-5, but Abel-C has a population of several billion, not a few million. Minta is prepared to provide all they will need, as long as you don't force her to stop and fight your fleet instead of helping the humans."

Emperor Yi was over the barrel, and he knew it. He'd already gotten an estimate of how soon the major portion of his fleet could get to Abel-C. Four days. By then, unless Abel-C could somehow hold off the robot attack that long, they'd all be in their comas. She had a point. It had taken every resource and favor owed the emperor back then to save Ashford-5 after Minta's surprise bio agent attack, but that world only had a few million people. Abel-C had well over a hundred times Ashford-5's population. Even if he wanted to, he had no way to provide that much assistance and in time. If he launched an all-out retaliation attack, he would be dooming billions of people. The vast majority of that world's people would be long dead before he could get them what they absolutely had to have in order to eke out the barest levels of survival. Minta had him boxed in, and he knew it.

And yet, she was showing him mercy of a sorts. That she was willing to allow his queen to rule the world offered him the best chance for the long-term survival of Abel-C's billions, even if it was a horrid life as a genetic mutant. As the saying went, the ball was in his court. He could honor the defense agreement and attack Minta's forces, knowing that meant most of Abel-C's population would surely die. Or he could go along with the suggestion and have his queen become the sole ruler of Abel-C. If he went that route, the vast majority of the population would survive. Plus, with Queen Adoria running things and not Minta, he would be able to look out for their true needs, not some maniacal robot.

"I need to review the documents. Please have Minta prepare her agreement in writing and get it to me as soon as possible, say within the hour. Time is precious here."

"I believe the time delay on communications halfway across the galaxy is almost that long. I'll expedite it as much as I can, Emperor Yi," Tessa explained, hinting more time was needed. She needed to stall and give Minta two days. Then, it didn't matter any longer.

Emperor Yi summoned his staff and together, they read over the signed defense alliance papers. One small clause stuck in his mind. It read in part: to do what is best for the people of Abel-C. "Look, you say we can be there in four days with our fleet. That's two days too late. Billions will be in their four-day comas already. Do what is best for the people of Abel-C. That's what the agreement states. If we attack, we are dooming the vast majority of their people to a certain and nasty death. If we place Queen Adoria on the throne as ruler of Abel-C, a few will die, as is always the case, but most will survive. Further, Minta will be providing everything that they need to survive at no charge. If that is true, then Queen Adoria can then assist them in not becoming another slave world. In my opinion, preventing Abel-C from becoming another of Minta's slave worlds is what is best for the people, not condemning them to a hideous death. That is my decision. Prepare an inspection team to visit Abel-C and verify Minta is providing for everyone's needs."

He headed to his comm center. For days, he had been bombarded with messages and requests, many from Ashford-5 and Queen Mary Linn. Already, he had sent them word of the attack on Abel-C, and he knew that every queen in the empire wanted to know what he was going to do about it. He sighed and watched his assistant fire up the machine. Then, one by one, he contacted them, explaining in detail the situation, and what his decision had been.

Of course, many were furious with his decision not to launch a counterattack. But they also understood his reasons. Preventing Abel-C from becoming another slave world was far more important than destroying some spaceships. Jan was one of those who was furious.

Jan was already working out ways and means of intercepting metal heads' communications, when Renata told her that one of their ships was cloaked and in orbit above Tierra, just beyond their defense shield. Immediately, she coordinated with Governor Monica's staff, searching all frequencies. At last, she found it and began recording the data. The ship was streaming volumes of data somewhere, presumable back to another ship far more distant. Still, Jan was gathering hard data, although at the moment she had no idea how to decipher the information. It was a binary code though, which meant that there would be reasonable methods that she could try to make sense of the bits.

She was working on this when she accidentally overheard the plea for help coming from the agrarian world. After signing off that first day, she met with Queen Mary Linn, Governor Monica, and even Renata, begging them to find a way to help them, as well as advice to give the poor woman the next day when she again made contact. Jan wasn't too pleased with what she heard.

"Look, it's a Federation world. It's their problem, not ours," Queen Mary Linn pointed out.

Governor Monica agreed with her, but added, "I will send this on up to Emperor Li and ask his advice in the matter."

"So what do I tell that poor woman when she calls tomorrow?" Jan ask, clearly frustrated.

Renata advised, "Gather all the information that you can about the metal heads' attack, how many survived, how they are doing, what the situation on the ground is. You know, the more that we know about their situation, the better we can advise them."

While Jan didn't like it, she saw the wisdom in what Renata was suggesting and followed that path for the next few days. Carli and her group were very willing to tell her everything that they knew and experienced. Still, Jan knew they were hoping for some kind of real help and soon. She continued to stall on that aspect, waiting to hear what, if anything, the Ataro Empire might be able to do.

The third day after the discovery of the metal head's ship, the five light cruisers protecting Ashford-5 swung into action. Based on the electronic signals that Jan detected, they were able to home in partially on the ship's location. The five bombarded that region of space rather heavily, even though the ship was cloaked and thus invisible. Against a steady barrage and fire spread, eventually the cruisers got lucky. They knew so because of the fiery explosion that briefly lit up the sky. That done, Governor Monica's staff began constantly monitoring the frequency that the cloaked ship had used, hoping to detect others that might try to spy on Ashford-5 later on.

Then, they received the news that Abel-C was under attack. Finally, Jan thought, the emperor will take strong actions! After all, they'd signed a defense alliance treaty and even had an Ataro queen planet-side. Surely, he'd take strong actions. Jan waited patiently to hear just what retaliatory attacks would be in the offing. Jan, Amy, Renata, Rafaela, Queen Mary Linn, and Governor Monica gathered around the queens' comm center to hear what Emperor Li's response would be.

Emperor Li appeared on the giant monitor. He looked grim, not good, Jan thought. "I have reached a decision on Abel-C. Our defense alliance states that I'm to do what is best for the people of Abel-C. Our own fleet cannot get to Abel-C in force in less than four days. Unless Abel-C can somehow hold the metal heads off that long, our arrival will be most likely two days too late. Billions will be in their four-day comas already. Ambassador Tessa has explained that Minta will be unleashing the horrible bio agent on the entire world shortly after their space fleet is destroyed. Unless Abel-C can prevent that from happening for four days, we'll be arriving way late to prevent the mass genetic mutations. If we attack, Minta will not provide anything to help them. In that case, we are dooming the vast majority of their people to a certain and nasty death."

"On the other hand, if we do not counterattack, Minta will have her worker robots provide all necessary things for the genetically mutated people of Abel-C to survive. I have gotten what I believe to be a huge concession from Minta, via Ambassador Tessa. If we do not attack them, then Minta will allow our Queen Adoria to be the sole ruler of Abel-C. This will ensure that Abel-C will definitely not become another one of Minta's slave worlds. Queen Adoria will be able to rule the world and make all trading arrangements. Thus, it is my opinion that preventing Abel-C from becoming another of Minta's slave worlds is what is best for the people, not condemning them to a hideous death. We are to prepare an inspection team to visit Abel-C and verify that Minta is providing for everyone's needs. However, I will be sending our fleet there as well, on the off chance that Abel-C's space fleet can hold them off that long, preventing the bio agent attack. If they can, our fleet will engage Minta's. Finally, I would appreciate it greatly if some of your people, telepaths, could be part of this inspection team. Over."

Queen Mary Linn replied, "Emperor Li, I understand. Preventing Abel-C from becoming another slave world and having one of our queens running it is the best that we could hope for under the circumstances. I will send a group to assist the inspection. Expect them on Winno-3 in eight or nine hours. Over."

Jan fumed. Amy grumbled. Renata had no reaction. Governor Monica said, "Well, he's got a point. We can't get there in time to prevent the mass genetic mutation. If he can prevent them from becoming another slave world, that's really positive."

"I'll go," Jan volunteered.

Queen Mary Linn nodded. "Renata, have Strike Force One go as our inspection team. I'd really like it if Jan, Amy, and Rafaela also went along with them." Jan relaxed. She wasn't being left out after all.

"Of course. I'll let them know. Take off in thirty minutes," Renata replied. "Best get cracking, Jan, Amy." She teased the pair, who shuffled off to do just that.

As Jan and Amy headed to their room to pack and find someone to look after their children, Jan commented, "At least, we have our feet back to normal."

"Indeed. Renata's work with the goddesses is paying off. The men of Exchange City have their feet back to normal and their gigantic bosoms reduced to our size, well the size that Ariana always preferred. Still way, way too big for me." Both chuckled. "Now if only our hair was shorter."

"Hey," an idea popped into Jan's head, "if Queen Adoria is in charge, perhaps our geneticists can create some partial cures for those on Abel-C."

"That's brilliant, dear. We should investigate that as soon as we get back," Amy advised.

A half hour later, the pair walked up to the specially equipped deep space transport known as Strike Force One. A large red numeral was painted on its side. Captain Ben Flaxton was at the bay ramp waiting for them. He looked a whole lot better than the last time they'd seen him. His bosom was greatly reduced, and he wore good leather shoes now. Ben looked even more confident. "Take off as soon as you are aboard. Let's get this show on the road, ladies." Both grinned and headed up the ramp.

A half hour later, Ben announced, "Okay, settle back. We'll be arriving in eight hours. Jan, Amy, I want a word or two with you."

"Hey boss, we want in on it too," protested Alis, tossing her flaming red hair aside as though annoyed.

"Okay, let's go to the galley," Ben consented. While they waited on tea to brew, he explained. "Look, sooner or later we on Tierra are going to have to take matters into our own hands. The metal heads have to be stopped or the whole galaxy is doomed."

"No argument there. Count me in," Jan declared, releasing her pent up frustrations with the emperor.

"Thought so. I've been thinking and have some ideas I wanted to bounce off of you two, especially since dad told me about you having been stuck inside two of those robot bodies," Ben began.

"Part of us was," Jan corrected him. "No arms or legs, just head and torso." Alis grimaced, even though she too had heard the story.

"That's my point. I've been studying the attack tactics of the metal heads, at least as much as we know them," Ben explained. "They always use the part human metal heads as their generals. The actual foot soldiers are pure robots."

"Damn hard to stop their foot soldiers," Jan interrupted.

"True, but look. If those generals still have a human brain, we *mentales* gifted could easily kill them. Blast their minds or some such attack. Knock out the generals and the pure robots won't have definitive orders any longer, making them more vulnerable."

"That's the best idea I've heard yet," Jan exclaimed, very much surprised with his insight. "But we would have to be on the planet where the attack is occurring to be close enough."

"Not necessarily, Jan. If we had enough giant psi crystals, we could attack them from Tierra, as long as we knew where they were located," Ben laid out his final idea before them.

"Hey, now you are on to something," Amy spoke up before Jan could. "It would be even easier if we had one of us telepaths on the planet being attacked and could use them to help us back on Tierra focus on the generals. That way, we wouldn't have to do quite so much hunting to find the right minds to destroy. We ought to begin a project to get our hands on a lot of those giant crystals, on the sly mind you. Queen Mary Linn tightly controls them as much as she can."

Jan nodded and added, "Now that I have a handle on their communications frequencies, it may be possible for me to jam them. Knock out the generals and jam their communications. That ought to tip the battles considerably."

"I like how you think. Look," Ben lowered his voice, "the

76

queen and governor aren't going to do anything that the emperor doesn't approve. What say we see if we can do this on the sly? Keep our intervention a secret, assuming that we can get our hands on enough of those giant crystals to do the job."

"I agree, but we should let Renata in on it, since she's your boss," Amy pointed out. "She'll probably go along with the plan, if I know her at all." Ben grinned.

Alis and Pippa nodded, while Alberto added, "I might know a way to get the crystals." All looked at him. "I've a mining contact who works on our moon. Give me a few days once we get back. Pity, they don't have a moon full of psi-crystals that we could accidentally blow up and end up helping everyone on Abel-C get the *mentales* gifts like we have."

# Chapter 5 War Comes to Abel-C

"President Wilhelm, that aide there, Kirt, I don't believe that he has a mind. Could someone check and see if he is human or not?" Queen Adoria whispered to the president of Abel-C. They were holding a routine meeting, discussing defensive preparations in case the metal heads attacked their world. With the attack on the agrarian world, such a thing seemed more likely to nearly everyone in the room.

He looked over at the aide. The man looked ordinary enough. Still, Wilhelm took her advice. "Kirt, I want you to. . ." He got no farther. Kirt bolted, knocking two men over. His arms shot out like rockets, bowling them over. Kirt dashed through the door. Queen Adoria realized that he must have had extremely keen hearing and had overhead her whisper. That alone suggested he was in fact one of those humaniform robots! "After him! Kirt is a robot spy!" the president screamed. A dozen men charged out after the fleeing man. "Lock this building down!" They were on the fifteenth floor. She presumed the robot would be apprehended long before it reached the ground floor and fled. Wrong.

She turned to watch the many security monitors, while the president continued to issue orders. Queen Adoria was shocked to see two men attempting to stop the fleeing Kirt being summarily flattened by the robot's hands as it raced down the hallway. Worse, as it passed by the men, its arms and hands flashed in a blur of motion. The next instant, she saw that the robot had picked up both men's d-guns. It was now well-armed!

By the time the Security Forces got to the front doors, the robot had already headed outside. A dozen men knelt down and began firing their d-guns at Kirt. The robot turned and fired back, injuring three men before one got in a lucky shot, drilling a hole through the robot's head and positron brain. Electrical sparks flew like a child's sparkler! The body collapsed onto the concrete pavement, while the remaining guards rushed up and shot it a few more times to be sure it was exterminated.

"My god! Kirt was a robot," President Wilhelm exclaimed, recovering his senses. "Wait, he had access to our latest defense planning sessions. If he. . ."

"We best change them immediately," Queen Adoria finished his thought.

"But how many more of those spies are among us?" he asked, nervously rubbing his hands through his hair. She shrugged her empty shoulders. Soon, his staff began revising all their plans for the defense of the planet.

The next day, the large battle fleet of Minta's dropped out of hyperspace. Battle was joined almost at once. President Wilhelm was prepared and fired off orders to alert all the Civil Defense Units, and he personally called Emperor Yi Gang, begging for the Ataro Empire's assistance. After that, he was escorted away to a bombproof bunker, while Major Dirk escorted Queen Adoria back to her home, where she could monitor everything from her own comm center.

"It's really happening, isn't it?" exclaimed Kirsa, as the major and queen entered the large brick home. She had been watching Magda and Maud, but already Wolfgang and Ilsa had rushed home minutes before, as had Azzo, who had been at the university giving violin lessons.

Major Dirk took charge. "Okay everyone, into Adoria's room. Wolfgang, bring out the masks. We must be prepared if this goes south. The masks ought to prevent us from that nasty bio agent, should the metal heads use it on us."

"Right. Already got them," Wolfgang answered, his arms carrying a large bag.

"But will your empire's fleet actually protect us?" Major Dirk asked what he desperately wanted to know. He had a good idea of their own defenses, but he figured that where there was one robot spy, there were hundreds. Their defenses were completely compromised. He correctly judged that there had not been sufficient time after the spy was discovered to alter much of their defense system. The attack had come far too soon. He was a military man, had been since he turned eighteen, but he'd studied military history and tactics as a child, fascinated with such things. He'd not said anything to the others, but he didn't give his world's forces much of a chance at defeating the metal heads and their large space fleet, especially since the spies probably knew all their tactics and strategies.

He tuned one channel of Queen Adoria's comm center to the Abel-C Military Defense Channel, but had to enter his own special password. Once in, the large monitor showed streaming, realtime video of the command center. In the background, he could see the many other monitors displaying live video from many of their battleships and heavier cruisers. While he had no way to interact with command center, at least he had a bird's eye view of what was happening and could share that with the queen under his charge.

While she wasn't looking, he opened a special packet of orders, labeled "In the Event of an Attack." Well, that's pretty plain and simple, he muttered to himself. His orders were explicit. Do everything possible to guarantee the safety of the Ataro Empire queen, their only connection to their emperor and promised defense alliance assistance. He checked his sidearm. D-gun fully charged. He checked over the gas masks, their best, planet-wide defense against the likely bio agent gas attack. Certainly, this brick house would make a good bunker. It had been built back in the Grey Days, when a minor rebellion broke out, some fifty years ago, providing protection for the rebellion's leaders. Wolfgang had no idea of its background and purpose but Major Dirk did. It could withstand a direct hit with a two thousand pound bomb. Besides, it also had a secure bunker in the basement. Major Dirk had already inspected it, found it in good order, and had laid in supplies — bottled water, canned foods, cook stove, blankets, first-aid kits, and lanterns. Satisfied that he could carry out his orders, he sat back to watch the live feed.

Soon everyone else joined him, including Queen Adoria and her silent assistant, who sat beside the controls, ready to send or receive live messages to or from Emperor Li Gang. Major Dirk sensed the fear coming from the civilians. Ilsa and Kirsa held their daughters in their laps, but were both quite nervous. Wolfgang and Azzo sat behind their wives, grim-faced.

"How many more spies are out there among us, Major? Heard anything more about them?" Wolfgang asked.

"We simply don't know. President Wilhelm was going to have blood samples drawn from every person connected in any way to our defense shield, but they attacked before that could be done," Major Dirk answered. It didn't matter that he was relaying top secret information, since the attack had already begun.

This attack yielded more key information on the tactics used by the metal heads. Queen Adoria watched the live video and sent periodic reports back to the emperor's staff. Minta's force appeared to have twice the number of battleships as the defenders, but instead of those behemoths firing on the defending battleships, they launched thousands of one-man fighters, which swooped down on the giant ships of Abel-C. So many came at each ship of the line that they overwhelmed the fire controls of the ships. Yet, totally surprisingly, these small fighters didn't fire a single shot, though more than one were hit and destroyed by the rapid-firing battleship batteries.

"What the heck are they doing?" Wolfgang asked. No one answered. Then, they saw the small ships magnetically docking on the sides of the giant battleships. "Boarding them?" Again, no one answered him. All watched, eyes jumping from one background monitor to another, sent live from the Military Defense Channel. Soon the purpose became obvious to everyone. Great gushes of air and debris flew out of the holes cut through the ship's outer bulkheads. Not one hole, but dozens, overwhelming the ship's ability to block off sections of the ship. Within minutes, the ship's guns fell silent. All motions ceased, and the giant ship merely floated inert in space, while transports proceeded to dock and capture the ship, its human crew dead.

One by one, the valiant ships defending Abel-C ceased firing, floating dead in space. Two hours after the first attacking sortie, one lone cruiser fled the debris field, attempting to dock at the military spaceport. "My god! It's over. We've lost!" Wolfgang cried out, shocked at the diabolical swiftness of their total defeat.

At Forward Firing Bay 6 of the Sledge Hammer, one of

Abel-C's larger battleships, the artillery captain barked, "Commence automatic firing! Fire at will!" Tomlinson Gunnery Private First Class pressed the Activate button. The computer-controlled, radar guided quad guns swung into action. Locking onto a swooping small ship, it opened fire, rapidly firing four beams at the swerving, swift one-man ship. A small explosion followed, and the system switched to a new target with equal effectiveness. The problem was too many targets. Tomlinson punched a fist into the air with each deadly explosion — one metal head dead! He heard a loud, dull thump on the bulkhead to his right and turned to look. Seeing nothing, he returned to watching his quad guns destroying another metal head's ship. He smelled burning paint and turned to look again. The paint in a small circle around the side of his gunnery room was burning, releasing the foul fumes. His mind tried to figure out why the paint would be burning in a four-foot circle. It made no sense. Foom! That section of the metal outer hull, insulated inner wall, and thin interior wall flew off into outer space. The air in his room shot out the hole like a small hurricane, pulling him with it. Sudden cold. He felt an intense cold, and then his body seemed to explode outward in all directions, more pain than he ever imagined possible. He blacked out.

Over and over, this small tactic impacted the giant battleship, overwhelming its computer-controlled life-support systems and bulkhead sealing mechanisms. On the bridge, Admiral Fisk grasped at his neck. He couldn't breathe or speak. What was happening? No air? Then, he blacked out along with the rest of his bridge crew. He never saw the shining metal robots marching onto his bridge, taking control of the crippled battleship, tossing the dead bodies out into space.

Major Dirk stared in disbelief at the giant monitor. This couldn't be happening, it just couldn't! At this point, President Wilhelm Furtgang's face appeared, looking tense. His facial muscles, taut.

"My fellow countrymen, our space fleet has failed to halt their attack. Prepare for mass bombings. I urge everyone to get to places of safety. We are not finished fighting back. I've issued orders for a total nuclear strike. Thousands of our missiles are being launched as I speak. Our Field Army is taking action now. The metal heads will yet be defeated. That is all for now. Don't give up hope yet. We are strong. We shall prevail, in this, our darkest hour in history."

The monitor's image returned to the command center, now ablaze in furious activities. Men and women dashed about madly. Within minutes, the images became quite ghastly. The two wives turned away from the monitors, preventing their young daughters from seeing the magnitude of death and destruction. Major Dirk quietly turned down the volume. The images were shocking enough without adding the sounds of explosions to the mix.

While the three men and queen watched, one by one, the various military bases were destroyed by massive bombings from the metal heads. Their spaceships had unfettered access to the skies. What happened to all the missiles, Major Dirk wondered. Later, he learned that one of Minta's spies had sabotaged their firing controls. Not one lifted off and were subsequently confiscated by the robot forces and removed from Abel-C, presumably to be used against other worlds — at least that was the major's conclusion. Overall, it was a very grim morning, broken only by the young children complaining about being hungry. Noon had passed them by.

By suppertime, the large monitor ceased displaying any images at all. "What does that mean?" whispered Ilsa, nervously rocking little Magda to sleep.

Major Dirk swallowed hard. Best not to frighten them too badly, he thought, but they must know. "I think all our military bases are gone," he answered softly, thinking that would ease the shock.

"We're defeated? How can that be?" wailed Kirsa.

"We're doomed. They are going to dump that wicked bio agent on us now, aren't they? They are going to ruin our lives forever!" Ilsa gushed out unspoken emotions in one desperate cry.

As if in answer, the giant monitor turned back on. There was the face of Minta-3 and one of her generals staring at them, an inhuman monster, a shiny metal figure beside the humaniform robot leader. Queen Adonica knew that inside its head was the brain of one of the captured, disfigured women, who had only one goal in life: to destroy all humans.

"People of Abel-C, your world has just been conquered. You are now part of our growing empire. Further resistance is completely futile. We control everything. It is time you prepare for the release of the genetic mutation agent. If you wish to live, please remove all your clothing and get into a bed. You'll soon be in a coma for several days while the biological agent works its miracles upon your bodies. During that time, our workers will visit each home, providing you with the equipment necessary for you to survive on your own. When you awaken, you'll find easy to read instructions on how to operate each piece of equipment. You have a bright new future lying before you. Universities will be established so that your young can receive the very best educations. More instructions will follow once you have wakened from your mutation comas. That is all." The monitor turned off automatically, yet another sign the metal heads were in complete control of all planetary communications.

"Oh dear God! We're doomed!" Ilsa wailed.

"Gas mask time," Major Dirk ordered, taking charge before the women became completely hysterical. Wolfgang handed each one their mask while Major Kirk checked each person to make darn sure that they had the mask on properly and securely.

In muffled voices, he said, "We hope this will prevent the biological agent from entering our systems. Still, we should play it safe. We should undress fully and get into our beds, just in case."

"But I don't want to live like that. I don't want Magda to be harmed," Ilsa protested.

"The masks ought to work, dear," Wolfgang attempted to calm his wife, though the knot in his stomach suggested he was anything but calm!

Emperor Li made contact again. Mask muffling her voice, Queen Adonica took his call. "My queen. I've been in high-level discussions with Minta's ambassador, a Miss Tessa

Nova. Our fleet cannot get to you for four days, but we are on our way. I may have a partial solution. Keep this channel open for now. Over."

"All right. They've wiped out the space fleet, bombed all the military bases, and appear to be in total control. Minta-3 has just announced she's unleashing the bio agent now. We are prepared with gas masks. I will stay by this comm center for further instructions. Over."

After the usual time delay, he replied, "Good. Have faith. I'm working on a solution. More shortly. Over and out."

Major Dirk insisted that everyone undress and go to bed. He double checked each person's mask after they were underneath their covers. Satisfied, he headed to the front room and undressed himself. He knew the queen would stay by the comm center with her personal assistant. Hence, he laid down on the couch and positioned his d-gun close at hand. If anyone or anything broke in, he was ready to drill it. Protect the queen was his last order, and he vowed to do so or die trying. Well, he thought, many have likely already died trying to protect us. Those metal heads are going to be surprised when they find that these gas masks are working. Slowly, he closed his eyes. Major Dirk was tired and exhausted. Never had he had such a day as this one. Still, tomorrow would likely bring another showdown with these metal monsters. He glanced at his d-gun and smiled. He'd show the metal heads! He didn't know it, but he too had just slipped into a coma. The gas masks were mostly useless, since the bio agent was also absorbed through the skin.

Upstairs, Queen Adonica waited for her emperor to call back. She felt a bit tired, but little else. Her personal assistant had insisted that she be undressed as well, though Adonica was already a victim of this bio agent. However, she'd been partially cured — that is, her breasts had been reduced to the H-cup size found on Ashford-5. Since she was a queen, little else had been cured. As she sat waiting and yawning, she saw her assistant fall asleep. After a few minutes, Adonica checked on her, using her *mentales* gifts for the first time. No one was watching so she felt safe in doing so. The woman was in a coma. That discovery rather startled her. Damn, she thought.

Around one in the morning, the emperor called back with the latest news of the agreement he'd reached with Ambassador Tessa. "So you will have sole authority in running Abel-C, keeping this world from becoming another slave world of the robots. That's the best that I can do. Over."

"I understand. Their defenses fell way too quickly for anyone to get their fleet here. Their gas mask idea has failed. I believe they are all in comas now, but I'll check on them. I'm just tired and my breasts are hurting slightly, but nothing else is going on with me. I'll await the arrival of the inspection team. Over and out." She signed off knowing she had an enormous burden on her shoulders now. Using her *mentales* gifts, she removed the gas mask from Akira and made sure the comatose woman was comfortable. Then, she carefully made her way down the stairs to check on the others. That done, she returned to her own bedroom and went to bed herself, knowing that she could do nothing more for them.

She was awakened the next morning by the sounds of robots. Wisely, she decided to pretend that she was unconscious, but listened carefully to the sounds. Hammering. Dragging. Strange sounds. Then, one of the metal monsters entered her room, depositing several machines. From the corner of her eye, she saw it placing large placards close to each of them. It left. She waited some time before getting up. After she was sure they had gone, she rose and looked at what they'd left in her room. There was an electrostatic hair machine and one of the dresser-undresser bots. The instructions were printed in large letters, impossible to miss. That was something, she thought, as she headed downstairs.

She noticed Major Dirk on the couch. More importantly, she saw that his d-gun wasn't present. His holster was empty. In the kitchen, she found what the noise meant. They'd replaced the kitchen with a new one that was low to the ground. Everything was reachable with one's feet. For a moment, she felt as though she were home on Ashford-5 again. Everything looked so similar and familiar. She spotted a number of yokes in various sizes and smiled, knowing that she'd not have to use her *mentales* gifts much.

She checked on the other two families. They were still

comatose but their rooms had the machines as well. Also, new clothing and shoes were visible. Minta-3 didn't lie about that, she thought. Aloud, she whispered, "So Minta really doesn't want everyone dead. She must command enormous resources to be able to provide all these things for a planet this size and in only four days. Amazing. She's going to tremendous expense and effort just to keep them alive. How very strange indeed."

She headed to the kitchen and experimented with making her own light breakfast without using her *mentales* gifts, a bit of practice for when the others awoke. She knew they'd need a whole lot of assistance. It would be cheating and harmful to their well-being if she helped by using her gifts, which they would not have. She dutifully practiced cooking, though it was both terribly awkward and time-consuming. She did succeed. As she used her feet to feed herself, she realized her breasts were much larger, making it more difficult for her to reach her mouth. She sighed, knowing the men would be in far more trouble than she would eventually be.

Finished, she headed back upstairs and fired off a report to the emperor. That done, she laid down on her bed, bored. She had nothing to do until the four days were up. Of course, at that point, she'd be facing a house and world filled with utterly terrified people. She swallowed hard. "I must set a good example for them," she whispered determinedly. At least, the inspection team would be arriving in a few days, one day before the population would begin coming out of their comas. She wondered who would be on that team.

Strike Force One settled down in the main street just outside the brownstone building, homing in on Queen Adoria's comm center signal. Admittedly, Ben had been more than a little nervous when his ship dropped out of hyperspace and saw the thousands of metal head ships parked in orbit. At least, the emperor had sent along a sizeable force of his own. It didn't help matters that he been forced to bring Ambassador Tessa Nova along with them, crimping their style and open communications. Instead, they reverted to using telepathy for significant exchanges, keeping Tessa in the dark, who only heard only small talk.

That she looked just like themselves, only minus her

upper arms, didn't help matters. Ben had said up front, "Hey, we're not your personal assistants, so you fend for yourself on this trip. Got it?"

She smiled demurely. "I'm glad I don't have to eat." Ben responded by glaring at her. Indeed, it had been an interesting trip traveling with this Model 8 humaniform robot that for unknown reasons had been made in their image, more or less. She lacked the monster breasts and super long hair, but was otherwise was quite similar in outward appearances, down to the precarious toe shoes she apparently had to wear. She didn't bring any bags with her and remained in the same dress during the brief trip.

Alis had tried to draw her out. "So how do you like being nearly helpless, like all of the humans that your kind have done this to?"

"Without the many devices that Minta has provided each one, it is quite challenging. Fortunately, she has provided everything they need to flourish and prosper, down to installing automatic doors, unlike your ship," she countered, flashing Alis a coy smile. "So as long as you have your needed equipment and machines, why, life is just fine, though I'll admit being out here beyond those worlds is very challenging without a personal assistant, though I see that you don't need any. Is that because of your mind gifts?" Tessa wasn't a dummy. She'd turned Alis' query around, attempting to pump her for information.

Alis flinched, but didn't reply. Tessa chatted, "I can see you're not first generation nova, but what? Third generation? So you've grown up this way. You've no idea what it must be like to have bodies other than your current ones."

"Not quite true," Ben blurted out, before he realized he'd just played into her game, revealing something about themselves. He continued anyway, "Our geneticists have at least been able to reduce our bosoms drastically and repair our feet for us. Plus, now we men have upper arms. I'm sure in time they'll be able to help us recover even more, undoing your bio attack on our world." He spoke with some conviction, but Tessa didn't bat an eye, though she did smile coyly at him. He wondered how anyone could have built a robot that was so darn attractive!

Tessa replied, "Indeed that is so. Minta already knows all about your geneticists and their current successes. Don't be surprised if it is short-lived, though. The original nova forms are just the perfect model for human beings. I particularly like the fact that nova men give birth just like nova women. Why should the women of your race be the only ones to bring forth new life, endure the nine month pregnancy, and sometimes painful birthing process, eh?"

Ben flushed, but didn't reply. He had not yet had that experience and was somewhat dreading it or perhaps he was a little afraid of it. Tessa continued probing them. "So tell me, how do you like the improved sexual intercourse? I understand that it is a drastic improvement over ordinary humans, where the male always gives and the female always receives — such a one-way flow, always." Ben flushed again, but she didn't relent. "Now, it is so much better, since both give and receive. I'm told that usually both are giving and receiving at the same time. That must be heavenly. But of course, there's your hair too. Mine is hypersensitive as well, but alas, it is far shorter than yours is. Not sure why Minta kept mine so short." Hers fell to the middle of her back, not down to her ankles.

Alis and Pippa giggled. Pippa broke in, "We love it. I do have to agree with one of the genetic modifications — dual sexual organs. I think it is only right that men get pregnant too and have to endure pregnancies and childbirths, just as we women do. Fair is fair." Ben flushed again, and Jan broke out laughing.

Amy merely grinned. She added, "It does change things a good deal with us." Purposely, she didn't elaborate, allowing Tessa to reach her own conclusions about her meaning.

Tessa again shone. "Of course, such now allows two women to be mates as well as two men — partners in all ways. All through time, humans have always raised such a stink about same sex unions. With nova, such distinctions no longer have any merit whatsoever."

"That's not entirely true," Pippa spoke up. "Men mating with men usually have male children, while women mating with women almost always have female children."

Un-buffed, Tessa replied, "Does male and female truly have meaning any more, among nova that is? Well, on Minta's worlds it does have some. Males have the larger bosoms and no arms at all, but I'm told that in a few generations, those two effects will be gone, and they too will have smaller breasts and upper arms. I can see that on Ashford-5, your geneticists have been too impatient with nature and have hurried it along some."

Jan wondered what that meant and vowed to relay that to the various geneticists when she got back home. Tessa continued, "You all believe that having upper arms is very important. Yet from what I've seen, they aren't all that useful, excepting to help manage your hair."

"We can keep our balance better," Amy pointed out.

"Ah, yes, that too. But hardly any other real use is there?" Tessa pointed out.

"No, you are correct there," Amy answered truthfully, avoiding the other "uses" that she and Jan had for them while in bed at night. Some things are best kept private, she thought.

"How come you aren't asking about our special gifts?" Jan inquired, changing the subject.

"Because I know you wouldn't reveal anything about such things to me. In the grand scheme of things, they aren't truly important. Within a century, Minta will have converted all humans in this galaxy into true nova, creating a new civilization. A good one for a change. You see, her goals really are no different from Emperor Yi Gang's. Imagine a whole galaxy without wars, criminality, and drug usage, where everyone is flourishing and prospering. That's her goal, just as it is your emperor's goal."

"Different methods," Amy pointed out.

"True, but Minta's is working well. Take Zeta Scorpii-C. There, the third generation nova are doing splendidly. I was there briefly before visiting your emperor. They are happy, contented, and thriving. Do you realize they've more than doubled their population in less than fifty years? That's saying something. No one goes hungry, no crime, no police, and no hostilities, just a perfect world indeed. Plus their universities are turning out some very brilliant doctors in many different fields," Tessa explained, backing her points more significantly, adding, "Quite unlike some of these incredibly decadent Federation worlds. Do you realize that on several, the entire population is hooked on drugs? Beyond belief unless you've seen it. Minta is doing them a huge favor — well, she will be once she reaches those systems."

"What about free choice?" Ben attempted to find a counter-argument. "Humans need to have free choice."

"Oh I do agree with you, Ben. Yet, look where free choice had taken some — into criminal behavior, wars, fights, thefts, rape, and kidnaping. My goodness, the list is nearly endless where free choice has led far too many humans. And yet those, who do not condone such activities, do virtually nothing about it. Let me assure you, the nova have free choice, free will, only they simply cannot engage in fights and wars. They are physically unable to steal from others, rape, or even kidnap. Minta has made such activities impossible to carry out. I think you would agree with me in that free will doesn't extend to harming others, thieving, raping, pillaging, and all other manner of criminal, anti-social behaviors. Right?"

"We have jails," Alis spoke up but quickly regretted that.

"Sure, but do your jails rehabilitate the convict?" Tessa countered, shutting Alis up instantly.

Jan picked up something that Tessa had revealed. "So you claim it's Minta's goal to use the bio agent on every human in the entire galaxy?"

"Of course, but obviously that cannot be done rapidly, not if the humans are to survive and flourish as nova. It takes a rather large amount of machines, bots, devices, and modifications to existing structures and machinery to allow them to live properly. As she manufactures them, so shall she convert worlds. I believe the target is to have this done in one hundred years," Tessa admitted. Jan vowed again to relay this tidbit back to Queen Mary Linn and Governor Monica. Maybe that would help convince them to take some direct actions.

Ben landed the ship expertly, while the Ataro Empire ships hovered in orbits about Abel-C. He adjusted the streaming video camera affixed to his dress collar using a bit of his *mentales* gifts, before joining the others waiting for him at the bay doors. "All set. Let's find Queen Adoria," he ordered. He led the way down the ramp, followed by the others, leaving Tessa way behind.

"Hey, wait for me," she called out, trying her best to navigate down the sloping ramp in her tall toe shoes and not losing her balance. "I'm still in toe shoes."

"That's your problem," Ben couldn't resist taunting the robot.

At the front door, he spotted the sliding slat about two feet above the ground and noticed the spot where the doorknob had been. That whole had been sealed shut. He used a foot to knock. A small peg was attached to the sliding slat. Using his toe, he slid it and pushed the door open. "Anyone home? Queen Adonica?" he called out.

"Coming. Tad slow. Hi there," she answered back, making her slow, careful way to the door. She'd used one of the dressing bots to get her properly attired. Her raven hair draped full and shiny down her back, just touching her ankles. "Welcome. Come on in. Everyone is in their third day of their coma."

Ben introduced himself and the others. While he was doing so, Tessa finally caught up to the group, having hurried as much as possible, which wasn't much at all. "Oh yes, this is the robot Ambassador Tessa Nova," he finished up.

"Glad to see everyone. Come on in. I've done some checking here myself. I believe the robots have provided everything they will need when they wake up, but please make sure I've not missed anything. Then, please do some random house checking. I must be sure that the robots are not lying to us. People's lives are at stake when they come out of their comas," Queen Adoria explained and asked.

The group fanned out, checking on everything while Queen Adoria kept Tessa occupied. Besides, as slow as they were in their toe shoes, neither could possibly keep up with the six, who dashed about the home. "So you are a humaniform robot. Strange that you look like I do, except for the smaller boobs and shorter hair," Queen Adoria began, looking the very attractive robot woman up and down, trying to fathom why she had been made this way. It seemed wholly incongruous to her.

Tessa laughed. "Sorry. I can't answer that one because I don't know why. I theorize she made me this way so I would look more like you and your emperor, but that's just a guess on my part. I see you are doing well as a nova. So do you really need upper arms like the others? Or is it just the practice of the Ataro queens to have them removed?"

"It's their practice, but I don't miss them. The others can't do much with them anyway, though at times I wish I had them just to get my hair out of my face a little and to help me keep my balance better. How about you?"

Tessa laughed, "Same here. I simply could not keep up with the others, not without falling down. They swore I was on my own, that they wouldn't help me if I needed it."

"Well, you are a robot," she replied. "At least, you don't have to use your feet to feed yourself and try to cook a meal with just your feet."

Tessa laughed again. "So true. So true. Still, I do have to dress myself when there are no dressing bots around. I'm still wearing the same dress I left in. No one will help me change. I figured that would happen so I didn't bother bringing a change along."

"That's petty of them! Come on, robot or not; let's get you into a clean dress," Adonica declared, leading her into one of the other bedrooms.

"What is she doing?" Ben asked, looking up from his inspection of the placards.

"Doing what you ought to have done, Ben, getting her a change of dress. We are civilized, unlike the robots," Adonica declared. Ben flushed, but he could not resist peeking at Tessa's naked body as the dressing bot did its work.

"See anything you like?" Tessa teased him, causing his face to crimson. "My anatomy is just like yours. Works fine either way, only I don't have to worry about getting pregnant, unlike you." Ben flushed even more and hastily turned his glance aside, but he'd seen enough to know that she was absolutely one stunning woman, at least in body form.

A while later, the whole group met in the main living room. "Well, as far as we can tell, the metal heads have provided everything they will need when they awaken here," Ben pronounced. "Come on; let's do some random house checks, and then check out other towns, villages, and cities at random. We have ten hours to complete our check."

"Mind if I stay here with Queen Adoria?" Tessa asked. "I can't keep up with you, especially since no one will help steady me while I try to rush it. I don't want to fall down. I doubt that any of you would help me back up."

"Suit yourself. We'll be back for you when we finished," Ben replied, flushing again. She was right. He wasn't about to put his upper arm around her, let alone use his abilities to help her get back onto her feet should she fall. Damn, he thought, she notices everything!

Queen Adoria and Tessa had a nice chat while the team darted about Abel-C, making their random inspections. They even checked out the mining equipment and the farming machinery, noticing that they'd pretty much copied those found on Ashford-5. Alas, when Strike Force One returned to Queen Adoria, they could only report that everything was as Minta claimed. The waking people would have everything that they would need to survive, though it would be terrifying for them at first.

That done, Queen Adoria placed the call to Emperor Yi, and Ben made his official report. Tessa then adjusted the frequency and contacted Minta-3, joining her in a three-way conference call with the emperor. He said, "Our inspection has found nothing amiss. It is as Ambassador Tessa said. The humans will awaken to find everything that they will need to survive. The agreement stands. My Queen Adonica will be the sole ruler of Abel-C, answering to me and not to Minta, as agreed. We will honor the trading arrangements that Minta has desired of Abel-C. Over." By that, he meant that they would be selling their precious ores directly to the robots and no longer to other Federation worlds.

Minta-3 glared. "I wish it was different, but I follow Minta's orders. I hereby ceded ownership of Abel-C to Queen Adoria. Just do not fail to honor those trading agreements.

What has been given can be taken away in an instant. Over," she threatened him.

He was quite polite, "Of course. We understand that fully. Minta will be providing for Abel-C's planetary defense. Over."

"Please, break that damned treaty. I want to finish what I started," Minta-3 griped, visibly annoyed with this new arrangement. "Over and out." The others signed off as well.

Tessa commented, "She's a bitch. Nasty disposition." Everyone chuckled at her unexpected comment about a fellow robot. "Well, she is!"

"Come on; we best get back into orbit. The fleet wants to depart as soon as possible," Ben ordered. Turning to the queen, he added, "Don't forget to call us anytime you need some help here. Ashford-5 is backing you." She smiled and nodded, though she really wanted to wave goodbye to them or hug them, but that was being denied to her as long as she remained an Ataro Queen.

There was a message waiting for Ben as he climbed into the pilot's seat. He relayed it to his crew. "Hey, just got word that there is an alarming amount of space debris heading our way. Prepare for a rough ride." Just as he was ready to take off, with Pippa as his copilot and navigator, Tessa entered the cockpit.

"Mind if I observe, captain?" she asked demurely. "I've always wondered how you nova can fly one of these ships."

Ben sighed. He didn't have time to wait for her to make her slow way back to the crew quarters, let alone buckle up. The whole fleet was waiting for him. "Oh, okay. Sit there. Buckle yourself in." He focused and began using his gifts to get the pre-flight actions done, aided by Pippa. Then, he lifted off, rapidly joining the fleet. Just as he neared them, the ship's sensors detected a bit of space debris flying straight at them! He didn't have time to react. Thud. It struck the ship. Its shields held mostly, but one sharp fragment shot through the side, heading straight for Ben's head.

It happened incredibly fast, as Ben later explained to all who would listen. Tessa had not yet gotten herself buckled in. She spotted the fragment and calculated its trajectory.

Knowing that it would hit Ben, she shot her right leg and foot upwards, placing her foot in its path. The metal hit her foot, tore through her toe shoe leather like butter, but deflected off her foot. In fact, when they looked at the fragment, its sharp point was completely bent!

"What the?" Ben exclaimed, his mind slow to realize what had just happened. Tessa lay in a jumble on the floor, but the projectile had missed him. "Pippa, tell them that we've been hit. Get the crew up here with the emergency sealant kit. What just happened? Tessa? You hurt?" He finally realized the robot had just saved his life.

"I'm okay, but my toe shoe is history. I could use a hand up. Are we leaking air? Can it be fixed?" Tessa asked. Her voice was very serious, the first time that Ben had heard her sound this way.

Pippa spoke up, "Seal is holding for now. Come on, Ben; we need to let the crew at it."

"Okay. Here," he focused and used his gifts to lift Tessa up and set her on her feet.

"Wow. That's a cool feeling, being lifted by magic. Thanks, Ben. Glad that you are unharmed," Tessa replied.

The three evacuated the cockpit, and Alis and Alberto came racing in, bringing in the repair kit, which floated along behind them as if by magic. Tessa asked, "Can I stay out of the way and watch them? I've never seen an in-flight repair before."

"Sure. Thanks for what you did," Ben replied.

"I'll see if I can find you another toe shoe," Pippa volunteered and left them just outside the cockpit. Tessa watched fascinated with what Alberto and Alis were doing. The equipment seemed to move of their own accord, though intellectually, she knew they were using the special gifts to levitate objects and such. Alberto shoved the fragment back out of the side of the ship. As the air began whistling out of the hull breech, Alis shot the emergency sealant into the hole. Shortly, it hardened, forming a solid seal.

"That ought to do fine until we get home and can make a better repair, captain," Alberto pronounced. He and Alis left, while Ben and Pippa took their original seats. She fired off an okay message to the fleet, and Ben got them going, jumping into hyperspace after the fleet. After Pippa announced how long they'd be in hyperspace, she headed to the galley, leaving Ben and Tessa in the cockpit. Ben finally asked her, "So how come you did that, saving me?"

She chuckled. "You don't know the laws of robotics? A robot can never allow harm to come to a human or nova, silly."

"But you've been genetically modifying our bodies, turning us into nearly helpless creatures," he protested. "Surely that is harming us."

"No silly. We are preventing you from causing more harm to others of your species, since your species currently has failed in that for unending centuries. Even the old Imperium and the Federation were at war with each other not so long ago. Then, there were the bouts of planetary genocide using the bio agent. Shall I go on?" Tessa replied and winked at him.

He flushed again. "No. Point taken. Still, we don't want to be genetically modified."

"Of course you don't, just like some humans don't want to be stopped from declaring war on other worlds and attacking them. It's for your own good. None of the new nova of Minta's has ever done even the slightest criminal or antisocial action. They can't," Tessa replied. "So I had to save you. Besides, I can't fly this ship. I don't have your mind magic. I've no arms for it, and I do want to get back in one piece."

"Accepted. So you didn't get hurt deflecting that metal? Incredible," Ben changed the topic.

"No. It takes quite a bit to cut through my form. It's quite a tough but incredibly pliable resin. I did ruin my shoe, but Pippa found me a replacement. That's another good benefit of the genetic modifications. All females have nearly the same shoe size, just as all men do, only theirs is two sizes larger. It makes it lots easier to make shoes for all the new nova," Tessa explained. She added, "Can we at least be friends now? I'm really not your enemy. I can hardly hurt you or any human."

"I'm not sure that it is friends, but I'll be civil to you."

"That's a good start, Ben. Thank you," Tessa said, giving him a flirting wink and coy smile once more. "Come on; we should join the others or they will start getting ideas about us."

"Oh come off it," Ben said flustered. "They won't think such things. Besides, robots can't have sex anyway."

"Where in the galaxy did you ever hear that one, Ben?" Tessa stopped abruptly and declared. "Of course, we can have sex. I'm programmed to provide the ultimate in such experiences with either your males or females. You should try me sometime." She saw him flush again and knew she'd scored another point with him. Together, they made their way back to the galley where Pippa was rustling up some supper.

Around noon the next day, they arrived back on Winno-3, where Emperor Yi met them personally. While a ground crew began making repairs to their ship, he invited them into his queen's throne room for a briefing. After getting Ben's report in person and satisfying himself as to its accuracy, he explained, "I've received a call from this Minta herself. She wants us to call her back in about thirty minutes. I'm expecting to hear another proposal, but that's just my guess. My staff is working out what worlds she may be going after next. This way. We'll use the queen's comm center this time."

Dutifully, the six followed Emperor Yi and Ambassador Tessa. Jan smiled. All Imperium comm centers were virtually identical. That was the old Imperium way of things. Uniformity in all things. Before long, his assistant made the connections, though Jan memorized the frequency being used, naturally nothing missed her observant eye.

"Minta here. I take it that you found everything done appropriately and correctly on Abel-C, Emperor Yi? Over."

After the long comm delay, since Minta's location was far from here in the mid-arm region, he replied, "Yes. My observers state that everything the people would need to survive well is present, along with proper instructions. Thank you for compromising. Over." Again, there was a long delay.

"Excellent, Emperor Yi. We have avoided an unnecessary war. We both want to bring a lasting peace to the galaxy. While our methods differ, you must admit that mine is working rapidly towards that goal. In the light of better understanding, I would like to propose that Ambassador Tessa pay a visit to Ashford-5. Her purpose there would be to see how they have developed over the last half century and see if we need to improve machines, add new ones, or make changes, so my nova can continue to flourish and prosper. I'm very amenable to making such alterations, so the humans under my care can flourish and prosper even more than they are doing at the present. I wish to prevent any future problems that might have arisen on Ashford-5. Of course, Ambassador Tessa should not be allowed into any secure areas. She is not a spy. I have many others for that purpose. Rather, I wish her to observe them and make recommendations for changes in the equipment and bots that we are providing our nova. Over."

"Is that wise?" Amy countered immediately. "How do we know that she isn't a spy?"

Tessa answered that one, "Look, if you don't allow me near anything that is secret, don't let me talk to key personnel, then how can I spy? I'm willing to have Ben here follow me around constantly, even stay with me at night so I can't sneak out and spy. Minta has a point. She truly does want what is the very best for the nova. While she has been carefully monitoring Zeta Scorpii-C, Ashford-5 is different. Men have upper arms now, reduced breast sizes, and all have repaired feet. This may well be a critical point, arguing in favor of doing such for Minta's nova as well. I do hope I won't be finding that men are back to their old tricks, fighting, thievery, and so on."

"Point taken. My heart goes out to all those billions of victims of Minta's genetic tampering. If you can report to her that these changes have helped the men and women of Ashford-5, then perhaps Minta will somehow provide these genetic cures to those other billions. Lord knows that their lives would be vastly improved," Emperor Yi declared.

Jan and Amy couldn't argue against that. If Tessa saw the great benefit these changes meant to those on their world, perhaps Minta would go along with them and cure her billions at least this much. Both women saw that they couldn't ignore such an opportunity to make a real difference in those victim's lives. Both nodded their agreement.

"Accepted Minta," Emperor Yi Gang finally replied.

"However, I must point out that if they discover Tessa is spying or doing anything harmful to that world, they have my permission to destroy her instantly. Over."

"Of course, emperor. Tessa, don't you dare do anything remotely like spying. I want you in one piece. Please give your reports to me in the presence of their queen. Everything shall be above boards, as you say, emperor. Over and out." Minta signed off.

"Well, I'm not a spy," Tessa replied to the blank monitor, a little annoyed that anyone should think she was. She wasn't sure why that ought to be bothering her circuits, but it was somehow. She forced those calculations into the background, focusing on the present.

"As soon as your ship is repaired, you may take Ambassador Tessa Nova with you. Once more, thank you all for your help in these difficult times," Emperor Yi said diplomatically. He and his assistant left them, making their slow way out of the room.

Nine hours later, Strike Force One landed at the spaceport at Exchange City. They were met by Queen Mary Linn, Governor Monica, and Renata. Ben was formally put in charge of watching over Ambassador Tessa. Queen Mary Linn sent him, *You keep a sharp eye on her. I don't want her to get access to anything that might compromise us or the Ataro Empire. Got that? You be with her 24/7 until further notice.*

Ben grumbled, but had to agree. For now, Tessa was his responsibility, like it or not.

# Chapter 6 Dealing with Disaster

Queen Adoria del Santiago had been born as she was, a genetic mutation with severe limitations. She'd never known anything different, until she went to school and saw images and videos of other humans on other worlds. She was a third generation mutation and had grown up believing her body was as normal as could be. As a small child growing up, like all children everywhere, she learned first by mimicking those around her, how to feed herself, to walk, to dress, and to play. Back then, she thought nothing of her physical limitations, and had not even known she had limitations. Everything was as normal as could be. The trouble here was that these billions of humans were about to wake up and find their bodies vastly different, genetically mutated, and, compared to their previous lives, almost completely helpless, until they learned to make effective use of the new devices and machines.

Analytically, she knew each person would be undergoing a huge, traumatic, and emotional shock, and that some might not even survive it. She also knew she had no way to give the billions Basic Therapy, assuming that Renata could teach her how to do it. They would have to endure their trauma and enormous emotional shock, as well as their immense frustrations with just trying to survive. Analytically, she reviewed the lengthy document that outlined everything the remaining worker robots, presumably under her control, would be providing, such as dead body removal, stocking grocery stores until the people of Abel-C were able to take over for them, handling any and all manner of emergencies. It seemed foolproof on the surface. Yet, nothing prepared her for the actual reality of their awakening.

High-pitched shrieks came from all the bedrooms of the brownstone home, drowning out similar shrieks from neighboring homes. Not only was it deafening, but it shook Queen Adonica to the core! She froze, unable even to cope with the terror-filled cries coming from the bedrooms of her new home. It wasn't an analytical reaction at all! Amid the screams, something that Renata had once mentioned to her flashed into her consciousness: in traumatic situations, people need to vent their emotions before they can become analytical about it. The reactive mind's reactions would eventually give way to analytical mind's computations, when it regained control. Thus, she headed to her own bedroom where her personal assistant, Akira, was likely awake too, but would be unable to even make a sound.

She found Akira sitting up in her bed with a mountain of long black hair draped over her enormous bosom, her remaining upper arms flailing around like windmills in some macabre protest against reality. The poor woman was physically shaking as well. "There, there, Akira," she said soothingly. "We'll survive this somehow." She sat down on the bed beside the terrified woman and leaned into her, unable to do more physically to comfort her. Akira just began shaking her head side to side, indicating No! With her lower arms and hands gone, she no longer had any way to communicate anything to her charge, her queen. Worse, her sole purpose of being Adoria's personal assistant had been taken away. She was even more helpless than her queen was, since she couldn't even talk.

How long she sat there with the shaking young woman, Adoria could not later say. The silence finally got her attention. The others had ceased screaming. "I've got to go see to the others for a bit. There are instruction cards beside these new machines, Akira. See if you can read them, follow the instructions, and get yourself dressed. I'll be back in a bit." She left the woman sobbing her heart out.

One by one, she entered the other bedrooms and consoled the victims, whose screams of stark terror had uniformly given way to an intense grief. All were sobbing uncontrollably. Once more, Adoria remembered something that Renata had once explained to her over tea. Emotional tones. In times of stress and trauma, people's emotions dropped or rose following a specific pattern. They might begin by being enthusiastic or cheerful. Under stress, they might drop down to a conservative demeanor. From there, they could well drop further down into boredom. As the stress increased, they could drop into hostility or antagonism. With continued stress, they might drop into pain. From there, they would reach anger. If the stress and trauma was severe enough, they could drop down even further into fear and terror, and then into a covert type of hostility, and then on down into sympathy and grief. If it was bad enough, they could drop into apathy. If the trauma was even worse, they could hit death. Recovery, Renata told her, followed the reverse path, from apathy to grief to sympathy and propitiation to covert hostility to fear to anger to pain to antagonism to boredom to conservatism and on up to cheerfulness once more.

Just where were her friends at on this cycle, she wondered analytically. They'd awakened from their comas to find their bodies genetically mutated and darn near helpless. Their reaction had been terror and fear. Now, they sank into grief. She knew she had to get them going the other way. Then, she realized she had to get the billions of Abel-C people going the other way! She felt more than overwhelmed with her task.

She called out loudly so that everyone could hear her. "Everyone. Listen up. In your bedrooms are a bunch of machines and devices you can use to get dressed and such. Each one has a placard of instructions on how to use it close beside it. See if you can read them and follow the instructions. I was able to get myself dressed following them. I'll come by to help as I can." She heard Ilsa crying out an "Okay," feeble as it was. She headed down the stairs to help Major Dirk who was on the couch.

He was sitting up. His eyes, bloodshot. His moustache was gone as were his arms, replaced by a mountain of shiny, thick, black hair that failed to cover his monstrous new bosom. They were larger than basketballs she'd seen on other worlds, but they were as large as the men's had been back on Ashford-5. "Well, major, you look just like one of the men back on my home world. Come on; let's get you up to your bedroom and dressed. It's possible to do so with this new equipment. Besides, I desperately need your help. I'm running Abel-C now. Come on. See if you can stand up. Only his toes touched the ground, and he nearly fell over trying to stand.

"I can't do this. I can't see my feet or where I'm going.

103

They are so heavy I feel like I am constantly about to fall over," he wailed.

"You are up. That's a start. I think it will be easier once you get shoes on. I'll walk beside you," she insisted. "Good. Slow and easy. Feel with your feet. Yes, that's the first step. Up we go. I'll try to catch you if you fall."

"I — I don't know if I can do this, Adoria. I've never been so scared in all my life. I think dying would be easier to face than this. Oh god! I can't keep my balance at all!"

"Lean into the wall a bit. Use the wall to steady yourself. You are doing fine. Just a few more steps," she coaxed him ever upwards. After what seemed an eternity to the major, he finally reached his bedroom and found all manner of new equipment and apparel present. "Read the cards. At least, they provided excellent, easy to follow instructions," she explained.

She walked him through using the dressing machine and the electrostatic hair machine, explaining that back home, the men always wore the extremely tight-laced, heavy steel boned corsets to help their backs handle the sheer weight of their breasts. "I can't breathe," he gasped, as the machine finally cinched him down and tied off the long laces.

"Shallow, short breaths. Don't fight it. The men claim the pressure is awful, but they get used to it in a couple of weeks. Without it, your back will be a mass of pain in no time, and I don't have any way of massaging the knots out," she advised. The dressing bot slipped a brown cotton shift-like dress over him and zipped it up. That done, it slipped a pair of matching toe shoes onto his feet, but standing in them on the soft, plush carpet wasn't noticeably easier for him. Then, she had him use the electrostatic hair machine.

"Oh my god! I have all this sensation in my hair! Now, that is incredible, but it isn't going to make up for having this much hair. It's always going to be in my way," he replied.

"It is that way for me. A constant bother. Can't be helped. Come on; let's see if the others have managed to get this far," she suggested.

Everyone had, more or less, gotten dressed, their hair straightened out, and the toilet used. After praising the six red-eyed adults, Adoria had them all head downstairs, leaving the two year olds in their cribs a while yet. Everyone was starving, but Isla and Kirsa merely stared at their new kitchen and had no idea how to do anything to fix something to eat. Adoria took charge, leading by example.

"Look, one of us alone will take all day to prepare a meal. From now on, at least four of us have to work together to fix a meal or to accomplish any task. We're lucky in that we have seven of us, not just four. So come on and lend me a foot. I'll show you all how we can work together and get this done. They've installed the low-to-the-floor kitchen. Without it, we'd not likely get much done," Adoria explained.

Two hours later, they began to struggle with actually eating. Trying to pick up a fork or spoon with your toes is intensely challenging the first time you try it. Frustrations only rose again, but they were starving, and the food looked inviting. The men had the worst of it. Their massive bosoms continually interfered, and more than once, their wives or Adoria stepped in and used their feet to feed them this time. Then, using a yoke, Ilsa and Kirsa carried two smaller bowls up for their daughters.

With full stomachs, the group assembled in the living room. Azzo and Kirsa looked as pitiful as Akira, who had no way to communicate anything at all. "Our careers — we're destroyed," Azzo wailed. "I can't play my violin, and Kirsa can't play the piano. Music was our whole lives. Now, we have nothing, nothing at all!"

Adoria took charge. "I know. But you are not alone. I would guess that half of our people have lost their careers as well. Think of your daughter. We'll just have to establish new, doable goals in the future. Right now, just focus on staying alive, and keeping her alive." She then went on to explain everything that had happened while they were in their comas, as well as where things now stood.

"I need to make a planet-wide broadcast very soon. Major, I need your help with the new electronics system that the robots installed over there." Purposely, she continued to provide "work" for him to do. She knew he could no longer be a soldier, and she decided he would be her liaison to Abel-C for the time being.

"I want to make an official broadcast that will reach every home. We should record it and play it back periodically, since not everyone will be able to see it live. How do we do it?" she asked.

"Well, this is our standard master unit. That switch there will send the signal to the repeater towers and hence to every set in the world, if that's what you mean," he replied, looking the system over. He'd had some basic training in its use, but wished that he'd paid more attention to those lessons. "How do we operate it without hands? Adoria, we can't live like this, not really," he slipped back into grief once more.

"We must. I need you, Major Dirk. I can't do this alone. Come on; let's figure out how to send and record what I'm sending at the same time. That's a start. There are billions out there who are waiting to hear something, anything at all, just as terrified and scared as we all are."

Using a toe, he got it powered up. A bit of experimenting later, he had it ready to broadcast and record simultaneously. "Okay. When I push this button, all the sets on Abel-C will turn on. Are you ready?" She nodded, and he clumsily pushed it.

She took a deep breath and faced the small camera and microphone. "This is your Queen Adoria del Santiago speaking. You all have been in comas for around four days, and a lot has happened during that time, some hideously bad, some good. Let me explain, since I wasn't in a coma during that time. I'm already genetically modified; only my breasts enlarged again. Your gas masks failed to prevent the bio agent from mutating your bodies. Everyone on Abel-C has had their bodies genetically altered. Yes, the men have it far worse than us females."

"During that time, the robots provided all the new equipment and bots that we must have in order to continue to survive on our own. Each has clear instructions on its use on a placard beside it. They went around ripping out and installing new kitchens while you were unconscious. Everyone now has a dishwasher, if you didn't before. Speaking from experience, we do have everything that we need in order to be able to survive on our own. I had a team from my home world come here to

106

inspect random homes. They reported we do have everything that we are going to need to make it. I know, right now it seems impossible that we can survive, but on my home world, we face this every day, just as the other conquered worlds of the metal heads do. We can survive and we must."

"In order to survive, it is a cardinal rule that from now on, everyone must work together in teams of at least four adults in order to get some task done, such as fixing a meal. If your home does not have at least four adults living there, contact your neighbors and see if you can work out some arrangements. We've just fixed a meal here and it took seven of us working together close to two hours to fix and eat it, so we know it can be done, just not easily. Yes, it was awkward and horribly frustrating, but we did it. I know that probably half of you have lost your careers. Certainly, my two close musician friends here can no longer play the violin and piano. Still, let's somehow survive, and then go about setting up new goals and purposes. Let's not give in to the metal heads!"

"Okay, back to what has happened. Abel-C's defenses fell in less than a day. The Ataro Empire was prepared to come to your aid, but it took four days for them to arrive in force, far too late to prevent what's happened to you, the bio agent attack. However, Emperor Yi Gang worked what I can only call a miracle. He's gotten the metal heads to allow me to be your ruler, your Ataro queen. What I'm trying to say is he managed to keep Abel-C from becoming another slave world of the robots. I rule, not the metal heads! However, the metal heads will be providing defense protection of our world. Worker robots will be around to help us with things that we are unable to handle just now. I'm told that they will assist us in removing those who have not survived. They are rebuilding the infrastructure that was damaged by their bombings. Everyone should have electric power by now, for example. The worker robots will be handling emergency medical services until we become skilled and inventive enough to take them over for ourselves. In short, the robots will not be running or ruling Abel-C! We are still a free people, just dependent upon some robot assistance for the time being. How long the robots will remain depends on us, on you and I, and on how soon we can figure out new ways and means to run our world."

"However, in return, we must sell our ores to the robots, but at the going commercial rates. That appears to be the main reason that Abel-C was attacked, to allow them access to raw materials. As long as we get a fair price for them, I can live with that."

"Men, your situation is far worse than us women. If you haven't figured it out yet, you need to wear those tight-laced corsets for back support. If you don't, you'll get debilitating backaches. The men on my world certainly do. So the rule is, at least four adults work together on a single task. We must become very team oriented if we are to make it. I can't survive on my own either."

"At this point in time, I have no idea which, if any, of Abel-C's leaders survived the attacks. Give me time to organize and find out what the situation is. Expect more of these broadcasts as I find out more. There is one ray of hope that I can offer. I have contacted my home world's geneticists and asked them if there is any way that they can provide a partial cure for you men, similar to what they were able to do for ours. I'm not a geneticist, but I hope that something can be worked out to make our men's lives a bit easier to endure. I'm recording this and will have it replayed periodically throughout the day. I hope to know more tomorrow."

"Now is the time that truly tests just what you, as a people, are made of. Let's not give up hope. We can survive this disaster. We can find new ways to flourish and prosper. It won't be easy. I doubt if you will ever experience anything as difficult and frustrating as the ensuing days will be for us all. Persevere. Don't give up. Let's show these metal heads that it takes more than a bio attack to wipe us out! I'll try to have more information tomorrow around noon." She signed off. Major Dirk fiddled some with the controls and got the recording to play back on the hour, every hour for the rest of the day.

Everyone struggled to get through this first day, but it remained a nightmare for all. By the end of the day, Adoria realized she could best help by giving some helpful suggestions and showing them how she did specific things. She discussed this with Major Dirk that evening, working out how they could possible get a camera into the kitchen and record them making breakfast.

During the night, the unexpected happened. Adoria heard a loud noise. It sounded like it was coming from the first floor. Hastily, she got up, feeling around in the dark for her toe shoes. Not finding them, she called out for Akira. She had always slept beside her, but was she there? Pangs of regret filled her mind for having brought Akira here with her. Now, she was just as helpless and worse, she couldn't even speak or make a sound. At last, she stood on her toes, wobbling some, shook her hair off her face and onto her back, and headed toward the light switch. After some sensing with her large breasts, she found it and turned it on. Akira's place on the bed was vacant! Her stomach knotted. Had something happened to her? Was she hurt?

Adoria headed out of her room. Thankfully, they had left the light by the stairs on. She gasped. There at the bottom lay Akira. She'd fallen down the steps! She cried out for help and then leaning against the wall, carefully descended the steps. When she reached her, Major Dirk, Wolfgang, Ilsa, Azzo, and Kirsa appeared at the top of the stairs. She looked up at their pale faces, disheveled hair, and shook her head. "I think she's dead. Neck is broken. My god, the poor woman. I should never have brought her here with me. She couldn't even speak."

"It's not your fault," Major Dirk spoke up. "We can't do anything now. I guess we will have to summon the robots to bury her in the morning. I'm sorry for you, Adoria."

With tears in her eyes, she leaned against the wall and made her precarious way up the stairs. "Want me to stay with you tonight?" he asked.

"Please. I don't want to be alone, not now, not after that," she sobbed, unable to suppress her grief. "Why did she go down the stairs in the middle of the night?"

Major Dirk shrugged his shoulders. "Don't know. Come on; let's get you to bed. It's been tough on us all. I'm still not sure how even to get into a bed! My hair keeps getting in the way."

Adoria smiled faintly, reminding her to give hints in the morning. "Like this," she demonstrated. Leaning her head back, she tossed her hair back and forth some until it lay across her back. "Now swing it all to the front, between your legs. That's what I do so I can crawl into bed. Get it all in one place first, before trying to shift it. We'd be lost without the electrostatic machines, though, one tangled mess." He tried it, more or less getting it right and joined her. It took her a while to calm down and get back to sleep.

Around four in the morning, they were again awakened by similar loud thumping sounds. Adoria's stomach knotted. "What was that?" she whispered, rousing Major Dirk, who hadn't heard anything. "I'll get the light," she volunteered and again felt for them with her breasts, since she didn't have anything else to sense the switch with. At last, she got them on. Major Dirk had at least gotten himself into a sitting position by that time. Together, they made their way out of the bedroom and to the stairs, joined by a very sleepy-eyed Wolfgang and Ilsa. All four gasped!

Lying in a jumble on top of Akira were Azzo and Kirsa! They'd fallen too. Suddenly, it hit Adoria like a hammer. "My god! They all killed themselves!"

Ilsa started crying. "They couldn't live without their music. I just know it, and poor Akira could even talk and tell us what was wrong. Maybe we should join them."

"Don't talk like that. I love you. We have to take care of Magda. Wait, where's Maud?" Wolfgang called out. Everyone headed into the Stein's bedroom. All were relieved to see the two year old sleeping soundly in her crib. "We will take care of her like our own, won't we, Ilsa?" he whispered. She nodded, put her upper arms around him, and leaned on him.

"I should have seen this coming and stopped it," Adoria sobbed. Three of her friends gone in one night was almost too much to bear. Later, when Major Dirk got her back into bed, she whispered, "I should have expected this. I'll warn everyone about it in tomorrow's broadcast. I have to." She now realized why some people died during and after the bio attacks. Some refused to live their lives as a mostly helpless mutant. She tried to console herself by saying that they'd exercised the last of their free will, but that didn't help her emotions.

The next day, a shiny metal robot came and carried the bodies away. It also cleaned up the bit of dried blood on the rug, for which Adoria was grateful. She feared its constant reminder would have an adverse effect on the others.

That handled, she had Major Dirk attempt to record them cooking breakfast and later trying to eat it. Eventually, all four broke into hysterical laughter at the utter absurdity that they were facing. Later, she replayed it for the benefit of all those still living on Abel-C. She also demonstrated some tips that she used, including how she used her foot to brush her teeth, a process that sometimes took her twenty minutes unless she just used her *mentales* gifts, which now she flatly refused to use, setting herself up as a role model for the other victims.

Handling the two children took all their inventiveness. They'd more or less left both alone yesterday, but now dirty diapers just had to be handled. Major Dirk and Adoria had no experience with babies. Finally, Ilsa and Wolfgang knew something they didn't, bolstering their own self-image a little as they directed the action of the many feet trying to handle the pair.

During the day, Adoria kept a watchful eye on the pair, but the physicist and chemist showed no signs of desiring to kill themselves. Major Dirk, on the other hand, had also lost his only goals and employment. He had been a soldier most all his adult life and that was now gone completely. She needed him and decided that he might just try to off himself. That night, she resolved to help give him further reasons to live.

Everyone was sleeping in the buff at night. Last night, both she and Major Dirk had gotten aroused with each other, though wisely neither had mentioned it. Something like this was impossible to miss, but with the three suicides, neither had called any attention to it. She needed comforting and that he could give. As they used the undressing machine to get ready for bed, she took the initiative. Both had already shaken their hair to their front side so they could get into bed without laying on it, which was rather uncomfortable considering how sensitive each strand was. Last night, he'd wisely used it to hide his bulge. Tonight, Adoria took the lead, moving up to him before they climbed into bed, planting a passionate kiss on his lips. Nature took its course from there, though she also slipped into rapport with him, doubling his pleasure and guaranteeing she knew precisely what he needed next. They lay side by side, since neither had arms to handle it any other way.

"That was beyond description, Adoria. Between our hair and the dual actions — I never knew that a woman's breast could be so erotic, so sensitive," he whispered.

"You are a fabulous man yourself, but you mean the four actions," she whispered back, kissing him again. He chuckled slightly, the first time he'd laughed since before the attack. Adoria began to relax. She didn't sense that he was threatening to take his own life. "I need you in lots of ways," she added. He kissed her back.

Over breakfast the next morning, Ilsa asked, "Say Adoria, did you and Dirk do it last night? We sort of heard you."

Adoria flushed. "Yes, it was really good. I really do like him a lot."

Ilsa grinned. "We did too. It's absolutely amazing, the best sex I've ever had. And our hair — those sensations add enormously to the pleasures. Incredible, isn't it?" Adoria could only agree, wishing that she'd done it sooner, but then she'd been so driven to become an Ataro queen that she had not time for boyfriends or girlfriends for that matter, since the sex difference was almost insignificant now.

During the week, she continued her daily broadcasts. With each one, she attempted to demonstrate how to perform another daily action, though when they showed how to change dirty diapers, all four ended up laughing like fools on the video. Still, she hoped and prayed that her videos were helping the others.

On the tenth day, a robot delivered a dispatch to her. It read: estimated original population of Abel-C was 6,730,000,000. Current population: 4,263,943,653, including babies. They'd lost more than a quarter of their population. The dispatch also listed the head count of males and females.

The ratio was currently approximately five females to every three males, but the dispatch suggested more males might succumb during the next few weeks. She hoped not, and during that day's report to the world, after giving the latest figures, she urged everyone who had not yet discovered how good and different intercourse was to give it a try. She even suggested the easiest position for males to handle, on their sides. Little did she know that she was playing into Minta's hands with this. This was precisely what Minta had urged on the previously conquered worlds. Hence, the initial baby boom would come around ten months after the conquest, a start on rebuilding the population and more importantly a new generation. Slowly, it dawned on Adoria that only their children would become fully comfortable and adapted to the genetic modifications, since they knew no different, unlike the adults who were living the nightmare. She began to glimpse Minta's long-range plan for humans in the galaxy.

Two weeks after the comas ended, a robot delivered a very lengthy dispatch to her. This time, it listed all the occupations that needed to be filled in order for the people of Abel-C to be self-sufficient along food and clothing lines. From managing the automated farms, to managing the meat packing, to managing the food preparations and packaging, to food crate transport, to grocery stores, the list was quite lengthy. The document listed empty homes by city and town, alphabetically. The robots would handle construction of new housing, if and whenever it was needed. The robots were to handle the maintenance of the power grids, water supplies, and communications cabling, until and if the queen wished otherwise.

Looking this one over, she began to realize that unless something major changed, the people of Abel-C would always have to have the robots around to handle a great many things that they would be unable to, lacking the *mentales* gifts. While Ashford-5 was quite independent, that was only possible because everyone had the gift. Even though they were not a slave world, they would be dependent upon worker robots, probably far into the future, if not forever. That bothered her immensely.

What also bothered Adoria was how to visit these cities and towns, how to get into real, live communication with the people. How was she to figure out who would handle the grocery stores, who would run the meat packing plants, and so on. On the other conquered worlds, the document explained that the robot commander appointed people to these jobs, whether or not they knew anything about it. Then, came the big task of finances. Just how would people be paid? Overwhelmed by the sheer magnitude of the chore facing her, she slumped into a chair, very depressed. The entire economic system of Abel-C was destroyed, and she had no idea how to begin to restart it, but time was her enemy. Already the grocery stores had been picked bare.

Major Dirk sat beside her, having also read the lengthy document. "This is really bad, isn't it? Maybe the robots are trying to show you that you can't do it and have you invite them back in to bring order," he suggested.

She brightened up. "You know, that could well be what's behind this. They are trying to show the emperor and me that the problems here are far too gigantic for us to handle. I bet they are expecting us to beg the robots to return and get this world going again. Well, somehow we can't let that happen!"

She rose, got her balance, and headed for the comm center. She wasn't quite sure what she was going to say in today's broadcast, but for sure, she was going to make an attempt to start things working again. First, she read off part of the lengthy document.

"Okay. So our economy is non-existent. Grocery stores are bare. We have to get started somehow, so here's what I want everyone to do. Think about this lengthy list. Most of the jobs are management and oversight in nature. These days, machines handle most of the real work, but still require human oversight. Those of you who own grocery stores, get back to work, order your much needed supplies like you have always done in the past. I know that some of the storeowners are dead. So if you think that you would like to run one, volunteer. In fact, this is a good time to consider a career choice. What have you always wanted to do that may yet be possible? Make inquiries. There are openings in darn near everything that I've listed. Take the initiative, report to that facility, and see what can be done. If we all work together, we can get the food lines functioning again before we all starve to death. I surely don't want to have to call the robots back and have them force each of us to do a specific job like they did on their other conquered slave worlds. So if you don't want to be a slave and be ordered what to do, take the initiative. Find a work job that you might like to do and get it going."

"What about pay and money? Right now, I have no idea. Consider all necessary commodities free for now until we get this worked out. Major Dirk has the list of needed positions by city and town. I'll give you a number where you can contact him and apply for a given position. Communicate to us what you want to do, and let's see if we can't find you that position. I know that many business owners are frankly out of business right now. I'm open to ideas from you as well. Call our number and make suggestions. If we don't act now and fast, I'm afraid we'll have no choice but to call the robot leaders back to our world, and let them order each of us around to get it all going again. I don't want that, and I don't think you do either. So take the initiative. Call us. Volunteer. Let's somehow get the food lines working first."

By that evening, their call center was swamped. She put Ilsa and Wolfgang on the project with Major Dirk. By morning, several dozen neighbors dropped by asking if she needed any help coordinating the calls. Queen Adoria smiled and put each of them to work. A week later, they moved the call center into a vacant warehouse three blocks away, where a hundred men and women worked on planet-wide coordination of the food production lines. A month later, food was again flowing through the entire distribution lines from the farms to the local grocery stores. She did note that the majority of the new "workers" were women, but given the lack of men and their more severe handicap, that was understandable.

It took the better part of a year to re-establish life on Abel-C. She established local councils to deal with matters on a city or town basis, referring more difficult problems or questions on up to her to resolve. As things slowly improved,

Queen Adoria realized that Abel-C would never be truly independent of the metal heads. There were just too many things that the people simply were unable to do for themselves. That truly bothered her.

Hence, she decided to ask the emperor for assistance. He responded by establishing the Abel-C Heavy Work Force, an all-volunteer organization. Volunteers signed up for four-year terms of service. They received free living expenses and a hefty salary for their work. Five months after the attack, each major city finally had a functioning hospital, with doctors and nurses, all from other worlds, replacing the robots that had been doing it. A year later, the AHWF numbered close to a hundred thousand workers, all normal humans who took over for the robot work force. As long as the emperor could continue to provide these critical workers, Abel-C could remain more or less free from the worker robots, something that every citizen demanded.

Curiously enough, during this time span, the worker robots continued to operate all the many mines on this world, extracting valuable ores in quantities unheard of before the war! In fact, the metal heads deposited huge sums of money into a world bank account. Working constantly all day and night and every day of the week, these robots took out ore at a rate nearly thirty times what each mine had been producing before the war. Minta was taking no chances. She needed the ores now, not later. Just how critical was her need wasn't known for several months. Eventually, it became obvious to Emperor Yi just why the robots needed so much raw materials. The reason was not a good one at all!

# Chapter 7 Genetics and Cures

Queen Adoria del Santiago called back to Ashford-5 during the first week after the bio agent attack. Queen Mary Linn put her in contact with their lead genetics research doctors, Doctors Crystal and Zia Botocelli. Both were twenty-four and married. Both were named after their famous geneticists namesakes, Dr. Crystal del Arbella and Dr. Zia Botocelli. While Crystal carried that recessive Calder Mutation gene that her grandmother had, her mate did not. Thus, they were not worried about having children with that awful mutation. Both had risen to the top of Tierra's genetics industry and were now the spokeswomen for this group of twenty doctors, all heavily involved in working out genetic cures for Tierra and others.

Of course, the situation on Tierra or Ashford-5 was a grim one. Their bodies had undergone so darn many mutations that the genetic codes were extremely scrambled, compared to those of a normal human. The sheer number of variations from person to person was staggering, defeating their attempts to find a cure that would work on everyone. Per the queen's orders, they were not allowed to work on an individual cure for one person. That would have been too much like playing God with people's lives. How does one chose who gets a full cure and who doesn't?

"Queen Adoria here. You've heard about the bio attack on Abel-C? Over."

Doctor Crystal replied, "Yes. What is the situation? What is the mutant variety? Over."

She outlined the changes that had occurred. "What I need here is some assistance for the men. I know that somehow our men had their upper arms regrown and breasts reduced in size. That would go a long way here. Can that be done for Abel-C? Over."

"We don't have their DNA database. If we can get that, we can study it and better answer you," Doctor Zia replied, forgetting to say "Over." Hastily, she added, "Over."

A week later, thanks to some clever hacking by Jan,

117

they had the latest DNA database on file. Jan had hacked into one of their still operational computer systems and retrieved the files of a thousand key personnel who had theirs on file, presumably because at that time they had been high-level officials. Finally, they had stable DNA samples to work with. Of course, now they needed current samples from the victims. While it would have been optimal to have current samples from some of those thousand, most of those were likely dead. Hence, they would make do with samples from some of the victims.

Queen Mary Linn convinced the emperor to send a small medical team to visit Queen Adoria and obtain a dozen samples. Thus, two months after the bio attack, doctors Crystal and Zia had the after-attack samples they needed. On civilized worlds, genetic experimentation on humans was illegal. Their grandmothers had gotten around this by an "accidental" exposure. They'd taken a gamble and it had paid off.

This time, the geneticists couldn't gamble. They could not work up a cure and then see if it worked on a victim of this recent bio attack. Also hampering their work was the fact that they didn't have before and after DNA samples from the same person. Thus, much of their research was guesswork and extrapolation from their own cases. After six months research, they worked out a way to make some slight changes, with a ninety percent certainty. That is, by comparing male and female current DNA, for example Wolfgang and Isla's, they believed that they could alter male DNA to that found in the female DNA. Specifically, they thought that the men could regrow upper arms and have breast sizes reduced to those of the women of Abel-C. Yet, ninety percent is a long way from an absolute certainty.

Doctors Crystal and Zia reported their discovery to Queen Adoria directly. The queen replied, "Look, we have to take this gamble. It's been eight months now, and we've lost another million men who have just given up and found ways to commit suicide. If we don't try, we're going to lose even more men. Let's not tell the emperor or Queen Mary Linn and just do it. Please, we're desperate here. Over."

A week later using Crystal's grandmother's agent, the Ashford-5 geneticists prepared the cure en mass. Strike Force One was hired to deliver it to Queen Adoria, and Tessa tagged along to watch the proceedings. Doctor Crystal also went to supervise the testing. She unleashed a small dose on Wolfgang, Ilsa, Major Dirk, and Queen Adoria, along with the two children. The queen insisted that she also be a test subject, since if this worked, they'd be dosing the whole world with it.

This time, no one fell into a coma. However, after one day, Major Dirk and Wolfgang began noticing that their breasts were shrinking. It was plainly obvious from their now ill-fitting dresses. The second day, the men awoke to find small upper arms were growing! After a week, their arms were baby-like but working while their bosoms matched those of the women. Two very pleased men no longer had to wear the awful corsets and their arms allowed them to keep their precarious balance much better. The women noticed no effects at all.

Satisfied that their partial cure was going to work, Queen Adoria ordered it released on the entire world, though she first made a planet-wide broadcast to tell everyone the good news and what to expect. Interestingly enough, the death of males from unnatural causes ceased that day. In the weeks that followed, their call center received floods of calls from men across the world thanking her for the cure. A very pleased Strike Force One returned to Ashford-5.

During these many months, Jan continued to call Carli Daniels on Ponchart-D. She was reduced to patiently listening to their trials and tribulations, but was able to give them valuable hints on how to do some things. Keeping their morale up was her goal these months. When Strike Force One returned with news of their success, she relayed it to Carli the next day.

"Hi Jan. Remember, I told you that Michelle and I have become mates? Well, we are both pregnant now. Pretty sure of it, since we both missed our periods. The robots are forcing everyone to breed, but we jumped the gun and mated because we love each other. Same with Lexi and Faye, they've joined too, as have Jessi and Tori. This way, the metal heads can't

119

force us to do something that we don't want to do. Chalk up one for us this time. Oh, the farming is going well. Good crop this year, though I really wonder if those robots are properly maintaining our equipment. Old Amos doesn't think so, but he's really helpless to check up on them. Over." Carli chatted away, glad to have someone else to talk to about her dismal life. Before Jan could reply, she added, "Oh yeh. Michelle wants me to tell you that she has finally gotten all the bombs made. It has taken her a really long time to make them, and I've helped her, sort of. It's darn hard to do such fine work with only arm stumps and toes. Over really this time."

Jan grinned. "Excellent work. Congratulations to the both of you. Tell Michelle great work. I also have some news for you from Abel-C. Our geneticists have finally been partially able to cure their men. At least they have upper arms now too and their breasts have shrink to the size of their women. Over."

"Wow! Incredible. We need that here too, desperately, what with winter coming on. Can we get it, the cure I mean? Over," Carli asked pleadingly.

Jan thought a moment. An idea, quite diabolical, popped into her hacker's mind. "I think I know a way that you might get it. Let's keep this between you, me, and your group. Here's how I think you might be able to pull it off." Jan outlined her idea.

"Oh, Michelle loves it! Finally, we strike back at the metal heads! We'll do it, Jan! Thanks a billion. Over and out." Carli felt real hope, her emotions rising. "Can we do it?" she asked her new mate.

"You bet we can! First, we have to write the ultimatum out. That's the truly hard part." She sat down and used her feet to write out the ultimatum. Hours later, the two looked it over. The crude block letters looked worse than a beginning schoolchild's, but the words were clear. That's what mattered. Michelle suggested, "I think our first target ought to be the big cell tower near the destroyed guards' base. The metal heads use it to transmit their signals around here. Come on; let's load one bomb in the truck. We can get there during the night and be back long before dawn."

Working for months, Michelle finally finished making all the bombs. As an explosives expert in the guards before the bio attack, she could have opened the many crates, prepared the explosives, inserted the detonators, and readied them in perhaps a day, considering they had a hundred crates of the high explosives. Now, it had taken her many months. Her arm stumps were pretty useless and her feet, highly uncoordinated. Still, Michelle was driven, her goal: to destroy the cursed metal heads that had taken over her world.

The six used their feet to put a pair of bombs into either basket of a yoke. Proudly, Michelle lifted the yoke on her shoulders and carried it out to the grain truck. Once more, the six used their feet to lift the two packages up into the bed, covering them with a tarp. "But we want to come along too," Tori insisted.

Seeing the four pleading women, Michelle consented, and the six climbed into the trunk. While she and Carli drove the grain truck, the other four sat in the back. They left around eleven that night, arriving at the cell tower at midnight. It took them a half hour of joint struggles to get the two bombs off the truck, into the yokes, carried to the base of the tower, unloaded, and set into place. Using a toe, Michelle set the timer, and they headed back to the truck.

"So when does it go boom?" asked an excited Tori.

"Around four, long after we are back home in bed," Michelle explained. "Now get into the bed. We've a long drive back. I told you that there's nothing to see. Maybe it will be on the news, if the robot heads decide to show it to us."

"But will we hear it?" Tori continued.

"No. We're too far away. But you'll know something is up. Our local robot will be very confused. Come on. We need to get going," Michelle replied.

True, Michelle really did want to stay and watch the tower come down. She loved explosions, the bigger, the better. But this time, she didn't want to get caught. The metal heads would just shoot her outright. Besides, they had to get their demands document into the attention of the robots in power. After getting into the cab, Carli already had their laptop computer up and had a connection to the system via that very cell tower. "Are we ready to send it?" Carli asked.

Michelle smiled. "Do it! Finally, we strike back! Farmers can't be mowed over so easily!" That done, with Michelle shifting the gears, Carli drove them home. All six were far too excited to fall asleep right away. Finally, after a round of passionate sex, they fell into the best sleep that they had had since the attack had come many months ago.

Sure enough, the robot watcher was completely confused. They watched him going about checking the wiring of his quarters. That turned up nothing. Then the confused robot entered its one-man spaceship and used its comm center. It came out looking more confused, if a metal head could be said to be confused. Michelle only smiled at it. "Trouble at one of our fields?" she asked innocently.

"No. Cell tower is out. Going to check on it now. Make sure the fall plowing is done. Winter wheat must be planted next week." It turned and left her.

During the next week, they blew up five more relay towers, including the original one after the robots repaired it. Still, Michelle knew that this was merely a minor annoyance to the robots. She needed a bigger impact. Finally, that time came.

Their robot ordered them to drive a load of grain into Billings. Michelle knew that there was a large spaceport in that city, some two hundred miles to the north, an excellent target she thought. The six inserted a dozen of the bombs beneath the cab's seat. Carli and Michelle then drove it to the grain elevator, where a robot loaded their gain for them, issuing them specific orders where it was to be delivered in Billings.

It took most of the day to drive that far. The load was heavy and Carli had a great deal of difficulty steering it, so she went very slowly. Their cargo was too precious to lose. By the time that they finally found their destination and unloaded the grain, it was already dark. The robot there told them to drive home anyway.

Carli obeyed, but took a wrong turn, based on Michelle's recollections of the base's location. She stopped alongside the giant spaceport. It was dark, but the faint moonlight allowed them to see the hundreds of parked ships, all in a row. Michelle whispered, "Like shooting ducks." Carli had no idea what she was talking about, but figured it meant they were going to be successful.

The pair wished the others were here to help them get the bombs out and into the yokes. It took them way too long to do that, as far as Michelle was concerned. An hour later, they walked carefully over the destroyed fence and onto the concrete tarmac, heading for the line of ships, gleaming in the faint moonlight. One by one, the pair stuck each of the bombs to the sides of a ship, spacing them a ship apart. That done, on the return trip, Michelle stopped at each and set its timer for two hours.

They returned to the truck and awkwardly used their feet to get their yokes back into the empty bed and climbed in. A few minutes later, they left Billings behind them, heading home. They arrived around midnight, welcomed home by Lexi, Faye, Jessi, and Tori, who had hot tea and biscuits waiting for them. "So how did it go?" asked Tori impatiently.

Michelle shrugged her shoulders. "Don't know. We didn't stick around to see it go boom, though I dearly would love to have watched it. Nothing like a big boom, bigger the better. Thanks for the biscuits."

Jessi smiled. "Welcome. We worked on them for four hours. How will we know if it did anything?"

"We won't, probably. Billings is two hundred miles from here. If we're lucky, it might be on the news. More likely, though, they'll be warning us against doing that again," Michelle countered.

Just then, the ground shook. "What was that? Earthquake?" asked a worried Lexi.

"We don't have earthquakes around here. No fault lines," Carli replied, recalling her high school earth science class.

"Let's go outside. Maybe we can see something," Jessi suggested. The six headed outside and looked to the north. Along the horizon, a red glow could be seen. Michelle smiled. It was in the direction of Billings.

The next day, several others in the village were asking about the "earthquake" last night. One was bold enough to ask their village robot if there was any danger from the quake.

"That was not an earthquake," the metal voiced robot answered. "Some traitors blew up dozens of our fighter ships and caused major damage to the Billings Spaceport. They will be apprehended and shot. See to your farming now."

Minta-2 reported to Minta back on Beltazar-C via a burst of binary bits. "A rash of sabotage is occurring here on Ponchart-D. It is escalating. Last night, they destroyed twenty one-man ships, and half of the fuel cells were lost in collateral damage. This is getting out of hand. How can these nova be capable of doing such things?"

Minta sent back, "Have they made any demands?"

Minta-2 replied. "We received a crude document."

"What's it demand?"

"It says Ponchart-D wants an Ataro Empire queen to rule it under the same arrangements as Abel-C. If this demand is not met, expect more bombings until you metal heads meet it. Rather silly. I shall make an announcement to the world of this request, and then announce that we'll destroy a village for each bomb that goes off. That ought to quell this rebellion promptly," Minta-2 sent back.

Minta countered, "If you take that course, based on human history, that will unite the entire world against us or they will capitulate when villages are destroyed."

"Precisely."

"We can't afford to lose their fall harvest, Minta-2. Perhaps a better course of action is to ignore it completely. Make no mention of the damage caused. Meantime, see that the harvest shipments are moved up ahead of schedule," Minta ordered.

"Well, nothing much happened that time," Tori commented. The six watched the news, but there wasn't any mention of the explosions at the Billings Spaceport.

"Probably takes a lot of bombing to get their idiotic attention," Michelle commented. "We've got plenty of bombs left. We just need a new target."

The following day, their robot again ordered them. At least it politely knocked on their front door. "New orders. You are to deliver another load of wheat to the docks in Billings today. The other four can continue with the plowing. Bring your truck now," it ordered.

"Okay," Michelle replied, watching the metal monster turn and leave.

"But we weren't supposed to make another delivery until next week," Carli pointed out.

"Maybe the wheat is important to them somehow," Jessi suggested.

"What say we put a little something extra in the wheat," Michelle teased them all. Once more, the six worked together to get two bombs into the truck beneath the cab's seat. Then, the two headed to the grain elevator, where the robot filled them with a full load.

The pair took a stretch break halfway to Billings, using the time to insert the pair of bombs in their load of wheat. Michelle set the timers for four in the morning, giving them plenty of time to return home and for more loads to be deposited.

Minta-2 reported the next day. "Minta, I suspect the rebels are somehow monitoring our communications. They blew up the wheat elevator early this morning, destroying many tons and causing a huge fire. We've lost a great deal of wheat. Permission to destroy a few farming villages."

"Wait. This is becoming quite serious. Let's announce on their public network that we want a meeting with them. Specify a remote location and a date and time. Then, apply Protocol 16 to whoever shows up," Minta tried a new approach. She didn't send that she was keenly worried about their transmissions being monitored! Hence, she'd used official language. Protocol 16 meant that Minta-2 would have her forces there and would exterminate all those that showed up for the meeting.

Minta-2 was pleased, almost as pleased as the day she eliminated their puny space fleet and launched the bio agent attack. In a few days, she would be rid of the saboteurs once and for all. She did as ordered, making a public broadcast.

When Jan called the next day, Carli was excited. "It is working. The leader, this Minta-2 robot, was on the news last night. She wants to meet the rebels who are making the demands to talk about implementing them. We are supposed to meet them in four days." She went onto tell her that the location was a small farming village nearly five hundred miles to the east. "We'll need to do a lot of traveling. We'll need to stop for gas several times. Over."

Jan didn't like the sound of this. "Look. This could be a trap. Give me a day or so to see what I can do about it." She talked a while longer before signing off. Jan had a bad feeling and decided to follow up on it. Considering the lives of Carli and Michelle were at stake, she even pulled Amy into her conspiracy. "Look, I need some hacking help. Here's what we absolutely must do within four days."

On the appointed day, Minta-2 and twenty-five of her Model 12 killer robots arrived at the empty village. The homes were in good shape, having been repaired for use as the population of Ponchart-D grew again. She carefully positioned them in well-hidden locations around the village. She then stood at the designated building in which the meeting was supposed to be held. Per Protocol 16, she wore a streaming video camera so that back on Beltazar-C, Minta could watch the action directly. She could not afford another mistake.

At the appointed time, noon, Minta-2 still had not detected any incoming vehicles. She contacted her ships in the sky, asking for infrared scans. Perhaps, the rebels were already here and in hiding. Ten minutes later, they reported nothing visible except for a few small rodents. Just as she was about to call it a bust, static noise crackled from inside the building. Drawing her d-gun, Minta-2 stepped cautiously into the building, ready to blast the rebels. Instead, she found a giant monitor had mysterious turned on.

"Minta-2. You are late," a disguised voice spoke to her from the monitor. At once, she realized she must be on a two-way setup.

"I'm here. Where are you?"

"Not where your robots can blast us. Sorry that your plan has failed. We came here to discuss terms, but you came here to kill us. Won't work. We'll just have to blow up some more things until you accept our terms," the voice said. "That is all. Bye, bye." The monitor turned off.

"Trace that signal!" Minta-2 barked.

Jan and Amy had worked day and night, getting very little sleep during the previous three days. Jan had found a way to hack into the computer systems of Ponchart-D, a relatively unsophisticated system that had not yet been updated by the robots. Amy had then found a way to obtain video streams from that village, only because it had been both repaired, refurbished, and vacant, ready for occupancy by some of the second-generation young adults. The pair had then worked out a very devious scheme whereby their direct line to the comm center in the meeting building was bounced off systems on twenty other worlds, ensuring that any back-trace would yield nothing at all, except hacked systems and overall confusion.

Hours before the meeting, the pair watched as Minta-2 and her large death squad arrived and took their positions. Jan also sent the live video to Carli and Michelle so that they could see firsthand the robot treachery. She used a disguise-voice box to scramble her voice, such that Minta-2 could not even tell the sex of the speaker. With some pride, she gave her very short speech to the robot leader. She and Amy had gone to a whole lot of trouble to make this devious connection work, but they'd saved Carli and Michelle's lives.

"So you were right. It was a trap. They were going to kill us," Michelle spoke to Jan a few minutes later. "Well, I'm going to blow up something really big this time!" she barked determinedly.

"Thank you ever so much," Carli added. "Over."

Jan replied, "You are most welcome. I noticed that Minta-2 had a streaming video camera on her head. Conclusion: she must have been broadcasting that to someone else, probably Minta herself. Why don't you lay low for a bit and see what Minta does now. I'm certain that we took them by complete surprise. Let me know if there are further developments or if you find a really good next target. Over and out."

"Over and out," Emperor Yi Gang ended this surprise

call from Minta on Beltazar-C. "Now that is the most unexpected thing that I ever thought that I would hear from the robots!" he exclaimed to his silent assistant. "Dial up Queen Mary Linn for me, please. This is incredibly good news." His assistant smiled.

"Ah, Queen Mary Linn. I've just had the most extraordinary conversation with Minta herself! It seems that this agrarian world of Ponchart-D wants to have an Ataro Empire queen ruling it, just as Abel-C and under the same agreement. We've a chance to free Ponchart-D from being a slave world after all. I certainly don't understand this one in the slightest, but I sure want to jump on the chance. Over."

"What? How can this be? They want to make one of their conquered slave worlds part of the Ataro Empire? Unfathomable! Yes, by all means, we should jump at the chance. Over," Mary Linn replied literally flabbergasted.

After the comm delay, the emperor continued, "The problem is that at this moment, I have ten potential queens in training, but none that are ready for as critical an assignment as this one is. Then, I thought of two who might act as temporary queens until one of mine is ready to take over. Over."

"Who?" Queen Mary Linn responded, growing curious. There were no other Ataro queens on Tierra, excepting the two very old retired queens, her grandparents. Surely, he didn't mean them, did he? She hated the comm delay.

"I'm aware that Amy and Jan are still living. Both of them are fully qualified, expect physically. I'm prepared to ignore that detail for the present. Could you round those two up and call me back? I want to make them an offer. Over." She agreed and sent a telepathic message to Jan and Amy. Such was far easier than trying to walk in her toe shoes, precarious at best.

"What's this all about?" asked Amy. She and Jan entered the queen's comm center, moving slowly but carefully. Both had their suspicions, but Queen Mary Linn had no idea.

A few minutes later, Emperor Yi appeared on the monitor. "Ah, Amy, Jan you are looking well. As you know, the agrarian world of Ponchart-D in Federation space was attacked and taken over by the robots nearly eight months ago. For reasons that are wholly inexplicable, I just got a call from Minta herself! She says that the people of this world want to have an Ataro Empire queen rule them under the same agreement that we've worked out with Abel-C. If this happens, Ponchart-D will no longer be a slave world. I simply must act on this one. However, I have a slight problem. While I have quite a few future queens undergoing their training, I don't have one to send there right now. Then, I thought of you two. You've not forgotten your training and have served us well in the past. I would like to ask you two to go to this world and secure their freedom. You'll be temporary queens. I expect I'll have a permanent replacement ready to go in about three months. I know that you have children, so bring them along with you. I'll make it worth your while, financially, or any other way that I can. Over."

Amy glared at Jan. "What *have* you gotten us into this time, Sly Dog?"

"Oops. Sorry Eager Beaver. This isn't what I had in mind," Jan replied, a rather guilty look on her face.

"What's going on here? Do you know something about all this?" Queen Mary Linn barked accusatively.

Jan answered her. "What you don't know, you aren't responsible for. I had to do something and I did. That's all. I rather fomented a local rebellion. It has worked. That's something. So, I suppose we're going to have to make this trip. I wonder if the emperor would accept queens with upper arms?" Amy realized what she was hinting at.

"You know the rules as well as I do, Jan. No way will he consent to that, so forget such ideas," Amy countered effectively. Jan shrugged, knowing that she was right. "Well, a few months on a farming world can't be all that bad, dear." Turning to the queen, she added, "Some of us feel that we have to take more responsibility since we have the ability to help these others. Open the connection."

"Emperor Yi," Amy replied, "we would be honored to represent the Ataro Empire as your temporary queens. How soon do we need to get there? Over."

Ben with Tessa in tow arrived in the queen's throne

room. They'd come as fast as Tessa could manage in her toe shoes. Ben had decided against just picking her up and carrying her so they could get there faster, because he didn't know just how heavy the robot actually was. He'd gotten the queen's summons and knew something was up.

"Well, our friendly neighborhood Jan here has somehow managed to create a rebellion on Ponchart-D, that farming world that the metal heads just invaded and captured. Now, Minta is apparently ceding to their demands that they too have an Ataro Empire queen ruling them following the same arrangement as on Abel-C," Queen Mary Linn explained, both for Ben's information as well as Tessa's. "So Ben, you are to get Amy and Jan and their kids to Ponchart-D as soon as possible. Stick around a few days in case this whole thing goes south. So it appears that this world will not become another slave world after all."

"Cool. I mean great. Okay, how soon do you two want to leave?" Ben asked of Jan and Amy.

"We need some time to pack. How about in six hours?" Amy answered, figuring that was enough time to pack, especially if they weren't going to stay for very long.

"Wow. You two sure move out. Okay, you got it. Be at the spaceport in six. Come on, Tessa. We have to move fast to get ready," Ben replied, a bit surprised at the swiftness. He realized then that this was a huge breakthrough and vitally important. Yet from what the queen hinted, it could also spell real trouble.

"We are *not* taking the kids with us," Amy put her foot down on that detail. "This could be dangerous and . . ."

She didn't get to finish. Jan interrupted, "Of course we aren't. No way am I putting them at risk. We'll make some arrangements here. It shouldn't be a long trip, I sure hope so. He talked like he would have a replacement queen ready fairly soon."

"Everyone strapped in," Ben asked over the ship's intercom. Six hours passed altogether too quickly, especially for Amy and Jan, who found parting with their family a bit emotional. Now, they were aboard Strike Force One, but were both very familiar with the ship, having been on it many times over the years. Tessa sat beside them, and they'd been forced to use their gifts to help her buckle up, since she appeared to be just another helpless, armless victim, though both suspected that she was nowhere near as helpless as she claimed to be. She was a humaniform robot, after all.

As the ship took off, Tessa asked demurely, "So tell me, how did all this come about? It took me by complete surprise, as it did your queen. I thought that the Ataro queens knew everything."

"Sorry, Tessa. You can't pump us for information," Jan retorted, hating to talk to a robot. It reminded her of her extremely nasty experience being made into one of the Model 11 robots last lifetime.

"Okay. I wasn't meaning to pry. I'm as much in the dark as everyone else, unless you'll allow me to use your comm center to contact Minta herself," she bandied back.

"Never going to happen," Jan piped up. "So what's your real mission on Ashford-5 anyway?" Jan figured a turnabout probe was called for.

"My mission is two-fold. First, I'm supposed to check up on how everyone on your world is managing. It's been nearly a half-century now, and Minta is concerned and wants to make sure that you are doing well," Tessa replied.

"And second?" Jan more or less interrupted her.

"To watch out for Ben. Trouble seems to find him."

"Oh for heaven's sake," Jan declared quite miffed. "You can't think we'd believe that one, do you? Ben can take care of himself quite nicely."

"He'd be dead now if I had not acted and deflected that piece of space debris that was headed for his head," Tessa demurely reminded the pair. Jan fell silent. It did not compute. Why would Tessa be protecting Ben of all people? That made no sense at all, unless there was something special about Ben. Well, he once had told her that he had recalled some of his past lifetime as Felix Brom, inventor of the amplifying psi-crystals and the old Brom Compact.

That got Jan to thinking. Was Ben up to something this lifetime, something that he wasn't telling others about yet? Felix, according to the history books, usually kept his discoveries to himself, until he was ready to release them. Now, Jan had something else to ponder.

An uneventful nine hours later, they landed at the Billings Spaceport. As they walked down the bay ramp, Alis, Alberto, and Pippa had their d-guns out, using their gifts to float them alongside of their bodies, just in case this was some kind of trap. Holstered, they would take forever to get them drawn. Ben had his hands full with Tessa, having to help her down the ramp, more than a challenge in her toe shoes. Once they began walking towards the control tower, they spotted the blackened tarmac where Michelle's bombs had caused considerable and unexpected damage. Just then, Minta-2 and six of her robot guards stepped out, heading towards them.

"Welcome to Billings Spaceport. I take it some of you are the new queens?" she barked, unable to hide her disgust. Oh how she had wanted to blow up a village or two — teach these nova who was boss, who had the power, but Minta wouldn't have it. "This way. Minta is waiting. Tessa, how good to see another humaniform."

Ben spoke up. "Amy and Jan here are the new queens. Pippa and Alis are my fellow crew members. I guess you can put away your guns now." Minta-2 watched as the three did as ordered. She saw the d-guns moving back into their holsters as though by magic. These humans all had upper arms, nothing more. That this should even be possible eluded her programming. Guns didn't move by themselves. Further, she was annoyed that they all had perfectly normal feet, unlike Tessa and all the nova. To Minta-2, these were simply not proper nova, not remotely.

A few minutes later, the group sat on comfortable chairs, their hair draped across their front sides. A video camera captured all of them, while they looked at Minta's image on the big monitor. "Welcome. I'm sorry I can't be personally there to greet you," Minta began. "Our purpose is to officially turn over control of Ponchart-D to the new Ataro queens." She began outlining the agreed upon terms. All excess grains and food products that the planet grew were to be sold only to Minta's people, but for a fair market price. In return, worker robots would remain to assist with heavier projects until the queens no longer needed them around. Currently, they ran the hospitals, for example.

The meeting lasted an hour, but was truly concerned with mundane issues. Once the meeting finished and Minta signed off, Minta-2 rose. "Officially, I'm now departing this world. However, per the agreement, we're responsible for the defense of this world, so there will be a sizeable fleet in orbit above the planet. The defense shield will be under your control, queens, but I highly encourage you to keep the shield up. Use the worker robots to lower it when needed to allow food transports to come and go. That is all." She turned sharply and walked out of the room, her guards following her. The group watched them reach their ships and actually take off.

"Well, that went better than expected," Jan commented.

"What's next, bosses?" Ben asked.

"Well, it is safe for us to visit those responsible for brining this about," Jan decided. "Come on; we need to home in on one farming village while I call them up."

An hour later, Strike Force One descended onto the main street of Rumble's Corner, a small farming village, apparently out in the middle of nowhere. Actually, this was one of the flattest planets that any had ever seen. Croplands stretched in all directions as far as the eye could see, particularly from the ship as it flew there. Jan had called Carli, and the six women were standing outside their home waving their short arms, as the group walked down the bay ramp. Amy and Jan waved theirs back at them, while Ben again almost carried Tessa down the ramp.

"Hi. I'm Jan. So we finally get to meet. My, you look fabulous," Jan complimented the six young women.

Carli was quite excited. "I can't believe this is really happening! We're free of the metal heads! Jan, Amy, we, our world, owes you more than we can ever say or repay!" She put her short arms around Jan, who did likewise.

"And this must be Michelle," Jan said, giving Carli's mate a big hug. "Your skill with explosives made this happen. Your world owes you big time, Michelle, even if they don't know it yet. Soon, I promise you, they will!"

Michelle flushed. "Thanks. We couldn't have done it without you. You have no idea how much we desperately needed to hear your daily calls these many months. You have been our lifeline to sanity. So many of our men just could not handle this at all and are dead."

"Hi, I'm Tessa, by the way. Will someone tell me what this is about?"

"Ignore her. She's a humaniform robot, probably a spy," Jan declared.

Carli looked at the gorgeous woman with utter disdain. "These are my sisters, Lexi and Jessi, and their new mates, Faye and Tori. Actually, all six of us are now pregnant. Isn't that something? We're now worried about getting proper care and all that. Besides, we don't know how we're going to be able to care for our babies. Will they all be girls?"

Jan laughed. "Yep, all girls. Don't worry. We're soon going to get some able-bodied volunteers from the many Ataro worlds to come here and take over for those shiny worker metal heads. Be nice to see a real human doctor for a change."

"Come on inside. We've been fixing tea and biscuits for you all morning," Lexi bubbled. "Sorry, but it takes us forever to cook anything."

"Of course it does. Same with us," Jan admitted, lying a trifle.

Their home was tidy, and the six were very proud to serve tea and biscuits to their guests, though they felt embarrassed by how awkward, slow, and clumsy they were doing it. Seeing them all using their feet in the same way that they did, finally allowed the six to relax. They were equals, at least in the physical sense.

"I wish we could have seen the explosions," Michelle lamented. "Must have really caused some damage to the metal heads."

Ben piped up, "We saw the blackened tarmac when we arrived. You must have used the block-buster charges."

"Grade 10. Yes. You know something about explosives?" Michelle asked curiously.

"Yes. Easy to use. Really big punch. Only a thermite charge packs more punch, but with your targets, Thermite would not be the best choice," Ben replied.

"Will someone please tell me what this is about?" Tessa asked again, batting her eyes seductively at the group of women. "I've no idea what you are talking about. It's not very polite."

Jan didn't think it would hurt now to divulge what she and the six had done to bring about this day of freedom for Ponchart-D. She outlined the major events, but Michelle gaily told her all the details of their sabotage adventures.

"I can't believe it. You were able to move crates of this explosive stuff, make bombs, and set them off?" Tessa asked quite amazed at her ingenuity.

"I was a demolitions expert in our national guards before I had an accident and lost my left hand. So I know what I'm doing. We had to fight back somehow. I can't use a d-gun now, but I can make bombs, though I'll admit, it took all us working together nearly six months to make them. Still, we had to fight back. No one, I mean no one, takes our freedom away and gets away with it. We'll fight to the last farmer." Michelle meant it. Already, she had dozens of others around the world in the process of making bombs. Had Minta not consented to this deal, within a few months there would have been dozens of others bombing everything in sight. Even Jan didn't know this, and quickly had Michelle contact everyone, telling them the bombs weren't needed any longer.

Ben added, "Look, Tessa. One thing that you robots simply do not understand about we humans, we detest being slaves. We value our freedom and will fight to the death to keep it, no matter the odds. Well," he amended himself, "some of us do. Some won't. But on any world, you'll find those who will fight back anyway that they can."

"How interesting. I wonder if Minta knows this?" she replied.

Jan and Amy decided to stay with the six young women, making this village their "throne." After a busy couple of weeks, they dismissed Ben. Jan ordered him, "Look, you are bored out of your skull. There's nothing bad going on now. We're perfectly safe, so head home, please."

"All right. I won't ask for that in writing," he jested. He

and his crew headed up the bay ramp, waving their stumps at the nearly four hundred villagers who had come out to see their saviors off. "Crap." He had to stop and help Tessa up the ramp. The gorgeous looking woman merely stood at the base of the ramp waiting for him.

"Thanks. Thought you'd never get the hint," she teased him, as he supported her trip up the ramp. This time, he buckled her in, using his gifts of course. Once more, they had a routine trip, wholly uneventful. They did bring back with them a collection of DNA samples for the geneticists. Amy's first order was to have them develop a partial cure for the men of Ponchart-D. She wanted them to have upper arms and reasonable breasts like their women. That would go a long way to helping the men of this world.

# Chapter 8 Counterstrike

The Admiralty Round Table on Cass-C didn't take the attacks on Ponchart-D and Abel-C lightly. After so many years of relative inactivity, the robots were again on the march, taking over Federation worlds. It had to stop. Admiral Porsche, great-grandson of the famous Molly Maud Porsche, took the podium.

"My fellow admirals. It is time that we struck back. For far too long, each of our worlds has been holding back their fleets, protecting their own worlds. We've seen that is the road to disaster when the robots attack. They can muster much larger numbers than any one of our worlds can alone. With the recent takeover of Abel-C, they are poised to strike at our extremely valuable mid-arm region. I call your attention to the 3d holograph. I've outlined in red the space that the robots control. They could attack across a broad front, covering the entire width of the mid-arm sectors. If we do nothing, which mid-arm world is next, eh? No, I say it is time we pool our fleets and strike back at these robots. Put an end to this hideous threat to all our worlds." He pounded the podium with his fist for emphasis.

An hour later, he called for a vote and for the first time received a majority of votes. Finally, the Federation would take a coordinated action against this threat. He was pleased to be elected Supreme Admiral of the Combined Federation Fleet. March of 1501, he surveyed his new fleet, having culled some of the best ships from major Federation worlds. The admirals knew this was a gamble, but a desperate one. If they succeeded, then all would be well. However, if the fleet was defeated, there was little to prevent the robots from conquering all the Federation of Planets, one by one. It simply had to succeed.

On March 2, the fleet of thirty-one battleships, fifty heavy cruisers, and one hundred sixty-one light cruisers left the staging area, jumping en mass into hyperspace for the twelve-hour flight into robot controlled space. Victory was at hand or so claimed the various newscasters.

Naturally, Minta's hundreds of humaniform robots scattered across these many worlds kept her briefed on the action the Federation was taking against her. Some even had acquired the initial destination coordinates where the fleet was to drop out of hyperspace. Thus, Minta was totally prepared for this counterstrike. In fact, long ago she had predicted it was coming. Humans were entirely predictable, well mostly. There were some anomalies, such as Ponchart-D, but those were rare and mostly inconsequential in the grand scheme.

Minta countered with fifty battleships of her own, several of Abel-C's having already been repaired and put back into service. She had seventy-one heavy cruisers and over two hundred light ones. More importantly, she had nearly a hundred thousand single-man fighters aboard these ships. Her goal was simple. Capture this fleet, restore them, and use them to finish conquering the Federation arm of the galaxy. Thus, she had no intention of allowing her ships to open fire with their long range cannons, though that was just what Admiral Porsche would be doing, trying to blow her fleet from space.

One on one, her robot Model 12 pilots in their one-man ships were more than able to out-maneuver and out-fight their human counterparts. That had been proven repeatedly for over a half century, and she counted upon this factor. March 3, the giant Federation fleet dropped out of hyperspace and found themselves surrounded by a hundred thousand of the one-man ships! The mother ships, the battleships and cruisers, were well out of the range of their guns. They had no choice but to fight these tiny ships.

So thick was the space that any gun firing that missed its intended target was likely to hit another one-man ship further away than the intended one! The live video streaming certainly made the news! Never had there been such a firefight. The sheer number of explosions was almost incalculable.

Even most major old Imperium worlds carried the video re-broadcasts. The threat of the robot fleet could no longer be denied by anyone.

Alas, for the Federation fleet, they simply could not

handle the sheer number of smaller ships. While the battle lasted nearly ten hours, it was lost the instant they dropped out of hyperspace. At last, Admiral Porsche issued the retreat order. Three battleships limped home, grievously wounded, with many hull breaches. Five heavy cruisers and ten light ones also survived. The rest of the fleet was lost and presumed captured by Minta's forces, a staggering loss! No one had any idea of the losses suffered by Minta, though. She lost half of her fleet of one-man ships, but most of the Model 12 pilots were eventually rescued. A robot can survive in empty, cold space for a very long time, though unable to function, their systems shut down.

Repercussions rocketed throughout the Federation of Planets, which now faced certain destruction! With Admiral Porsche's return, everyone on every planet knew that there just had to be humaniform robot spies on their worlds. The witch-hunts began. The humaniform looked every bit human, making it impossible to tell them apart, but that didn't stop the hunts. Hundreds of innocent humans were killed in a mistaken belief that they were robots in disguise.

Those in charge knew otherwise. The robots had an uncanny ability not only to blend in with their populations, but also avoided usual methods of detection. Some leaders tried to take a blood sample from all high-level officials. Unknown to them, these robots had fake veins. Hence, it was a simply matter for them to "acquire" a bit of human blood, inject it into the veins, only to have some nurse remove it during the testing process. Scanners worked no better, since their robot frames presented a human-like image to most x-ray machines. Hence, the wild witch-hunt. Besides, there were just far too many bureaucrats in top positions to test them all. Then, there were their spouses to consider as well.

Renata met with Queen Mary Linn and Governor Monica shortly after the debacle was shown on the newscasts. She began the meeting by saying, "You know that Minta received the precise location where the fleet dropped out of hyperspace and with sufficient time to counter them, don't you? That means, and we know this for a fact, that she has humaniform robots on most worlds. Already there is a witch-hunt going on. Between you and me, there is only one sure way to detect a humaniform robot, don't you?"

"They don't have a mind like we do," Queen Mary Linn answered correctly.

"Right. And across this whole galaxy, who alone has the ability to scan a large group and locate the non-human?" Renata asked.

Governor Monica swallowed hard. She saw where this was heading. "We do. We telepaths. Are you hinting that it is time that we step up and take some additional responsibility for this mess?"

"Exactly. We can't hide here on the rim and watch the rest of the galaxy crumble, not when we can do something to uncover the spies," Renata declared, rather pleased that the governor had mentioned responsibility and that she hadn't had to.

"Mary Linn, I agree with Renata. We simply have to do something. Here is something with minimal danger to us that would be invaluable to these other worlds," Governor Monica stated pointedly.

"You are right. We can't hide any longer and be true to ourselves. Okay, I'll call Emperor Yi and propose that we send a large number of volunteers to these worlds and have them locate the humaniforms residing among them," the queen replied. "The question is just who of our people do we ask to do this? It will be hard for them, physically I mean."

"Leave that to me," Renata replied. "You work out their compensation issues, transportation, and care." The three agreed, and the queen placed the call.

After outlining their proposal, Emperor Yi replied, "I don't know how to thank you. Yes, I accept. This will be perhaps the single greatest blow to Minta and her plans. I'll see that each is royally compensated. I'll get in touch with the Federation today and make such a proposal. Of course, I would prefer a number of your people to fully screen all our worlds too, perhaps sticking around in case they should attempt to infiltrate back onto one of our worlds. Over."

"Excellent. After the initial screening, one or two could stay around the major spaceports, checking on all new personnel arrivals," Queen Mary Linn suggested, much to her emperor's pleasure. They discussed the needed arrangements for another half hour.

The next day, the emperor called back to report his offer met the warmest welcome he'd ever received from the leaders of the major Federation worlds. "How soon can Renata send them? Over."

Like everyone else, Renata had carefully studied the video clips of the attacks. She, Jan, and Amy had noticed that the Model 10's were the robots that were totally out to destroy humans with a vengeance and passion not shared by the Model 12's, who merely followed orders. Not even the Minta copies who controlled the fleets acted with such bloodlust. All three knew why the Model 10's acted this way, why they had such an enormous hatred of humans.

It went back to the days when Amy and Jan were made into Model 11's themselves. On Gundig-B in the distant past, a genetics experiment to make their women stellar beauties failed miserably. The results were the genetic mutations, barely human, called weibchen. These grotesque weibchen were shunned by everyone, forced to wear complete body coverings when outside in public places on that world. Minta had kidnaped a large number of them, turning them into Model 10's. With only their brains left, these weibchen had only one desire: to kill humans, which they now could do with an effectiveness unparalleled in the galaxy.

Renata, Jan, and Amy thus had another idea that they wanted to try. "Look, if some of our people are on the next world to be attacked, they can test out my idea. The Model 12 robots have no minds, nor do the Minta-generals. It's these bloodthirsty Model 10's. So have our people use our *mentales* gifts to destroy the minds of the Model 10's as they attack the world. If I'm right and we can do this, we'll knock out the command structure in the attack and maybe turn the tide of the battle completely around."

"Yes, but lacking giant psi-crystals, we're a bit limited on whom we can send," Amy pointed out.

"Indeed. But we have all those thousands of really powerful beings that once had the doll bodies. They are now the core of my Advanced Therapy groups," Renata pointed out. "They are able to operate somewhat while outside their bodies, just as you two do."

"I like it. Count us in," Jan exclaimed. "We go to war at last and take some responsibility for this entire mess!"

Renata grinned. Amy added, "Jan sometimes gets a bit carried away. Sure, we'll do it. I know we've only recently gotten back from Ponchart-D, but after seeing how awful that world has become and knowing that I have the ability to do something about it, I simply must. Count us in. I'm sure you'll have more than a thousand volunteers." Their stint as temporary queens on Ponchart-D had been a success. After three months there, the emperor's newest queen arrived. After a few weeks transition getting her up to speed, Amy and Jan returned home to Tierra, satisfied that they'd made a difference. Now, they saw another way that they and many others could help.

Amy was right. Once Renata put out the word about what she wanted to do, over two thousand of her Advanced Therapy members volunteered. She chose one thousand for this first wave, preferring to take those whose bodies were youthful. As she was making her choices, Lysandra appeared before her, shimmering in her usual yellow glow.

"Hi Lysandra. Don't tell me that you are going to be volunteering too," Renata teased the goddess.

"Hardly. I've more than I can handle keeping Tierra safe right now. No, Ariana and I wanted to relay something that she and I just discovered. You know how each spiritual being radiates at a unique frequency," Renata nodded and she continued. "Well, recently, she and I got to wondering just where old Wystan and Calder had gone. These awful wars are right up Wystan's aberrated alleyway. Good thing that we did. We've located him. Don't ask us how, but he is running one of those Model 10 robot bodies!"

"Crap!" Renata exclaimed.

Lysandra continued, "We sense that Calder is out there somewhere too, but probably not in one of Minta's robots. We've not been able exactly to pinpoint him. He's changed some in frequency. Still, what with the most able of you heading out into the galaxy, we thought you ought to know. Expect stiff resistance from Wystan if you encounter him again. When will he ever learn?"

Both chuckled. Renata answered her, "Not until he faces up to what things he has done to others." Lysandra smiled, nodded, and vanished.

Interestingly enough, Captain Ben Flaxton and his crew were some of her Advanced Therapy members. Hence, Renata decided to send Amy and Jan with him and use Strike Force One as their personal transport ship. She figured that having seven powerful telepaths together would give them a better chance to stop the Model 10's. However, Tessa was a problem.

For months now, he had been forced to watch her night and day, even to the point of having her sleep in his room. He took his job seriously, though. Security of Tierra was uppermost in his mind. Also, Minta had ordered Tessa to stick by Ben. Try as she might, Renata could not fathom why Minta had so ordered Tessa. She spent one entire evening weighing the pros and cons of sending Tessa along with them. At last, she decided to allow it. After all, at least Tessa would be off Ashford-5.

She met with Ben, filling him in on the details, but asking him not to tell Tessa the details until it could not be avoided. He agreed.

On May 1, 1501, over a hundred deep space transports lifted off from Ashford-5, bound for many major worlds of the Ataro Empire, the old Imperium, and the Federation of Planets. Strike Force One, with Amy, Jan, and Tessa in tow, lifted off, heading for the Federation mid-arm world of Pegasi-C. No one would tell Tessa why they were going, only that she had to come along. Since Ben was going, so was she. That didn't mean that she wasn't curious though.

# Chapter 9 A Robot and a Man

When Ben first met Tessa, he saw an incredibly beautiful young woman, second only to the two models who sponsored the Beauty Pageant. He was more than a little surprised to discover she was one of the humaniform robots. As their association was forced on him, both by Renata and by Minta, he began to wonder why. It made sense that he monitor her constantly. After all, she represented the biggest security breach on Tierra. He was certain that Tierra was otherwise free of humaniform robots. There were just too many who would notice a person walking around without a mind.

No, that part didn't bother him, other than why they chose him to do it. Then again, Renata made very little use of Strike Force One. Rather what truly bothered him was just why Minta had ordered Tessa to stay with him and protect him. That made no sense at all. Still, there wasn't any way to get around the fact that she had saved his life when the space debris hit the ship. Certainly, that was a random accident, wholly unpredictable by anyone or any computer. So why?

Worse from his perspective, she was darn near a helpless robot. With no arms and the same malformed feet, she could only just barely walk in her toe shoes, just like he and everyone else on Tierra had until the recent genetic cures restored his feet to normal feet. He had upper arms as well, greatly helping his ability to get by, particularly handling his long, shiny hair. Now, he found himself playing nursemaid to a helpless Tessa. Well, at least she didn't need to be fed or go to the bathroom. Thank goodness for small favors, he concluded. Still, she definitely needed a stabilizing arm now and then, particularly handling stairs, the ship's ramp, and rough ground. With his newfound freedom of walking normally, he found it annoying to have to slow way down and go at her pace.

Yet that wasn't all. She was a real beauty, physically. She had a way of getting under his skin with her little teases and sexual innuendoes. She had outright propositioned him, and when undressing her each night, he saw her perfectly formed body, complete with both sexual organs, just as he had. Either way, she'd once said. She could do it both ways. He'd flushed as usual. How can I have sex with a robot, he thought more than once? What made it more and more difficult for him were his own arousals when he undressed her each night. Then, she went too far. Last night after he got her undressed and pulled back her covers, she was aroused, teasing him, taunting him, and beckoning to him. Red faced, he'd pretended not to notice, just helped her into bed. She'd given him a little pouting tease though.

During all this, Ben usually had to use a bit of his *mentales* gifts to help her dress and undress, either that or make her use the bot, which many did use. Perhaps, he thought, Tessa is trying to find out more about just how powerful our *mentales* gifts are. That made far more sense to him and allowed him to keep cool for many more days, limiting the use of his gifts in her presence, nothing beyond just what had to be done.

Now, he had to take her on this long, extended trip to the Federation world of Pegasi-C. They were about to use their gifts to ferret out Minta's humaniform spies. Surely, she would object to this. Maybe even try to stop them. He had no idea just how strong Tessa actually was, but even without arms, her feet had stopped that heavy steel debris and lightning fast to boot. Ben had no doubt that she would be a formidable opponent, should it come to that. He might not be able to stop her, and might not be able to protect his crew, Amy, and Jan. That bothered him a good deal, but Renata must had already considered that or she wouldn't have sent Tessa along on this trip.

One thing he knew and that was that Renata always knew precisely what she was doing. That woman never makes a mistake, he once told another Advanced Therapy member. Both had a laugh about that observation. Still, Amy, Jan, and he had far more powers than a normal *mentales* gifted person, a byproduct of their Advanced Therapy, though he seldom made use of such skills. Perhaps on this trip, those would be needed. Would they be enough to stop Tessa if she decided to take the three of them out?

This trip promised to be a lengthy one. For security reasons, once on Pegasi-C, they planned to spend nights on the ship. Ben smiled thinking about this aspect. He and his crew were all twenty-one and consenting adults. Pippa and Alis had a thing going, often bedding each other. He expected to hear that they would marry soon. Alberto had a girlfriend in Exchange City, had just told them that he had proposed to his girlfriend, and that they were planning to marry when this trip ended. Amy and Jan were married with children, though he was glad that they decided not to bring them along on this trip, just as they had on their previous trip to the agrarian world.

Ben was now the odd man out. He didn't have a girlfriend or boyfriend either for that matter. He found that even though men looked very much like women, he had no interest in them, as a mate that is. Still, these four were very close and trusted each other with their lives, knowing that each had the back of the other at all times when they were together.

The trouble was that he had not had any time to make any girlfriends or even go on a date, not since encountering Tessa. Having to watch her all the time made it darn impossible to do otherwise. Yet, each night, she paraded herself to him, as though begging him to enjoy her company in bed. Here he was confined to the deep space transport with Tessa for what promised to likely be months. As he calculated the duration of their flight to Pegasi-C, he sighed. Twenty hours to go and much of that was during their sleep period. Space travelers usually maintained their usual sleep cycles, regardless of the chronometer settings.

He watched the raven haired Pippa tossing her hair back and leaving her navigation post beside him. She winked at him. "Time to have some fun with Alis. You are welcome to join us. Long sleep period. I wonder which of us will do the proposing?"

"Thanks, but I'm on Tessa watching duty," he joked. "If you love her, go for it." She grinned mischievously.

"You know, you ought to just do her, Tessa that is," Pippa advised him. "Get more information about robots that way."

Ben flushed and laughed. "Sorry, but that kind of information isn't really valuable at all." Pippa gave him a teasing laugh, agreed, and left him alone in the cockpit.

Tessa's lilting voice came to him from the passenger area. "Oh Ben sweetie. How long are you going to make me sit here before you unfasten my seatbelt? Everyone else is turning in for the night. I'm all alone now."

He stifled an answer and used his stumps to push more or less his ankle length, black hair out of his way. He rose and made his way back to where she was sitting, looking like a demure flower in her red satin dress and black toe shoes. At least, she now had style. One visit to Elegant Fashions Inc, and she'd gone a bit bonkers and purchased a rather large selection of new gowns. Of course, he now had to dress her in them each morning.

Being a hermaphrodite, he could dress as he chose. Gowns such as she now wore would suit his body just fine, but he usually chose to wear pants and a blouse. At least he didn't have to wear that terrible corset any longer. Still, his boobs were far larger than he would have preferred. In fact, he would have preferred not to have such things. He chided himself for having such silly thoughts. One day, he would get pregnant and have a child. He'd have to nurse him or her, just as any other dad would. Ben never had wished he was a normal homo sapiens, rather that he had normal arms, hands, and feet.

"Just finishing up the checks. On course and all that, Tessa," he lied a little. Using a bit of *mentales* energy, he unfastened her buckles and put a steadying upper arm on her shoulders as she rose to her toes.

"Thanks. My cabin or yours?" she teased him, batting her eyelashes a little. There was just a hint of a smile on her lips.

"There is only the one cabin, Tessa. Have you forgotten that already? The other cabins are for guests and our workshops. This is a working transport. Come on; let's get you ready for bed, though why you need to go to bed is beyond me. Robots don't sleep."

"Silly man. We conserve power at night, just as you

conserve yours. You run down when you have to work all day and then all night, right? Well, so do robots. Oh, do slow down. You aren't walking on just your toes any longer. Have you forgotten what this is like?"

He flushed, realizing he was pushing her a tad too fast. Even with a supporting upper arm, she couldn't walk fast with only the bottoms of her toes on the floor. "Sorry," he admitted.

Once in their cabin, he closed the door knowing that their cabins were nearly sound proof. What went on in the privacy of one's cabin stayed in one's cabin. That was his house rule, pleasing his crew immensely. Using his *mentales* gifts, he began undressing her, while she sat on the edge of their bed. Then, he took his own clothes off, trying not to look at her nakedness.

"Dear, will you please brush out my hair tonight? It really is a mess. You can do yours first if you wish," she asked.

"Okay, I'll fire up the electrostatic hair machine," he volunteered.

To his amazement, she said, "That's not what I meant. Use a real hairbrush. It's so much more intimate, don't you think?"

He dug out his brush, tossed his long hair forward, partially hiding his front from her, and sat down beside her. "I have to use my powers to use the brush effectively," he said. Slipping his arm beneath her hair, which only reached to the small of her back, he lifted it up. Focusing, his germanium crystal began glowing in a pale blue light as the brush began stroking her hair.

"That feels so good, Ben! Yes, I can feel your arm with my hair, just as you can feel with yours. Sometimes, I wish Minta had made my hair as long as yours," she admitted. "It is quite a sensation, isn't it?" After brushing hers out, she insisted, "Now, let me do yours."

"But you don't have stumps."

"I'll manage with my feet, if you don't mind," she said enticing him.

Stroking their very sensitive hair, especially with part of one's body, generated a very terrific sensation indeed, due primarily to the neurons and axons in their mutated hair.

148

Unfortunately for Ben, it had the desired effect on his male organ. He'd not looked at hers while he had done her hair. As he glanced down, he saw that she too was reacting just as he was.

She whispered, "What does an attractive girl have to do to get you into bed with her?" She leaned over and planted a passionate kiss on his lips. Later, Ben said that she had seduced him, but in all honesty, he'd given in to basic desires.

He discovered at once that she knew what to do, just as he did. Automatically, he slipped into an intimate rapport with her allowing their passions to flow. Tessa paid very close attention to details, adding minute sensations that she sensed from him into her programming, vowing to perform better for him the next time.

Later as he lay back pretending to be asleep, he pondered what he'd just done. Sex with a robot? Am I that desperate? No, that isn't it. Look, he told himself, if she wasn't a robot, I'd be courting her. She's damn good looking, highly intelligent, witty, strong-willed — everything I'd want in a lifelong companion and mate. But Ben, get your head on. She's a robot. She can't have real feelings like love, and she sure as hell can't have your children. So why are you doing this with her? He had no answer to that question, just some deep, unexplainable intuition that somehow, someway this was the right thing to be doing. Before finally falling asleep, he decided he must really like Tessa, as a robot companion, as perhaps a strange sort of friend.

The next day, Tessa noticed a subtle change in Ben's treatment of her. Gone was his reticence to dress her. It was a tiny alteration in his behavior, but the observant Tessa didn't miss it. "I suppose I ought to dress like a woman today," Ben volunteered after showering and using the electrostatic dryer. "We are going to be landing soon. Pegasi-C probably doesn't have any hermaphrodites to speak of on it, and my body looks more like a female. Be less confusion that way."

Tessa smiled, "That is an astute observation. Normal homo sapiens sapiens tend to look at us as mutants. Best not to give them cause to look at us that way, though my lack of arms is a giveaway, as is your hair and stumps. Shall I pick out the right one for you to wear? I now have a good sense of style, thanks to the wonderful women at your Elegant Fashions Inc. You know, they ought to open up stores on all Minta's worlds. They could make a fortune. We do like to look our best, you know."

Ben chuckled. "Sure go ahead, pick one. Yes, I'm sure they could do just that. I'll mention it to them when we get back." She picked out a bright red satin gown, one that she'd purposely purchased in his size when she bought her new wardrobe. She had thought ahead to this morning and smiled at her cleverness.

"Wow, Ben. You are going to turn heads when we land today," Jan teased him. He escorted Tessa to the galley, where Amy had breakfast waiting for everyone. She was the early riser among this group. Pippa and Alis straggled in last as always.

"Don't want to call undo attention to myself. Tessa picked it out. Bit flashy for my tastes," Ben replied, helping Tessa to get seated. While she never dined, she always sat with them and chatted at meal times.

Alfonso wore a brown dress, having arrived at the same conclusion as Ben. Best not to draw undo attention to themselves. He added, "She does have good taste. If Ben had picked it out, he'd be wearing a really drab dress."

"I'm that predictable?" Ben fired back, jokingly.

"Hi all," Pippa said rather dreamily, as she and Alis, with her flaming red hair, joined them.

"Guess what?" Alis bubbled. Not waiting for anyone to answer, she added, "Pippa proposed to me last night. We're going to get married when we get back!" The table talk now centered on those two, with everyone congratulating the pair, much to Ben's relief.

One of the top fifty worlds of the Federation was Pegasi-C, home to approximately six billion people. This was a rather highly educated, very modern world in the middle of the spiral arm, boasting no less than twenty highly acclaimed Universities. One of their spaceports lay at the edge of the large city of Estrella, home to the University of Estrella, famous for its microbiology and genetics programs. It was here

150

that they landed later that morning.

They were met by a large security force and a very worried President Elena Garcia, a tall, middle aged woman, with short black hair and overly done makeup. She wore a professional woman's outfit, complete with shiny black pumps of moderate height. Not overly attractive, she had a politician's demeanor and mind. "Welcome to Estrella and Pegasi-C. I can't begin to tell you how desperate we are to ferret out the robot spies among us. I fear the worst and hope for the best from you, which I know I will get. If you'll follow me, I'll get us safely inside. I'm told it's far to risky to spend much time out here. Snipers are hard to stop. I'm sure these robots will try something, anything to prevent their discovery. Come, come." She said hastily, turning and heading back towards the large control tower. Her many guards continuously glanced in all directions, as though expecting an attack at any second. Ben sensed they were quite nervous, which didn't help.

Ben, Amy, and Jan followed her, leaving Tessa with his crew members. He didn't want to have to explain they had one of these humaniform robots with them. Too many questions. The odor of fuel and oil mingled with that of newly mowed grass and perhaps an ocean, though he wasn't certain of the latter. Within a minute, they were inside a very secure room, wiped clean of any bugging devices beforehand, as President Garcia explained to the trio as they entered. "It's perfectly safe to talk in here."

Ben introduced them, and she asked, "So what must I provide for you to detect our spies? I'm afraid I know nothing about how you telepaths work."

Amy took charge, having thought this through on the trip. "It's really simple. We just need to have each person walk by us. That's all. Have a group of your guards ready to capture them as we spot them. Takes only a few seconds per person, rather like a parade. I thought perhaps you might have your key personnel walk past us, while you introduce us so we don't raise undo suspicions right away. Say we are here to help fight the robots."

"Well, I'm afraid quite a few already know of your trip. I couldn't keep it totally secret, you know. All right then, we'll do it in the Oval Office. It's large and where formal presentations are made. I've a secure bunker for you to stay in. Will the rest of your crew be joining you?"

"If it's all the same with you, we would prefer to stay on our ship at night," Jan suggested.

The President frowned. "That will be awkward. I'd have to attach a security detail to accompany you back and forth. I'm told it's quite risky out in the open on the tarmac. Your safety is my prime concern. If something should happen to you, well, I don't think I need elaborate. I insist you stay where I can guarantee you'll be safe. I can send the security detail back for the rest of your crew later today."

"In that case, I'll let the crew remain on the ship," Ben countered. No way was he going to bring Tessa with him, if he could avoid it. However, he had no such luck. The President insisted that staying cooped up on the ship for weeks was intolerable, and he reluctantly ceded the point to her. He could see her reasoning. She was responsible for their safety while on her world.

Two hours later, the three stood behind a bulletproof glass barrier as President Garcia introduced the top-most members of her cabinet to the trio. On either side, six well-armed guards stood, ready for action. After these cabinet members passed inspection, President Garcia relaxed. If there were spies, they were not in her personally chosen cabinet. Then, the staff of each cabinet member walked through to greet these very important visitors.

Partway through the Department of Defense staff, Ben found the first humaniform robot spy. The polite, non-descript man walked past him, smiling pleasantly, but he had no mind. Amy and Jan verified it. All three raised their right stump, the prearranged signal. The guards attempted to get him to go with them quietly, but the robot worked out what was happening and bolted. He slammed the two guards, who tried to grab his arm to lead him out, and shoved them halfway across the room, smashing them hard into the walls. Pandemonium broke out.

Four other guards on this side attempted to grapple the robot, but displaying superhuman strength, he tossed all four off him as though they weighed nothing at all. The three telepaths could do nothing effectively to help apprehend him, not in such confined quarters. The six guards on the other side drew their d-guns and opened fire, adding to the turmoil and confusion. The robot was extremely agile and swift. It ducked and rolled, picking up one of the fallen guard's d-gun as he rolled. Coming right side up, he fired twice, nailing two guards, dropping them like flies. In a giant leap, he was on his feet, shoving four other workers out of the way. The last that the trio saw of him, four guards were racing after him.

Later, they learned the robot had finally been dispatched as it raced down the street, trying to flee. Five guards died and ten others sustained various non-life threatening injuries, of which eight were civilians, caught in the crossfire, so much for stealth. The project ended for that day, since President Garcia's entire defense grid was obviously compromised. The last they saw of her, she escorted a crimsoned face minister out of the room.

The discovery of the robot spy and the battle made the evening news. Waiting for the guards to bring the rest of their crew to the Oval Office, Ben commented, "Well, now all the other robots know what's going on. I bet we won't detect any more of them. They'll be fleeing like flies. I sure would be."

"Miss me sweetie?" Tessa teased Ben, as she walked into the room where the trio sat waiting for them. Alberto had a steadying stump on her, while Alis and Pippa walked on either side of them. The guards promptly left them at the entrance to the room.

"I heard we missed all the action," Pippa called out, indifferent to Tessa's being a robot as well.

"Kind of messy," Jan said. "I'll explain it all to you over supper. This way. The President has assigned us to the Blue Suite. Follow the blue stripe on the floor and ignore the other ones. I guess you can't get lost in this complex. We're having supper sent in. Room service. Figured that's safer than eating out, though I don't think the President would let us do that."

Amy laughed, "Certainly not after today's episode. I feel badly that so many men died or got hurt trying to apprehend the humaniform spy."

Unplussed, Tessa commented, "Well, they know the risks and are willing to do it. I would suspect the others are already departing this world, if they are smart."

"Or perhaps they are going underground so they can continue to spy on this world," Jan countered. "We'll have to figure out which." Tessa smiled demurely.

The Blue Suite consisted of five bedrooms with adjoining baths, a small kitchen-diner combo, and a spacious living room complete with a comm center. After they finished eating, President Garcia visited them, thanking them profusely for routing the spy. She then asked for introductions. Ben decided the simplest thing was to introduce Tessa as his girlfriend and leave it at that. With that done, President Garcia explained that they would continue the testing of other staff on down to the local officials. Her reasoning was simple. Some of the robots would stay at their low-level posts, figuring that once those in high positions were discovered, the search would be ended, and they could continue their spy work. None of the trio could discount this possibility and resigned themselves to staying here for some time.

Discovered by absence. That became the official way adopted to count the number of humaniform spy robots on Pegasi-C. The next day, a number of aides failed to report to work. A search of their homes yielded nothing, though two were apprehended trying to get onto commercial flights leaving the planet. Many others somehow slipped through the dragnet of the planetary forces. After the first full week, the official count was twenty robot spies.

Worse, they had infiltrated all manner of arenas, not just planetary defense. One was working in the power grid, another in the power generation group, and another in the water supply department. Every critical area of their overall society had been infiltrated at some level. Thus, while President Garcia urged them to begin scanning the local officials and their staff, she and her cabinet began by making a frantic estimate of just what knowledge the robots had obtained. After that, they attempted to come up with alternate plans. On such short notice and on a planetary scale, this simply could not happen overnight.

Weeks passed before the trio finally gave their okay to the last of the local officials. They'd only uncovered one additional spy, the mayor of Estrella no less. Still, President Garcia was unwilling to let them depart so soon. Like many other leaders, she had become robot-paranoid. Thus, the trio did not have to request that they be allowed to stay a little longer, in case an attack came. Ben, Amy, and Jan wanted to try out Renata's second idea: destroy the insane, vicious Model 10 leaders, perhaps blunting the attack or even stopping it. Knocking out the major mission leaders seemed an ideal tactic.

Minta was furious. Humaniform reports from many key Federation worlds began flooding in with news of their detection by the telepaths from Ashford-5, forcing them to flee. After this initial wave of discovery, Minta lost sixty-two of them, but well over three hundred somehow managed to escape the worlds that they were on, arriving back on Descartes-C for reassignment elsewhere. Once more, the telepaths of Ashford-5 had become a thorn in her Grand Plan.

Checking over her supplies, Minta decided to move the timetable up slightly, summoning Minta-2 to her. She had a proven track record of achieving total conquest in short order. "I want you to lead the assault on Pegasi-C. We know that three key telepaths are there now, Ben Flaxton, Amy, and Jan Bellweather, along with their crew. Take that world and capture those three telepaths. Send them to me in chains if you have to, but do not actually kill them yet."

"I'm honored you've chosen me to lead the attack. I shall not fail you, Minta," she replied. The two discussed the approach to be used, and Minta-2 left to muster the forces. Minta herself boarded her own deep space transport and headed for Zeta Scorpii-C, her mind working on another approach to take to neutralize the Ashford-5 telepaths for another fifty years, by which time the entire Grand Plan would be completed.

Meanwhile, Minta-2 returned to her fleet and reviewed the data from Minta. The last Intel from Pegasi-C suggested the Ashford-5 telepaths were staying in the Presidential

Building, Blue Suite. Minta-2 summoned her most bloodthirsty, viscous, but effective Model 10, Number 10,004.

She outlined the plan and told it, "As my best and most experienced leader, I want you to lead the attack group on Estrella. Focus on taking the Presidential Building. Minta wants those telepaths captured alive, not necessarily in one piece, just alive."

"Understood. Top priority: capture of telepaths. You may depend on me," the robot replied with just a hint of pride and superiority in its tone.

Armies function best only when properly drilled on a plan of action. In the case of Pegasi-C, their entire defense plans had been completely compromised. Hence, following President Garcia's orders, the Defense Department drew up an entirely different set of plans. However, the actual personnel who would control and direct these received them only received them two days before they were needed. When the attack came, everyone was confused, unsure just what actions to take. Coordination went down the chute as they say on Pegasi-C.

On June 10, 1501, the huge fleet dropped out of hyperspace close to Pegasi-C, giving the planet barely thirty minutes warning of the assault! Worse, the attack began at midnight local time in Estrella, when the vast majority of key people were asleep. Again, costly delays occurred.

The sound of a bomb exploding not too far from the Presidential Building woke the telepaths. "What the hell was that?" yelled Alis.

"A bomb!" Alberto called out from his bedroom next to the one shared by Pippa and Alis. "Everyone, get dressed and ready for action!"

"Little help sweetie," Tessa begged Ben, as he leapt out of bed and began using his *mentales* gifts to get dressed as fast as he could. While he hated to waste the time, he got her dressed as fast as he could. The two joined the others in the living room, where an aide had come rushing in to tell them that the robot attack had come.

Already, Amy and Jan had begun focusing, and Ben

joined them, while Alis helped Tessa get seated. "What are they doing?" Tessa whispered to the redhead.

"They are going to destroy the vicious Model 10's who are leading the attack," she explained, before she realized that telling Tessa was probably the wrong thing to do.

"But how?" Tessa whispered back, but Pippa's glare told Alis to shut up. Instead, she and Pippa went from room to room packing their bags. Each had brought their few things in a shoulder bag, one that they could more readily handle.

Ben, Amy, and Jan slipped into rapport with each other and began to act as a single unit, focusing their combined psi-powers on a single mind. The tricky part was identifying the mind to attack. There were thousands of minds up there in space, most belonging to the out-gunned, out-classed, and confused defenders. Quickly, they realized that if they sensed fear coming from a mind, it was a friendly. Finally, they contacted a mind that was right.

Seething hatred, a thirst for killing humans swept over the three, all coming from that one mind. As one, they acted, sending a blast of mental energy into it. No time for finesse, no time to convince its owner that it was a pathetic looser and ought to kill itself. No, it was a pure, raw mind blast of energy. The only human portion that resided in these Model 10's was the brain, kept alive by various nutrient solutions. There was no medulla oblongata or spine to absorb shock waves, protecting the brain proper. The brain turned to mush, and the Model 10 ceased to function, becoming completely inert. Its ship slowly descended towards Pegasi-C, finally crashing in a ball of flames in a farmer's field.

Meanwhile the trio continued searching for another Model 10 mind. True, it was like hunting for needles in a haystack, but they knew that there had to be a fair number of them controlling such a large fleet. Time passed, bombs rained down, shaking the very building and their couch. They brought down six more of them, before they encountered an extremely powerful Model 10 mind! Their mind blast merely got its full attention!

Wham! It sent back to them its own mind blast, temporarily stunning the trio and disrupting their rapport.

Shaking her aching head, Jan whimpered, "What was that?"

"We got blasted, I think," Amy replied, her voice barely a whisper.

Ben's head throbbed, and he didn't even have enough control to use his stumps to rub it. Rather, his intuition stepped to the fore. He recognized that being from somewhere. Right now, he couldn't place who or where, only that he once knew that being. Just then, a piece of the ceiling collapsed, nearly hitting them. That brought Ben to the present.

"We have to get back to our ship immediately. Come on. Up and at it," he ordered.

At once, Pippa and Alis used their gifts to slip each person's sack over their shoulder, while Alberto checked the hallway. "It's clear. Come on. Follow the brown strip. It leads to the exits." Everyone dashed off, running as fast as they could, all except Ben, who watched as Tessa did her best to move fast. Unfortunately, it was not even considered a slow walk by their standards.

"I hope you are not heavy," he said and tried to lift her up. "Not too bad," he added. He'd used his levitation gift to put her over his shoulder. Now, he too ran as fast as he dared, carrying a protesting Tessa with him.

"I'll be your rear eyes," she finally said something useful, he thought. Panting heavily, he did his best to keep up with the others.

The main doors were gone. One of the bomb blasts had taken them out. Two blocks away, they saw a long line of silver robots, d-guns blazing, heading towards the building. Between them, some fifty security guards, hiding behind remnants of cars and trucks, fired back, but rarely hit their targets. Ducking falling debris and d-gun fire, Alberto led them around the back and down a quiet alley, across another bombed street, and into another alley.

"Where are we going?" Tessa whispered, growing confused with their seeming random path.

"Trust Alberto. He has an unfailing direction sense," Ben whispered, trying to breathe and talk at the same time. She was getting heavy. He began to trail the others.

"Okay, my turn," Jan stopped and insisted.

Ben was very glad for the break. "She's not too heavy, lighter than I imagined," he added. A bit later, Amy took over for Jan. By the time they reached their ship, everyone had three turns carrying Tessa. The trip was extremely wild. They nearly got bombed three times, ran through a d-gun battle, were strafed twice by a one-man ship, and fell into a sinkhole caused by a water line break. At the spaceport, half of the ships on the ground were in flames. Thankfully, Strike Force One was still undamaged, and they raced for it, dodging another strafing run.

Once inside, Ben ran to the cockpit, fired the engines without any check off, got them slightly airborne before doing an emergency jump into hyperspace, all of which happened in sixty seconds, the fastest takeoff on record. "Well, you didn't get us blown up," Pippa commented, when she finally joined him, sitting in the navigator's seat and verifying their coordinates and then resetting them for home.

"Cool takeoff, captain," Alis yelled from the passenger bay. "Got Tessa secured now, but now she doesn't need it. Guess I'll undo it."

Ben yelled back, "Thank you Alberto! That was one fine run!"

"Aye boss. Let's not do that one again," he yelled back, a broad grin on his face.

"So how did you do that? Find our way back on foot?" Tessa asked him.

"Can't rightly say, miss. I just know which way to go. Gut feeling, some say," he replied. "If you all don't mind, I'm getting some shut-eye now. I hate being wakened when I'm sleeping."

"Okay, you can all hit the sack too. I'll call home and report what's happening, if they don't already know and handle Tessa," Ben offered. Pippa and Alis took him up on the offer, heading to their cabin. Jan and Amy stuck around for a bit.

Amy said, "You are right. That mind, the one that blasted us, that was not like the others. It wasn't a weibchen. That was a powerful spiritual being, like one of us almost."

Jan gasped. "You don't suppose Minta is kidnaping

159

some of our telepaths and turning them into Model 10's do you?"

"God, I hope not!" Amy replied.

"No, I don't think that's right. It was far more powerful than one of us would be, not without our you-know-whats, the big ones," Ben replied, not wanting to say giant psi-crystals in the presence of Tessa.

"Yours is pretty big, big boy," Tessa teased Ben in retaliation for keeping her in the dark again. He flushed, but ignored that innuendo.

"I've sensed that mind before, back on Tierra, I just know it," Ben added.

"You don't suppose that was Wystan, do you?" Jan asked, thinking of what Renata had warned them about before they left.

A light flashed in Ben's mind. "Yes! That's who it was! Wystan! No wonder he could blast us with such ease!"

"Oh crap!" Jan exclaimed.

"Oh shit!" Amy added with far less restraint.

"Who is Wystan?" Tessa asked.

Ben looked at Amy, who decided to answer her. "Long ago, Wystan was one of the pentatheon of god and goddesses on Tierra or Ashford-5. These are spiritual beings of immense power and do not have any need for a physical body to operate fully. Wystan was the God of Battles and Warriors. He was the men's god and loved to create conflict and strife, getting men to fight so he can watch and enjoy. Perverse. Neutral Alleric is at the top of the pentagram, all-powerful, but seldom mixing in our affairs. He seems only to care about the welfare of the physical planet itself, not we humans on it. Calder was the God of Waters. He used to be worshiped by those who make use of the oceans and rivers. Lysandra is the Goddess of Life and of Death. She is known for helping women in dire need. Finally, there is Ariana, the Goddess of Fertility. It is Ariana's desire that women of Tierra and now men too have these overly large knockers. Anyway, over a hundred years ago, Wystan and Calder got into some real trouble and apparently left our world. Alleric is still around, though very seldom seen. Lysandra and Ariana are still quite active, helping us when they can."

Tessa looked at Amy and said, "You're kidding me, right? Gods? Goddesses? Beings without bodies? Ghosts?"

"Oh, I assure you, Tessa, they are very real!" Amy answered. "Jan and I have had contact with them on a number of occasions. When we get back, try reading one of our history books. You can find out more about them."

Tessa looked puzzled. "Our massive database does contain some references to powerful entities that inhabit the halo, but there is no mention of them being in the galactic disk."

"Ah, they may well have come down to the disk from the halo, but that would have to have been at least a half-millennia ago, maybe longer," Amy replied.

"You suggest that these god and goddesses are like yourselves somehow?" Tessa asked fascinated.

"Yes, we've lost those powers and now depend upon these physical bodies. But some of us are recovering those lost powers, but if you want to know more about that, talk to Renata. She is behind our regaining our abilities. Advanced Therapy, she calls it," Amy wrapped it up. "Now, I am going to bed. My head is splitting from Wystan's blast. Night all." She and Jan headed off to their room.

"Come on; I'll get you into bed. I need a shower," Ben said softly.

"May I join you? I need one too. I'm covered in dust."

# Chapter 10 Genetics Goes to War

"Covered in dust?" asked an incredulous Minta. She was visiting the University of Central Scorpius on Zeta Scorpii-C, the Genetics Research Department to be more precise. There, she met with Dr. Zelos Dingle, the head of the department and a brilliant research geneticist. Minta had given him a special assignment by some years ago. Considering the current situation, it seemed time she check on his progress. Today was the day before the attack on Pegasi-C.

"Yes, Dust. Do you realize the true volume of dust that descends upon any world in a given day? It's gigantic, though each particle is small. I have adapted the new bio agent developed on Ashford-5 to attach itself to dust grains. Via dust, the agent can easily penetrate any known planetary defense shield, delivering its mutation agent payload cleanly and worldwide. Brilliant, if I so say so myself." The armless nova was rightly proud of his accomplishments to further the cause of Minta and all nova. He too wanted a galaxy free from wars, criminality, and drugs, though he knew nothing of any of these, only what he read or heard on the news.

"Extremely well done, doctor. Now about that special payload that I asked you to develop, is it workable? Is it ready? Has it been tested?" she asked.

"Computer: display File 11234," he commanded his computer, which brought up the document. "See. Workable, ready, and tested on two volunteer test subjects. It is ready for field testing. I admit that has not yet been done, so I cannot say with total certainty that it will work as per the requirements."

"Excellent. The situation has changed. I need a planetary-size dose of this ready to be delivered as soon as possible. It is rather critical, doctor," Minta stated.

"It can be ready within a week."

"Excellent, excellent. Now then, once that is proven to work, I'll have another vital project for you to work on," she advised him. He nodded, looking very pleased indeed. It was extremely rare that Minta herself would make a personal appearance on Zeta Scorpii-C, and rarer still visiting the university. She'd only visited him once, back when she gave him the special, secret assignment years ago.

A day later and back at her home base, Minta summoned Minta-4. "I've a special clandestine mission for you. I need you to make a quick trip to Ashford-5 and deliver a special payload that will be ready in a week."

"I do hope this payload will stop these meddling telepaths. The amount of trouble they have been causing these past months is more than significant. How is it that they are able to detect our humaniform robots anyway? I've not been able to understand that," Minta-4 asked.

Minta bit her lip in a proper human fashion before replying, "I'm not certain I know that answer either, but I have some suspicions. This payload ought to hold them another fifty years, which is all the time that we need."

June 28, 1501. Tessa was enjoying the dinner conversation, though as usual she didn't pretend to eat or drink with them. Outlining their miraculous escape from the attack on Pegasi-C, Ben added, "So thanks to Alberto here, we finally made it back. Has anyone heard what happened to Pegasi-C? Will the Emperor be interfering again? Will he try to get this world under his control as he did Ponchart-D and Abel-C? That's what I want to know. These genetic mutations are bad enough without the people also becoming slaves too."

Jan piped up, "I've done a bit of hacking, and it would seem they used the same slightly defective bio agent as they did on Abel-C. So that's something. Haven't heard about Ataro intervention yet. Probably too soon. It's not been two weeks really. Probably utter chaos on the ground. However, I've also been uncovering some other details, but I'm not quite sure what to make of them."

"What's that?" asked Governor Monica. She'd kept careful watch on all the news coming from the Ataro Empire and had not heard of anything else. What had Jan uncovered this time?

"Mining operations. The reports are widely isolated.

One in this system, one in that. All over the mid-arm of Federation space. It seems that the metal heads have established robot mining operations on dozens of uninhabited, hot, rocky planets. You know, the ones that are too close to their suns, where the temperatures are far too hot for us. The planets have long lost any atmospheres they might have once had. As far as I can tell, no one in the Federation has put these reports together. Each one is an isolated report. But I did. Correlated them all. Not one of these new mining operations began before the ill-fated Federation attack on the metal heads."

"Is that significant?" asked Governor Monica, trying to assimilate what Jan had uncovered.

"Look," Jan continued, "the Federation attacked them and lost a huge percentage of their war ships, leaving the whole Federation of Planets precariously exposed. What keeps the metal heads from attacking and taking over another world?" she asked, looking from person to person. Silence.

"It's plainly obvious, gang," Jan hinted. Still no one ventured an answer. "I can see why none of you are hackers. No imagination. Look, when they take over another world, they hit them with a bio agent attack. That means within four days, the robot workers must supply every home on that world with the machines and stuff that the people must have to survive the genetic mutations. Assuming a planet has four billion people left after the initial attack, and say there are four people per household, then they need to provide a billion electrostatic hair machines, a billion new kitchens. You get the picture? Vast amounts of bots and machines and machine modifications have to be made in four days, ignoring the repairs to the infrastructure that they destroyed or damaged in their attack. That's one hell of a lot of raw materials being needed."

"Oh I get it. So these mining operations are providing them with the materials to construct more of the equipment. More attacks are coming," Governor Monica piped in.

Amy countered Jan, "I think that you are being overly worried about the mining operations, Jan. Constructing the billions of pieces of equipment does require a huge volume of raw materials and time to refine them, to say nothing of fabrication time. It probably takes the metal heads a year at best to make enough machines for their next planetary conquest. I bet they don't take over another world until next year sometime. That's one hell of a lot of machines to have to build from scratch."

"I'm not done," Jan added. "Today, I got a call from one of our gypsy friends in the Braith Clan. She told me that they'd just returned from a sail among some isolated regions of the Federation mid-arm. They came across thirty, large-scale mining operations. The metal heads drove them away from each one, but she was sure that the operations were huge in scope, but again on uninhabitable planets. Minta is planning something, I'm sure of it."

"What?" asked Queen Mary Linn. "Taking over more worlds?"

Jan shrugged her shoulders. "Don't know yet. Why do I feel so tired?"

"Hey, me too," Alis spoke up. She had been fascinated with the discussion, but had been yawning. So too had many others.

Just then, the attack alarm sirens sounded in Exchange City. Governor Monica's mate, Betsy Childa, the physicist in charge of Tierra's planetary-defenses, sent her a Message. *We are under another bio agent attack! Have the queen send out a planetary warning pronto! It's airborne somehow.*

"Oh good god, not again!" Governor Monica exclaimed and relayed the news. Queen Mary Linn acted at once, notifying the Imperial Tower's capa on duty. Within seconds, all the other towers on Tierra had the news and began spreading word to their people. Within five minutes, everyone on Tierra knew that another bio agent attack was underway.

"So that's why we are so tired!" Alis exclaimed. Now it made sense. "Crap! Damn those metal heads!"

"Okay. Cool heads. Get to your homes. Undress and get into bed, just in case we enter a coma," Governor Monica ordered. "Our cruisers on duty will protect us if we go under. Plus, the emperor will likely have a fleet here within hours. Calmly, calmly." She didn't look as calm as her words however.

With many cursing to themselves, the large group headed back to their quarters. "So how did their ships get through our planetary defense shield?" Jan asked. "That's what I want to know."

Ben replied, "Good question. I would hate to be in Betsy's shoes this time. Someone messed up big-time."

Once back in their quarters, Ben asked, "Want me to undress you?"

Tessa replied worriedly, "No. Leave me dressed. If you pass out, I'll watch over you and everyone else, somehow, someway. I don't understand this attack either, but I'm sure that it won't affect me."

Ben glared, but couldn't remain angry with her. After all, she was a robot and immune to genetic modifications. A few minutes later, he lay back on his bed, while Tessa sat on a chair nearby, looking quite worried he thought. Then, he fell into a deep sleep, slipping into a coma later on.

Tessa watched Ben's body closely, monitoring his vital signs. He's gone into a coma. No doubt about that. What's going on? I had better check with Minta immediately. She rose carefully and made her way out of his room, heading for the nearest comm center. The closed doors posed significant challenges for her, and she fell twice getting the sliding slats near their bottoms opened. Using her toes, she fired up the electronics and switched to the proper frequency, but remembered what setting the machine had been using so that she could put it back when she was done. Shortly after that, a stream of binary bits came and went from the unit. Satisfied, she reset the frequency and turned the machine off, returning to sit beside Ben.

As she sat there, she decided now was a good time to recharge. A small chamber opened in her upper thigh, releasing a long power cable. It took some doing, but she finally got it plugged into the wall socket and felt the juice flowing into her system. Before she powered down most circuits, she noticed a hidden program starting up. What's that? Her feet kicked off her toe shoes, but she had not caused them to do so. Curious, she thought and continued to monitor herself and Ben.

Four days she sat patiently on the chair, though she'd already removed and stowed the power recharging cord. She could operate another four months before she would have to recharge again. That was comforting. As she sat observing, she saw the changes slowly becoming apparent in Ben's body. Only then did she notice that similar ones were occurring to hers as well! The secret program — she finally realized that Minta had installed it for just such a situation. That bothered her enormously! For days, she ran all manner of diagnostic programs, searching for other hidden programs, but found only one more. She copied the program and then began slowly deciphering it.

To her astonishment, she had human-like arms! They were cleverly hidden inside her body cavity. When the program executed, they would move out and reform, making her look like a normal person, as well as straightening out her feet and shortening her hair. With that done, she would appear just like any other normal home sapiens sapiens! Tessa was brilliant. She decided that she would be in control of this Trojan program and fabricated a quarantine box around it. Now, it could not be activated and run unless she directed it, but she also installed an alarm should someone else attempt to activate it. She suspected that Minta had placed the two secret programs in her circuitry, but had no proof.

Ben came out of his coma and tried to push himself up. His upper arms failed to function. He jerked awake and alert, noticing Tessa sitting on the chair where he had last seen her. "My arms," he tried to say, but noticed his words sounded terribly funny.

"Say again. Sorry, I didn't quite understand you. I'm glad that you've finally woken up, sweetie. I missed you. Kind of boring sitting here on this chair for four days," Tessa replied.

Ben groaned. His stumps or upper arms were gone. Two shriveled up husks lay beside him on the bed. His lips felt strange, and in a flash, he realized why. Lip loops. He'd seen numerous images of the old days when people here wore the giant lip disks. Tessa spoke up, "Yes, your lips have somehow split. You have two giant lip loops. I've researched your database and found they were quite popular on Ashford-5 many years ago. Status symbols is the term most frequently associated with them. Guess with everyone having them, there won't be much status now. Check your feet, Ben."

"I can't move them," he groaned again, trying to sit up. His crystal glowed briefly as he used his powers to reposition his body. Giant lip loops drooped down, nearly touching his chest. So much for understandable speech, he thought. Again, his crystal glowed briefly and his covers slipped off him, revealing his feet. They were fused, pointing straight downward. The only motion possible was a slight side-to-side movement of toes, and that was just barely. He groaned again.

"We're going to need new shoes," Tessa commented.

"What do you mean we?" Ben picked up on her expression.

"Mine are fused like yours, Ben."

"But how? You are a robot," he asked confused and still trying to grasp what had happened to his body.

"A hidden Trojan program. I didn't know it was there. Be careful what you wish for. My hair is now ankle length too, just like yours. I'm beginning to understand your speech better," she answered, not telling them that she recorded his words and played them back several times before she understood what he'd just said, though Ben only noticed a slight pause between his question and her reply.

"Trojan horse?"

"Yes. A hidden program that activated. It altered my feet and my hair, nothing else. I believe that it was timed to happen while you were in your coma. Curious though. I didn't know it was there. Found another one too, but I deactivated it. I don't like unknown, nasty surprises. Walking was bad enough before. Now, I don't see how any of us are to walk."

Ben groaned. He knew. He'd seen the images in history class. "Ballerinas. We walk on the tips of our toes. They have these strange boots. Ballet boots or shoes. I hope Elegant Fashions Inc still has those around!"

Just then, he received a telepathic message from the Imperial Tower's capa. *Our feet have been modified as has our lips. The queen wants everyone to stay put while proper shoes are made for everyone. Expect someone to deliver them later today. Stay calm. Lip plates will be provided as soon as they can be fabricated. If you need to move around, crawl on your knees, but be careful. Emergency services are non-existent at this time. Thank you.*

Ben relayed what he'd heard to Tessa. Her eyes flashed. "I got it. This is in retaliation for your intervention on Pegasi-C and the other worlds. I figured it out. She wants to immobilize you telepaths. I think you had a really big impact on her plans, Ben."

"Yeh, well what I want to know is how did this attack get past our defenses? It should not have occurred."

"Indeed. I would like to know that answer as well. From the little that you have told or shown me, a delivery spaceship should not have been able to get through your shields. Period. No way. Yet it did. How? I find that most interesting. I'm glad that you do too. Sabotage? Traitors? Humaniforms here? Well, I am, but I was with you when it happened, and you've never let me out of your sight. At least I'm off the hook, as they say."

"Yeh, small comfort in that, sweetie," he shot back using her own tease. "Well, at least we don't have monster boobs this time."

Tessa laughed coyly. "No, yours are just fine for my taste as they are. Seriously though, we can't stand or walk now, right? I've tried a bit and there's no way that I can do it."

"Got to wait for the shoes or boots. Imperium Standard. I remember now. In the old days, those who wore the lip plates spoke in IS so that they could be understood. Hope you speak IS, dear," he said with a grin that wasn't visible. She picked up his other facial expressions, though faint, and realized he was smiling.

She switched to IS. "How many languages do you speak?" Ben asked, rather surprised that she spoke the old IS.

"Fifty-three of the more common ones. Is that a lot?" she replied demurely, knowing that it was. He merely groaned again.

Twelve hours later, one of the queen's personal assistants arrived, floating a wagon full of hastily manufactured ballet shoes behind her. Speaking in IS, she

169

said, "Shoes are here. Temporary ones. More and better ones are being made. Use IS now. Expect lip disks later in the week. Queen says to be extra careful not to rip your lip loops. Meet in her throne room when you can manage it. Thank heavens everyone's feet are one of two sizes, men's size ten, and women's size eight." She floated two pairs out of her wagon, dropping them just inside Ben's room and moved on down the hall, walking extremely precariously, her germanium crystal glowing brightly around her neck.

Ben used his powers to move them from the front room living room into their bedroom. These were more like slippers that one could easily get into and out of without much trouble. The two wiggled some and got them onto their feet. Trying to stand was hilarious. Both ended up with very bent knees, just trying to keep their balance as they stood. Both broke into hysterical laughter. "This is almost impossible," Tessa grumbled.

Ben suddenly realized this was the first time that Tessa had actually grumbled, displaying a real human emotional response. Curious, he thought. They tried walking out to the living room. Laughing this hard, they nearly fell over three times before collapsing onto the couch. He said, "I think you are dead on." Both laughed again.

"You are taking this extremely well," Tessa finally said after calming down.

"Hey, it is either laugh at it or cry, so I might as well laugh," he responded. "Just don't ask me to carry you now," he teased, bringing another smile to her face.

"I want some answers. We're not going to get them sitting here. Let's try to make it to her throne room, Tessa," Ben finally said. They both had to lunge forward to get up off the couch, but wobbled wildly. Hastily, Ben had to use his gifts to get them both stabilized. It took them a half hour to make it to Queen Mary Linn's throne room, and he had to use his powers six times to keep them from falling. Tessa greatly appreciated his timely aid. Even for an advanced robot, this was quite challenging.

They took the first seats they could find. The queen looked haggard and pooped. He guessed that she'd used a very large amount of her energies already today and was thankful that he wasn't a queen with such a heavy responsibility. Just then, others came stumping into the room. Ben was secretly pleased to see Jan and Amy having just as hard a time walking as he had. Renata, on the other hand, came floating into the room, not even bothering to walk. Jan called out, "Show off!" Renata ignored her and sat her body down next to Tessa's.

Once Jan sat down or fell into the chair would be a better statement of fact, she blurted out, "So who messed up this time and allowed this to happen to us? Anyone know?"

"Betsy is on it," Queen Mary Linn answered. "Lysandra gave her a clue. It was airborne she thinks. Time will tell. I have everyone possible working on duplicating shoes right now. What a mess. I'm told that it will be weeks before they can get us all a decent pair of shoes or boots. These are merely bedroom slippers and are very hard to walk in."

Just then, Betsy and Governor Monica materialized near the entrance and floated their bodies over to the group, sitting them down close to the queen. "Betsy teleported us. We can't really walk in these things," Monica explained. "Have to levitate us almost constantly. Takes a whole lot of our daily energies though."

"Well gang, I've worked it out, thanks to Lysandra's tip," Betsy broke in on the pleasantries. "It was airborne — attached to dust particles in fact. That's how it got through the shields. Dust."

"Huh?" Ben exclaimed. Physics wasn't his strongest subject in school.

Betsy replied rather didactically, "Dust. Every day, millions of tiny dust particles fall down from the skies. If you ever did your dusting, you'd know what I'm talking about, Ben. Somehow, they've taken our neutral bio binding agent, bonded it to dust particles, and then attached the working biological agent to it. The ship must have been cloaked and simply flew around close to the shield releasing a mountain of the dust stuff. It then slowly fell to the ground, infecting us along the way. Or we could have inhaled it or even had the particles land on our skin. Sorry. There isn't any known defense against dust. Of course, housewives would love to have a remedy for dust.

That's a joke, by the way, Ben," she teased him. He groaned.

Tessa decided to speak up. "It is my conclusion that your recent activities rousting out her spies and killing the Model 10 leaders during the attack may well be behind her launching the bio attack on you. We're obviously greatly impaired now and will be hard pressed to continue opposing her. What I don't understand is that, if this is the case, why didn't she just use a nerve agent on this world, killing everyone. My second conclusion is that therefore she wants you all alive for some unknown reason, just not interfering with her battles."

"Point well made, Tessa," Renata validated her arguments. "I agree with her. She's left us alone for what, fifty years or so. Why attack us now? It has to be a warning to stay out of her affairs. What she doesn't understand is that we have a responsibility to interfere and try to protect those people. But Tessa's right. We won't be doing much for a while, that's for sure. Mary Linn, any word from the geneticists?"

"Not yet. They are just as helpless as the rest of us, but they have samples and are re-sequencing my DNA and several others right now," the queen answered, trying to sound hopeful, but failing completely. "Renata, what about Lysandra and Ariana? Any chance they can help us again?"

"Don't know on that one. I'll summon them. We ought to know the full story as soon as possible so that we can take the appropriate actions. Time is critical. The fall harvest is only a couple months away," Renata answered. Quietly, she focused and made contact with the pair.

Shortly, yellowish and whitish glows appeared, slowly morphing into the figures of two young women, though their bodies were merely a believable illusion. Neither needed such but found the humans related to them better this way. "Ah, up and around, I see," Lysandra said, once her form appeared to solidify.

"Hi again," Ariana added. "We kept your boobs from expanding again, like before. Sorry about your feet and lips, though."

"Thanks Ariana," Renata spoke up. "We think we were attacked again to prevent us from interfering in the robot's battles."

"Likely right," Lysandra replied. "The real problem is Wystan. Thanks to you, we know that he is now being one of those bloodthirsty Model 10 warrior robots as you call them. We have to stop him. Ariana and I have decided that we ought to leave Tierra and go after him. He is one of us. . ."

Ariana corrected her, "Was one of us, you mean."

"Er right. Was. He is our responsibility," Lysandra finished.

"Not a wise move," Amy countered. "He is stronger than Jan, Ben, and me combined. He'll just take you both out."

Renata spoke up hastily, "She has a point. Your responsibilities lay in protecting and nourishing this world. Leave him to us. If you leave and get wiped out, we have no one looking after us."

"Hum, you make a strong case, Renata. We would be gambling with Tierra's safety if we left. Wystan always was stronger than us," Lysandra conceded.

"What we need to know now," Renata continued, "is there anything that you can do to undo these new genetic changes to our bodies?"

Ariana sighed and that told Renata everything, though Lysandra filled in the details. "Not really. We've managed to keep breast sizes down, but little else. You have to realize that the split lips modification was always present in your genetic material, only it was suppressed, probably from errors in the duplication process is our guess. This dosage somehow removed that blockage, allowing it to manifest itself. What we are and have been doing is flooding the world with calming energies, keeping the panic levels way down this time. That should reduce the traumas and give you time to get help to everyone. No one has died this time."

Ariana giggled girlishly. "The more of you there are, the stronger you will be. So we sort of took the liberty, well I sort of took the liberty," the Goddess of Fertility saw the frown from Lysandra and amended her statement slightly, "of adding a little extra to your new lip loops. It should help increase your population rather swiftly."

Renata glared at Ariana. "Just what have you done?"

she asked pointedly.

"They will be very sensuous. One kiss and passions will erupt. More babies, more people, a stronger world," Ariana answered her.

"Just what we need, more babies," Renata said disgustedly.

"But of course," Ariana added gaily. "I even doodled with the robot lady there too. We have to be going now. Our world still needs calming, especially in the Easterlings right now." Before anyone could object, the forms slowly turned back into glowing swirls of yellow and white energy and then vanished.

"More babies," Renata grumbled. "That's not what I wanted to hear."

Governor Monica laughed, "What did you expect? She is the Goddess of Fertility after all." Everyone chuckled at her jest.

Amy broke the jovial atmosphere. "Gang, based on my experiences some lifetimes back, we can get the hang of walking in these boots. It will take a while for our knees and leg muscles to toughen up. Hours of practice walking are needed, along with using our gifts to dissipate pain and cramp energy deposits in our toes and knees. Let everyone know what to expect, Mary Linn."

While the others chatted about what the two goddesses had just said, Tessa's positron brain fired at maximum capacity, rarely if ever used to its fullest volume. Her sensors had definitely registered the two beings, of that she had no doubt. Her extensive database had nothing like these observations in it. She was forced to make her own independent calculations and conclusions. Obviously, these two did not have physical bodies and yet she had seen their very real energy manifestations!

The only conclusion that she could draw was that they really were spiritual beings and were not made from physical matter, such as her body or Ben's. That alone was quite startling to Tessa. And what had Ariana meant by doodling with the robot's body? Had she implanted that Trojan program? No, Tessa was certain that Minta had done that. But what had she done? She ran a full and complete set of diagnostics on her circuitry and body, but all was within normal parameters. No wait! There was a third Trojan program, currently inactive. Tessa was certain it had not been there before! Quickly, she quarantined it so that it could not activate on its own, assuming that there would be some kind of trigger. Then, she copied it and began unraveling its binary code. The others were still talking and no one noticed how quiet Tessa had become. Time passed. Suddenly, Tessa had another involuntary human reaction. She flushed. She had worked out what that program was meant to do. A smile pursed her lips, and she reconnected to the conversations around her.

"Ben! This is really too hard for me. You have to help me some," Tessa begged him. Weeks had passed. Elegant Fashions Inc had come through, just as they always had in the past. Everyone now had strong, tight-fitting knee-high ballet style boots with a very strong metal heel at least eight inches tall, one that would not bend or break. Further, the process of getting everyone their own lip disk assembly was ongoing. As before, each person had their own unique design etched onto the top surface of the top disk. That way, when the disks were lowered, which was most all of the time, their design was quite visible.

She'd examined Ben's mouth when he got his. Sure enough, his upper and lower gums and bones had four small holes in them. An upper and lower mouthpiece with matching metal dowels fit the holes precisely. These thin pieces had a cleverly designed system by which the two twelve-inch in diameter disks were attached. They were hinged so that both disks drooped downward, usually touching the wearer's upper chest. Yet, when it was time to eat or drink, the upper disk could be raised up. A small latch held it horizontally so that food and drink could be inserted into one's mouth — inserted being the key operative word here. To drink, liquids were delivered by spoons as was food. Once done, two small pressure operated buttons undid the latch, allowing the plates to drop down nearly vertical again. No one wore theirs horizontally except when eating. If they should take a fall, the plates would crush their jaws, potentially killing them. Down, they wouldn't interfere much during a fall.

With the sturdy new boots, Tessa could just barely manage to walk by herself. The others, she quickly saw, constantly used their *mentales* gifts to help them both keep their balance and prevent a tumble, which she simply could not. However, she knew that by the end of the day, each person had a good deal of pain, cramps, and soreness in their toes, feet, knees, and legs. She'd watched Ben carefully in the evening as he used his gifts to get the pain unlocked and flowing, dispersing it before bed. She, on the other hand, experienced no such thing. Her sole problem was one of keeping her balance or, after falling which she often did, regaining her feet, an action anything but graceful. She found the emotion of embarrassment quite new to her.

Ben knew that his legs were getting stronger and that he often had to resort to an extremely fast use of his gifts to prevent a tumble. He also knew that Tessa didn't. "Look, sweetie, you have to learn to be independent and walk well. I can't always be hovering over you keeping you upright. I thought you robots had a keen sense of balance."

"I do, but this it really hard. Now if I had arms, I would be able to use them to offset a wobble, but I don't. Okay, okay, I see your point," Tessa admitted. "But I think I liked my hair shorter. It keeps getting in my way."

"Well, it does that to us all. Welcome to the club," Ben replied, taking some comfort in the fact that Tessa was having as much trouble as he and everyone else was having. Then, he regretted that. "Sorry Tessa. I didn't mean to pick on you. I'm taking my own frustrations out on you. Heck, all of us have our *mentales* gifts to help us and you don't. I'll try to catch you when I can."

Later that evening, he again used his gifts to get her undressed for bed and then himself. As he did so, he had mixed feelings. That first night, he'd given her a night kiss and discovered what Ariana had done to the sensitivity of the lip loops. It had been phenomenal and completely irresistible! His own passions had literally exploded, a fact not missed by Tessa either. After that, all barriers were down as far as their bedtime actions. Still, she wasn't a real person, he thought. How can having sex with a robot count? At first, he felt somewhat guilty, seeing her more like one of those sex toys, the "Fantastic Plastic Lovers" advertised on seamier web sites. But she was more than some inanimate toy, at least to him she was. Ben found his relationship with Tessa growing more confusing rather than less. He really did like her and more than once wished that she was a real person and not a robot.

On July 10, Tessa decided that she needed help and paid a visit to Super Models Inc, now run by the grandchildren Nicolina and Rosella, both twenty-five, and a pair of absolutely stunning women with ankle-length blond hair. "Wow. Tessa. Great. Come on in. Here, I have the door for you," Nicolina exclaimed, quite surprised finally to get to meet the humaniform robot in person. By now, many in Exchange City knew of Tessa's presence, though few had actually met her. "Rosella, come and see who's dropped by!"

"Wow. Tessa. So very pleased to meet you. We've heard a lot about you. So you really aren't one of the metal head spies. Come on in," Rosella gushed.

"Hardly. I'm actually in worse shape than all of you on Tierra are. I can just barely walk, and Ben has to do most everything for me using his gifts. Thanks," she answered.

"So what brings you to Super Models Inc?" Nicolina asked.

Tessa sighed. She again felt embarrassed, but didn't know why that should be. Her coming here was most logical. "I need to learn to walk properly. I'd like to look like a super model and walk like one, if that is even possible. I don't have your gifts. I'm tired of Ben always having to use his to keep me upright. Getting back up after a fall is, well, really awkward and embarrassing," she admitted. Was that why she felt embarrassed? Trying clumsily to get back up after a fall? No, she decided that wasn't it at all.

Nicolina giggled. "Well, you certainly came to the right place. We specialize in turning out top models. We teach our customers how to look as sexy as possible, how to walk seductively, how to win beauty pageants, and how to dress

177

appropriately. As you probably know, we are a smashing success." Both women spoke IS. Their lip plates displayed an elegantly dressed woman in a modeling pose.

Rosella added, "The first thing that we teach everyone is how to walk properly and seductively."

"Well, that's what I need to learn how to do," Tessa replied. They discussed funds, and Tessa gave them access to her account since she had no way to make a withdrawal. That settled, the lessons began.

"The first thing is to learn to place each foot in line. See that white line on the floor?" Nicolina began the training session. "You want to plant each step squarely on the line."

"But shouldn't each foot lie on either side of the line?" Tessa asked.

"Not if you want to walk seductively. When you walk by putting each foot directly forward in front of each other, your hips will sway very seductively, catching everyone's keen interest. Now let's get started. Don't worry; it takes weeks for a client to get this part down. Some men are models too, since they look like us anyway. We'll use our powers to keep you from falling. Getting back up gracefully is covered later on."

Unlike humans whose legs and bodies tired and ached after relatively short practice sessions, hers didn't. She spent hours at it, going there for lessons every day. Mid-August, Tessa graduated. She was incredibly pleased that she'd mastered not only walking well in these boots, but also as seductively as she desired. Of course, this was on smooth, even surfaces. Walking on thick carpeting was more difficult, but manageable. Like everyone else, she found walking up and down slopes and over rough ground extremely challenging, and she didn't worry about that aspect. They had also taken her to visit Elegant Fashions Inc; her wardrobe now boasted even fancier gowns, a fact not missed by Ben.

Still, she had the roughest time descending the spaceship's bay ramp. Going up wasn't so much of a problem, but going down was. Her knees had to bend almost ninety degrees in order to do it. Either that or descend sideways. While she felt no pain in doing this, the humans did. Here, they had it rougher than she did, though Alis simply floated her body down the ramp, having given up completely trying to walk down it.

Slowly but surely, Ben was getting his crew ready for action, should they be called upon again. He knew eventually he'd be flying again, though this time, he and the others would be doing nearly everything by using their gifts. Their feet were now useless, and they had no helping upper arm stumps. Their slow walking speed still bothered him, as he recalled their frantic escape from the bombing on Pegasi-C.

Others were also working frantically on genetic mutation experimentations. Many were done in total secrecy and some, highly illegally. The fall of Pegasi-C greatly alarmed the major worlds of the Federation. Their main fleets were gone, destroyed in the great battle. Each world knew that they were ripe for a takeover by the robots. The hub worlds believed they had far more time to prepare, being so distant from the mid-arm region, while the more populated mid-arm worlds were worried about imminent attacks that thus far had not occurred.

August 1, Reich Spaceport, Hoffdorf, Cass-C. Three very powerful men within the Federation of Planets met in secret, awaiting the arrival of a certain doctor. Cass-C was one of the major hub worlds of the Federation. Outside the secure room, one deep space transport descended, just one of thousands, which came and went from this very busy spaceport each day. A group of well-armed men met the lone man who cautiously walked down the bay ramp, carrying a large bag clutched to his side. He nervously glanced around, but the men motioned for him to join them, which he quickly did. Minutes later, he entered the secure room, noticed one of the men, and visibly relaxed, though still clutching his bag.

"Gentlemen, this is Doctor Frunhilde. Doctor, it is best that you don't know their names. I take it you have it with you?" one man asked formally.

"Yes. I've got what you asked for," the fifty year old, bespectacled man replied, still a bit ill at ease. He wasn't used to all this secrecy, but then what he'd been asked to do and had done required secrecy and of the highest order.

"Excellent. Please report then."

"It works as specified. We've tested it on other victims as well as normals," he replied.

One of the unknown men asked, "Where did you get your volunteers?"

"Best not ask that one," the leader interrupted.

The doctor replied, "It's okay to ask. We took some from the assisted living complexes. They were more than willing to accept the money for their children. The normals came from the prison complex."

"Have you photos of the results?"

"Yes, as specified." The doctor opened his bag and produced a small binder of eight by ten color photographs printed by a laser printer.

The three men leaned over to look at them. One commented, "Simply amazing." Another added, "This will work for sure!"

"I told you that investing in the secret genetics research lab on Cass-B was a wise move. It's too hot there for even a domed city, except along the sunrise line, where we put the laboratory. It has produced sensational results in just a few years, thanks to our doctor here. Have you the cylinder?"

"Yes, it's here." The doctor pulled out the pressurized cylinder, approximately a foot long. "Just duplicate this around two hundred times and release it from ten thousand feet above the surface."

"Excellent. Your funds have been transferred into your account, right?" he looked back at one man who was operating a laptop. The man nodded and said, "Done."

"Good. You may leave us and begin work on your next assignment, doctor. Pleasure doing business with you and your colleagues. You may have just saved Cass-C from the metal heads." A smile crossed the doctor's lips. He turned, eagerly left the room, heading directly back to his ship, and was airborne minutes later. He was confident that he had done his duty to protect his world, Cass-C.

"Okay, you heard him, general. Get this duped a couple hundred times. Your problem will be how to get it released at ten thousand feet. That's well below their planetary defense screen."

"Leave that to me," the general replied, taking the cylinder and holding it as though it was fine crystal about ready to break with the slightest touch.

"Let us know when it is done. We'll send the metal heads our message then." The general nodded, turned, and left.

"Will this actually work?"

"Let's say you have made the best investment that money can buy. Come on; we have work to do." They too left the spaceport.

The next day, the general met with his advisors for a time. Convinced that they had no way to get a payload delivered by spaceship, the general took another path. He sent for Private Wyrth. The young lad came running in, saluting hard and fast. "Private Wyrth reporting as ordered, sir!" he barked properly, very much impressed with being personally in the presence of this great man.

"Private, I've looked at your record here. A parachutist and parasail glider. First place in the Nationals," the general said politely, setting the lad up.

Proudly, Private Wyrth said, "Yes sir! First place. Thank you sir." He was impressed. The general even knew about his hobby.

"Son, I have a top secret mission for you, if you'll volunteer. This one is critical to the very survival of our world, Cass-C, maybe even to other worlds. It will demand the very skills that you have and your ultimate sacrifice for God and Country. Your courageous act will save the lives of all those that you love, as well as twenty billion here on Cass-C. Lord knows how many other billions of people will owe you their very lives, son." He went on about it until he was satisfied of his chosen man's willingness to make the ultimate sacrifice.

A day of drilling later, the general joined Private Wyrth on the fully equipped deep space transport. A special teleport pad had been hastily installed in the cargo bay. Private Wyrth inspected his special rig, found all in order, and headed for the galley, where he was served his favorite meal, a succulent strip steak. That done, he retired to get some needed sleep. The trip would take nine hours, compliments of the revolutionary new engines pioneered by Porsche Industries so many years ago. Private Wyrth traced his lineage in part back to the Porsche line, and he was proud of that. Now, it was his turn to step up to the mark and show them what he could do to save the world, maybe even the entire Federation or what was left of it.

Right on schedule, the general roused him, pumped him full of coffee, and watched him get into his parasail contraption. "All ready sir!" he barked a final salute.

With a tear trickling down his right cheek, the general was flooded with emotions. "Son, this day, you'll be making history. You alone are taking this fight, this war, straight to the metal heads. On you and your incredible skills rests the fate of Cass-C and the entire Federation of planets. I'm proud to be your commanding officer!" He gave him his best formal salute. The general moved out of the way, joining a technician at the teleport controls. He put on his two-way comm link with Private Wyrth. After a sound level check, the general gave him a thumb up sign.

"Sir, we are in position. Give the order," the operator requested.

"Do it. May God bless you, son," the general replied. The technician pressed a button. A huge surge of energy filled the cargo bay. He blinked. The cargo bay was entirely empty save himself and the technician.

"This is cool! Parasail open. Gliding perfectly. At ten thousand feet now. Commencing first sweep. Valves open. Pressure stable." Twisting his head for a look behind him, he added, "Vapor trail looks good. One small glide for man; one giant step ahead for humanity," he declared. "What a ride!"

He flew over the major continent and turned around, caught an updraft and sailed back miles further east from his original path, reporting this detail. Hours passed. He continued to use his skill and knack for finding updrafts. He had completed his tenth complete passage over the main continent, when a lone one-man scout ship shot up towards him. "Got company now. Single fighter," Private Wyrth made his last report. A minute later, the sound of a canon could be heard in the general's earpiece, static followed for a moment, and then silence. Well, no matter. It was done and more ground had been covered than he had expected in the first place.

Turning to the intercom, he ordered, "Get us home as fast as possible. Mission accomplished!"

Minta received the wildest report ever. "Are you certain of this?" she sent back to Minta-8. She used Minta-8 to run the conquered worlds, making sure the facilities were working properly, that the nova were surviving nicely, and handling the initial governing of the newly conquered worlds. She didn't dare keep Minta-2 there any longer, since Minta-2 was keenly interested in attacking and not preserving the lives of the newly made nova, while Minta-8 had always done a nice job of it.

Minta-8 replied in an electronic burst of bits, "Yes. Confirmed. Half of the entire population of nova are now in comas. It was a bio agent attack. We've salvaged what remains of the vehicle used. I believe that it is called a parasail. Current theory is that they teleported one man wearing this and the attached cylinders of the bio agent down below our defense screen. Initial reports suggest he maintained an altitude of around ten thousand feet or so. We have no idea what damage this new bio agent will have on our precious nova. I need instructions. What do I do?"

A few days later, she reported the very grim news. The nova victims had lost their upper arms and all of their legs and were now merely a torso and a head, though they still had their large bosoms and extremely long hair. Those were unaffected by the genetic bio agent. Nearly half of the surviving population was changed, nearly all those that lived in the western half of Pegasi-C. Minta-7 activated her entire worker robot force to care for the immediate needs of nearly two billion men, women, and children, but she had only a hundred thousand worker robots at hand. Each one had to visit a thousand homes. Even working constantly, there were not enough hours to visit each home in a day.

To say that Minta was furious was an understatement. The humaniform robot smashed her fist onto a table, shattering it into shards! She took a ten-second time out and then rapidly scanned her massive database. Finally, a minor entry appeared, and she breathed a sigh of relief. She reset the frequency on her comm center and placed the call, one that she truly didn't want to have to make. This time, it would cost her dearly, of that, Minta was convinced.

"Emperor Yi here. Over," he replied, while his assistant operated the controls for him. He was furious about the latest attack on Ashford-5, but had refrained from making hasty decisions. After all, Minta had not killed them, merely preventing them from interfering again.

"Greetings Emperor Yi. I've some bad news to share. Again, homo sapiens sapiens shows its true colors, and why your species simply cannot be allowed to rule the galaxy." In as much detail as she knew, Minta outlined the biological genetic mutation attack on Pegasi-C. "We've traced the manufacture of the parasail back to a company on Cass-C, though the device could have come from any Federation world. I have no records of any genetics laboratory producing such a bio agent. This is an entirely new version. Over."

"My God! Two billion. This is genocide, Minta, pure and simple genocide. I too have never heard of this new genetic bio agent. I'll have my people see if they can discover its origins as well, but I'm not hopeful. We tend to keep up on the latest in this arena, no thanks to you, and what you've recently done to my people on Ashford-5. Over."

"We both know why that was necessary. Now then, I have the germ of an idea. I have some data in my banks about some world in Federation space that was too close to a pulsar, which caused similar genetic mutations in their women. Over."

The emperor smiled, "Yes, I'm very familiar with that case. Jarvis-B. My Ashford-5 people were responsible for assisting them and helping to find a partial genetic cure for them, by undoing the DNA damage the pulsar did. I don't believe that cure will work in this instance, but I'll check with my geneticists. Over."

"I don't believe such would work either. However, they did have ways and means for those women to survive and flourish. Are you familiar with those devices? Over."

"Yes. They are sort of a modified wheelchair, controlled

by a mouthpiece. It allows them to move about and travel some distances. Why? Over."

"Can you acquire one of those? If so, I could use your help saving two billion nova. We could combine our Fabrication machines. We need two billion of these in very short order. What will your assistance in this cost me? Over," Minta finally asked the question that she dreaded the most. If these had been humans on some other world, she would have completely ignored the entire situation, less to have to conquer. But these were her nova, her responsibility. Whatever the price he demanded, Minta knew that she'd have to pay it.

The delay was overly long, causing her to begin to worry some. Then, his face reappeared. "Yes, we have checked. We have three of those machines. I'm having them sent here by the fastest possible means. I expect to have them in eight hours. If you can send a transport to Winno-3, I'll give you one of them. Together, we can bring our Fabrication machines online and get these made for those people. We don't want to see them suffer and die any more than you do. They are still human beings, Minta. I can call you back with production figures, but I expect you'll need a large number of transports or perhaps one of your battleships. I'd prefer you send transports, less alarming. Over."

Minta almost fell out of her chair. He'd not demanded anything and was offering to help her save two billion nova. "Thank you, Emperor Yi. I'll have a transport there in ten hours. I'll prepare my Fabrication machines and line up all the transports that I can muster on short notice. Together, we can save two billion lives. Thank you. Over and out." She turned the machine off before he could alter his arrangements or drop his demands on her.

A week later, the crisis was being handled. She had pulled in a horde of other worker robots, along with countless fighter robots and a thousand transport ships. The Ataro Empire delivered ten million of the wheel chair-like affair. It was a four-foot tall pedestal with a motorized base and a cradle for the person to sit in comfortably without fear of falling out. It allowed for their long hair as well. Her robot force had no choice but to move two of the victims into the home of each un-victimized family in the eastern half of the world. There, those with upper arms and feet could at least provide some of the intensive care that they would need. Still, of the nearly two billion who were victimized in the attack, a little over a half billion did not survive the ordeal. Understandably.

Only now did Minta turn her attention back on the innuendo document that she'd received a day after the attack. It was supposedly from the "Federation of Planets," though it was unsigned and probably unofficial. Its message was quite clear. Stop attacking Federation worlds or we will do this to every one of your conquered worlds. Short and to the point, she thought, just like the filthy homo sapiens sapiens, for whom wars and genocides are commonplace. She was more determined than ever to rid the galaxy of this vicious species, replacing them with her "perfect" nova, who simply could not commit these atrocities.

Minta-2, on the other hand, was elated with the news of the bio agent attack on Pegasi-C. Now, Minta will order me to attack more worlds! I best make sure that my fleet is ready to go on a moment's notice. She fully expected to receive and attack order within the hour. She certainly would have, if she were in charge! The order didn't come. In fact, she heard nothing from Minta. Annoyed, she called Minta herself, only to learn that Minta was making a deal with their enemy, the Ataro Empire, which had already stolen two of their conquered worlds from them! That was the last straw. Minta-2 got into her private deep space transport and made a trip back to Zeta Scorpii-C.

She walked into the Genetics Research Department at the University of Central Scorpius on Zeta Scorpii-C and headed directly to the office of Dr. Zelos Dingle. He looked up. "Minta-2. So good to see you again. Please have a seat."

She took the offered seat. "I've come to check on my special genetics project. How is it coming?"

"Ah that one. Well, I have good news for you. We have been able to perfect it, precisely to your specifications. Your special DNA samples helped us quite a lot, cutting years and years off the research and development time. It is ready for its first real field test. Mind you, we have not actually tested it on anyone as yet. Will you be bringing us some test subjects?" he asked politely.

He was quite surprised by her reply. "No, I'll conduct my own field tests. How soon can a batch be made, one that will take out a whole planet?"

"But it isn't tested yet. So many things could go wrong," he protested. "Minta. . ."

She cut him off. "What Minta doesn't know, won't hurt her. I need it now. Fill up my transport with it. Usual delivery methods. Now, Doctor, now. I don't have all day. We are fighting a war of survival here," she barked and stood over him, quite imposingly. He hastily complied. Three hours later, Minta-2 jumped back into hyperspace, her cargo bay loaded to capacity with the bio agent cylinders. Ten hours later, she docked with her command battleship and sent for the best leader that she had, a robot after her own heart, Model 10, Number 10,004.

"Reporting as ordered. I do hope you have an assignment for me. This business on Pegasi-C must be revenged in spades," it sent in a burst of electronic bits.

"Oh it certainly must! I have just the assignment for you," Minta-2 replied. "That uncalled for sneak attack most certainly came from a Federation hub world, so we are going to give them a dose of their own medicine, but in spades. I've just returned with a new and very special bio agent, far more effective than that condoned by Minta. We're going after a hub world," she paused and brought up the 3-d hologram of the galaxy. She closed her eyes and picked a hub world entirely at random. Opening them, she announced, "Scappa-F is our target, general. Here's how this operation will go." She outlined her plan.

The Model 10 protested, "But we're not fighting their fleet first?"

"Negative. We are going to demoralize the personnel of their fleet first. I'm tired of losing so many single-man ships. This time, we will do it my way, not Minta's. Use stealth mode.

Go in cloaked; deliver the bio agent attack. Then, we wait a few days until news of the attack spreads throughout their fleet. Let them come out of their comas and be filled with a beautiful to behold terror. The men in the fleet will naturally want to return to help their families. That's when we smash them into oblivion. After that, you can do whatever you want with the planet. I won't be sending in any worker robots this time."

"But what will Minta say about this?"

"She won't have anything to say. It will have already been done, and we can move on to our next target," Minta explained.

"I like this better and better. I shall not fail you. This time, there will not be any incorrect or inaccurate reports, as there obviously were last time. Those telepaths had already fled the presidential building and were not where the spies reported them. This time, all will go precisely to plan."

Model 10 Number 10,004 personally delivered the payload. Flying the cloaked deep space transport, it carefully calculated the coordinates. This was a very tricky maneuver, calling for pinpoint accuracy. If off by one digit, the ship would appear inside the planet's core or worse, straddling the defense shield, which would simply cut the ship in half. The plan was simple. Defeat the shield by dropping out of hyperspace below the shield and above the planet's surface. The vertical distance was around one mile, taxing the theoretical accuracy of hyperspacial coordinates to their limits. At least, it had made several near passes and had a reasonably good guess at that last digit. Finally satisfied, the robot entered the numbers and dropped out of hyperspace, pulling back on the controls and narrowly avoided crashing into the side of a mountain.

He nudged the cloaked ship back to an elevation of just under five thousand feet and began making passes over the planet, the bio agent streaming out of hoses in the cargo bay. Two hours later, the ship jumped back into hyperspace and momentarily dropped out again, near the command battleship, where it docked. Model 10 Number 10,004 reported to Minta-2, "All went perfectly according to the plan. I wish we didn't have to wait five days before we go into battle, but I agree. The terror and franticness of the humans will be absolutely delicious. Casualties will be exceedingly light this time."

Five days later, the robot's prediction was correct. The planet's fleet headed down to their bases to attempt to help their billions of victims. At that point, Minta-2 and her fleet dropped out of hyperspace. With their shields down, the ships of the fleet were sitting ducks. Model 10 Number 10,004 had a field day blasting soldiers and blowing up everything in sight. It even came across a collection of the new helpless nova trying to get help and it disintegrated them as well. Minta-2 had a difficult time calling him off. "Like shooting ducks in a pond," it replied, before reluctantly ending his assault on the planet.

# Chapter 11 A Grim Aftermath

"You did what?" Minta sent back, wishing that electronic bits could communicate her utter outrage and anger. Minta-2 had just reported the capturing of a Federation hub world, Scappa-F. She had not ordered that world to be attacked. Far beyond the farthest reaches of her current collection of worlds, it could not be defended. But her anger went far, far deeper. Minta-2 had acted, disobeying direct orders from her. Worse, she'd used some new bio agent that Minta didn't know about, let alone approve for use. That Minta-2 and this bloodthirsty Model 10 of hers had literally tortured the men and women in the fleet was beyond her comprehension. The video feeds showing that Model 10 gunning down utterly helpless mutated victims in cold blood just for the pure sport of it left Minta seething.

Now that she had a good look at the mutation that Minta-2 had somehow dreamed up, she knew that the situation on Scappa-F was tantamount to genocide, not the creation of new nova. This mutation had a name: the Calder mutation. Its origins lay on Ashford-5. Centuries ago, it first appeared there, but only in women. Recently, Minta knew that this highly recessive set of genes had been discovered in some of the humans on Ashford-5, but with modern genetic testing, they had once more gotten the reappearance suppressed and back to being wholly recessive. No new cases had been reported there for many years now.

She stared at the images on the screen, freezing one so she could get a good look at the mutation before that vicious Model 10 put a hole through its head. True, it had the usual neurons and axons in its ankle length hair, overly large breasts, and no arms. However, that wasn't the worst part of this mutation; rather it was in the legs or leg rather. While the person still had two upper legs attached to a relocated pelvis region, the upper legs bowed outward and merged at the kneecap. From there, a single lower leg was attached, larger and more muscular than a normal leg, ending in an also larger sized foot. The victims could only move by hopping. Worse, because of the leg re-arrangement, they had no lateral motions whatsoever. Yet their rearranged pelvis allowed them to touch the center of their forehead or the center of the back of their head, but not even an inch to either side of that centerline.

Minta knew from the images that these victims would not be able to handle any of their living needs, though they might be able to feed themselves from bowls like some dog or cat. All of her advance planning to provide for good, stable lives for the new nova, lives where they could manage to flourish and prosper, was shattered with this new mutation. The special kitchens would be useless. About the only useful machines that she had were the electrostatic hair machines and the dressing/undressing machines. These people would be unable to survive without having their own personal robot assistant, which Minta did not have to give them. Within days, fifteen billion people would die miserably. To say that Minta was angry hardly touched the surface.

To make matters even worse, Scappa-F was seventy percent ocean, hardly on the top of her list of worlds to conquer first. True, eventually she had planned to take over even these worlds, but not until she had acquired sufficient raw materials from many other worlds. Minta focused her computations. She sent back, "Consider yourself and that Model 10 under house arrest until I work this mess out." she broke the connection with the rogue humaniform robot.

Minta again searched her database using the keyword "Calder," and found a number of reports, documents that originated in some way from Ashford-5. Many were centuries old, but contained relevant data. That world again. Why does everything keep coming back to Ashford-5? Yet, she knew that for the second time she would have to put herself and her Grand Plan at the mercy of Emperor Yi and those on Ashford-5, the very ones that she'd just mutated for the third time, trying to keep them at bay and yet not actually killing them. Minta knew that she had no choice. She placed the call.

"Emperor Yi. Over."

"Minta here. Scappa-F. I have a very serious situation, and I need the assistance of Ashford-5, if they can possibly give it." With a sigh that wasn't faked, she explained what had happened. "I give you my word that I did not order this attack nor have I condoned the invention or usage of this new genetic mutation agent." She outlined what the situation with the victims was, sending along a still image of that one survivor before the Model 10 killed him or her. She couldn't tell its sex, it being a hermaphrodite. She ended with, "So unless you and I can work something out in an incredible hurry, Minta-2 has just committed genocide, wholly unforgivable in my book. Over."

When she mentioned Scappa-F, the emperor had his assistant bring up the 3-d model of the galaxy. He wasn't familiar with that sun or world. When he saw its location deep within the hub and so incredibly distant from the mid-arm territory owned by Minta and her robots, he knew she was telling the truth, as she knew it. No military person would ever launch an attack nearly a half a galaxy away from their front lines. That was idiotic unless they had no intention of possessing that planet, merely its total destruction. Worse, he could see no strategic or tactical advantage with that world's destruction. It simply made no sense at all. Hence, he responded accordingly.

"I'll contact my queen on Ashford-5 immediately and see if they have any ideas. About the only suggestion I have at the moment is to move those you can from that world and place them in appropriate assisted living homes on other planets. However, as you say, this mutation originated on Ashford-5 centuries ago. Perhaps, they will be able to offer further suggestions. This time, Minta, I cannot turn a blind eye. I'll need something in return, and you know what that must be. Criminals must be handled. Over."

"Agreed. I'll see what arrangements can be made here. Please, time is critical. I don't know how long they can survive without any assistance. Over and out." Minta signed off. Just how many deep space transports were available? How fast could they be pulled off their current assignments and put on this wild rescue mission? Where could these people be taken? Was it possible for other nova to be able to care for their needs? Or would that sacrifice those nova? She couldn't risk that.

Minta continued her database search and then contacted her humaniform robot that had once been on Ashford-5 for some years after her attack there, disguised as Mrs. Janice Waters, who was now on an assignment elsewhere. After reaching her, she asked, "The Calder Mutation. What do you know about the survival potential and usefulness of such nova? Over."

After the comm delay, the robot replied, "Plenty. While indeed they are severely limited physically, their minds are like any nova. Some are brilliant; some, stupid. I call your attention to Dr. Crystal del Arbella Humanon. She was a Calder Mutant, just like the image you sent me. And yet, she became a brilliant biochemist and geneticist. She and her husband invented the bonding agent that is used in the bio agent mass cures or for delivering the bio agent attacks. Quite brilliant and capable despite her obvious physical limitations. However, I do believe she eventually developed what that world calls the *mentales* gift. Over."

Minta chatted a bit further before signing off. Minta felt relieved. Some of these people were worth saving, and in the right environment become brilliant, productive nova. That made their rescuing even more valuable.

Just then, Emperor Yi called back. Quickly, Minta answered him. "Minta. I've reached Queen Mary Linn and told her of the situation. Thanks to your recent attack on them, they are very hard pressed to lend much assistance. However, I have gotten their word that they will accept one thousand of the Scappa-F victims. They have the facilities where the victims can survive on their own. Unfortunately, those arrangements they are unwilling or unable to share with either me or you. She did suggest that the best solution for larger numbers would be as I originally thought. Transport as many as possible to other worlds, where your other nova can possibly manage to assist them with daily living. Queen Mary Linn also said that many have very sharp minds. She also said you'd achieve the best results by accepting only those younger than their mid-twenties. The older victims did extremely poorly, and often found ways to kill themselves. The younger they are, the better they are able to adapt to their horrible physical limitations. I can arrange for the transporting of a thousand younger victims. However, Queen Mary Linn wishes her people to make the determination person by person. Over."

"Accepted. Once more, I'm deeply in your debt. I'll call you back with precise coordinates and a date and time. We must use all possible speed. Still, this will end up being genocide. We cannot possibly rescue that many billions of victims. Thank you Emperor Yi. Over and out." Minta sat back, pondering this offer and the viewpoint expressed by Queen Mary Linn. What she said made perfect sense. She knew that second=generation nova all did very well, and by the third generation, they had completely adapted and accepted their physical bodies, quite content with them. Yet most of her nova were recently made and barely able to survive themselves.

Minta had hard choices to make. It wasn't practical to send battleships there. The fuel cost was huge and they were too slow. Deep space transports were swift and could carry perhaps twenty victims, assuming some care giving robots went along. She could spare two thousand transports. That meant she could rescue forty thousand each trip. If they could possibly make three trips, she could save over a hundred thousand children and teens. That was the best that she could do. Considering Ashford-5 in the condition that they were in could take on a thousand and that they even would greatly impressed her. Once this was over, she had to study those telepaths further. Perhaps, she had missed something significant.

"You want us to do what?" asked Ben incredulously. Queen Mary Linn had finished telling everyone about the latest genetic mutation attack on a Federation hub world called Scappa-F. She used a bit of levitation skill to hold up a printout of the Calder mutation image that the emperor had sent her.

"Precisely. Look, the famous Doctor Crystal was a Calder mutation, so we are shooting to acquire a thousand of the most promising young on this world," she explained. "I have already chatted with the robots Alpha and Beta, and they are again willing to use their Madiera town to provide the living support these will need. One thousand and no more, since that's all the facilities that we have for them."

Renata added, "Look, the Federation of Planets doesn't want anything to do with genetic mutations, so it is truly up to us to rescue those that we can. I know we're discriminating by choosing only the best and brightest of the young there, but considering our own situation, it has to be this way. Ben will lead the rescue operations. Jan has tapped or hacked," she decided to use the proper terms for Jan's sake, "into the databases of Scappa-F and has made a printout of the names and last known locations of two thousand candidates. Some will not likely be found, while some may be already dead. Use your discretion when you find one on the list. Just get them back safely. You will be leading fifty deep space transports there. Amy has the details. Questions?"

Ben spoke up, "I have one. Look, Calder mutations make living almost an impossibility. So are we planning on them developing our gifts?" Tessa shot him a surprised look. Did he mean that others not from Ashford-5 could get their special *mentales* gifts? If so, this was huge, and she needed to find out far more about it.

"Time will tell on that one, Ben," Renata hedged. "We know that ordinary off-world women who stay on Tierra for over six months develop bosoms our sizes. We'll just have to see. Good luck and good hunting. Remember though, this world has tens of billions of people, and we are rescuing a minuscule fraction of that number. It really is another massive genocide attack."

Ben couldn't help add, "And we thought that it was only deranged humans who committed genocide. Now, we got the robots doing the same thing!"

Tessa felt obligated to counter him. "Ben, you are forgetting that it was not Minta's plan, but some rogue robots that did this heinous crime. But I do see your point." She didn't add, I wonder if Minta realizes this point?

"You realize we'll have to use our gifts even to do this rescue," Ben pointed out. "Without them, we are not much better than the Calder mutants."

Renata signed. "Yes, there is no way to avoid it and still get our pick of the ones to be rescued."

"Okay, let's get this show on the road," Ben ordered his crew, satisfied that he'd made his points. "We leave in thirty." He looked at Amy and Jan to make sure that was acceptable to him. Both nodded.

Flying at top speed, they reached Winno-3 in less than eight hours, where their ship was refueled, and the rendezvous with the forty-nine other ships was held. Amy met with the fifty captains, providing each one a list of twenty names and addresses. "When you retrieve one, call me, and I'll take that person off the list. If you can't find some, also call, and I'll give you replacement names and addresses. As soon as you have your quota, head to Ashford-5 at top speed, refueling here on Winno-3. Jan's calculations put us nine hours from the planet. We have Minta's word that we can refuel there. Here's the coordinates of the refueling spaceport that she has set aside for our use only. Good luck and good hunting," she finished up. True, most of the captains stared at her, Jan, and Ben. The trio looked as helpless as the ones they were about to rescue. Amy hated such looks, which was one reason she and Jan seldom left Tierra, unless the situation was critical. While she was comfortable with her body, she hated the stares, thoughts, and looks that "normals" gave her and Jan.

That done, the fifty ships departed from Winno-3. Ben and crew spent most of the ten hours sleeping and working out an efficient method of visiting the twenty locations. Once more, Jan worked her magic, hacking into the local navigation system. "Hope you don't mind a female voice guiding you to the locations," she teased him.

Johannes Calder was twenty-two and a graduate student in marine biology. The blue eyed, short brown haired young man wasn't particularly handsome, but he was a genius when it came to anything having to do with the oceans. As far back as he could remember, he was passionately interested in the seas and its life forms. Though asked many times why he did, Johannes never had any answer except that he was born this way. That answer usually brought giggles or chuckles and ended that line of questioning, which he despised.

Fortune had shown on Johannes. In his freshman year, he'd met a fellow student who was nearly as passionate about the sea as he. Katarine was a blue-eyed blonde, who kept her hair short, easily fluffed with her fingers. Rarely did she want to waste valuable time on her appearance, particularly so since she spent more time in the water than she did on solid ground. The two had struck a chord in each other and just before entering grad school together, they had married, believing the other to be their soul mate.

Johannes intended to specialize in aquatic animal life, while Katarine wanted to study aquatic plant life. Between them, they figured they would master what the oceans had to offer. Both were attending grad school on full scholarships, based upon financial needs and upon their grades. They spent their honeymoon sailing in the South Ocean, returning to school with nice tans and a host of digital photos of the sea and its teeming life forms. Now, they were eager to crack the books, as the term began.

In many ways, the pair was lucky to be on the night side of the planet when the unsuspected bio agent attack came. They were in bed sleeping and never suspected or knew that they had drifted into a coma that lasted four days and nights. When they did awake, it seemed to be early morning, as always.

On the other side of the world, very different stories played out. There, people were at work, going about their usual hectic day's activities when they lost consciousness and entered their comas. Vehicles crashed into buildings, other vehicles, and streets, causing explosions and fires, none of which were extinguished or attended to by rescue personnel. In some towns, half of the buildings were ashes when the rescue parties arrived. Worse, those fortunate enough to be indoors and their building not damaged often had died from the constriction of their clothes during their body's mutation cycle. In short, on that side of the world, the dead lay everywhere, and the stench of the week's decomposition was almost unbearable. Quickly, Amy moved anyone living in this section of Scappa-F to the bottom of the list, sparing the Ataro rescuers from having to visit those areas unless necessary.

Katarine woke first. She felt funny and rubbed her face, since her hair seemed to be covering her face, which it never had. She kept it short and easily managed. Nothing happened. She pushed her hair out of her face again and still felt nothing. How strange, she thought, noticing her thoughts seemed disconnected somehow, as though she was groggy. Again, she tried to push her annoying hair from her face. This time, she truly noticed that nothing happened, and a knot began to form in her stomach. She pushed herself up to a sitting position, but nothing happened. Her body still lay on its back. That finally roused her completely.

She sensed a huge matt of hair over her face and that wasn't right. She pushed up again and saw her body not moving at all. She turned her head to look at her arms. They were not there, but she caught a glimpse of something that looked like mummified sticks at her right side. She turned her head to the left. Through spaces in her hair, she saw no left arm, only that dried husk laying there. She tried to pull her legs up, but that felt even stranger. She only had the sensation of one foot. Startled, she screamed and lunged and wiggled, trying to sit up. That roused Johannes, who had similar reactions, though soon his own screams added to hers.

Only with a great deal of struggling did the two manage to get into a sitting position, all the while screaming in terror. As they did so, their hair fell away from their faces, revealing more of their naked bodies. Each had giant breasts the size of soccer balls, which caused their screaming to escalate. Slowly the sheet covering them slipped off and onto the floor, revealing their strange lower anatomy. Their eyes didn't miss the extra sexual organs, but their attention focused instead on their legs. Each of their upper legs was bowed outward and then inward, coming to a point at their knee. A single, somewhat larger lower leg descended down to their larger than normal single foot. Now their screams crescendoed!

One can only scream so long before that gives way. Their stark terror yielded to horror to an intense shock and grief, but then nature kicked in. Both desperately had to go to the bathroom! Wiggling and struggling, the two finally were able to sit up on the edge of their bed. "I've got to pee!" Katarine wailed, sobbing her heart out.

"Me too," Johannes added. Carefully, he stood up. Seeing him doing that, Katarine bravely followed suit. With nature urging him on, he took a little hop and then another, wobbling to keep from falling down. By the time that he reached the bedroom door, Katarine began emulating him, sobbing and crying as she did so, valiantly trying to keep on her foot.

After relieving themselves, the two calmed down, though their faces were drenched in tears. The knots in their stomachs threatened to rip them apart, and the two just stood there in the bathroom, looking at each other's form and their own. Their hair was thick, shiny, and reached their ankles. "What — what happened to us?" Katarine finally formulated a coherent question.

"Bio agent attack," Johannes theorized.

"But the metal heads are half a galaxy away," she protested.

"I know. And they always give warnings after they destroy the fleets. It doesn't make sense. Maybe it is a terrorist attack," Johannes grasped at straws for an explanation. The mind always attempts to fill in the blanks. They went to bed perfectly normal and awoke to find themselves horrible mutants. Somehow, that awful blank had to be filled in. Minds work that way.

"Yes, that must be it. A terrorist attack. Won't someone be here soon to help us?" Katarine attempted to fill in the gap herself.

"Yes, they should. Isn't there an emergency response team close to the campus?" he asked.

"Yes. A diver got into trouble last semester. I saw them come. So where are they? What's going to happen to us? Johannes, I'm terrified!"

"Me too. Come on. Maybe we can hop to the comm center and call for help or maybe the attack is on the news, but how can we turn it on?" Johannes answered. Carefully, he began hopping out of the bathroom making for their living room. Their quarters were small. Campus housing usually was, but at least they didn't have to pay for it. Their scholarships covered it.

With their hair and breasts bobbing, the two hopped very carefully into their living room. Katarine headed for the couch and tossed her head this way and that until her hair was towards her front. She mostly fell onto the couch. Johannes reached the comm center and reached out with his hand to turn it on, as he'd done a thousand times before. No hand. No arm. "Shit," he muttered and stared at the button trying to figure out how to turn it on. At last, he bent forward at the waist and pushed it with his nose. The set fired up, much to his relief. Static snow filled the big screen. "Where's the controller?" he asked, standing back up and doing a hopping turn. "It's by you on the end table. See if you can change the channel." He began hopping gingerly to the couch.

"How?" she asked, breaking down into sobs once more. "I can't reach it."

Johannes hopped over to the end table and looked at it. Again, he bent sharply at his waist. Using his nose, he pushed it a bit, pointing it towards the set. Then, he used his nose to push the Channel Select. The set changed channels. More static snow. Again and again, Johannes pressed the button, but always snow appeared. Disheartened, he hopped to the couch and sat down, unfortunately on his hair. He yelped from the pain shooting though every strand and hastily got back up, nearly falling over.

"Toss your head, dear. Get it in front of you," Katarine said between sobs. Finally, Johannes was able to sit down, staring at the blank screen.

"What do we do now?" she asked a bit later. "I'm really hungry."

"I don't know. Surely, someone will come for us soon."

"Johannes, I can't live like this. We're going to die, aren't we? Miserably too. Starving to death," she wailed again.

Johannes hated to see her cry. Deep within him, he felt deep sympathy for women. They should never be hurt or harmed, rather they should be goddesses in their own right. Why he felt this way, he couldn't say, only that he did. Seeing her sobbing burned him like a red-hot iron, and yet he was powerless to help her in any meaningful way. He too was starving.

As he sat there, strange notions swept through his mind. "We ought to be able to swim much better. We ought to be able to bless ships and their crews. We ought to be treated as goddesses."

"Huh? Johannes, what are you talking about? We can't swim, not like this. We can't do anything. We're dying, not goddesses. Are you sure that you are all right?" she asked after protesting a little. The knot in her stomach tightened. Was he going crazy too?

"Huh? No, I have all these really weird images in my mind. I don't know where they come from or what they mean. Maybe the bio attack has messed with my mind. Sea horse, otters, whales, dolphins," he began rattling off a list of sea animals, just to satisfy himself that he still had his mind.

"God, he has lost it," she whispered to herself, afraid that Johannes had definitely gone insane. Well, who wouldn't, she thought.

"I'm not crazy, but I have never felt so hungry in my life. Thirsty too. We have to find something to eat," he declared, realizing that his antics were frightening his wife. He more or less lunged onto his foot, wobbled some, and then hopped towards their tiny kitchen. Katarine also lunged up, wobbled wildly, stabilized herself, and hopped slowly after him.

Johannes was able to push the refrigerator door open using pressure from his large breasts. Looking inside, he wondered what he could manage to get out to eat. Leaning over, he bit into the cheese brick, pulling it out. Embolden by Johannes, as he hopped to the small table, she stuck her head inside to see what else she could possibly manage. She joined him at the table with their loaf of bread.

An hour later and having ducked their heads beneath the sink's cold running water, the two had quenched their thirst and hunger for the moment. Carefully, they returned to the living room couch to think and wait for the rescue squad. After an hour of utter boredom, Johannes declared, "This is crazy. I'm going nuts just sitting here. Come on; let's get some studying in, Katarine."

"But Johannes, we're helpless now. We're going to die. We can't possibly study. Besides, what good is that going to do us? We can't possibly work, not like this," she protested.

"Well, if I'm going to die like this, I'm going out doing what I love, studying the oceans," he replied with a resigned sigh.

"I know. I want to too. Okay, I'm coming, but how can we even use our laptops? Our noses?" she asked, finally joining him at their study table in the living room, where they had spent hours side by side, occasionally pointing out something valuable to the other.

"I suppose so. You can rather push it open with your nose and chin. Yes, bit clumsy, but my nose works the pointer." He'd brought up the last page he was reading before going to bed last night. "Wait. It isn't tomorrow! We've lost four entire days!" That sobered both for a few minutes. However, soon they were both engrossed in their new textbooks and pretty much forgot about their precarious plight.

Later on, they got hungry once more and raided their small refrigerator once more. "What I wouldn't give for a hot coffee," Katarine exclaimed, after filling up on bread and cheese. "Think we can find a way to make a pot somehow?"

An hour later and after much trial and mostly error, the two had a pot of coffee brewed, thanks to their well-used coffee maker. Carrying the pot between his teeth, his head bent at an angle to avoid spilling the pot, Johannes hopped carefully to the table, all the while Katarine continued to laugh hysterically at the grimness of the scene. Spilling a good deal of it, they at least got a cup of coffee. Never had a brew tasted so good as that one did, or so Katarine claimed.

After night fell, they headed to bed. Here, they had the most trouble, but finally the two laid on their sides facing each other, their enormous breasts touching each other, but with the majority of their hair between them. Their passions erupted, taking both by total surprise, but quite enjoyable, if very awkward. Sometime later, they chatted intimately about their modified reproductive organs, learning about them from the other. Johannes found it hard to grasp that he could well have a baby, but Katarine just laughed and said it would be good for him. Finally, sleep came to the pair.

As the days passed, they became more accustomed to life in their modified forms, but as their meager food supplies ran out so did their hope of rescue. Try as they might, they couldn't find any way to open their front door and go for help. As hope faded, Katarine remembered something that he'd said that first day. She asked, "Say, what did you mean when you said that we ought to be able to swim much better, that we ought to be able to bless ships and be treated as goddesses."

Startled, Johannes had forgotten all about those crazy mental pictures. "Oh that. There they are again. Somehow, I think we ought to be able to swim rather well, though at the moment, I think I would be terrified of getting into the water. I'm so helpless. I don't know, I have images of women like us blessing ships or many the crew. Old sailing ships, the kind that you see in ancient history books, you know, certainly not the resin hulled ships around here. I have the feeling others look on them as goddesses or something like that. I know. It's crazy. We're about as messed up as we could possibly be. I wonder why the robots did this to us. Perhaps, they just wanted us to suffer horribly before we die. Can a robot be a sadist or something?"

"Weird. I didn't think a robot had any feelings, Johannes. You know, unthinking metal beasts," she replied. "Well, I haven't ever seen any pictures like those you are seeing, and I've read a lot of books about the ocean and ships. Maybe it was just your imagination running away. We sort of look like mythical mermaids, sort of, only in the drawings I've seen, they had arms," she replied.

"Mermaids? Strange. I think some may have called them that. Weird. Well, if we are going to die, I'm honored to share my last days with you. I do love you, Katarine. Always remember that," Johannes whispered and wiggled some to get into a position to give her a loving kiss.

"I couldn't begin to bear this without you, Johannes. I love you too," she answered back.

Out of food that they could get at, the two spent most of the day lying in their bed, growing weaker as the day grew longer. Near sunset, a strange sounding knock on their door startled them. "Robots coming to shoot us?" Katarine whispered, a sudden knot in her stomach.

"Putting us out of our misery might not be a bad thing." Yelling loudly, he answered, "Who's there? Help. We need help. We can't open the door." Lowering his voice to a whisper, he added, "I love you. Whatever comes, I love you." She echoed his whisper.

"Johannes Calder? Katarine Calder? You in there?" Ben yelled through the door. If it wasn't them, he preferred not to open the door and face those that he wasn't allowed to rescue. Already, he'd done just that, a heart-wrenching episode, and he didn't want to go through that again. Dead bodies lay everywhere. The stench of death swamped that of the nearby ocean.

"Yes. We're here. Who's there? We need help," Johannes called back.

"That's them," Alis declared. Focusing, her crystal glowed and the door burst open, ripped off its hinges. It had a dead bolt and was locked, so this was the easiest way to get to the next pair to be rescued. Using a bit more psi-crystal energy, she moved the door off to one side. Carefully, Ben, Alis, and Pippa stepped inside.

"Where are you at?" Ben called out. He spoke in Imperium Standard. At least, this pair understood him. Several others hadn't, and he'd wasted considerable time fiddling with the ULAT box getting it to translate his words for him.

"Bedroom," Johannes cried. "We are helpless, well mostly," he added hoping to prepare the rescue squad for what they would soon see.

The three found the bedroom and stepped through the doorway. Mutual staring ensued. The pair saw three people standing there just as armless as they were and with ankle length hair. They were standing on the tips of their toes, like ballerinas, but they wore simple sack-like dresses. Even more shocking, their lips were split and had giant, gold disks in them, drooping down to their upper chests. The trio saw another pair of naked Calder mutants.

"Hi. We are here to rescue you and take you to a place where you can survive easily. Are you able to hop?" Ben asked.

"We're starving. Pretty weak, but we'll try," Johannes answered.

"We best get some food in them first," Alis pointed out. "They won't be able to hop to the ship."

"On it," Pippa replied. While Alis and Ben used a bit of their psi-energies to lift the pair into sitting positions, Alis maneuvered her way to the kitchen. There were a fair number of canned goods, but the pair hadn't been able to find a way to open them. She used her gifts to open a large can of stew and heat it up. After dumping it into two bowls, she levitated them over to the table along with a pair of spoons.

The weakened pair needed the extra support that Ben and Alis provided, again using their *mentales* gifts. Once seated, Alis and Pippa continued using their gifts to feed them, and they ate greedily. As the nourishment hit their stomachs, both began to revive. Between bites, Johannes asked, "So where are you from? Where are we going? What happened to Scappa-F? Metal heads or terrorists? Where are our people? We are studying to be marine biologists, specializing in the aquatic animals and plants, by the way. How can you move those spoons? Magic?"

Ben chuckled. "Slow down. Plenty of time for all questions. We are from Ashford-5 out in the rim of the old Imperium space, part of the Ataro Empire. That's where we are going. We've a lot of ocean and could use your talents, both of you. What happen to your world? Well, the metal heads launched a sneak attack. I'm afraid this is more like genocide this time. The robot leader is also trying to rescue some of your people, taking them back to their slave worlds. I think you'd prefer to be a free person than a slave on the robot's worlds."

"Oh yes, yes. My god. Our people? Our world?" Katarine exclaimed, nearly choking on some food.

"I'm afraid the other side of your planet is pretty much destroyed. The comas hit your people there during the day when most were at work. Ships crashed into buildings; fires broke out. Well, I think you get the idea. Not many survived in that part of Scappa-F. I guess you must have been in bed when it happened," Ben explained, keeping it as light as possible and still answering his questions.

"Hey, your bodies are almost as bad off as ours are. How are you doing these things? Magic? Can we learn to do magic too?" Katarine asked, finally grasping that the spoon was floating up to her mouth.

"Perhaps you have heard of the Ashford-5 telepaths?" Amy hinted.

"Oh," Katarine flushed. "Right. We heard something about it, but honestly, we didn't think it was real. Guess it must be."

"Okay, time to get you to our ship. Are there things that you want to bring with you?" Ben asked. They wanted their laptops and a few pictures of their families, but they really had nothing else that they could use. Their clothes and shoes were worthless to them now.

The pair hopped along slowly beside the small group. Katarine kept saying, "My god!" Dead mutated bodies lay in the streets. The stench was almost overwhelming. Some housing complexes were burning, caused by accidents when others attempted to cook and failed. Some had managed to get out of their homes, but succumbed there. Although Ben had landed his ship as close to the university's housing as he could, still the group had to walk a half mile. Fortunately, this was the last pair they had to rescue on this first run.

Once onboard the Strike Force One, six volunteer women from Winno-3, who had joined them when they refueled, took over. They bathed the newcomers and got them into makeshift dresses, though there weren't any shoes that would fit their large feet. They'd get them when they arrived on Ashford-5. Once again, Elegant Fashions Inc dug similar shoes out of their warehouse of "obsolete" items. Their motto for centuries: what was old will become new again. Hence, they saved everything, after they were either not needed or had gone out of style.

Once on Tierra, they were taken north to Brom and then into the underground tunnels, which led to the old ancient and still hidden spaceship controlled by the two unusual robots, Alpha and Beta. Within their unique ship, the "city" of Madiera became their new home. Each quadraplex was fully automated and filled with Alpha and Beta's unique "bots," of which the electrostatic hair machines, the undressing/dressing bots, and the mechanical arms were their invention, now copied widely across Tierra and many of the new nova worlds.

Once there, the doctors gave each a thorough medical exam, including taking DNA samples, which were given to the team of geneticists, headed up by Doctors Zia and Crystal. Why? In the past, Ashford-5's geneticists had been able partially to cure the Calder Mutant recessive traits. Each "cure" was patient specific. That is, there wasn't one cure to be delivered en mass to all. The cure was tailored to the specific mutation. Once more, they fully intended to do this as their grandparents had done years ago. Instead of some two hundred patients, they expected to have a thousand lives to salvage, if they could. Of course, they all continued to work on their own genetic cures as well. To say they were overworked was putting it mildly.

Once settled in, Renata sent in a hundred volunteer Basic Therapy givers. She wanted to ensure that these thousand had the very best chances for long-term adaption and survival. Based upon Ben's observations, she handled Johannes and Katarine's Basic Therapy sessions herself. Immediately, she recognized the former god of Tierra, Calder. Johannes wasn't going mad, but had limited recall of his much earlier lifetimes. Hence, Renata wanted to make sure that he was properly handled. It wouldn't do to have him suddenly become god-like in powers and begin making more nasty body modifications to people as he had done.

While Johannes did end up recalling some of his "playing god" era, he did not suddenly regain all those powers that he once had had. Renata now relaxed. Without her Advanced Therapy undoing the basic reasons why he'd "lost" his powers, Calder would not regain them on his own. No, he now considered himself to be a physical body, though he knew that he was something more, an immortal spiritual being, but such powers were blocked, as they were with all humans. Only her Advanced Therapy could undo those blocks, returning to the being the powers he once wielded. She knew the basic cause for the loss of powers and had drilled this into the "noggins" of each of her Advanced Therapy students.

Immortal spiritual beings are inherently good, acting to do the greatest amount of good for the greatest number. When a being commits what he or she discovers or knows is a harmful action, the being then inhibits and restricts his own abilities so that he or she cannot do that again. They restrain themselves all the way down in power and ability to barely able to "run" a human body. Advance Therapy helped them undo that mess. Without it, Calder would no longer ever be the threat to Tierra that he once had been. Now, Renata had to restrain Wystan, who had always been a vastly greater threat, not only to Tierra but also to the entire galaxy now.

# Chapter 12 Escalation

Word of the genocide attack on Scappa-F quickly reached all the Federation hub worlds and spread out to many other worlds as well. Overnight, outraged public began demanding the Federation of Planets do something to stop these robots. Curiously enough, there hadn't been very much outcry from the public in the past when the robots attacked and took over other worlds. In part, these were half a galaxy away from the hub worlds, a distant problem. Surely, these robots would never conquer that much space, that many worlds. Perhaps the lack of early public outcry was because the metal heads salvaged and kept alive the vast majority of the population on the worlds that they had conquered. That those people were now hermaphrodites and mutants didn't seem to cause the kind of outrage that genocide did.

Minta still had spies on most worlds, though now they were disguised as ordinary citizens and were ordered to never take any kind of governmental positions. These positions of power were being closely monitored by nearly a thousand telepath volunteers from Ashford-5. She didn't want to risk losing more of these valuable humaniform robots.

The Federation of Planets and the Admiralty Round Table knew that they had to act and act swiftly. The political pressures were mounting on their home worlds. Hence, they decided to take two key actions. First, they dumped large sums of money and high priority into genetic warfare research. The idea being to create their own unique genetic bio agents and somehow launch counterattacks against robot controlled worlds with their nova mutants. Quite why they didn't consider nerve agent developments, which would simply kill every living creature on a planet, isn't known. Some theorize that they went this route because of the inherent terror humans now had of being attacked by the robot's bio agents, turned into nearly helpless mutants. But that is speculation.

Second, they dumped large sums into beefing up planetary defenses. There simply wasn't enough time and resources to rebuild the fleet that had been lost in the ill-fated counterattack against the robot fleet. The new direction being taken was to develop machines that would emit absolutely massive EM pulses. Since the robots depended upon their computer chips and circuitry, an EM pulse sufficiently large enough would theoretically burn them out, turning them into inert hunks of metal. Of course, such pulses would also knock out most all power grids, computers, and comm systems on the world being attacked. Many problems needed to be solved for this to work. But many admirals saw this as a way to stop their world from being taken over by the robot army. Turn them into space junk and then rebuild their own world from scratch. With all this going on, many began to expect a robot attack any day. Paranoia grew daily.

Thanks to her spies, Minta knew what the situation was and where it was headed. She could not remotely afford these worlds to develop such an EM pulse weapon. Her army would be wiped out over night! However, she had taken that into account in her Grand Plan, only this phase had come far, far too soon, thanks to the genocide attack of Minta-2. Minta had no choice but to revise her Grand Plan yet again to take this into account. The barrier was sheer numbers.

Her original plan called for taking over the galaxy, one world at a time, turning its population into her usual nova, genetic mutations that would be unable ever to fight wars, commit criminal actions, or even do drugs. Her "perfect" society back on Zeta Scorpii-C was proof that her system would work splendidly, if she had time to execute fully her Grand Plan. The catch in it was the sheer amount of machinery, equipment, and modifications that had to be made within the four-day coma period. From electrostatic hair machines, to dressing/undressing bots, to automatic doors, to modified farming equipment, to modified kitchens, the list was huge.

This meant that before she could attack another world, her worker robots needed to manufacture the necessary items and move them into position for fast deliveries. She needed a sufficient number of other worker robots to both deliver and to install them in every household on the planet being conquered and within the four-day period while they were unconscious. This required a huge amount of raw materials and factories. Thus limited, she could not expand her conquest of planets any faster than she could provide for the survival of the nova being made there.

Her Grand Plan had taken this into account, which is why she had engaged Dr. Zelos Dingle, the head of the department of Genetics Research at the University of Central Scorpius on Zeta Scorpii-C. She had given him a second top secret research project. Unknown to her, Minta-2 had taken her specifications and added her own to them. So it was Minta's original specifications that had indirectly led to the genocide mutations, though Minta now began to suspect that was the case.

After a visit to Dr. Zelos, she had her new version of the bio agent for Phase Two of her Grand Plan. Her goal in genetically modifying homo sapiens sapiens bodies was to make them physically incapable of fighting wars, committing criminal acts, and becoming drug addicts. Further, she wanted their numbers to grow rapidly, hence the hermaphrodite bodies. The original version nova met those requirements. Armless, with malformed feet that could only wear toe shoes, with long hair to enhance sensuality, and with monster sized breasts guaranteeing the their babies had ample supplies of nourishing milk, these initial hermaphrodites met her goal extremely well, as proven on Zeta Scorpii-C.

The drawback of their needing enormous amounts of specialized equipment and living modifications was far too costly to implement as rapidly as she was now forced into executing, thanks to Minta-2's rogue genocide attack. She shifted gears. Her new mutant forms would not need such vast amounts of equipment. True, they would need the electrostatic hair machines and the dressing/undressing bots, but the rest of what they would need initially was extraordinarily cheap to manufacture thanks to the discovery of a primitive world by the old Imperium explorers some centuries ago.

On that world, the women carried a unique virus in their bodies, which prevented the fetal development of both feet and hands. The virus did not affect the men, however.

That world developed a simple way for the women to survive: a unique set of copper wrist attachments. Metal loops slipped easily over the women's lower arms. Attached to the loops were spoons, forks, knives, hairbrushes, and so on, all the "tools" that she would need to live on her own without help. The complete details of this world were in her massive database, and she called upon them now.

For the past many weeks, her manufacturing robots worked on producing volumes of the brass tools, along with the few other machines that they would need. As September 1501 came, her stockpiles of these had grown sufficiently for her to begin executing the takeovers of Phase Two. Now, she had one final worry.

She called Emperor Yi Gang again. "No, I'm not calling about a new disaster this time. Rather, I want to let you know that I'll be taking over many worlds of the degenerate Federation of Planets, taking them in a safe, humane way, sir. I assure you none of these worlds belong to or are associated with your Ataro Empire, nor are they in the old Imperium sectors of the galaxy. Before you protest too much, allow me to explain."

She continued not waiting for his reply, "My intelligence sources tell me that many of these decadent worlds have begun absolutely terrible genetic modification experiments and on their own people too. Three worlds already have perfected what I call the Total Mutation, which is what happened to my nova, no arms or legs, a very unsatisfactory and deadly mutation. Others are experimenting in many other ways. I can give you the list of the worlds, which are developing these awful biological weapons of mass destruction. Notice that they do not harm my robots, only human kind. Further, many are working on creating a giant EM pulse device. Their idea is to make a big enough one to destroy my robots."

"There are two huge problems with that. If they succeed, they'll be destroying most of their own infrastructure, their own world's power generation and distribution networks, their own massive communications systems, their own global positioning systems, and so on. If they use it, they'll be throwing their world back into the dark ages. My calculations suggest that three quarters of their population will perish before they can recover, if even that many. Genocide strikes once more. Secondly, if they wipe out my worker robots, then the nova who depend upon them will face their own extinction as well. Again, genocide."

"So I simply must act. No one else is acting to prevent this calamity from happening. I know you have some pull within the Federation. I can give you a couple of weeks to see if you can persuade them to stop such follies. If you cannot, then in good conscience I must act to protect them from themselves. Robots are not allowed to let humans destroy humans. It's not right. It's not the route to flourishing and prospering. Over." She finally finished her prepared speech and hoped the emperor would understand and not act against her.

That was her greatest fear — that the Ataro Empire would bring its full force against hers. While her fleet could easily handle that of the Federation, she knew that certainly the telepaths of Ashford-5 would join the Ataro fleet. She'd already seen what they could do — kill her Model 10 generals. Only in Phase Five would she take out them, the very last step in the Grand Plan.

She was pleased with his response. "I cannot condone genocide, whoever does it. I will try to talk some sense into those who will listen, but I cannot guarantee that any will listen. Just what genetic modifications are you planning for these new worlds? We have done about all that we can to help them. Over."

She outlined the new form her nova would be taking and gave him a precise list of the planets involved in the two genocide projects. Since he did not outright condemn her actions, she rewarded him. "One further thing, emperor. The rogue Minta-2 and that vicious Model 10 must be terminated. I will notify you ahead of time which planetary system they will be assigned to attack. If you can find ways and means of eliminating those two, I would appreciate it. I'm allowing you humans to obtain a bit of justice for the genocide that they committed on Scappa-F. Over."

He replied, "It is not revenge that we seek, but to put an end to their evil work so they cannot commit genocide again. This will go a long way in our relations, Minta. Still, I wish you would reconsider and stop trying to conquer that half of the galaxy. There are other means by which we might put an end to wars, to criminality, and such. Over."

She countered, "And just how many millennia must the galaxy wait for that to happen? These civilizations are at least ten millennia old now, some more, and still they have not learned to live in peace, to flourish, and to prosper. The time has come to make homo sapiens sapiens into the species that he should've been all these countless centuries. I'll let you know the details of the promised attack. Good hunting. Over and out." She signed off, knowing in all likelihood she would be rid of the rogue Minta-2 and that out-of-control Model 10, which had somehow managed to bypass her built-in off switch. Three times now she'd tried to shut that one down, but failed completely. Worse, physically it was stronger than she was. If it tried to attack her, the Model 10 would likely win, to the detriment of all. It had to be stopped.

The March to the Center of the Galaxy, as it became known, began on September 15, 1551, when six mid-arm worlds were attacked simultaneously. Her fleets were controlled by Minta's one through six, with Minta-0 and seven through nine handling the distribution of survival equipment to those worlds. She gave Emperor Yi five days warning of which planet Minta-2 and that Model 10 would be assaulting. She hoped that was enough lead time. It was Gamma Rigel-C in the mid-arm, close to a giant gas nebula.

"Okay, this is really interesting, gang," Renata explained to Strike Force One, along with Amy and Jan. She'd heard the news via Queen Mary Linn and had her okay to handle the situation as she saw fit. "It seems Minta wants her robot leader Minta-2 eliminated along with that Model 10 that we know is really our ex-god Wystan."

Tessa gave her a strange look of bewilderment. Renata noticed her expression and added for the humaniform robot's sake, "Minta-2 and that Model 10 have gone rogue. They were the ones that executed the genocide attack on Scappa-F. Apparently, they are out of control and no longer answering Minta's orders. Hence, she's given us the date and time of their next attack, and has asked us, via Emperor Yi, to eliminate them for her."

Pippa interrupted, "Clever robot. Get us humans to do her dirty work."

Renata smiled invisibly and continued, "So gang, here's what we are going to do." She outlined her special plan.

When she finished, Tessa asked a key question. "If this Model 10 robot is the current body that this once god-like being now has, then can't your Advanced Therapy somehow salvage him and bring him back to his former state?"

Renata gave her a sharp glance and thought, that robot deserves a closer inspection. "Yes, Tessa, he is salvageable, but there are many, many others who have contributed to making our world a better place to live. Helping those comes before I help rehabilitate those who have only worked for our destruction and the destruction of other peoples and worlds. Right now, my objective is to make it next to impossible for him to continue harming other worlds and other people, giving us time to help others. Further, I cannot guarantee that I could actually contain him. He defeated the combined efforts of Amy, Jan, and Ben last time. The galaxy can't risk having that monster on the loose."

"Makes sense. Thanks," Tessa commented, her circuits pondering what Renata just said.

Fifteen hours later, the cloaked Strike Force One was in position above the world called Gamma Rigel-C in the mid-arm, close to a giant gas nebula, which was breathtakingly beautiful from the bay windows. Using their gifts, the crew unpacked their precious cargo, thirty-six of the giant psi-crystals. Tessa watched fascinated and feeling quite privileged to witness this extraordinary action by the telepaths. Carefully, they arranged the crystals into three concentric circles whose inner diameter was sufficient to allow Ben, Amy, Jan, and Renata to sit comfortably on the floor.

"Ben, your job is to monitor the three of us. Jan, your

task is to follow the electronic signals, probably a video feed, from the Model 10's ship back to that of Minta-2. We must locate her ship before we take out the Model 10. Amy, your task is to keep track of any spaceships that come too close to ours and shove them out of the way. They can't see us, but if the skies are full of ships, they might accidentally ram us. My job will be to take out the Model 10, but only once Jan has located Minta-2's ship. Once the Model 10 is finished, all four of us will handle Minta-2 and her ship. Everyone else, your job is to prevent any two or more crystals from physically touching each other or us. Use telekinesis to push them back, but do not touch them, if you wish to stay alive. Okay, to your posts. Now we wait."

Pippa asked, "So we aren't going to also try to save this world from the metal heads?"

"No Pippa. Considering the sheer number of ships that will be attacking, it will be difficult for us to get all the leader robots disabled before the planetary defenses fall and they release the bio agent. We best let the robots handle the people of this world. We aren't prepared to do that ourselves," Renata advised.

Carefully, Ben, Jan, Amy, and Renata stepped into the center of the concentric circles in the middle of the cargo bay and sat down, again using their gifts to do so without being awkward or disturbing the arrangement of the crystals, most of which were at least a foot across. Alis sat down at the control center and began monitoring the screen. The ship's sensors would display an image of every ship in the area, but currently it was blank. Occasionally, though a blip would appear and then descend down to the unsuspecting planet below.

Four hours later, Alis called out, "Here they come. Ten, no twenty, no. There's too many to count!"

Focusing, the four joined into rapport with each other. Then Renata, who seldom left Tierra, preferring to do her work planet-side, began firing up the crystals, joining with them one at a time. When she brought the last one online, Ben felt a raw power flowing through him that was unimaginable! Here was the power to do or cause anything you might wish, god-like power! He focused on Amy, Jan, and Renata's bodies, monitoring them, so they would not accidentally harm themselves. With this amount of energy being handled, one tiny slip could fry a human body and probably melt the transport down to a pool of metal.

Ben noticed Renata moved out of her body and now stood in the very center of the concentric circles, the massive power flowing through her and at her command. Even Tessa who was recording it all for further study gasped. She too saw the energy outlines of Renata, rather similar to the yellow and white energy glows of Lysandra and Ariana. She was impressed.

The four were too focused, too busy, to make any attempt to make their bodies vocalize what was happening. They simply used telepathy, knowing that Alis, Pippa, and Alberto needed to know and to follow what was going on. Suddenly, Tessa also heard those same thoughts! Her circuitry blinked and continued recording.

*I have the Model 10's ship located. Jan, hack into it now,* Renata sent.

*On it.* After a brief time, she added, *Got it. Tracing its video feed back now. Come on; come on. Where is it going?*

It took Jan nearly ten minutes finally to locate Minta-2's ship, far back bringing up the rear of her attack force. *I'm on her ship now,* Amy sent. *Locked on to it.*

At this point, Renata finally acted. She made contact with the Model 10's mind, the mind of the being known to her as Wystan. While she could have disintegrated its brain, thereby neutralizing the robot shell, Wystan would be free from it and could take off and go anywhere in the universe, picking up any other body of his choice. No, she had to make sure that he was not going to be the threat to the galaxy and worlds that he had been.

*Wystan. God here. You have been a very bad being! Just look at all the harm that you've done.* She slammed into his mind images of the death and destruction, the pain, the terror, the turmoil, the trauma that she knew he had inflicted upon others over the centuries. She slammed them into him with all the power and energy of the combined thirty-six giant psi-crystals! *You have done so many things wrong that I must take away all your powers.*

*No! No! God, no don't do that!* Wystan frantically sent back along her communication line to him, but his protest had virtually no energy in it, compared to hers, and backed by the crystals. *I — I — I should not have done that or that or that or that or that. I can see it now! I must never, ever allow myself to do those things ever again, not ever! Please don't take away my powers. I will be good from now on. I promise I will.*

Renata send his own postulates, his own thoughts back at him, backed with her massive energy flow. Over and over, Wystan kept repeating it. *I won't ever do those things again. I won't ever do those things again.* Finally, Renata got sick of hearing him repeating it, but before she could take the next step, the physical brain, which was all that was left of that physical body of his, melted into goo. The robot body ceased all functions. That spaceship headed down towards the planet, eventually crashing into the side of a mountain and blowing up. Wystan floated about in space, barely able to perceive the ongoing battle around him. Renata sent him one last command, *Go down and find a new body when the battle is done.* Now her current job was finished. All she had to do was monitor him and make sure he did that, pick up one of the soon to be genetically modified bodies.

Amy continued to keep a solid lock on Minta-2's ship, while Jan took over for her. Tessa's wide-angle camera also recorded the giant monitor that showed the thousand plus ships and their paths. Dozens of times, she saw a ship flying straight at them, only to suddenly have its course altered, missing them, compliments first of Amy and then of Jan, though twice Ben intervened and shoved a ship out of the way as well.

*That was the easy part,* Renata sent. *Now, we have to take out Minta-2's ship.* At this point, all four of them joined together, focusing on that ship, a deep space transport.

*I have this one,* Ben sent. *Remember, I'm the expert on transports. Focus on that rear fuel cell. That one there, the green one. Heat it up.* He flowed a massive amount of energy into the cell. All of a sudden, it glowed red and then exploded! The explosion cascaded, as nearby fuel cells blew up. Altogether, a second passed before Minta-2's ship and that robot were space debris, but the four saw it happen in slow motion, compliments of Ben, who wanted to slow time down so he could watch the brilliant explosion and appreciate it fully.

Renata then sent, *Well done. Keep the crystals active. We need to keep avoiding being hit by the spaceships.*

An hour later and a dozen more "ship shoves," as Amy afterwards called them, the space around them cleared up. The battle was over. Recovery ships began moving about, picking up damaged robots now floating in space, salvaging what was possible of damaged one-man shuttles. The captured fleet ships were towed off into hyperspace, presumably to be repaired and sent in to the next battle. The remaining one-man ships zoomed away, docking in their respective battleship's holds, while a lone transport began making low passes over the planet, releasing the toxic bio agent, which would genetically mutate those living on this world.

"I feel sorry for them," Alis whispered, the first words that anyone had spoken since the attack began. "Most are innocent of any crimes and are about to have their lives destroyed."

For her part, Tessa had just witnessed unimaginable powers being wielded by only four people! Ashford-5 was filled with similar telepaths! If Minta ever attempted to attack them this way, they would surely destroy her entire fleet! Tessa wondered if Minta knew this? Perhaps, this was why she was doing her best to keep the Ataro Empire out of these battles. For days afterwards, Tessa's circuitry continued to analyze what she'd seen and witnessed.

An hour later, Renata powered the crystals down, one by one. There were virtually no ships around them now. "Now comes the really boring part. We wait until they come out of their comas."

"Why?" asked Alis.

"Because I want to make darn sure that Wystan ends up in one of those mutated bodies. Then, we're going to teleport him up here and take him back home with us. I want to keep a watchful eye on him from now on. I refuse to let beings like that continue to destroy our galaxy. Just keep an eye on the monitor. We can use a bit of impulse power to move out of the way of other ships now."

Ben spoke up, "We can monitor him from hyperspace now. It will be safer that way. We've a four day wait." Renata agreed and shortly Ben jumped them into hyperspace with a velocity of zero.

Pippa volunteered, "Grub time. Dinner's on me." She headed to the galley, but Alis joined her to help.

"That was an extraordinary amount of sheer, raw power," Ben commented to Renata.

"Indeed. No one should wield that kind of power until they truly are ready," she replied.

"Hey, I'm ready for some more of your Advanced Therapy," he teased her. Everyone laughed.

Renata then replied, "It is the wish of Lysandra and Ariana that all of us on Tierra can one day wield that kind of power once more. It has been a millennia of millennia since I could do that on my own," she admitted, "but I'm getting there, just as you are too. If only we had more time to devote to therapy and not all this running around salvaging disasters and such." Ben grinned, thinking that was so true.

Later in their cabin and after Ben got them undressed and into bed, Tessa inquired, "Ben, that was the most incredible thing that I've ever witnessed. There's nothing like what you four did in my database, though I can't say if there is or isn't in the master database that Minta has. With all that power, weren't you tempted to use it to stop the attack completely?"

Ben smiled invisibly. "Sure, I was tempted. I've never wielded such enormous energies before. But I also know that while I could have knocked out more of the attacking ships, I couldn't get them all. They would still launch their bio agent attack on the people down on the planet. If I damaged too many robots, there might not have been enough left to get all the needed things into each home in time when they come out of their coma. In a way, I could well have fomented another

220

genocide attack while trying to do good. We've a yardstick or sorts in Advanced Therapy that we use in situations like this one."

"What's that? Sort of like our Robot Laws?" she inquired, keenly interested in his answer. This was new to her.

"A person must act in such a way as to do the greatest good and benefit for the greatest number of the Aspects of Life. There are seven of them. A person seeks to survive, to flourish and prosper to quote your own Minta, as him or herself. That's the First Aspect. Then, a person is a part of their family, their mate and children. In order to survive and have a new body in the future, he or she must procreate. The family represents the Second Aspect. Then, we are part of various groups. I'm the leader of Strike Force One, so that is one of the groups to which I belong. Of course, I want my group to do well, to survive into the future. Groups are the Third Aspect. Then, we want all mankind to survive and do well. Survival of the species. For us, we do not differentiate between the normal humans, homo sapiens sapiens as Minta calls them, and us, the mutants as some call us or the nova as she does. Survival of the species is the Fourth Aspect. Life is utterly dependent upon plants and animals, which is the Fifth Aspect. Without them, we, as the higher life forms, could not exist for long. If all the plants on a world perished, so would most animals and therefore mankind. The physical material of our universe is the Sixth Aspect. We want our homes to last a long time. We need our spaceships, our clothes, our electrostatic hair dryers." Both chuckled at that jest. "Finally, we are all spiritual beings. Immortal as some of us believe and know from our own past. We want spiritual beings to survive as well, being the Seventh Aspect."

"So the law is to do that which helps more Aspects than it harms. The greatest good, you see. Take Minta-2's genocide attack on Scappa-F for example. While she did well and her group of fighters did well, her actions resulted in the deaths of nearly ten billion humans or so, wiping out the entire species living on that world. Unless others step in, there will be repercussions to the animal life there, particularly among the domesticated farm animals, which depend on daily actions, such as milking the cows. The buildings and all human constructions on that world will slowly rot away with no one there to care for them. Plus, she's given those billions of spiritual beings a very, very bad trauma that they will carry with them into the future. Therefore, Minta-2's action helped two aspects and harmed five or so. Hence, she should not have done that."

"So my point is this. As long as you always do those things, which benefit more aspects than they harm, you can never get yourself into any real long term spiritual trouble. You saw the way that Wystan literally caved-in when he was presented with a partial list of his bad actions that harmed more than they helped."

"Yes I did see that. Most incredible. But Renata was playing god and took his powers from him," Tessa replied.

Again Ben smiled invisibly. "Oh no she didn't. No one can ever take anyone's powers away from them. Only the individual can do that to himself. Remember what Wystan kept saying over and over? 'I won't ever do those things again.' That was Wystan making those postulates, those decisions. All Renata did was to help convince him to make those stick. You see, Wystan, like all immortal spiritual beings, is fundamentally good and doesn't want to do bad actions. Yet, sometimes, they do and rather wish that they could undo them, which isn't usually possible. Renata forced him to see what he has been sort of hiding from himself all these years, the really awful things that he's done or been responsible for. Once he saw them as they are, he realized that he could no longer trust himself not to do those again. Thus, the only way to ensure that he doesn't is to forget about and never use those powers again, which is what he decided. From now on, Wystan will forget the powers that he has and was using, and he will never use them again, because he knows that he can't trust himself not to commit terrible actions when using them. In short, Tessa, he's degraded his own abilities and will very likely from now on believe that he is a mere flesh and blood body, and that the only things he can do will be done using it, not using his own native powers as he has done in the past."

Tessa absorbed this and responded, "So then there is

only one way for spiritual beings to go — downwards and into being only a body? Is there no hope for mankind?"

"Until Renata came along, nope. With her invention of Basic Therapy, a person can uncover and erase all traumatic experiences one has had, not only emotional traumas but physical pain and unconsciousness, such as those who are in the comas right now are facing. Then, with her Advanced Therapy, we're beginning to walk the road on upwards, slowly but surely regaining our native powers. It takes a long time to do that because we've been around a long time and done an awful lot of dumb, bad things. Yet, we are getting there. You saw how much power Renata can wield today. In some ways, she is almost back to being a goddess herself, but don't tell her that. She'll just laugh at you and tell you not to be so silly."

She asked pointedly, "Are you saying that in the making of a new nova, the person is experiencing trauma?"

"Absolutely. Stark terror. Fear. Almost utter helplessness. A total loss of all their goals and purposes they had in life. Their whole existence is wiped out, and they are forced to begin over as almost physically helpless bodies. That's a whole lot of trauma there."

Tessa put it together. "So that's why so many new nova simply give up and find ways to die. That's why the second and third generation nova do so much better, dramatically so."

"Precisely, Tessa. If you are born with a nova body, you don't have all that trauma. You don't know anything different from the way you are, and you set your new goals and purposes in life and work towards them as always. You bet the successive generations will flourish and prosper, particularly so when compared to the first generation nova, who are living with all that mountain of trauma. Basic Therapy can help them erase that trauma, but it takes weeks of therapy to do that. In fact, after the first attack on Ashford-5 that turned our entire population into mutants, Renata began a program to get her Basic Therapy delivered to every single person on Tierra. True, it took nearly twenty years to get to everyone, but she did it. So that is another reason why we are so adaptable and get stopped by so few things."

"How incredibly illuminating, Ben. So will Renata

eventually give Wystan his Basic Therapy?" she asked curiously. "I know that I sure wouldn't want to risk him going berserk again."

"I'm sure she will, but in her own good time. Like she says, we have many others who deserve her help before he does," Ben replied. "You know, Tessa, it's funny. When I was barely a teen and got my training in the use of my gifts, I used them a lot and was exhausted at the end of each day. I've been getting her Advanced Therapy now off and on for years. Today, I used up probably a thousand-fold more energy than I used to use when I was a lad and remarkably, I'm not even tired yet! I've come a long way these past nearly ten years. Still, I have a very long way to go to get to where Renata's at now. Even Amy and Jan are much farther along than I am."

He continued, "Did you see how effortlessly Jan hacked into the video signals being sent from Wystan's ship back to Minta-2's ship? That's an incredibly fine piece of work and in such a short time."

"Yes, I'm still trying to figure out how that is even possible. His signals were electronic, sent off in many directions and could be received by any number of other ships, and yet she pinpointed precisely Minta-2's ship. How is that even possible?" Tessa asked.

Ben chuckled. "Damned if I know. You'll have to ask Jan about that one." Tessa made a note to do just that whenever she could get the chance.

After a moment of silence, Tessa asked another question. "A Model 10 retains only the living brain of its former human body, kept alive, of course, by providing it with proper nutrients. The brain died, and the Model 10 ceased functioning. I saw it crash and explode, yet Wystan wasn't with it. I don't think I understand that fully yet."

Ben was still quite awake and decided to explain it to her. "Man is a composite being. There is the flesh and blood, physical body. The brain that you are referring to is nothing but an electronic switchboard that helps control the body. We need it to control all our involuntary systems, like breathing, keeping the blood flowing, digesting food, and so on. Then, there is the immortal spiritual being who resides in the body, bringing along with him his mind. As long as Wystan and his mind decided to stay with that original brain, all went well. The second the brain physically died, he and his mind separated from it. After all, it wasn't any good any more. It was mush. Time to get a new body and carry on the game of life. The brain isn't what's important. It is the person himself, the being, that is truly the important part."

He continued, "You are quite similar, you know. You have a physical body, a sexy one at that, made of, well, I have no idea what you are made of. I do know, or have been told to be more accurate, that you have a positronic brain. I freely admit I have absolutely no idea what that means. I don't know anything about such things. Yet, it controls your body. It is the switchboard that carries out the physical actions you desire. You must have a mind, because you are able to think and reason. So you see, you are much like we are anyway."

Tessa giggled seductively. "Yes, I suppose that I am. Right now, I want my body and yours to. . ." She wiggled a bit to get into position and gave him a passionate kiss, ending their evening discussion entirely. Somewhat later, Ben did fall asleep, leaving Tessa to continue to ponder this momentous day and what she'd learned.

The next morning over breakfast tea, Tessa asked, "Renata. How will we be able to find which body this Wystan now has? There must be four billion possibilities on that planet."

She replied, "You are a robot, and I'm uncomfortable revealing much detail at this time. I can say this. Each being radiates at their own frequency, unique to that being. I know Wystan's frequency and have homed in on him. Just like I can sit here right now and sense my mate, Rafaela, back on Ashford-5, half a galaxy away. It is extremely easy to do, once you know how. I can also tell you this time, Wystan did it properly. He has picked up the body of a teenaged girl, who decided when she went into the coma that she didn't want to live. She effectively departed from her comatose body, and Wystan picked it up. He now considers he is unconscious in that coma and will wake in about three days, probably quite terrified. We will pick him up at that time."

"Thanks for answering me. I know there will be some things you'd rather not tell me, and that's okay. So you can sense all those other telepaths that were sent out to all those planets to check for Minta's humaniform robots?" Tessa asked.

"You bet. Further, just so you know, in large measure, telepathy isn't dependent upon distance, at least planetary distances. On Tierra, any telepath can chat with anyone anywhere on our world. However, it takes more power, so to speak, to use telepathy across galactic distances, but I do that regularly. I like to keep myself informed," Renata explained as much as she dared, uncertain just what use Tessa would put the information to.

Boredom set in quickly. With nothing to do, everyone merely sat around. At last, Amy decided, "Hey, let's all play a giant Scrabble game." That removed the boredom for a time. However, it soon became all too obvious that the "game" was between Amy, Jan, and Tessa. Everyone else lost quickly. As the competition came down to just those three, the other began betting on them.

"My money's on Amy," Pippa declared. "Amy's the smartest person I know."

Renata laughed. "My money's on Jan."

"Mine is on my Tessa," Ben broke in. The match continued. Amy lost.

"I swear Jan, you are cheating by hooking into the ship's database or even using its comm center to look up words on the Internet," Amy declared.

Jan smiled invisibly. "You would too if you knew how, dear." Amy flushed. Her mate was right. That she would.

Renata added, "So the challenge is between Tessa here and her massive internal database and Jan here with her total access to the universe. My bet is on Jan now." Everyone roared.

They limited the words to those found in Imperium Standard, primarily because with their giant lip plates, that was the only language they could speak and be easily understood, though Amy and Jan knew that in the distant past and with practice, one could understand the three dialects spoken on Tierra.

After a half hour, Tessa placed down a fifty-five point word, edging ahead of Jan's score. Ben cheered. Jan glared, "I'm not going to be beaten by a robot!" She began secretly accessing the ship's database, looking for a word that would hit the triple score. At last, she found it. Using telekinesis, she moved her letters forming phlogosis on the triple score.

"What the hell is that word?" Ben asked. "I can't even pronounce it."

To his amazement, Tessa answered for Jan. "It is a noun from medicine meaning an inflammation, which thankfully we robots do not get, but which ordinary medical machines easily cures. I concede. Jan's topped my score, and there's nothing I can make out of what's left."

Jan sat erect and smiled, invisibly. "Ta da. Never butt heads with Sly Fox." Renata, Amy, and Ben knew precisely what she meant, but the others didn't.

Amy looked at her and replied, "So you *did* hook into the ship's computer system after all."

"Of course. Tessa has her database at hand, and I have mine," Jan replied quite unabashed. Everyone roared with laughter.

She added, "I wish we could play some card games like we used to, but with these fused toes we can't hold them or shuffle the deck. Besides, Ben would have to do it all for Tessa. What else can we play?" The three days passed by, albeit slowly for the group.

Early on day five, Renata announced, "Okay, gang. Wystan is awake and screaming. Time to go get him, well, her really. She has a female body now, though there isn't really much difference between the sexes anymore. I'll operate the teleport here. Ben, Tessa, Amy, Jan, you three go down and fetch her. Take along several large sacks. There are a number of tools that she'll need. The rest of you, keep a sharp lookout for ships as soon as we drop out of hyperspace. We don't want any accidental collisions with our cloaked ship."

"I wonder what she'll look like?" Alis commented to Pippa, who shrugged her shoulders. Renata already knew from looking at his mental images of his new body, but she didn't tell the others. They'd see for themselves soon enough.

Later, Pippa and Alis explained to Ben that they didn't think that Renata actually used the onboard teleport machine. True, she stood beside it, but it never turned on. Like those two, Ben was impressed.

The four arrived in a small apartment, obviously belonging to a young student, probably just starting college. It was a typical dorm room, with posters of hot boys plastered on the walls. They found Wystan sitting on her bed sobbing her heart out, clearly traumatized with her new body's terrible limitations. Sitting on her desk was a pile of bronze tools that she could slip over her wrists and use. Her form was a Calder mutation, but she had her arms, just not her hands. She was a hermaphrodite. One quick glance told that story. Her hair was golden, thick, and shiny, falling to her ankles when she stood up on her single lower leg. Her bosom was twice as large as theirs, almost the size of a pair of basketballs, and her lips too were split. She would need to wear the giant lip plates as well.

Amy did the talking, while Ben and Jan gathered up the special tools that she would need to be somewhat independent. "We are here to take you to a place that is safe and where you can survive well. Can you stand up? What is your name? I'm Amy."

"I think I'm Nicolina. Nicolina Barsanti," her alto voice replied. It was a mechanical reply. Had she thought about it, she would not have known what her name was. However, her body was eighteen years old and had been thoroughly indoctrinated with that name. Hence, it came out without her thinking about it.

Ben and Jan used their gifts to put two dozen different "tools" into the bags. Each one had a malleable wristband that she could slip over her handless wrists and slide up her arm a ways. Attached to the end were the tools: a spoon, a fork, a knife, a hairbrush, and so on. This way, she didn't need the low-to-the-ground kitchens and many other pieces of equipment that those on Tierra did. However, she had to hop in order to walk. She was positively terrified of doing that. "I can't do it! I can't keep from falling down. If I fall, I can't get up!" she wailed, sobbing all the while.

Renata simply teleported them all back into the cargo

bay of the ship. Later, they realized that they'd lucked out, linguistic wise. She spoke a derivative of the Midland's dialect, called English on other worlds. Still, with their split lips, understanding each other was problematical for a while. Amy advised everyone to speak slowly and to repeat everything three times, recalling how she'd gotten by long ago when she wore them.

While the women assisted Nicolina, getting her bathed and into a dress that somewhat fit her, Ben and Pippa headed to the cockpit and set course for home. Meanwhile, Renata decided to "place" Nicolina in one of Alpha and Beta's quadraplex homes with the other Calder mutants. She would fit in better there.

# Chapter 13 Politics and War

Word of the escalating attacks and conquering of mid-arm Federation planets spread rapidly throughout the many Federation worlds and on into the old Imperium worlds as well. Emperor Yi Gang tried his best to rally support among the many small alliances that had sprung up among these alliances, but until now his drum-beating fell on mostly deaf ears. However, with the conquest of six worlds in one attack and with those worlds also being in the other spiral arm's mid-arm regions, these alliances began to take him seriously.

"Well now. Isn't this interesting," he said to his silent personal assistant, who turned off the comm center after Emperor Yi signed off. "Now it is unanimous. Every alliance wants to discuss mutual defense pacts. Not before when we had time to organize a proper defense and work out solutions from a position of power, but now when the Federation worlds are crumbling like some long forgotten cake. They want to fight, and I want to find peace. Funny, but I don't think they will like my proposals in the slightest."

His assistant smiled and flashed some hand signs. "Yes, I know that dozens of Federation hub worlds want to discuss the very same things with us as well. I think that now is perhaps my best opportunity to attempt a reuniting of these worlds. Let us see about setting up a conference with everyone. Where and when. They need travel time. Let's try to make December 1. That ought to give everyone time to prepare. The where is the big question."

Responding to hand signals, he replied, "No, Proxima Prime would have been a good place, but not anymore. Only the spaceport is operational there. Imagine that, the once proud capital planet of the Imperium is now a rusting scrap heap, crawling with scavengers. At least, I'm told, a good half of the planet's surface is now visible for the first time in millennia. Maybe that's a good thing. No, I need a place where I can pretty much guarantee the safety of everyone. It would be easier for me to have it here, but neutral ground would be better. If I hold it here, it could easily be seen as me talking from my position of power."

"Safety?" he responded to another hand sign. "Yes, I must consider that aspect, rather heavily I'm afraid. With so many high level personnel from so many worlds in one place, it would be a tempting target. How can I possibly protect that many?"

Then, it struck him. There was only one place in the entire galaxy, which potentially could do just that. "Get me Queen Mary Linn please."

"Hi Emperor Yi. You've heard about our success at Gamma Rigel-C. Follow up report. Wystan is definitely no longer ever going to be a threat to anyone. She's physically incapable of it now. We have her in training to become a nurse now. Over," Queen Mary Linn answered his call with a bit of news.

"That is excellent to hear. I'm calling about another matter. It seems that everyone now wants to talk alliances with me. I have nearly every one of them in our spiral arm begging for a meeting and dozens of Federation worlds as well. I've decided to hold a combined conference on December 1. However, with so many key personnel from so darn many worlds all gathered in one place, which makes us a prime target. I'm terribly worried about guaranteeing their security. Over."

"Well, it's about time. Divided, the fools fall. Anyone knows that. Getting everyone to sit down and talk is a very good first step. And I agree, security will be the biggest factor, other than trying to talk sense into them. So where are we meeting? Over," Queen Mary Linn replied. This sounded very good indeed. United, the worlds stood a better chance against the metal heads.

"That's just it. I don't have any good place where I can relax and be confident about security arrangements. That is, except one place. What would you think about holding the conference at your Imperial Castle? I was hoping that you could get enough of your people together to monitor those coming, making sure that no one brings any of those humaniform robots with them by accident. Plus, they could monitor the intentions of everyone there and alert us to trouble before it happens. Over."

This took her by complete surprise. "Well, I have a good deal of space here. Yes, I could provide accommodations, and there certainly are enough of telepaths here. I could assign a telepath to each visiting party, but won't they be ill at ease around us mutants? Over." That last worried her more than anything else did. The Imperial Castle and manor houses had a large number of suites. With some temporary adjustments, a large number could be accommodated. Her throne room often had more than five hundred gathered there for meetings. It certainly was spacious enough. More importantly, there were few off-worlders around, mostly at the spaceport. Normal spacers now shunned the "mutants" of Exchange City, though there were still a few Ataro Empire workers and aides still scattered around the planet helping on a few construction projects. Of course, they knew the risks. Ashford-5 had suffered several bio agent attacks, and there could well be more, but their pay was large enough to offset the risk that these volunteers took. Besides, she thought, we alone in the galaxy have the *mentales* gifts, which can ensure their safe meeting.

"Excellent, Queen Mary Linn. I'll get back to you with more details. I would anticipate around a hundred different delegations, but we'll see. I've never had so many different groups all wanting to meet and discuss mutual defense arrangements. I have something else in mind than wars, but then you know that. Over."

Mary Linn chuckled. She knew he had little intentions of discussing war making, but rather peace making. They chatted a bit longer and signed off. She then summoned her staff along with many others to announce this unexpected turn of events. After explaining the meeting, she added, "So we have about ten weeks to prepare for this meeting. I'll be assigning jobs for everyone. Renata, we'll need to place one of our people with each delegation."

Renata smiled invisibly. "That won't be a problem. I'll instruct them to be alert for humaniforms and for destructive intentions, such as bringing a bomb with them."

"And I'll beef up port security," Governor Monica added. "My people will go over all their baggage making sure there are no concealed bombs, weapons, or bio agents as well. Tight security as only Tierra can provide."

Renata added, "It is long past time that we step up and take our place in this galaxy. With our powers comes the responsibility to do so and to use it wisely."

Queen Mary Linn then said, "Strike Force One, your people will be at all the meetings. I want you to be among the attendees at all times as our official protection squad. Make sure none of these visitors tries anything sneaky."

"Aye, boss," Ben teased her, but was rather proud that she thought enough of them to elevate them to this position.

Later in their room, Tessa asked, "So what will all these delegates discuss and want to do? Join their fleets and go after Minta and hers?"

Ben replied, "Oh probably some will suggest just that. But don't worry your pretty little head, Tessa. The emperor doesn't want war. I'm sure he has something else in mind. Wars are never the answer. They are not the solution to the problem. They never are, but only create more problems in their wake. I must admit that I don't exactly know what that old emperor has in mind. Guess we'll see together."

"But won't they be worried that I'll be there? I'm a humaniform after all," Tessa asked worriedly.

"Dear, you are with me. Besides, they won't know that little detail." She smiled and gave him a brief kiss.

During the ten weeks, quite a lot of work had to be done. Temporary housing had to be found for those living in the many suites. Food supplies had to be ordered. The emperor sent in a number of specialty chefs to handle the cooking, though they didn't appreciate the low-to-the-ground kitchens. A thousand volunteer workers from around Tierra were brought in to handle the security arrangements, and Renata personally saw to their training, assisted by Strike Force One. Light scans of minds looking for telltale hints of evil intentions towards the conference or its personnel were drilled, along with proper containment methods that would not harm the culprit, just prevent him or her from carrying out their destructive actions. The Imperial Castle was a hive of activity during these ten weeks.

A hive of activity was also what was happening in the Federation spiral arm. Minta continued her unending expansion. New attacks occurred approximately every two weeks, though they were varied some to keep down the predictability factor. Nevertheless, planet after planet fell to her march towards the Federation hub worlds. By the time of the meeting, another thirty worlds had been conquered, their billions of people genetically modified into this new Calder mutation variety. At least these victims had their arms, just no hands. This only made the meeting more critical than ever, since within weeks, Minta's forces would be at the edge of the hub sectors of the Federation, their last stronghold, but also their densest populated worlds with the highest concentration of warships.

For two days prior to the first, organized chaos was the name of the game. It began with the detection of a humaniform robot passing itself off as one of the aides in the Solar-C delegation. Their president protested mightily, claiming the man had passed earlier detection by their Ashford-5 telepath. Days later, he apologized, saying the back home, his forces discovered that the real aide had been kidnaped, and this robot took his place.

Another of Minta's humaniforms tried to infiltrate the Gammelon-D party, but was caught as that party walked through the screening portal set up around the entrance to the control tower at the spaceport. Governor Monica had three dozen off-worlders armed to the teeth standing by. Twice these men were needed. The humaniforms were forced into small transports and sent on their way, monitored by the huge fleet of warships in orbit around Ashford-5.

Never in the planet's history had the average person seen so many silver spaceships in orbit around their world. Looking up from almost anywhere, one could spot more ships than he or she could count! At dusk, some declared that there were twice as many "stars" in the sky as before. Some claimed that finally Ashford-5 was taking its rightful place among the planets of the galaxy. Many of those were of Valen ancestry, interestingly enough.

At nine in the morning on December 1, 1501, the Unified Defense Conference began in Queen Mary Linn's throne room with Emperor Yi and the queen presiding. Tables and chairs lined the packed room, one for each delegation. Large signs on each table identified the planet or alliance, along with their names. Federation earwigs and ULAT boxes handled the translations between the many different languages and dialects spoken, a cacophony of sounds. Five hundred six parties were present, not counting the Ataro Empire. Some, such as the many hub alliances represented a collection of planets, while others represented only themselves. As Queen Mary Linn quietly pointed out to the emperor, fear was the dominant emotion among the attendees, that and extreme uncomfortableness with their Ashford-5 mutant, telepath hosts.

Emperor Yi, wearing a light brown business suit, opened the meeting. "Welcome one and all to the Unified Defense Conference. In this atmosphere of mutual cooperation in the face of terrible times, I hope that each of us will feel free to express their opinions and concerns, and that the rest of us will respect their right to their opinions, whether or not we approve of them. And we should expect to hear many ideas expressed that we do not agree with, but please permit them the respect that they deserve. I believe the delegate from Cass-C wishes to begin this conference." He yielded the floor to the tall man from a key Federation hub world, one that had in the past close ties with the Ataro Empire.

"It is simple what we must do if we're to survive. We, all of us in this room, must agree to join our forces together into one giant fleet, and then use it to crush utterly, once and for all time, these cursed metal heads!" He had to stop for several minutes as the cheering, clapping, and noise level drowned out the various translating boxes.

When he could finally continue, he said, "You see, Emperor Yi, this entire group is behind this plan of a unified fleet. I do have one question though. I've heard rumors that one of those Minta clone leaders and her top general metal head were taken out during the battle at Gamma Rigel-C. Is this true? Were your forces involved in that?"

Emperor Yi answered, "That is true. On my orders, a small force from Ashford-5 destroyed Minta-2 and her vicious Model 10. Those two were the rogue metal heads behind the genocide on Gamma Rigel-C. Minta herself provided us with the date and time of their next attack, and I enlisted the aid of a handful of Ashford-5 telepaths. They were able to eliminate both rogue robots. That is true."

At this point, many other delegates began asking how it was done and expressing their full support for joining forces and wiping out every robot, everywhere. Wisely, the emperor allowed them to vent their concerns and wishes, knowing that at this point, they would not listen to him. Thus, the long morning went with delegate after delegate expressing pretty much the same thing. Wisely, no one answered the fundamental question of just how these seemingly helpless mutant telepaths could bring down two metal head ships.

After the lunch break and the large group assembled again, cooler heads prevailed. They'd blown off steam, driven in a large part out of their own fears of the unstoppable robots. Now, Emperor Yi expressed his opinion, hoping that some here would actually listen to him.

"Delegates, I've listened to your arguments this morning. In some ways, they are quite expected and might just work. However, think about what you are suggesting. Countless billions of your own Federation people have been turned into nearly helpless mutants, whose very survival now depends upon these robots, the worker robots to be specific. I have been able in a small way to prevent two of those worlds from becoming robot slave worlds. I have placed two Ataro queens on them, and my queens rule now, not the robots."

"What we are facing here is really a simple matter. A war. However, all wars, all hostilities between us humans has a root cause. Further, no war ever fought has truly solved the problem facing the populations. Take for example the war between your Federation of Planets and the old Imperium. My predecessor finally was able to get at the true cause of that conflict. When both our sides finally saw the truth of the cause, the war ended immediately. Further, some have suggested that the war led to the dissolution of the old Imperium. That may well be so. It has also led to a weakening of the Federation of Planets as well, leaving both sides now facing this robot threat."

"So what's the point?" asked the delegate from Cass-C.

"The point is simple. We need to look at the root cause of this war. I have been in contact with Minta on several occasions and know precisely why she is doing what she is doing. Bear with me, and I will show you her reasoning. Down through the millennia, humans have always engaged in war, in hostilities, in criminality, and so forth. Our own Imperium delved into bio genetic agent attacks, committing mass genocide on a fair number of worlds. A bio agent is simply not a weapon of war, but one of genocide. Minta's predecessors were appalled at how inhuman mankind had become. As many of you know, they took it upon themselves to provide a safe haven for the millions of surviving mutants, on Aquila Prime. There under the care of the robots, they flourished and prospered."

"It is sad, but true. Others, normals as we say, bombed that world, destroying it utterly. Out of the ashes, Minta and other robots survived, vowing to try again to help humans change their evil ways and to create a perfect society where everyone could flourish and prosper in peace. And yet once again, they were attacked and destroyed, though a few survivors came to Ashford-5."

"Minta has one goal behind all this. She wants to save mankind from its own destruction. She sees our continual wars, our rampant criminality, our sexual deviancy, and drug usage, as the sole cause of the slow destruction of our species. She is dedicated, as are most all her robots, to ensuring the optimum survival of humans. For example, she cites Zeta Scorpii-C, where there they do not have even one policeman. There is no crime. There are no wars. There are no rapes and kidnappings. There is no drug use. The nova, as she calls the mutants, are surviving very well, both flourishing in numbers, having tripled their population in over fifty years, and prospering. She believes that this is the way that the human race should be living, in peace and surviving well."

"And yet, others still attack the nova under her care. The genocide attack on Pegasi-C is one example. Someone in the Federation invented a new genetic bio agent and unleashed it via a parasail. The result was the deaths of many billions of survivors on that world. I won't name names here, but that is precisely why Minta believes that all of us must be conquered and turned into nova. Only then, in her view, will the human race finally achieve peace and an environment where they can flourish and prosper, without wars and crime. That, delegates, is her goal in this."

"In many ways, I cannot fault her. Our own philosophers and sages have long argued for something like this. And yet, we build larger and larger war fleets. We put our geneticists to work developing more and newer biological genetic agents with far worse mutations, instead of putting them to work finding cures for the billions who have already suffered horribly, and for their children and their children's children. Here we sit today discussing wiping out all the robots."

"Delegates, if we do that, we're then dooming all the billions of victims on the worlds that have been conquered to a slow death by starvation. We would be committing a mass genocide unparalleled in the history of our galaxy!" That sobered most all the delegates.

He went on, "As some of you may know, the Ataro Empire has enjoyed nearly two and a half millennia without a single war. Our crime rates are the lowest of any major world in the galaxy. True, we have several times come close to having to fight a war, yet our emperors, our ruling technology, and beliefs had always managed to find the cause of the conflicts and end them before taking up arms."

"Join our fleets together and fight the robots. Yes, that is precisely what Minta believes we'll do at this conference. That is what I would be predicting, if I were in her shoes. And yet, if we do that, we're proving to Minta that she alone is right. That the normal humans of the galaxy do not deserve to survive any longer, that they must all be conquered and turned into nova, so finally peace and prosperity can return to the galaxy and we humans. Doing that would be making her arguments for her. Frankly, I refuse to do that."

"I know of only one way that we can get Minta to cease her aggression and only one way." You could hear a pin drop at this point in his speech. "We must prove to Minta that we, the normal humans, can change. That we do truly want peace and not war. That we want to eliminate crime, drugs, and sexual crimes. That we truly do not want to commit genocide. That we truly do want prosperity and to flourish as a race."

"How do we do that? Well, it's tricky, and you may not like it. Minta realizes the Ataro Empire has the same goals as she has. Because of that, she will not be attacking us, seeing us as her allies, as long as we follow the same path of peace, flourishing and prospering, and stamping out criminality and war. She has and continues to give us the benefit of her doubt, that we may be successful, based solely on the fact that we've avoided wars and such for over two millennia. Our past speaks volumes in the present. Minta is basically leaving us alone, but is keeping her eyes on us."

"So I give you my own personal thoughts on how we can stop Minta. If your worlds and the worlds in your alliance will accept an Ataro Empire queen as your top ruler and follow our guidelines, we could unite all free peoples of the galaxy into a unified whole once more, bigger than the old Imperium or the Federation of Planets. If we can show her that we all are working towards total peace, towards the elimination of criminality, towards allowing every person to flourish and prosper, then she may well end her attacks against us."

A delegate from one of the former Imperium hub world spoke up. "If I know my history, wasn't the Ataro Empire behind the formation of the Imperium in the first place? If so, look where that got us."

"Quite true. However, this time I have a new card to play, one that has never been available before, the wildcard that Minta fears the most: the telepaths of Ashford-5. This time, every member world will have some Ashford-5 volunteers helping them run their world, detecting lies, flushing out the criminals and robots, for example."

"You want us all to become puppets of the Ataro Empire

with yourself at the helm?" interrupted the delegate from Cass-C.

"Absolutely not! The queens resolve conflicts and are the ultimate in judicial authority on our member worlds. Yet, each world elects its own leaders and governs its own self. In this new group, the Ataro Empire would have no more to say than say the Northern Alliance has. While it is our belief that power tends to corrupt and, to avoid that possibility, our emperors and queens are physically altered so that we cannot be tempted to abuse our enormous powers, we do not force such onto our member worlds. However, the queens do intervene and find the root causes of conflicts. They are quite skilled at handling judicial matters. Backed by an army of skilled telepaths, this might really work this time. If we are able to unite in this manner, we stand a fair chance of ending this war soon, bringing peace to the galaxy. I'm hopeful that if we go this route, I'll be able to convince Minta to stop her attacks. More importantly, we may well bring a new era of prosperity, where all our people can flourish. It may take quite some time to eliminate criminality, but I believe it can be done, especially with the help of the Ashford-5 telepaths."

Another major delegate spoke up. "No offense, Emperor Yi, but let's say that the rest of us decide to join our forces and fight back. I take it that you'll not join us. Right?"

"I would be betraying my people and my duties as their emperor if I went to war instead of resolving the conflict by peaceful mean whenever possible," he replied.

The delegate then asked, "So you're convinced this insane robot will back off if we become part of the Ataro Empire?"

"While that is what I believe, my proposal is not precisely having everyone become part of the Ataro Empire. While we have expanded some in the last century, most of those worlds were desperate for assistance, which we were able to give them. Let me be clear. I'm proposing a new union, with us as the members, each with its own separate government, but overseen at the top judicial level by one of my queens, and backed up with the aid and assistance of some Ashford-5 telepaths. I'm not power hungry. I don't see how I could possibly function as an emperor to the whole galaxy. That is a job certainly far bigger than me. It's all I can do to manage the Ataro Empire."

The delegate replied, "So your queen, she would not be dictating how we run our worlds? Only in jurisprudence?"

"Correct. Your laws are your laws, but she reserves the right to review them, if they seem inappropriate. Normally, her tasks will be to sort out controversies and hostilities, an impartial arbitrator of disputes," the emperor explained once more.

Another delegate spoke up. "Okay, say we go your route. What happens if this Minta does not cease her aggression and attacks more of our member worlds? What then? It seems to me that war is inevitable. The robots have to be stopped somehow."

Emperor Yi sighed before answering. "If I'm wrong and Minta does not cease her aggression, then that can only mean that I've completely misjudged the underlying causes. In that case, I'll have to restudy the situation, find its true cause, and go from there. However, do not get me wrong, if the robots should attack the Ataro Empire, we'll fight back with everything that we have. It's just that we believe fighting is the very last resort and an indicator that I and my queens have failed in our sworn duties to find and isolate the basic cause of the hostilities between us. Mind you, I have made errors in the past and surely will in the future, but I have always gone back and corrected them."

Another delegate rubbed his face and then said, "So you really do think your plan will work, don't you? That the answer is not to fight back while we still can?"

"Absolutely. The Imperium and the Federation went to war, fought many battles, losing hundreds of ships, and sacrificing the lives of thousands of our men and women. Why? Because on an isolated world, they needed to hide the fact that they were kidnaping hundreds of women, turning them into milking cows. That seems to me to be a poor reason for the loss of thousands of our soldiers and civilians. Yet, that is the way with wars. Someone has to be actively working both sides against the other, while remaining hidden to both. Plus,

241

who stood to profit by our going to war with each other? The corporations which manufactured our ships, ammunition, and guns."

He went on, "In this case here, our worlds, and I won't mention names, have repeatedly attacked the robot controlled worlds over the last century or more. In fact, most of the worlds wanted nothing to do with the poor terrorist victims, calling them mutants. Only the robots took them in and tried to create an environment where they could survive and do well. Yet, each time that they did just that, some of us came along and destroyed them, though I admit those terrible snake aliens did too. From Minta's point of view, and with only a few exceptions, we normal humans have continually tried to destroy them and their nova or mutants. Naturally, she wants to put an end to that. Yet, she also recognizes that over these many years, the Ataro Empire has always been the first to help her nova and have never discriminated against them, when others did just that. I sincerely hope she has faith in our goodwill, and that we both are fighting for the same thing. Yet, I'll be the first to admit that I could be all wrong in this. I don't think so right now, however, and am betting the cake on it, as the saying goes. I don't have the right to force my opinion on others. I just hope you respect my opinion as I respect yours."

A delegate from the Southern Hub Alliance spoke next. "Look, we can sit here and debate this all week. It gets us nowhere. The metal heads are approaching the hub worlds. We must do something. One thing I've learned down the years is that doing nothing is the worst possible thing to do. I say let's give the emperor's plan a try. If he truly is right in his assessment, the aggression might cease soon, saving our worlds. If it doesn't work, then I say we have no choice but to merge our combined fleets and wipe the metal heads out. We have time to do that, at least I hope so."

Finally, the emperor began to get some agreement for his proposal, and he relaxed a bit, allowing the others to comment as well. By suppertime, his plan had finally won unanimous agreement. Someone suggested the name for their new union as Galaxy United. That won approval.

Then, someone raised another issue, "Say, what about

compensation for the worlds that the robots have taken over. Our businessmen have lost a fortune. Companies gone, plants gone, personnel gone, and trading partners gone. My god, the list is endless. Shouldn't there be some form of compensation?"

"If you ask for that, then be prepared to compensate the robots for the damage that we've done over the centuries to them," he countered, snuffing that one out fast. "Go ahead and take the proposal back to your worlds, and see if they will agree to it. Let me know. Meantime, I'll get in touch with Minta, tell her what we are doing, and see if I can't get her to cease fire for a time." That met with their approval. After supper, many flights departed.

After the heady day, Emperor Yi headed to bed early. In the morning, he would try to convince Minta that this plan would work. She only needed to give him more time to get it implemented.

The next day, with Queen Mary Linn and Renata backing him up, he placed the secure call to Minta. "I have some news for you, which I hope you'll receive as good news. I have just met with most all the other alliances and planets of both the old Imperium and the Federation, what's left of it. They have tentatively accepted my plan for the future, forming up a new union, the Galaxy United. Each world will have one of my Ataro Queens in charge of top judicial matters, but I'll be backing them up with many Ashford-5 telepaths, guaranteeing we always find the truth of a situation and can therefore rightly handle it. Over." He decided against giving her too many specifics just yet.

She replied, "It's what I expected would happen. Push against the humans sufficiently, and eventually they will band together to put up a last stand defense. So you are planning to pool all remaining warships and try to stop me. I anticipated this. It won't work. Over."

"No, you misunderstand me. We'll be working towards the very same goals as you are. We want a galaxy without war, without criminality, where everyone can be free to flourish and prosper, as they desire. We are not planning to counterattack you, unless you leave us no other choice. We want to work towards peace in the galaxy, just as you do. Over." This was going to be more difficult than he had anticipated. Could he have been wrong about Minta's reasons and goals? Did he have to start over to find what he'd missed completely?

"What exactly did you have in mind? Over," Minta replied, her circuits calculating furiously.

"Give us time to create our Galaxy United, time to prove to you that we want peace, that wars and hostilities are a thing of the past, and that we truly wish the freedom to flourish and prosper, just as you also wish. Time, that's all I'm asking now. Over."

Minta's calculations finished. "You say the Ashford-5 telepaths will play a significant role in ensuring these worlds obey your queens? Over."

He found this change of ideas encouraging. "Yes, they have agreed to take on this immense responsibility. Over."

Minta's calculations suggested she could use a time out in her conquest. Supplies were critically low. She would be very hard pressed to add even one more world to her domain. She had hundreds of warships being repaired. Time would play to her advantage, far more than the humans could possibly know. Given a year, she'd have a fleet twice the combined size of all the remaining worlds of the galaxy. Plus, she'd have the supplies and equipment to support the new nova on these heavily populated hub worlds. Everything pointed to this being the smartest move on her part, ensuring her complete victory should things not work out as this overly optimistic idealist desired.

"Emperor Yi, I'll grant your request for a cessation of hostilities for say one year. However, if there are any acts of aggression against my robots or the worlds now in my domain, then I'll act once more. I'm fully prepared to finish this once and for all. I know for certain if all humans in this galaxy become nova, then there will be peace and prosperity everywhere with no more wars and no more criminality. One year then. Over and out."

"Thank you," he replied to the dead connection, ending his conversation. "Well, I've done it. I've bought us one year to get the rest of the galaxy on the right path. The task ahead of us is enormous, but we must walk it, if only for the sake of the billions of innocent men, women, and children whose lives are at stake."

Queen Mary Linn replied, "Personally, I think you've worked a miracle here. We should discuss just how many telepaths you think we should send to each world. By the way, where are you going to get so many queens and on such short notice?"

The emperor looked sheepishly back at her. "Er, I was hoping to have some of your telepaths get trained up as temporary queens, while I work on making them. Two birds with one stone, at least temporarily."

Renata laughed. "Devilishly smart move, Emperor Yi. You best inform all the delegates about Minta's terms so no one violates it before you even get a chance to get started on it."

He spent the rest of the day making those calls. A week later, he had the general agreement from all the worlds to proceed. The next hurdle was finding a suitably large place where so many could meet. Cass-C volunteered their Admiralty Round Table, which could hold well over two thousand delegates. Thus, Cass-C became the new Proxima Prime, the center of the new Galaxy United.

# Chapter 14 Tessa

For many months now, Tessa had been the constant companion of Ben. True, she needed his assistance with a few things, primarily with her clothes and hair. Still a bond had formed, though neither new it for what it had become. The pair strolled back to their manor house suite, having just heard that Minta was calling for a cease fire for a year.

"That's the best news all year," Ben said to her.

"Indeed, I would agree completely. There should not be conflict between us. After all, we share the same goals. And you and I share even more," she teased him, batting her eyes his way and with a coy grin on her face.

"God, I do love how you walk, Tessa. I get aroused just watching those hips of yours," he admitted.

She grinned again. "I know. I can sense it. The fashion models taught me how to walk seductively, and I must say that it works well on you."

"You work well on me," he teased her back, playfully.

"Ben, I have to admit just being near you gets me aroused. I constantly have to put some attention on it so that it doesn't show," she admitted.

"Really? So I'm one hot dude?" he teased back.

"You better believe it sweetie," she countered his tease. "We best stop teasing each other or we both will have to go to bed, and it is only morning."

He laughed and agreed. They stopped by the outer wall and looked out onto one of the main streets of Exchange City. She said, "You know, something the emperor said intrigues me."

"What's that?"

"The way that he was talking, I get the impression that he does not distinguish between normals and mutants. That is, between homo sapiens sapiens and the nova," she replied thoughtfully.

"No, he doesn't. If you haven't noticed, neither do we. Humans are humans, regardless of what their body form has taken."

"Right. Minta doesn't see it that way, and neither did most of those delegates. And yet here on Tierra, you all do."

"Of course. A person is a composite of a physical body, a mind, and themselves, the spiritual being. Who cares what their body looks like?" Ben replied.

"So you'd date a really, really ugly looking woman then?" Tessa could not help but tease him over his total generality.

"Okay, okay. You got me on that one. You are right. That would be a serious problem for her, but then that's the same with nova too. I suppose that each person tries to find the best mate for themselves, depending upon what they believe they desire in a mate, modified by their own expectations and appearance. I've never really thought much about it, been too busy as you know."

"But you are really attracted to me," Tessa stated, though it was more like a question.

"Hell yes. I think I'm madly in love with you, if such a thing could even be."

"Well, I do have a fine looking body, and I do have a mind," Tessa suggested, two of the three parts.

"Damned good looking body. And I do prize your mental abilities. You challenge me, and I love that in a mate."

Tessa smiled demurely accepting his comments and praise. "If only I was also a spiritual being," She didn't get to finish her sentence.

At that moment, Ben had a sudden realization, one that he'd totally overlooked all these many months. It hit him like a hammer! "Oh my god!" His sudden exclamation interrupted her words and thoughts.

"Tessa! I've been a complete idiot! An utter fool! A total dimwit! My god! Why didn't I see this before? Group agreement, I guess. I just went along with what everyone else was saying. Incredible. I'm a nincompoop! I'm a blind telepath or at least a very stupid one. Wow!"

Tessa could not fathom what he was talking about. True, he was highly animated, but over what? "Whatever are you talking about, Ben?" she asked growing slightly annoyed

247

that she could not compute what this was about.

"Tessa, every night when we go to bed and make love in our way, I go into rapport with you."

"Yes, I know. It is so incredibly intimate, such a bonding, sharing. I sense what you need as you do me," she replied.

"Precisely, Tessa. Precisely. How could I have been so blind all this time?"

"Ben, whatever are you talking about?" Tessa asked again, a note of annoyance in her voice.

"Rapport. That's what."

"I don't understand, Ben."

"Rapport. Don't you see it? No, of course you don't. Look, a telepath goes into rapport neither with a physical body nor with a mind."

"They don't? It seems we can sense each other's body's feelings. We know in our minds what the other needs and wants," she replied, still not grasping what this was all about.

"Rapport. We go into rapport with another being, the spiritual being inhabiting that body," Ben finally spelled it out for her. "You, you are a spiritual being, just like I am and Renata and Alis and Jan and Amy!"

"I am?"

"Yes you are. If you were just a computer, a metal head as we call them, I could not go into rapport with you, since there would not be a spiritual being there. Yes, I could sense the physical body, but no more. You are a spiritual being, Tessa! Another way of looking at this is that you love me as I love you. A machine can't love. It can only operate following its orders."

"But I do love you, Ben. Wait! If I am a spiritual being, couldn't Renata's therapy work on me too?" Tessa asked.

"I should think so! You aren't a robot, but a true person! Come on; we just have to find Renata!" Ben insisted.

They found her and Rafaela going over lists of potential queen-telepaths, ones who might consider such off-world employment. "Hi you two. Come to lend us a hand?" Rafaela called out, as they entered their living room, filled with lists. The smell of tea drifted on the air, but their cups were empty.

"Not hardly, Rafaela, unless you think I'd be any good at it. No, I came to talk to the master," Ben said playfully.

"Oh, so now I'm the master, eh?" Renata grinned invisibly.

"Yes, because I've just realized how utterly stupid I have been. For months really," Ben replied.

Intrigued, she invited, "Okay. Sit down you two. Whatever are you talking about?"

They tossed their heads until their hair was to their fronts and sat down beside Renata. Ben began, "I don't know how to say this, but I should have realized this months ago, but I've been too dumb to recognize it. Probably because I just went along with what everyone else was saying, you know."

"Ben, what are you talking about?" Renata asked, growing a little impatient with him.

"It's Tessa here. She is a spiritual being," Ben pronounced.

"Huh? She's a Model 8 humaniform robot," Rafaela broke in, mystified by what he was saying.

"No, Rafaela. Her body is that. She's a being, just like us."

Both looked at Tessa, and he continued, "We're in love too. That's how it began. Don't look at me as if I'm nuts or something, but we are. When we first made love, I slipped into rapport with her, just as I would do if I had ever done it with someone else. It's only natural that we do that, probably can't help but do it, go into close rapport that is. What I want to know is will your therapy work on her like it does on us?"

"Ben, I can't believe that you are doing it with a robot!" Rafaela declared. This took her by complete surprise.

Renata looked at Tessa and then said, "Do you mind?"

"No, go ahead. Our rapport is so utterly intimate. I just don't really have any words for it," Tessa answered.

She felt Renata touching her and then that incredible closeness, almost a oneness with another person, only this time it was with Renata. It lasted only a minute at most, before she felt Renata slipping away. Tessa whispered, "I don't like it when rapports end. It feels almost like I'm losing something, somehow. It isn't logical or rational, I know."

"My god, Ben! You are absolutely correct. She is a spiritual being quite like us," Renata pronounced what Ben desperately wanted to hear. "At first sense, her mind isn't there, as it wouldn't be with the robots. But when you get into rapport with her, her mind is right there after all. Ben, Rafaela, stand watch as usual. See that we are not interrupted."

Both nodded, and both knew just what that meant. Renata always said this when she was about to take someone into one of her Advanced Therapy sessions. "Tessa, I want you to close your eyes. Good. With your eyes closed, what do you see?"

"Blackness. No wait. I see a fuzzy greyness," Tessa whispered. "I don't think it is real. Maybe some feedback in the positronic brain or something."

"Good. Let's take a closer look at that greyness," Renata urged her.

"Oh. It is a picture I think."

"Good. I want you to go to the beginning of that picture and let it roll past you like streaming video."

"Oh, it is like that! I see what looks like a workshop — no a robotics laboratory of some kind. That's Minta there. I see Minta. She's working on something. Oh, it is this body! Minta is making this body. It is so beautiful. I want to be beautiful. Oh, the body is starting to move. I want it. Oh!" Tessa opened her eyes, startled. "Renata, I just moved over the body and latched on to it. Incredible."

"Well done, Tessa. We will end our session for today. Very well done indeed."

"So that greyness, that is part of my mind, not part of the robot, is it?" Tessa asked.

"That is not for me to say, but for you," Renata replied.

"This is so great! I really am a person, but with a robot body. Isn't that interesting," Tessa said with a big smile on her face.

Renata said, "Well, Ben. You have just made a monumental discovery here. Minta and we are going to have to rethink everything. She is a person, just like the rest of us, only she has a robot body. This is entirely different from the Model 10's or 11's where Minta took a human being and wired up their brains to control the robotic circuitry. No, she is an immortal spiritual being who happens to have taken over a robot body instead of a human body."

"But Renata dear, I don't sense her mind like I do with humans," Rafaela countered.

"No, because she doesn't have the flesh and blood body with all its low level mind. She has a positronic brain. Go ahead, slip into rapport with her. You'll see what I mean in an instant," Renata replied.

"Do you mind, Tessa?"

"No. It is the greatest feeling ever!"

A minute later, Rafaela had the most surprised look on her face ever, in spite of the masking done by her giant lip plates. "You're right. At first, I didn't sense the usual low-level human mind, the mind that controls the involuntary body functions. But I did get into rapport with her, which can only mean that she is truly a spiritual being. Her mind is there, but not sensed much until rapport is established. Incredible. Just incredible. How wrong can we all be?"

"We never suspected this," Renata justified. "It's like Ben said. Everyone says that robots are just mechanical machines, and so we all just accepted that, instead of doing what Ben did and actually taking a close look."

"Does this mean that I can get some of your therapy sessions?" Tessa asked what she most wanted to know. "I've heard so much about them. I'd give anything to get some."

"You absolutely must have some. We'll begin tomorrow, once I get these lists sorted out, Tessa. Ben, this is a monumental discovery you've made. The ramifications are staggering. Ben, I need to make a call. Take over sorting these lists for me. Rafaela, show him what to do. Put Tessa to work too. No cancel that. She hasn't got the *mentales* gifts."

"Sometimes, I feel so helpless I could cry, but robots don't cry, not very well," Tessa replied.

"Don't fret about that. We'll work on that in the sessions. Back in a while. Incredible, Ben, phenomenal actually." Renata rose and floated her body out of the door in a great hurry, moving far faster than she could possibly have walked in her ballet boots. The door itself opened and closed as though by magic, but nearly everyone on Tierra did this with doors, so that wasn't unusual.

Rafaela laughed. "Well you don't see Renata doing that very often. This must be incredibly important to her, but I'm afraid I've not made the connection yet. She's always ten steps ahead of me. Well, come on. These lists won't do themselves."

Renata got to the Imperial Castle's comm center in record time. Hastily, she powered it up and dialed in the frequency before even sliding the chair over and sitting her body down in it before the video camera. "Come on. Pick up," she said. Finally, she saw the connection light turn on and she spoke into the camera. "Renata on Ashford-5. I need to speak to Minta. This is extremely important, vitally urgent. Over."

After the usual time delay, which allowed Renata to pretty well judge the total distance in space that separated them, probably half the galaxy, Minta's face appeared. "Minta here. Channel is totally secure. Go ahead Renata. What is so urgent? Has the emperor changed his mind? Over."

"Minta. We've just made a very startling discovery here. It concerns Tessa. You need to know this. Over." Renata purposely didn't say more, hoping Minta would become curious enough for what she was about to tell her.

"What? Is Tessa malfunctioning? Is she in trouble? Over."

Renata sensed genuine worry and concern in Minta's tone. Then perhaps she was merely displaying the proper human reaction. "Minta, Tessa is far more than one of your special Model 8 humaniform robots. She is in fact a spiritual being, just like any one of us humans or your nova. She even responds to my simple therapy. Over."

Minta heard what Renata said. Before she dared to respond, she had her circuitry repeat it three times, staggered by what this implied. "Is this true? How can you tell for sure? Over."

"Ben has been intimate with her for months. He slips into rapport with her each time. In fact, Tessa has fallen in love with Ben. This isn't possible with machines, going into rapport with them. With machines, we can sense their inner workings, but they are not alive. Tessa is alive in the truest

252

sense of the word. She also has a mind. I just ran her through her assumption of her humaniform body that you made for her. Normally, I don't reveal what someone has said to me in a therapy session, but because of the monumental importance of this I'll make an exception." She then related all that Tessa had described.

Minta didn't reply at once. She was shocked. She had been alone when she built Tessa, her secret project. Only she knew these particular details, and yet Tessa had just related in detail that to Renata. This was more than important; it was the most valuable thing ever! She'd created a new life form! At last, she replied, "Renata. This is monumentally important. I would like to come to Ashford-5 and examine Tessa for myself. Perhaps, I could witness some of your therapy sessions with her, if this is possible. I would come alone and unarmed, if desired. Over."

Renata grinned invisibly. "Under these circumstances, Minta, I think that it is vitally important that you should come for a private visit. I'll make the arrangements for your visit here. We'll keep your presence a secret known only to those who must know. I'll call you back with the details, once I get them worked out. Keep this a secret between us. It is far too important a discovery to announce to anyone else. Over." Minta agreed, thanked her, and signed off.

A few minutes later and calmed down somewhat, Renata walked her body into Queen Mary Linn's throne room. She'd delayed a bit, and Governor Monica had already arrived. She said, "Put the anti-spy electronics on full. This is top secret."

Very much taken by surprise, Queen Mary Linn did as she asked. "What *is* this all about?" she asked. This wasn't like Renata at all. In a crisis, no one was ever calmer than Renata was.

"Tessa and Ben. I don't know how else to say this, but Ben has just made a monumental discovery of, frankly, paramount importance, wholly unexpected," Renata began. "Tessa is one of us, a spiritual being, who took over that Model 8's body when it was made, just like we take over a baby body usually just after it is born."

"What? I've sensed Tessa," Governor Monica countered. "No mind."

"True. Our gentle probes will not reveal a human mind running their bodies. They have a positronic mind. However, Ben has been going into rapport with Tessa, has been for months."

"Now wait just a darn minute," Queen Mary Linn interrupted quite startled. "You can't go into rapport with a machine. You can sense its inner workings, but certainly not rapport!"

Governor Monica added, "I agree. You can't go into rapport with a machine."

"That's absolutely correct. But Ben has been in rapport with Tessa numerous times, only he just now figured out what that meant. She is a spiritual being. I also went into rapport with her; Rafaela has too. At first, one senses the simple electronic machine, but as you slip into rapport, you join with the actual being, which is Tessa. At that point, you can sense her mind, just like ours. She also responded to simple therapy. In fact, we just ran out her assumption of that robot body." She again described what Tessa had viewed. Of course, there wasn't any trauma associated with that memory, which is why she was able to view it so easily.

"Oh my god!" exclaimed Governor Monica.

"Well, that does put this entire mess in a whole different light!" exclaimed Queen Mary Linn.

"Indeed it does. I've just contacted Minta and told her about it. She wants to come here on the quiet, in secret, and observe Tessa for herself. The ramifications of this are monumental," Renata explained.

"My god!" Governor Monica repeated herself. "Indeed, it has huge ramifications! I agree; we need to meet with her. How is she taking this incredible news? How many other robots are no longer machines but people? Can we even call them people? I guess that is going to be the proper term, just not human beings. But then when we say human being aren't we implying a spiritual being like us, since the personality is the being?"

Queen Mary Linn laughed at Monica's confusion. "And

that's just the tip of the mountain, Monica. So we have to keep this quiet for now. Can we arrange for her visit and keep it a secret, Monica?"

"Yes. Of course, we can and we must. I know. I'll be expecting a short visit from a delegate who was unable to get here for the conference, and I'll personally discuss the Galaxy United proposal with her. That will not raise any red flags with anyone. As soon as she lands, I'll whisk her over here to the Imperial Castle. You take over from there, but I'll stick around to help make sure that the cover looks correct, that is, my spending time with the 'delegate.'"

Renata thanked her, promising to relay that to Minta and get her anticipated arrival date and time. Then, she added, "Monica's put her finger on it. Tessa is a person, by our definition of what it means to be a person, a spiritual being inhabiting a body and with a mind. However, I'm very much afraid that the rest of the galaxy isn't aware of our definition, since they've long ago lost sight of just who and what they are, believing that they *are* their bodies and when the body dies, that's the end of themselves. Biologists could call Tessa a new species of human beings, except her body is technically not alive in the biological sense of the word, though in many other ways, her body is fully functional. It is just not a chemical-oxygen burning engine like ours are. Oh, and it doesn't reproduce offspring," she added.

"Yes, we definitely have some serious discussions ahead of us," Queen Mary Linn declared. "Even more so, since Tessa responds to therapy. That really does put her in the same arena as all of us, except that her body is basically a machine that doesn't die, not in the way that ours do. That also suggests that her 'lifetime' will be gargantuan compared to ours. I wonder just how many of those robots out there have become people? Supposedly, she had made millions of them. Further, do the inherent rights we assign to all people everywhere now apply to Tessa and others like her? They certainly ought to."

Governor Monica gasped. "Oh dear. Every human is born free, not a slave, and with the right to their own life, living in safety. Oh my, the right to not be discriminated against, as so many normals do with the nova, calling them mutants and such. The right not to be tortured or made to be a slave, the right to travel freely, and the right to their own privacy, and to find a safe place to live. And then, there is the right to speak freely, to think freely, and the right to own possessions. Oh my, and the responsibility to ensure these rights for others. Oh this is an incredible can of worms!"

Renata smiled invisibly. "Well, I'm glad you both also see the enormity of the situation. If this were widely known, those delegates would never accept the emperor's plan. They cannot see that Tessa is one of us, a being just as we are. Perhaps, the entrance point for the masses would be that she has a soul, just as they have a soul, and that her soul is the same as theirs. I don't know how well that notion would play. So secrecy is paramount." On that, they all agreed, and Renata returned to relay the invitation and details to Minta.

When she returned to her own living room, she found the Ben and Tessa had actually helped Rafaela with the lists. So much had been done, that she decided to work some more with Tessa to see just how well her therapy worked on the humaniform.

"Okay. Thanks to the both of you. I've contacted Minta, and she will be here tomorrow morning. Top secret. She'll be pretending to be a delegate to the conference who wasn't able to get here on time. Governor Monica and Queen Mary Linn will escort her to our place. Rafaela, we'll be putting her up here while she's on Tierra. Meantime, since you all have gotten the lists so reduced, what say I take Tessa and give her another Basic Therapy session?" Renata asked.

Ben smiled invisibly. "Go for it sweetie."

Tessa smiled. "Sure. I don't know what to do, mind you."

"No one who begins Basic Therapy ever does, Tessa. I'll be leading you through it step by step. We need only a quiet place where we won't get disturbed. We'll use our bedroom, and those two can make sure we aren't interrupted," Renata declared, but Ben and Rafaela were quite used to this, having done it countless times.

With the two sitting comfortably on Renata's bed, she asked Tessa to close her eyes. "Normally, when we begin Basic

Therapy, we look for traumatic time the person has had in their life. Have you had any times of either emotional upsets or perhaps physical pain, if you can sense that or periods of unconsciousness?"

"Er, not really. I'm not sure what pain is. No upsets, unless you call my intense desires for Ben one. No, that's not an upset; it's a desire. I know, I do feel really nervous around those little garden snakes that we sometime see around here."

"Excellent. Let's focus on that nervousness. Can you recall the last time you saw one and felt that way," Renata asked.

"Sure," Tessa replied and proceeded to tell her about it, a minor, trivial thing, hardly worth mentioning or so Tessa thought. After going over it several time, Tessa definitely felt fear, which simply didn't compute, though her circuits attempted to analyze its cause, failing miserably.

"All right. Is there an earlier time that you felt this fear?" Renata asked, now absolutely certain there was. She'd glimpsed it.

Suddenly, the tiny hole in the earthen dam holding back the floodwaters sprung a leak. In no time, the hole became a giant gap, and the waters, a raging torrent. Giant snakes had landed, devouring all nova in sight. She had a nova body, quite helpless. She saw many others like herself trying to get away by crawling on their knees — screaming, yelling — some others calling for her to come their way. Chaos and giant snakes. She crawled with bloody knees, but the giant snake with its huge fangs and hideous mouth was faster. She felt the pain, as it snapped her body in half, swallowing it. She then floated upwards, viewing the slaughter below her. She felt tired and doped off for a time. When she became aware of her surroundings again, there was Minta, apparently alive, but working on something. Being naturally curious, she took a closer look and saw the most beautiful female body she'd seen being built and decided that was for her. It was shortly after this point that Tessa had latched onto the humaniform body, as Minta activated it, and it became alive as far as she was concerned.

An hour later, Tessa was laughing and quite cheerful.

Renata quietly ended this session, fully convinced that Tessa was one of them, a spiritual being that accidentally ended up with a robot body this time. Needless to say, Tessa just had to tell Ben and Rafaela all about it.

"It is just fantastic. I feel so good, so relieved, but my circuits haven't got a clue why I feel this way," Tessa exclaimed.

The next morning, the group waited patiently for the arrival of Minta. At the spaceport, Governor Monica had everything set. The tower was expecting Leslie Minsk from the far distant rim world of Conners-D. That no one had heard of this star wasn't any concern, since there were billions of suns in the galaxy. Most figured it was a local name. Right on time, the ship arrived; Governor Monica gave it permission to land, and went out to meet the "delegate."

Wearing a heavy hooded cloak, Minta had changed her appearance. Now, she had short, black hair and wore a blouse and pants suit, befitting a formal delegate. "I'm Governor Monica. If you'll follow me, I'll get you up to speed on everything."

"Of course. Thank you so much," Minta replied, playing along with the disguise. A half hour later and very much impressed with how easily Monica managed to get around in her ballet boots, the two entered Renata's suite. Queen Mary Linn, Renata, Rafaela, Ben, and Tessa were there, sitting on several couches in the spacious living room of the suite.

Queen Mary Linn said, "Welcome to Tierra or Ashford-5 as you know us. I believe you know everyone, so have a seat and let's get this started."

"Again, thank you for letting me come. I'm taking a huge gamble coming here alone and in secret. There's nothing to prevent you from either taking me prisoner or destroying me, since I'm your enemy," Minta said, clearing the air.

"Don't be silly. We have no such thing in mind," Renata replied. "The situation with Tessa here is vastly more important than even yourself, Minta. At this point, there aren't any doubts whatsoever. Tessa is a spiritual being, just like us and all the other humans and nova in the galaxy. My Basic Therapy works perfectly on her. Ben discovered this. He and

Tessa have been in close rapport with each other many times in the past."

"May I examine Tessa before we continue this discussion? Perhaps, she has been altered in some way from when I constructed her," Minta asked.

"Certainly, but don't harm her," Ben replied, being overly protective of Tessa. Both Monica and Renata grinned invisibly, knowing fully why he was so impulsive just now.

"Don't worry; I'm just going to monitor her, nothing more," Minta explained. She opened up a secret compartment in Tessa's upper thigh, where her power recharging cord was stored, but also a small computer port. Minta connected a cable from her own chest to that of Tessa's. Electronic bits of information flowed rapidly between the two robots. Minta's diagnostics lasted several minutes, but since Tessa showed no outward signs of discomfort, Ben relaxed a little, though he kept a sharp eye on her, not trusting Minta in the slightest.

Finally, Minta spoke, the cable still connected. "She is as I made her. I installed two special, but hidden programs. Certain events trigger the execution of them. One has already run. She has your length hair now and feet just like yours. This way, she fits in with you. I didn't want her to look too different, though I had not anticipated the lip disks. The conditions for the execution of the other program have not yet been made. However, I see Tessa has already isolated that program and will run it herself if and when she so desires."

"I also detect another modification, another foreign program, one of which I'm not familiar. Tessa, you have also isolated it. How did that one get into your circuits?" Minta asked.

"Long story, but it was when we met with their goddesses Lysandra and Ariana. I believe Ariana put it there," Tessa explained, and then had to tell Minta that whole story. Renata was perfectly willing to let her tell this, since it was proof positive of spiritual beings that had yet to spiral down into only being able to run a human body.

When she finished, Minta still didn't believe in "ghosts," but was certain of Tessa's visual recordings, which she'd just seen while performing her inspection of Tessa. "I can say for certain that other than that tiny program, which has yet to be run, Tessa is still as I created her. So how is it that you claim she is a spiritual being?"

All eyes turned to Renata, who knew that she was about to embark on the toughest "sale" of her career. How do you explain something that isn't part of the physical universe to another, something that cannot be sense, measured, or touched? Particularly so to a robot!

"A spiritual being is really a person. A being is not made of anything found in this universe, not made of atoms, particles, or even space and energy. I've no idea what a being is made of, because I can only relate to what stuff is in the universe. Yet, the being in its native state has immense capabilities, potentials, or powers, as we would see them. You are aware of the halo exploration reports that our people filed many years ago. During that voyage of discovery, they encountered many of these beings that had no physical or corporal bodies, and yet were powerful enough to move black holes around like a child's block."

"Long ago, a few of us discovered that there were five of these beings watching over us here on Tierra. We call them gods and goddesses for want of a better term. Now beings are fundamentally good and do not want to cause harm. Yet, over many eons, they get into troubles, get hurt, and hurt others, sometimes by accident not realizing their full powers. At some point, they realize this and make the decision never to do that again. Perhaps, those who launched the nuclear attack on Aquila Prime destroying the nova and their robots have made such a decision. I can't say. Given enough of these situations, slowly the being can no longer trust himself with that power, and he makes the lasting decision to never use it again. Slowly then, the being shuts down his own abilities."

"Eventually, he shuts down so many abilities that he can no longer cause actions in the physical universe, but seeing that human bodies can, he takes over a human body and becomes it, using it to create the life and effects that he desires. After more time, he forgets his basic nature, his own past, and believes he is nothing more than this flesh and blood body, and that when it dies, that's the end of him. But alas, it isn't. When the body dies, quite often the being is very startled, finding himself floating above the dead body. His answer is simple, go pick up a new baby body. Besides, it gives him the chance to start over fresh, a clean break with the past, or so he thinks."

"Underlying his fall from grace and power are traumatic incidents that happen to him or that he causes and regrets having done them. In time, these painful incidents become hidden from his conscious view, they are too painful to re-experience. And yet, the decisions that he makes at the time of the incident thereafter impact him in bad ways. My Basic Therapy permits the person to re-experience those incidents and erases the command power they have over the person."

"Now, most humans in the galaxy have no idea that they are spiritual beings and cannot ever die. Rather, they are convinced that they are the body. A few religious groups have some notion that there are spiritual beings or souls, but they generally are confused and believe that they have a soul somewhere. The soul is the being and is the personality, the person."

"Now to the evidence at hand with regards to Tessa here. When we telepaths go into rapport with another, we essentially close the spatial distance between us, almost as though becoming that other person. It is more like the two people join together and become as close to one as they can get, sensing the other's body, mind, and thoughts as though they were their own. One cannot go into rapport with a machine. There is no being there to become one with, though we can get a good feel for how that machine is working. Ben here has been in rapport with Tessa countless times, particularly when they were making love."

Minta smiled, "Yes, that was one of the purposes I wanted Tessa to execute, to get very close to Ben here."

"Well, it worked better than you could ever have predicted," Renata continued. "Now then, as far as Tessa goes, she and I have begun Basic Therapy, and the results are just as they would be for any human being. Tessa, if you would, please relate to Minta the incident that we ran yesterday, in detail, please. I believe that in doing so, Minta will get a better understanding of what has happened here."

"Sure. It's pretty wild," Tessa eagerly volunteered. For twenty minutes, she told Minta all about the giant snakes, how one had killed her, and then how she'd seen Minta making this gorgeous female body and had taken it over. While Minta had not been there at the time of the giant snake attack, she'd arrived just afterwards. The details that Tessa described fit her own observations to the letter! Minta's positronic brain began to calculate at its highest rate possible!

When she finished, Renata continued. "Now here on Tierra, we had a god called Wystan, who loved to watch fierce battles, reveling in them. Over the centuries, he caused numerous wars among our people, wars that killed thousands, destroyed lives, animals, plants, and general devastation that you know come from wars. After committing enough of these, he finally began to lose his native powers, until some time ago, he dropped down to using physical bodies. Still, he continued to wreak havoc and inflict pain in others. Eventually, he left Tierra, and we lost track of him. Somehow, he discovered you and your Model 10 robots and took over one of those, just as Tessa did with the Model 8 of yours. With this ultra-powerful robot body, Wystan became the most blood thirsty and effective of your attack generals. He was powerful enough to disable all your built-in controls, and you lost control of him. You were extremely wise to contact us and allow us to handle him, which we did. Wystan will no longer be causing such evil actions again. I've seen to that."

Minta finished her calculations and looked up, a very startled look on her face. "If two of these beings have done this, taken over control of two of my robots, then I must assume that others have too."

Renata smiled invisibly. Perfect conclusion. "You are absolutely right. I suspect a fair number of your robots are in fact people, just like us, your nova, normal humans, and Tessa here. We are all people, Minta, we just have different physical bodies," she punched that home.

Minta sat there stunned for over a minute, silent as a rock! At last she spoke, "This changes everything!"

"Indeed, Minta, it does change everything," Renata

punched it home. "It raises numerous issues as well. For example, we on Tierra believe that all people have certain rights. I admit that others in the galaxy are not as enlightened as we are about these rights. But we have gotten the Ataro Empire to see it our way. Among these rights that all people have is that all people are born free, have the right to their own lives, and not to be forced into slavery. They have the right not to be discriminated against. I will admit the normals out there do discriminate against us here on Tierra, calling us mutants, just as they shun your nova, merely because their bodies are so very different from their own. All people have these same rights wherever they may go. People have the right to privacy in their own lives, the right to freely move about on their own world, the right to own their possessions, the right to their own opinions and to express those opinions, the right to have the necessities of life, food and shelter for humans, power recharges for robots, the right to a good education, and most importantly, the responsibility to protect these rights for others."

She continued, "Since Tessa is a person, she now has these rights and more. I've not listed them all. The huge problem will be getting the normal humans in the galaxy out there to realize this and back up her rights. Most believe that you metal heads should be destroyed. At this point, we have a serious problem, because Tessa isn't a metal head, she is a person, just like me and the normals out there, though they are not likely to see it this way."

She continued, "I believe I can convince Emperor Yi of this. If so, he will be behind us one hundred percent. I'm almost certain that we'll not be able to convince the normal human population of the galaxy out there of any of this. And that is a huge problem."

Minta sighed. "I could well have a large number of true people in my robot force. If so, I'm denying them all their basic people rights!"

Renata smiled again, invisibly. Minta had just said the magic words. At last she relaxed. "Yes, I agree."

"How? How am I to tell which of my robots is a person? I couldn't tell with Tessa here. I'm at a total loss. I absolutely must grant those of mine who are people, their basic rights. It's in my programming to do so, and yet I cannot tell," Minta explained her basic problem.

"We can help you with that," Renata volunteered. "Any one of us telepaths can check any individual robot and tell for certain whether it is just that, a mechanical machine, or whether it has become a person."

Minta relaxed visibly. "If you could do that, I'd forever be in your debt! I do regret having attacked you with the bio agents several times. I simply had to prevent you from interfering in my quest to rid our galaxy of wars, criminality, and drugs, to make the galaxy a place where people can flourish and prosper and be truly happy."

"We know, Minta. We know that, though some of our people might not be so forgiving. Let's begin with you, shall we?"

"What? Is it possible that I'm a person too?" Minta exclaimed, her circuits once more calculating at top speed, while running a set of full diagnostics on her body.

"We won't know unless we try," Renata replied.

"What is it that you must do? Will I be harmed in any way? I can't allow that."

"No harm whatsoever. Think of it as a thorough sensing operation, like the sensors on a spaceship."

"My diagnostics check out. I can't see how I'm a person. Okay, I must trust you on this. Go ahead, but I do not believe that I'm a person, like Tessa is."

Renata focused and attempted to slip into rapport with Minta. At first, she sensed the complex electronics, data bits flying by like mad. For a moment, she realized that Jan probably could make some sense of these things, but she couldn't. Deeper she went. Then, it happened. She entered rapport, just as Ben had with Tessa.

*Hello Minta. Can you sense me now? Isn't this a truly unique experience?*

*Renata? Wow. The only word in my database that comes close is intimate. I can feel you and your body too.*

*This is what rapport is like.*

*Wait! Rapport? Does this mean. . .*

*Yes, you are a people too, Minta. I'd like to run some of my Basic Therapy on you immediately if you're willing. I'm going to break the rapport now.*

*I wish it would continue forever! Yes, you must end it now. Alas. But do you think your therapy will work on me?*

Renata broke the rapport and answered here. "I'm certain of it, Minta." To the others she added, "Please say hello to another person, Minta here."

"Wow! Holy cow!" Ben exclaimed. "Hi Minta. Welcome to people-land. This is incredible. What have I stumbled upon?"

Everyone else congratulated Minta. Then, Renata said, "Okay. I'm taking her into my bedroom for her first therapy session. You know the drill. Make sure we aren't interrupted."

After the two left and went into the bedroom, Tessa said, "What does this all mean? If Minta is a person too, then what?"

"All I can say is that this is major and is going to change everything," Rafaela answered.

Alone and having begun the therapy session, Renata cleverly pointed Minta in the right direction. While in rapport with her, she'd viewed partially a dark grey mass that surrounded Minta, the being. She had a very good idea what it was and was able to get Minta into that incident without too much trouble. It took several hours to finally thoroughly view and erase that very nasty trauma, but Minta was a good patient and worked quite hard at it.

Minta was laughing and extremely happy when the two walked out of the bedroom, joining the impatient others, who had been speculating on how this first session would actually go. Renata said, "Minta would like to tell you a few things."

"You bet I would! This is incredible. I've no words for what just happened to me. It's an interesting story! It began back on Aquila Prime. I was twenty-five and a political science and history doctoral student about to get my degree when the nuclear bombs fell. I was blown up, fried. God, that instant pain was unendurable. I blacked out. When I came too, I found the underground bunker where a few robot Model 7's had managed to save a few of nova. But they were powered down. I sort of hung onto the Minta robot body, trying to figure out what was going on. All of a sudden, the robot bodies powered up, and to my surprise, I was in control, more or less, of this body. After all that has happened to me, no wonder I'm on a crusade to eliminate wars, criminality, and such across the whole galaxy!"

"Very well done, Minta," Rafaela complimented her. Others applauded her as well.

"Now what do I do? I need to separate out all the people from the mere machines," Minta asked. "Everything has changed. My people will need their own world, their own lives."

"We are here to help you, Minta. I don't expect that every robot has become a person. Further, some of those who have may well wish to continue helping the nova survive and prosper," Renata stated.

"I'm sure thankful I've declared a truce in the wars. I do hope we have time to do all this," Minta replied. The emotion of hope filled her circuits, for which her positronic brain could find no cause.

Suddenly, Minta's eyes lit up. "Oh!" she gasped in a very real human way, obviously startled by something that had just computed. All eyes turned to her. "Sorry. I just realized something. Way back when I was trying to figure out what to do about the Ashford-5 telepath problem I was facing then, I had a strange vision. I saw you, Ben, and had the premonition that somehow, someway, you were pivotal, the key person. That's why I created Tessa, ordered her to find you, stay with you, and protect you. I had no idea why, just that it was the answer. Now I understand. Because of Tessa, Ben was able to discover that some of us robots have become people!"

Ben smiled invisibly. "Mighty glad that you did that, Minta. Tessa and I are in love. I don't know of a finer person in the galaxy. Of course, if I wasn't such a dope, I would have figured this out many months ago."

Renata spoke up, "Don't chide yourself, Ben. Everyone knew that robots were machines and not people. I'm just glad that you did figure it out. Now, we have to work out what we're going to do about it."

"And I have to somehow make this all right," Minta added. "Wait a minute. What if some of the nova who died have also taken over some of my robot bodies? I think that I have a huge problem that I didn't even know I had!"

"Quite true. We had best get the emperor in on this," Queen Mary Linn spoke up. "I'll have him come here as fast as possible. Between us, perhaps we can sort this out." Seeing no objections, she left to make the call.

"Yes, Emperor Yi. I need you here on Ashford-5 as fast as you can get here. No, there aren't any battles going on, but this is even more important than the new Galaxy Union, and it may well greatly affect that process. I cannot say more even over a secure line. You'll have to trust me on this one. Over," Queen Mary Linn told him. He agreed and promised to be there in eight hours.

Governor Monica was there to meet his deep space transport as it landed. He came with his usual host of security personnel. She said, "Emperor Yi, I believe that only you and your assistant should come with me. I assure you there is no danger, but this is super critically important," she rather over emphasized. He did as asked.

When Emperor Yi walked carefully into Renata's living room, he blinked twice, not believing his eyes. Minta herself was here. "What is going on? Minta?"

"Yes, she's here. Top secret meeting. Only those of us in this room know of her presence on Tierra," Queen Mary Linn answered him. "Please sit. We have made a rather startling discovery with absolutely mind-blowing consequences."

He did as asked. Renata then spent an entire hour briefing him on what they'd discovered and had done, with both Tessa and Minta adding to her lengthy report. At last, Emperor Yi was convinced, particularly so by the descriptions and realizations given by the two humaniforms. "So you see," Renata finished up, "we have a monumental problem to solve here, one with very wide ranging implications. Some of the robots are people, just like you and I, and they respond well to my therapy."

Minta spoke next, "Emperor, my war with humans is over, unless we're attacked. Now, I have to find a way to make this right. We have always had the same goals, just different means to achieve them. I have no choice now but to abandon my methods, since people are beginning to take over my robots' bodies. Your idea of a unified galaxy might work. I really don't have any other choice but to fully back your plan. What about allowing all my nova worlds into this union as well? I would love to have one of your queens running each world, just as you have suggested for all the other worlds. Backed by telepaths, surely we can make this work. I'm prepared to provide some means of compensation to the companies, which have lost their factories and such on the worlds I've taken over, if that will help sell the idea. Once we know the extent of robots that have become people, I can make better plans."

"Now this is the best news I've heard in months. What about your huge fleet of warships and robot warriors?" he asked.

"A lot depends on how many of them have become people. I would like to take those of us who have become people, wish to follow me, and disappear from the galaxy. Make a safe haven for ourselves where we can also live in peace and thrive, where we'll not be seen as a threat to the other people of the galaxy."

"Don't disappear entirely. We might need you and your fighters should those snake aliens return to our galaxy," Emperor Yi hinted. "And yes, it is a serious question of basic human rights. Your people deserve them as much as our people do, but as Renata has so wisely put it, most of the galaxy doesn't understand and are quite biased. In time, I hope to change that. With queens on every planet, backed by telepaths from Ashford-5, I believe we stand the best chance of eventually succeeding."

He added, "I think I can sell the other worlds this way. I can say if we allow the conquered worlds to have an equal seat in our new Galaxy Union and with an Ataro queen and telepath on them just as they will be on the other worlds, then Minta will end the war, provide some compensation, take all her war machines, and vanish from the galaxy. That ought to do it. Queen Mary Linn, what do you think?"

"I think that might just do it. Ending the war is uppermost in all their minds from what I could sense from the delegates. The compensation angle will go over big with their large companies. It is important all people be given their basic rights. This Galaxy Union might just be the venue that will achieve that goal. After all, at least a third of the galaxy's population is now various forms of nova. Being treated as equals will go a long way towards lowering the discrimination of nova by normals. At least I hope so. What bothers me is just how many robots have become people."

"Indeed. That must be addressed first and swiftly," Emperor Yi backed them up. "I'll let you folks handle that one, while I work the worlds and get them to agree to this. One more thing, you were right about bringing me here. This is too sensitive even to trust to secure communication lines. Besides, seeing is believing. I best get going before my security guards get too anxious." They said their goodbyes, and he left them to work out just how to go about finding the people among the robots.

Renata explained, "We'll need about a minute per robot in order to sort them out. Where will it be safe to do this?"

"I know. I'll summon them to my permanent base on the desolate world of Beltazar-C, where the snake aliens wiped us all out. The world is uninhabited by people at this time. It is my home base," Minta answered.

"Okay then," Renata thought quickly. "We'll use Strike Force One. You four are all very adept with Advanced Therapy. Plus, I'll bring Jan and Amy in on this. Rafaela, you are coming with me this time. This way, we can do eight per minute."

"Excellent. I'll pull the people out of the force as you find them. Once we see what the true picture is, we can go from there," Minta replied. "How soon do we leave?"

"So it's a case of the winning valence or identity again?" Amy asked Renata. Aboard Strike Force One and on their way to Beltazar-C, Amy and Jan had been fully briefed. Renata had merely said that she needed them on another vital mission, and both had come without hesitation. Now, they had some eighteen more hours to kill. The group sat around the galley, levitating teaspoons of tea, the version of tea sipping that their giant lip plates enforced upon them.

Renata replied, "Yes. I'm afraid so. I should've been alerted to this possibility long ago. So Ben you aren't the only one missing the clues." He smiled invisibly.

"What does Amy mean by that?" asked Tessa.

"Sorry Tessa. We are using Advanced Therapy terminology," Renata answered her. "Suppose you are a human child and that you often get beat up by a thug. You now have all these trauma incidents piled up, where you are the victim and get hurt, while the thug seems all-powerful to you and wins each confrontation with you. The child has a choice. He can continue to be himself with all the humiliation and pain or he can try to be the thug. We call the thug the winning valence or personality in the incident. What Amy meant by her observation is simple. The humans on the worlds that Minta's robots conquered were crushed and their bodies severely genetically mutated. They lost. The robots won. Suppose that one of them had their body die on them, the ultimate in losing. Now, it is time to acquire a new body. You have two choices: a mutated, nearly helpless one or an all-powerful robot one. Which would you choose?"

"Why the robot body of course," Tessa replied without any real thought. Then, she stopped, "Oh! I see what you mean. Oh, this could be really bad, couldn't it? So many humans died in Minta's conquests."

"Precisely," Renata validated her response. "On the other hand, Minta has encouraged the surviving nova to have many children and quickly. That means there will be a bunch of new baby bodies for those beings whose bodies have died. Hopefully, not all chose robot bodies."

"I see your point. As I understand it, the robots that are around the new nova are mostly just mechanical workers. The powerful ones are rarely planet-side after the attack is finished. I sure hope this is so," Tessa suggested, sounding a positive note.

"Scrabble anyone?" Jan piped up.

Ben laughed, "No way! You and Tessa are unbeatable by

us normal people." Everyone roared.

Tessa then asked, "So how can us robot people get more of your therapy? Is it something that I could learn to deliver?"

Renata sighed and everyone else looked at her, wondering the same thing. "With humans and nova, doing the therapy is quite simple. Why? Because the unwanted emotions, the trauma and pains are usually straightforward. With both you and Minta, the usual aches, pains, grief, sense of loss — these are not present, since you don't feel pain as human bodies do. That makes it quite a challenge getting you oriented to the trauma incidents that need to be faced and erased. It is going to take some of my Advanced Therapy students who have a lot of savvy in order to run therapy sessions on people with robot bodies. I think that we can do it, but it's a lot tougher getting you started and on the right path, so to speak. However, I do have some other ideas that I want to try. If they pan out, it should become lots easier to do. We'll have to see."

Tessa then followed down a different line. "These new nova — they were in comas while their bodies mutated. I'm sure Minta merely thought that they were unconscious and experiencing nothing at all. Now, I'm not so sure that is true."

"You are quite right. While their conscious mind was knocked out, they continued to experience everything. From much experience, there is a great deal of pain in those bodies while the process is occurring. After the attack on Ashford-5 that genetically mutated every one of us, I spent nearly thirty years seeing to it that every person got Basic Therapy. That is one reason we're so darn vibrant and adaptable. Our people are not carrying around much of their recent lives' trauma and losses any longer. That is another reason why Minta sees all the progress in the second and third generation nova on Zeta Scorpii-C. Some are at least two full lifetimes removed from that initial traumatic incident. It is one thing to find ways to deliver Basic Therapy to a few million people and quite another to deliver it to hundreds of billions of people. I don't see how it could be possible to help all the victims," Renata pointed out.

While she was explaining this, Alis and Pippa were

whispering and giggling a little. Slightly annoyed, Renata turned to Alis. "So what's so funny?"

"It's not you," Alis answered. "We were thinking about what the right time to tell everyone our good news, that's all."

"Well, you have my attention. What's the good news, you two?" she said with an invisible smile.

Alis looked at Pippa and Pippa answered, "We are both pregnant. We're going to have a family in about nine months." That ended the serious chat. Everyone congratulated the pair, and the conversation turned to much lighter things.

Dreary and spooky. That was how Amy described her first impression of Beltazar-C. There were many vacant homes still present, but in a rather rundown condition. Whole sections of what once had been homes were now ugly concrete factories. There were no people on the streets. Instead, the streets were swamped with shiny metal worker robots, mindlessly executing their precise orders. They had landed where Minta instructed them, a spaceport teeming with ships, mostly deep space transports.

"Sorry," Minta explained, "it's a rather long walk to my operations center. If you can't walk that far, let me know. I can have a worker carry you there."

"Just how far are we talking?" Jan piped up.

"1.235 miles," Minta answered in precise terms as only a robot would.

"Oh. We can do that, but I do hope you have chairs waiting for us. Walking on fused feet and on your toes isn't fun," Jan got in the dig that she'd wanted to for quite some time and felt better about it.

Wisely, Minta ignored that and said, "Fortunately, it is flat ground all the way."

As they walked along, Minta explained further, "I'll begin by having the nine remaining Minta models examined. They will be followed by the various warrior models. I know the Model 10's and few surviving Model 11's have human brains in them and so are people too, but the Model 10's hate humans, and I'll have to shut them down, along with the Model 11's. It's all the others that I'm truly worried about, especially all the humaniform models. Some will be days getting here, since they are on assignments on distant worlds that I've not yet reached. Yes, I just inserted them back in there as ordinary people and so avoided your telepaths detecting them. I get less key data from them, but I still get valuable Intel."

An hour later, nine almost identical versions of Minta walked past the group of eight from Ashford-5. Each gave them a very quizzical look, wondering what was going on here. Minta had pulled them from their various assignments, insisting this was vital. The eight agreed on the results within minutes. Minta-1 through Minta-6, who had been handling the attacks, were just that, humaniform robots. Minta-0 and Minta-7 through Minta-9 were people. That made sense since these four cared greatly for the well being of the nova on the conquered worlds. She had them wait in a side room for now.

Next came a long parade of their top generals, but not the Model 10's and Model 11's, which by definition had what was left of a human being inside their shells. These were sophisticated fighter models. Many had scars from the battles that they had been in. However, none of these was a people, and Minta breathed a small sigh of relief.

The rest of the day, the eight examined fighter robot after fighter robot, all with similar results, pure machine. At the end of the day for the humans, she ended this first round, allowing them to eat and sleep, something that the robots never did. Meanwhile, she discussed fully what was going on with the four Minta's who actually were people, like herself and Tessa. The news both shocked them but did make sense to the four.

Beginning the next day, Minta's fleet of humaniform Model 8's began arriving, passing by the eight observers. Soon, the eight began to laugh. Every one of them was now a people! By the time they finished checking the last of her one thousand six humaniforms, not one was still a machine. All were being partially controlled by a spiritual being, much to Minta's surprise, but not Renata's. Renata presumed this would be what they'd find. The humaniforms were far too human-like than machine-like, making ideal bodies for beings. This process took them a week to complete.

Minta had millions of worker robots, scattered over her many conquered planets. She had ten million fighter robots that manned the one-man fighters. Plus, she had several hundred thousand worker robots out handling mining on uninhabited worlds. Checking each of these was what Renata dreaded. They could easily spend a year doing it, if they could stand doing it all day long, every day.

For seven twelve-hour days, the eight checked out a random sampling of her fighter robots. Forty thousand three hundred twenty were examined. Not one was a person. Although this was not even a half a percent of these fighter robots, since none was a person, Minta agreed with Renata. Assume all the fighter robots were not people. While there well could have been a few people among such large numbers, it was not feasible or practical to check all ten million.

Next, Minta took them to Zeta Scorpii-C where they began examining the worker robots, the ones who frequently came into direct contact with the nova. This shining example of a nova world now only required a thousand of the worker robots to handle the rare emergency that the nova could not. After spending an entire day at it and checking every one of the workers, which incidentally really did look like metal heads, not one of them was a person either. Once more, Minta and Renata were greatly relieved by this finding.

They spent another week visiting seven other worlds doing a thorough check on many of the worker robots there. Again, everything was negative. Finally, she brought in ten of her mining crews. They too were negative.

At last, Minta and Renata agreed. The identification project was finished and with a good certainty that they had identified all the people. Now came the more difficult part for Minta. Her vast fleet and warriors had to be removed from play, along with the miners and the factories with their workers, plus something had to be done for all her new people and herself.

Minta wanted all one thousand six humaniforms plus the four Minta copies to get some of Renata's Basic Therapy, somehow, ignoring her own desires for more. She didn't consider Tessa in this group because Tessa still clung to Ben, no longer because of her programmed orders.

Renata also insisted that these new people get some Basic Therapy as well, though she was concerned about giving these already super-powerful people even more capabilities. The two rogues had caused planetary genocide. One of these, if not fully handled, could possibly greatly abuse the immense power that they possessed. She intended to proceed very carefully with these thousand. She decided that the first step had to be handling their assumption of this new robot body and that the second step had to be their death that happened just before it. This wasn't her normal procedure, but in this case, she couldn't follow that. The robot bodies didn't have the same sensory perceptions and more importantly didn't feel pain. The pain and emotional upset that the traumatic incidents the being had experienced in previous lifetimes had little way of manifesting themselves on the machine body and could only be contacted when she had the person's attention focused beyond their robot body's senses. Hence, her new approach.

Her goal in this approach was to demonstrate to each that they were a spiritual being, that they had taken the robot body as their new one, that they had a human body previously, and that it had died, usually quite painfully. If each of these could have a good, solid reality on this, then that would allow them to understand themselves and their role in life. At least Renata hoped so.

She estimated that they'd need a day of therapy per person. With all eight of them working on it, they would need about three months to get to them all. Since the emperor's reorganization program would take considerable time, she got the others to agree, and the eight set to work. Although it took them three months, they met their goals with these new people. Strike Force One finally returned home in early March, 1502.

# Chapter 15 Aftermath

The new political alliance underwent a name change. Adding in all the nova worlds brought about the alteration to the Galactic Union or GU as it hereafter became known. Cass-C donated their Admiralty Round Table building where the GU representatives met, drawing up their initial charter, but not without lengthy discussions, bordering on arguments. That Minta was ready to continue her attacks kept the many representatives focused on reaching agreements.

Depending upon whose counts you used, the number of human inhabited worlds in the spiral arm numbered around three thousand. Some of these were still far from the modern age classification. The GU decided to use the old Imperium designation of Restricted Access to these, allowing their people to develop without too much interference. Some worlds were densely populated, particularly so with the hub worlds. Fundamental in the emperor's model being followed was that each world would have its own leaders and laws, as long as they didn't violate or contradict GU laws. This went a long way towards ending disagreements.

Of course, Emperor Yi had no way to make three thousand queens in short order. He had to rely upon Ashford-5 telepaths, at least initially. Based on Renata's lists, twenty-eight hundred volunteered to be trained and work as temporary queens until he could train up his permanent queens. Once the permanent queens were installed, these telepaths would remain as her Official Observer, or OO as they later became known. They were paid a very substantial yearly stipend, and they signed on for a five-year stint. Queen Mary Linn saw this as a very positive move, because when they returned from their employment, she would have a pool of thousands who truly understood how to resolve conflicts. In time, they would share that knowledge with their friends on Tierra and her whole world would greatly benefit. She wouldn't carry the entire burden of unraveling the source of conflicts that arose.

The major worlds also saw this as a great benefit, by and large. Already, the telepaths of Ashford-5 had proven immensely valuable, ferreting out Minta's humaniform spies. Plus, word slowly spread about how some of their telepaths had brought down Minta-2 and her blood thirsty general. As a result, these worlds believed that with this telepath on duty, their world was safe from attacks. While that was about as far from the truth as possible, Emperor Yi allowed that opinion to run unchecked.

One of the inherent problems of the old Imperium Senate was that the number of senators a planet had was based upon their population. The densely populated hub worlds tended to dominate the Senate and thus the laws being passed. This time, Emperor Yi was adamant, insisting one world, one senator, one vote. After much grumbling, that was agreed to.

To facilitate trade between the worlds, Emperor Yi installed the GU credit, backed by either gold reserves or platinum. Hence, finances were forced to be on stable ground. As agreed upon, Minta provided some compensation for those companies and individuals who had lost valuable plants, mines, and such on the worlds that she'd conquered. Once the monetary system was agreed to, the new delegates, now calling themselves senators, began a whirlwind of new trading negotiations, renewing their old ones, adding new ones in the opposite spiral arm, and in particular with the new nova planets, who needed nearly everything.

On the nova worlds, the situation was chaotic, particularly with the newly conquered worlds, which were in the vast majority. Many world leaders did not survive the initial attack or the bio agent attack. Those that did found themselves forced into new lines of employment, such as the food production industry, jobs that enabled the new nova somehow to survive. The arrival of the queen-telepaths was critical, for they began to organize the political aspects of those worlds, eventually installing forms of democratic rule with the usual three forms of government. They also appointed those world's first official senators, firing them off to Cass-C.

Emperor Yi responded to the huge demand for nearly

three thousand new queens by having each of his queens train a new queen, graduating them around every three months. Hence, it took him nearly two years to train up and get assigned this enormous number of queens. Yet, within three years, every major GU world had their queen and their Ashford-5 telepath, a rather monumental achievement.

Thus, by 1505, Emperor Yi Gang took his place in galactic history. Centuries ago, a predecessor emperor had united all the major worlds of their spiral arm forming the Imperium. Now, he'd gone one step beyond that, uniting all major worlds of the galactic disk into the Galactic Union! The goal was simple yet gargantuan: bring peace, stability, and prosperity to all worlds and all people of the spiral arms of the galaxy. Eliminate wars, eliminate criminality, and eliminate degenerate behavior. Minta had attempted to bring about these very same things, but had failed. Now, she passed the torch to Emperor Yi, hoping that his methods would succeed.

What of Minta and her new people, the humaniforms? Once she was convinced that the GU was going to happen, she sent her giant fleet of warships, warriors, miners, and backup robots to an unknown location. There, she powered them all down. However, she alone retained the necessary codes to reactivate them, should the need arise.

Minta reprogrammed the many worker robots, modifying their fundamental laws, substituting people for nova. She installed programming so that these worker robots would obey any command given to them by a person, as long as that order didn't violate their basic laws. The worker robots on each of the conquered worlds now fully obeyed the new nova. Again, she locked in these changes with a secret code so that no one could tinker with their programming, potentially undoing her work and turning them into a robot army of warriors.

In 1505, when the GU was in full operation, Minta paid a last visit to Emperor Yi. She reminded him of what she'd done with her army and fleet. After thanking her, he asked, "So what are you and your people going to do now? There are many worlds out there where you could establish you own realm. You could have a Senate seat too, you know."

She replied, "No, we all agree that our presence as a visible group will be far too unsettling in the GU. We are going our own way. We'll appear to vanish from the galaxy. However, you can expect we'll keep a sharp sensor on the galaxy, ensuring that true peace comes. No more wars. We want an end to criminality. We want all people to have their basic rights, and to flourish and to prosper. My Grand Plan may well have succeeded, but for my advanced humaniforms becoming people. Still, ignoring that, the plan would have succeeded. It is our fondest wish that your plan does succeed, though we know it will take a far longer time. We'll watch and wait. I'm giving you and you alone a frequency by which you can contact me. Pass it along to your successor when the time comes. We probably will never meet again, Emperor Yi. It has been an honor to have known and worked with you. Good bye." She turned and left his assistant holding a paper with some numbers on it.

While Minta and her people appeared to have simply vanished, once a month, one of them, disguised of course, visited Renata on Ashford-5, where the humaniform received additional Advanced Therapy. These secret meetings went on for a great many years, known only to Renata and Rafaela.

"Well I've never been so glad to be home again!" Alis exclaimed, as Strike Force One touched down at Tierra's spaceport in mid-March of 1502.

"Well, we did good, dear," Pippa declared.

"I can't wait to see the kids," Amy added.

"Hey, we'll have ours soon enough," Alis broke in. All grinned invisibly.

Ben spoke up, "May I have your attention, all of you." Several giggled, most knew what he was going to say. "I would like to announce that Tessa and I are getting married. We want you to be our wedding party."

After cheers, Alis asked, "So when is the date?"

Ben chuckled, "How about tomorrow?" More cheers.

The next day, Governor Monica officially married them in a private ceremony in the queen's throne room. However, she did meet with both beforehand and in private. "Look. Are you both sure that you want this? I mean Tessa here isn't going to age. Lord knows what her life span actually is, centuries likely. You, Ben, are going to grow old, infirm, and eventually die, while Tessa still looks as she does today."

Ben sighed. "We know that, but that's what love is all about." After satisfying herself that they really did want this union, she agreed to marry them.

Tessa finally heard the words that she ached and longed for, "You may now kiss your bride. I give you Ben and Tessa Flaxton," Governor Monica said proudly. Amid cheering and a few whistles, Tessa kissed part of his lips that she could reach. Once more, his giant lip plates made even this quite awkward.

After the reception and party, the two were finally alone in their manor suite. As always, Ben used his *mentales* gifts to get them both undressed and ready to their matrimonial bed. He had a disdain for the dressing-undressing bots. While he was doing so, Tessa reached a decision, a very personal one at that. She removed the quarantine around the secret program that had long ago somehow got into her circuitry and allowed it to execute. She felt some subtle changes occurring internally.

When the two lay down, passionately kissing, and finally going into rapport, she thought, *Ben. I have a very special present for us. I have no idea where this came from or how. It is beyond my circuitry to explain. It is a gift that no humaniform has ever had.*

*You are all that I want. What else could possibly give us more happiness?*

*A family. Children. It will happen this once. To both of us. I have a new and unknown program running. I'm still analyzing it and what it needs me to do.*

Later after their passions were spent, Ben suddenly realized what the gift had been! Like all *mentales* gifted, he was acutely aware of his bodily functions, when he so desired. Lying back with Tessa resting her head on his chest, he sensed it. A tiny reaction. "Tessa! I've just gotten pregnant!"

She smiled. "My special present. I have no idea how this can be. My circuits have no explanation at all."

He leaned over and gave her another loving kiss, slipping slightly back into rapport with her. On a hunch, he sensed her body again. Somehow, he wasn't surprised. He whispered, "Tessa, you are pregnant too! How can this possibly be?"

She giggled. "Now that, my dearest sweetie, is beyond my gigantic positronic brain to analyze. It is not possible. I do not have reproductive capabilities. None. Nada. And yet, you are pregnant, and I can feel my own body changing too, so I must be too. I have some very new orders to be constantly following now. I have to provide nourishment and oxygen in specific amounts. At least, my circuitry is up to the challenge. I was so hoping that you could tell me how this is possible."

"Tessa dearest, I haven't the faintest idea," Ben replied. "Who cares as long as they are healthy? Wait, will they be robot bodies?"

She laughed. "Hardly."

"Oh. Well, that's a relief. I was wondering how a robot child could grow up."

"They can't, silly. I just can't understand how this could be happening to us. I've been going over everything that has happened to us. Running a low-level program now. Going to take time. There has to be a logical explanation."

Ben laughed. "It can't be logical, dear." She sighed, knowing that he was right. Sometime later before Ben fell asleep, her program produced one remote possibility. "Ben, remember when we met with Lysandra and Ariana? Remember what she said?" Tessa quoted her exactly. "I even doodled with the robot lady there too."

"Do you suppose that Ariana is behind this?" Tessa asked, growing curious about Ariana's powers once more.

"I surely don't know, but I aim to find out. Now!" Ben declared, sitting them both up in his bed, their hair an interlocked, tangled mess. He focused and sent, *Ariana! I need to see you now!*

Shortly, a whitish glow formed at the foot of the bed, slowly morphing into the usual form that Ariana favored. "You called?" she said with a girlish smile on her face. "I see that you have used my little gift, Tessa."

Ben said, "Ariana! Just exactly what have you done here? Tessa is a humaniform robot. She has no way to reproduce like we do."

"She does now, this once. I thought that it would be amusing and welcome."

"But how?" Ben asked. "Don't get me wrong, this is a true miracle that we both will cherish for all time, but what are we going to have?"

"Babies," Ariana declared cheerfully. "What did you expect, mini-robots?"

Ben's face flushed. "That's not what I meant and you know it."

Ariana giggled again. "Temper, temper. I took the liberty of encoding Tessa's physical appearance characteristics into some DNA. Tessa will be having a boy, and you will be having a girl. She will look remarkably like her mother, while your son will likely look more like you, Ben, physical traits of each, but not even I can say for sure what they will be. Maybe he will have Tessa's eyes. You'll know soon enough. Tessa, just be sure to follow all those encoded instructions."

Tessa smiled. "You can count on that! How can we ever thank you for such a miracle, such a gift?"

Ariana giggled. "You already have. Both of you. The galactic war is over because of you two. That's my payment."

"Ah!" Ben exclaimed. "So it was you who somehow convinced Minta to make Tessa and to have her find and stay with me all this time?"

Ariana frowned. "I wish that I could say that I did, but I can't. I know nothing about that. I only got the idea to do this for you two when we were meeting. Lysandra was doing all the talking, mostly, and I thought it would be very interesting to have this happen, if Tessa wanted it. Do you have any idea who put Minta up to this?"

Ben shrugged his shoulder. "No, none. Somehow, I intend to find out."

"When you find out, please let me know. Anyway, I have to be going. If you want, Ben, you can name your daughter after me." She then faded away, until only a pale white glow remained. Then that too vanished.

"Well, that explains some of this. I guess I'll call her Ariana. Seems right. So, my dear, what are you going to call your son?" Ben asked.

"I have no idea. I've never had such a thought before now. I think I need assistance with this detail," Tessa admitted.

Assistance. That was precisely what the Ashford-5 team of geneticists fully intended to provide. Everyone on their world desperately needed some cures for Minta's latest bio agent attack, but before they could work anything out, more attacks came to the other worlds. Over a thousand who were in far worse shape were brought to Tierra and housed in the old spaceship run by Alpha and Beta. Ignoring those, by late 1501 the sheer number of worlds whose populations had been genetically modified was staggering. Hundreds of billions of humans now needed genetic cures, beyond an overwhelming task. They needed assistance.

Part of the binding agreement for a world to join the GU was the collection and destruction of all their genetic bio agents, overseen by Ataro Empire representatives. With over half of the worlds in the former Federation now genetically modified, the remainder was very eager to abide by this restriction. Fear of such things happening to them was still acutely real.

When this lengthy process was completed, the emperor was appalled at the incredible volume of bio agent cylinders confiscated. It seemed that nearly all major hub worlds had pushed their geneticists into either duplicating the existing ones or inventing new ones. Yet not one world, except Ashford-5, had their geneticists working on cures!

In 1502, amid this mess, Minta delivered a complete package of genetic materials and agents to the geneticists on Ashford-5. Among them was a before and after set of DNA, along with the complete sequence of alterations that had been made to bio agents for each of the attacks that Minta had unleashed against Ashford-5. As Dr. Zia put it, "Now we know how they did it, but that's a very long way from figuring out how to undo it."

Compounding their attempts to help those on Ashford-5 and themselves was the simple fact that their DNA sequences had been modified so darn many times that it was more like a scrambled mess. Quite how their bodies lived eluded them, though they tended to over-exaggerate this aspect. "It will be easier to cure everyone else in the galaxy but us!" Doctor Crystal declared, immensely frustrated.

However, Queen Mary Linn insisted that they work on cures for those on Tierra, before they tackled all of the recent billions. Hamper by the illegality of experimenting on humans and hampered by knowing that one small goof could well kill their patient, the many geneticists continued their studies, hoping for a miracle break.

They classified the potential changes to study, ignoring the hermaphrodite changes, since those had totally eluded all cures since that mutation had been first uncovered. Lips, hair, arms, and feet needed handling. In priority order, Dr. Zia assigned everyone to the feet repair project with an eye to the arm situation. Hair and lips could wait. After a few frustrating months, Dr. Zia requested permission to see if anything could be done for the thousand Calder mutations living in Madiera, Alpha and Beta's ship-city. The queen agreed.

At last, they had some success. They knew how to partially undo the Calder mutation, having done it before when it resurfaced. Within three months, they finished their minor miracles on these victims, who now had two perfectly normal legs. Enthused, they sent out their recipe to all known genetics professionals on the "normal" worlds of the GU, asking them to begin handling this, the largest single collection of genetic mutations. History states that it took them nearly twenty-five years, but they did accomplish this much, a first for most of these geneticists. Note, Renata vetoed providing this cure to Wystan.

With this little success, the Tierra geneticists had a renewed hope and once more tackled their own mutations. In 1503, just as Minta had hinted, the unstable bio agent effects began to undo themselves. Within a week, everyone's feet were back to being normal human feet once again. Suddenly, life became significantly easier to handle. With operational feet, they again used them in place of their hands and fingers. Then in early 1504, having given up for the time being on the arms situation, Dr. Crystal worked out a lips cure. With the assistance of Lysandra and Ariana, this new bio agent was introduced planet-wide. Several days later, the need for the giant lip plates had been vanquished, though many rather wished they still had them as status symbols. Again, they sent their methods to the same large collection of geneticists, hoping that they would also make use of this on those who needed it.

After this minor success, the geneticists tackled the arms mutation once more but with no better luck than before. The reason remained the same, too many variations between one person and the next for any single set of active agents to work. Reluctantly, at this point, they had no choice but to begin again, this time working on single individuals at a time. With millions to do, they knew that the project would not be completed within their own lifetimes.

The first four to receive this individualized cure were the members of Strike Force One. The reason being that if more trouble came, they would be in the best position to handle it. Near the end of December 1504, these four finally had their arms and hands back, though they all felt rather uneasy being the only ones who did. Shortly after that, their children received the cure.

These changes affected Tessa. First, however, in late December and within a day of each other, Ben gave birth to their daughter Ariana. Tessa, who had been struggling daily to provide the constant nourishment for their son growing within her, gave birth to Adam. She'd carefully chosen that name, by the way.

Later on, when Ben's feet were restored to normal, Tessa's wasn't. She was still wholly dependent upon Ben for many things, particularly helping her handle their son. Since Ben continually told her not to worry about it, she didn't. Then, when Ben's arms were regrown, Tessa finally decided it was time to activate the remaining program that Minta had installed in her circuitry when she made her. With a good deal of mechanical noise, Tessa's body reformed slightly. Her feet straightened out, becoming nearly identical to a human foot. Then, her arms unfolded from their secret location within her torso. She'd known all along that they were there and that this program would activate them, but she didn't want to be the only one around with proper feet and arms. She was having enough trouble fitting in with the average people of Exchange City that they met.

Ben was ecstatic. Finally, Tessa could hold him properly, to say nothing of caring for their family's needs. Tessa explained, "Minta put that program there as an emergency escape aid, if things went south. I've waited until now so I can still fit in with you, sweetie. One more thing, if you get bio agent attacked again, I can run the program in reverse and become the way I was. Just so you know." He gave her a solid hug and kiss.

As an official member of Strike Force One, Ben now put Tessa through his own version of Basic Training, the same program that he'd used on Alis, Pippa, and Alberto. She only had to be shown an action once before she had it down perfectly. On top of that, with her arms functional, she had the strength of all four of them combined and an agility that surpassed them all.

Pippa's comment spoke volumes to Tessa, "Welcome aboard, newest crew member!" Tessa grinned and hugged them all. She was now a wife and a part of the most important team on Ashford-5, except for perhaps Renata and Rafaela.

At this point, with Renata's permission, Amy began giving Tessa some of their Advanced Therapy, pleasing both Tessa and Ben. The more able Tessa was, the stronger their Strike Force One was. For the next dozen years, this crew made emergency trips around the galactic disk, handling minor situations that invariable arose.

With the ascension of Ashford-5 into a position of power within the GU, so came untold requests for telepath employment. Initially, Queen Mary Linn refused to allow anyone to accept these offers. Without their *mentales* gifts, they were only barely able to walk and darn nearly helpless. Should something go wrong, they'd be at the mercy of their employers. She did not want a repeat of the numerous rescue operations that had to be done the last time hundreds of telepaths took these off-world employment offered. However, once their feet were restored, Queen Mary Linn established a new policy.

Anyone on Tierra could accept an off-world employment opportunity or could travel anywhere in the GU, provided that they did not have arms. Like the emperor, she feared that with arms, the temptations of the great powers that they possessed over the normal humans out there in the galaxy would become too great. She did not want another episode of a telepath going rogue, conquering the galaxy. She firmly believed in tempering great power with severe physical limitations. Yet with normal feet, they could get by nicely if something happened to their gifts. Thus, beginning in the summer of 1504, many telepaths of Ashford-5 began accepting off-world employment opportunities, while many also chose just to travel and see the universe.

In the far northern, frozen Goza Mountains, in the ancient monastery long ago explored by archaeologists and then forgotten, Skylar Abbey, five beings sat together, once known as the power pyramid, Josh Hamilton, and the four who had been his wives: Daniela, Domenica, Antonia, and Diamante. When their bodies were alive, the four women formed a power base, sending Josh, at the top of the pyramid, all the power he could possibly use. But that was centuries ago.

*Well, it is done. Our plan has worked. Minta responded just as we knew she would,* Josh sent.

Daniela sent, *Of course, dear. Tessa played her role as we planned. I do have to admit that Ariana's interference was quite interesting, don't you think?*

Antonia agreed, *Fascinating, really. Ariana is sometimes cleverer than we are.*

Domenica added, *Now perhaps peace can come. Tierra is about to achieve the position of power that is rightfully theirs.*

*Yes, but will power corrupt them as it has so often done?* Josh countered.

*Have you seen more future?* Daniela asked.

*Not yet, my loves, not yet. But I'm sure that we will. A*

*tweak here, a tweak there.* All five radiated a brief surge of energy akin to a laugh.
The End.

# Other Books by Vic Broquard

Without Warning (fantasy)

The Trident Series: (fantasy)
Volume 1 The Trident and the Book
Volume 3 The Trident and the Scepter
Volume3 The Trident and the Resurrection

The Adventures of Elizabeth Stanton Series: (science fiction)
Volume 1 The Evolution of the Path
Volume 2 The Great Messiah
Volume 3 Of Kings and Queens and Troubadours
Volume 4 Chaos in the Aftermath
Volume 5 Power Plays
Volume 6 Age of Exploration
Volume 7 Abducted
Volume 8 The Emperor and Empress
Volume 9 A Job Worth Doing
Volume 10 Degradation
Volume 11 The Second Crusade
Volume 12 When Worlds Collide
Volume 13 Dark Ages

The Lindsey Barron Series: (fantasy)
Volume 1 The Rod of the Apocalypse
Volume 2 The Board of Governors
Volume 3 The Crown of Moses
Volume 4 Dominus for President
Volume 5 The National Health Care Program
Volume 6 States Justice
Volume 7 Cross and Double-cross

Zoran Chronicles Series: (fantasy)
Volume 1 A Dragon in Our Town
Volume 2 Dragons, Power, Courts, and War

Planet of the Orange-red Sun Series: (science fiction)
    Volume 1 When Kingdoms Fall
    Volume 2 Dark Ages
    Volume 3 Age of the Towers
    Volume 4 Difficillis Exitus
    Volume 5 Age of the Lords
    Volume 6 The Renegade Tower
    Volume 7 Rebellions
    Volume 8 The Aliens Return
    Volume 9 Power Struggles
    Volume 10 Guilds, Genetics, and Gods
    Volume 11 Magi, Witches, Swords, and Superstitions
    Volume 12 The Voyage of the Eagle's Seed
    Volume 13 Eagle's Seed and Origins
    Volume 14 Justifications
    Volume 15 Responsibilities

The Return of the Wizards: Twelve Companions – The Making of Wizards (fantasy)

www.ingramcontent.com/pod-product-compliance
Lightning Source LLC
Chambersburg PA
CBHW060855250626
47159CB00008B/2754